PRAISE FOR
AFTER THE FIRE

"Genuinely different…thrilling and spellbinding."
—Patrick Ness, *New York Times* bestselling
author of *The Rest of Us Just Live Here* and
the award-winning *A Monster Calls*

"Absorbing, gripping, and darkly fascinating… A must-read novel."
—Sarah Pinborough, international bestselling
author of *Behind Her Eyes*

"It will keep you up late until you get to the very end."
—Maureen Johnson, author of
13 Little Blue Envelopes

"A master class in suspense."
—Amy Alward, author of *The Potion Diaries*

"One of the most brilliantly realized characters in contemporary
YA."
—James Smythe, author of the
Australia Trilogy

"Powerful and beautiful."
—Maggie Harcourt, author of *Unconventional*

"A gripping story of survival with a big heart. Scary, exciting, and
uplifting all at the same time."
—Juno Dawson, author of *Margot and Me*

AFTER THE FIRE

AFTER THE FIRE

WILL HILL

sourcebooks
fire

Published by Sourcebooks Fire, an imprint of Sourcebooks, Inc.
P.O. Box 4410, Naperville, Illinois 60567-4410
(630) 961-3900
Fax: (630) 961-2168
sourcebooks.com

Originally published in 2017 in the United Kingdom by Usborne Publishing,
Ltd., an imprint of Usborne House.

Library of Congress Cataloging-in-Publication Data

Names: Hill, Will, author.
Title: After the fire / Will Hill.
Description: Naperville, Illinois : Sourcebooks Fire, [2018] | "Originally
    published in 2017 in the United Kingdom by Usborne Publishing, Ltd., an
    imprint of Usborne House." | Summary: Moonbeam, seventeen, survives a
    devastating confrontation between government forces and the cult she grew
    up in, but will need a lot of help to heal mentally, emotionally, and physically.
Identifiers: LCCN 2018010641 | (hardcover : alk. paper)
Subjects: | CYAC: Cults--Fiction. | Survival--Fiction. | Hospital
    care--Fiction. | Psychology--Fiction.
Classification: LCC PZ7.H5576 Aft 2018 | DDC [Fic]--dc23 LC record
available at https://lccn.loc.gov/2018010641

Printed and bound in the United States of America.
LSC 10 9 8 7 6 5 4 3 2 1

Go tell that long tongue liar,

go and tell that midnight rider,

tell the rambler, the gambler, the backbiter,

tell 'em that God's gonna cut 'em down.

I sprint across the yard, my eyes streaming, my heart pounding in my chest.

The noise of the gunfire is still deafening, and I hear—I actually hear—bullets whizzing past me, their low whines like the speeded-up buzz of insects, but I don't slow down, and I don't change course. The Chapel is burning out of control, its roof engulfed by roaring fire and sending up a huge black plume of smoke, and the amplified voice of the Government booms across the compound, repeating its demand over and over again.

"Put down your weapons and come forward slowly with your hands in the air!"

Nobody is listening. Not the other Governments, and definitely not any of my Brothers and Sisters.

In the distance, back near the Front Gate, the tank rumbles

forward, crushing the flimsy wire fence and churning the desert floor. Somewhere, over the engines and the endless rattle of gunfire, I can hear screams of pain and pleading shouts for help, but I force myself to ignore them and keep going: my gaze is fixed on the wooden cabins at the western edge of the Base.

I trip over something.

My feet tangle, and I go sprawling onto the cracked blacktop of the yard. Pain crunches through me as my shoulder hits the ground, but I grit my teeth and get back on my feet and look to see what I fell over.

Alice is lying on her back, her hands clutching her stomach.

Her shirt has turned red, and she's lying in a pool of blood that seems too big to have all come out of one person. She's still alive though. Her eyes are dim, but they find mine, and she looks at me with an expression I can't describe. There's pain there, a lot of pain, and shock, and fear, and something that looks like confusion, like she wants to know how things ever came to this.

I hold her gaze. I want to stay with her, to tell her it's all right and that she's going to be okay, but it isn't all right, nothing is, and I don't know very much about bullet wounds, but I don't think she is going to be okay.

I'm pretty sure she's going to die.

I stare at her, wasting seconds that the still-functional bit of my brain screams at me for wasting, then run toward the west barracks. Alice's eyes widen as I start to turn away, but I don't see anger in them. I think she understands what I have to do.

That's what I tell myself, at least.

A figure emerges from the swirling smoke, and I skid to a halt, my hands raised. But it isn't one of the Governments, with their black helmets and goggles and guns. It's Amos, his eyes red and puffy, one arm limp at his side, a pistol trembling in his good hand.

"Where's Father John?" he asks, his voice hoarse and torn. "Have you seen him?"

I shake my head and try to circle around him, but he grabs my arm and pulls me close.

"Where is he? Where is The Prophet?" he rasps.

"I don't know!" I scream, because the tank has reached the yard, and the gunfire is heavier than ever, and the fire is leaping from building to building faster than I can follow.

I push Amos as hard as I can, and he stumbles backward. He swings the pistol at me, but I'm already moving. I hear shots behind me, but none of them find their target before I plunge into the smoke.

It's instantly hard to breathe. I clamp one of my hands over my mouth and nose, but the thick, bitter smoke slips between my fingers, and I start to cough. I see my fallen Brothers and Sisters all around me as I run, dark shapes I stagger left and right to avoid. A few are moving, dragging themselves across the ground or twitching and spasming like they're having a fit, but most of them aren't.

Most of them are still.

The west barracks appear in front of me, their walls and flat roofs wreathed in acrid smoke. The gunfire is constant behind me, and with so many bullets flying through the air, it feels like a matter of time until the inevitable happens. As long as I unlock the cabins first, I don't care.

I really don't.

I stumble out of the worst of the smoke and toward the nearest cabin, fumbling the skeleton key out of my pocket. I grab the padlock hanging from the door, and there's a sizzling sound. I don't understand what has happened—until pain explodes through me, and I wrench my hand away. Most of my palm stays stuck to the metal lock. I fall to my knees, clutching my ruined left hand against my stomach, and a scream that doesn't sound human bursts out of my mouth.

It's overwhelming. The pain.

It feels like someone has pushed my hand into a jar of acid and is holding it there, and as my brain tries to process the agony, everything else fades away: the smell of the smoke, the heat of the fire, the noise of the guns. Gray creeps in from all sides, like the volume of my senses is being turned down. Then something shoves me from behind, and everything comes hurtling back as I tumble to the ground.

A Government is standing over me, its face hidden behind its mask, the gaping muzzle of its gun pointing between my eyes.

"Hands where I can see them!" It's a man's voice. "Show me your hands!"

They tremble as I hold them up. "Please," I say, my voice a raw croak. "Children. There are children in these cabins. Please."

"Shut up!" he yells. "Not another word!"

"Please," I repeat. "In the cabins. You have to help them."

The Government glances at the buildings. My head is spinning, and my stomach is churning, and I feel like I'm going to pass out from the pain screaming in my hand, but I force my eyes to stay open, force my reeling mind to focus on the dark figure above me.

"Padlocks," I whisper, and hold out the skeleton key. "Please…"

My strength fails me. The Government looks at the cabin. Looks down at me. Looks at the cabin.

"Shit!" he shouts, then grabs the key from my hand and spins toward the door. I watch him grip the padlock with his gloved hand and slide the key into the lock, and I wonder for an awful moment whether this is all going to have been a waste of time, whether there are some locks that even a skeleton key can't open. Then the cylinder turns, and the padlock springs loose. The Government hauls the door open, and my coughing, spluttering Brothers and Sisters come flooding out, their eyes red and streaming with tears.

"Go to the Front Gate," I manage to croak. "Stay together. Put your hands up…"

At the back of the crowd, I see Honey, and I feel something in my chest that overwhelms the pain in my hand. Her eyes are swollen and puffy, and her skin is pale, but her mouth and jaw are set in familiar lines of determination. She's breathing, if nothing else.

I wasn't sure she would be.

She helps the last few crying, panicking children out of the cabin and leads them south, toward the Front Gate. The Government races to the next cabin, shouting into his radio for backup. Something breaks loose inside me, a surge of relief so powerful it's almost physical. It breathes new life into my exhausted muscles, and I drag myself into a sitting position.

The children make their way across the yard, their little hands raised in surrender, until a rush of Governments come sprinting out of the smoke and scoop up my Brothers and Sisters and carry them out through the gaping holes in the fence. I can hear them crying and shrieking for their parents, and my heart breaks for them, but they're alive, they're still alive, and that's all that matters, that's the only thing that matters as the world burns.

I hear a scream, loud and high-pitched enough to cut through the gunfire and the roar of the inferno, and I turn my head toward it. Near the blazing ruins of the Chapel, two of the Governments have caught hold of Luke and lifted him off the ground by his arms and legs. He's thrashing in their grip, howling and bellowing for them to put him down, to let him go with the others, to let him Ascend.

His voice, full of fury and fervor and desperate, frantic panic, is the last thing I hear before everything goes dark.

A
F
T
E
R

…I drift…

…my hand feels like it's wrapped in fire. My eyes open and everything is white and there's a beeping noise and something that has no face looms over me and I try to scream but nothing happens. I'm so scared I can't even think. My eyes roll back and…

…a man looks down at me, and his face is just eyes above a white mask. He shows me a huge needle, and I just stare at it because I'm too scared to move, and when he pushes it into my arm I don't even feel it because the pain in my hand is still so huge that it blocks everything else out. I know what doctors are from when I was little and TV was still allowed, but I've never seen one in real life until now. The Prophet is screaming in my head that doctors are agents of *THE GOVERNMENT*, that every one of them is a *SERVANT OF THE SERPENT*, and his voice rattles and shakes my brain, and my stomach churns, and I'm so scared I can't even breathe while the doctor tapes the needle that's inside my arm to my skin and connects it to a tube that leads to a bag of milky white liquid. He says something I don't understand, and then the liquid starts to flow. I watch it creep down the tube toward my arm. I can't move a single muscle, but I manage to form a thought over the noise of Father John howling in my head: I wonder what is going to happen when the white liquid goes inside me, and I wonder if I'm still going to be me the next time I wake up…

…the lights above me are blinding, but the pain is much less, and the plastic bag at the end of the tube is empty. I can just about raise my head far enough to see the big mitten of bandages that has been wrapped around my left hand. Sometimes a doctor stands next to my bed and stares at me and sometimes I hear raised voices in the distance and sometimes I start crying and can't stop. I'm too hot and too cold and everything is wrong and I really want to go home, because even that was better than this. A man wearing a hat and a uniform asks me my name, but Father John roars in my head, so I don't answer. He asks again, and I don't answer again, and he rolls his eyes and walks away…

…a woman in a uniform tells someone to sit me up. Hands reach underneath me, and fingers press into my skin and drag me along the bed until I'm propped against a pillow. The woman in the uniform says, "That's better," and I almost laugh because nothing is better, nothing is even *remotely close* to better. "Can you tell me who started the fire?" she asks, and I shake my head. "Who handed out the guns?" I shake my head. "Did you see John Parson after the shooting started?" I shake my head. "What happened inside the main house? What did you do in there?" I shake my head. She stares at me, and when she speaks again, her voice is cold. "People are dead, girl," she says. "A lot of people. You need to start talking." She leans over me. I don't know what's she's going to do, so I turn my head away. I see a gold badge on her belt stamped with the words LAYTON COUNTY SHERIFF'S DEPARTMENT, and my heart stops dead in my chest and then I hear myself screaming, and the woman in the uniform jumps back, her eyes wide with shock. I hear running footsteps, and my heart starts back up. I thrash on the bed and scream and scream. I feel hands pin my arms and legs, and a doctor lowers another needle toward me, and…

…the faces of my Brothers and Sisters swarm out of the darkness, people I've known my whole life, their hair on fire, their skin melting off their skulls, and they're screaming two words over and over and over again: *Your fault your fault your fault your fault YOUR FAULT.* I turn away from them and try to run, but the ground turns to quicksand beneath my feet. I sink to my ankles as fingertips brush my shoulders and the back of my neck and I'm terrified, but I can't scream because my mouth won't open. All I can do is wade through inky blackness, dragging myself forward, trying to find the way back…

…a man wearing a dark suit stands beside my bed. I'm soaked with sweat, and my hand really hurts, like it's covered with biting insects, and I don't think I've ever been so tired. My body feels like it is made of lead and concrete, and my eyelids are the heaviest things in the whole world. The man tells me I'm being moved and I try to ask where, but all that comes out—as Father John bellows in my head *Never talk to Outsiders, not under any circumstances*—is a rasping whisper. The man says he doesn't know, and I summon every last bit of strength I have left and ask him who made it out of the fire. He grimaces and walks away…

…there's a paintbrush in my hand, and it's dripping with corn-flower blue. I know I'm dreaming, but I don't care because I don't want to wake up. I paint the wooden wall in front of me, and I hear the distant crash of waves at the base of the cliff, and I smell smoke as it rises from the chimney, and I know that if I look down, I'll see green grass beneath my feet, but I don't look down. I paint the wooden board in front of me and the one next to it and the one next to that…

…a different man in an identical dark suit reads a list of names from a piece of paper. I hear Honey and Rainbow and Lucy and Jeremiah, and I burst into tears of relief. The man gives me the first smile I've seen since I've been lying on this bed, and he carries on reading names, but not for long. My relief gives way to grief, and my tears keep coming because the list is so very, very short…

…the ceiling slides by as two doctors wheel my bed along a cor-ridor and into an empty metal box that shudders and rattles and makes my stomach spin. I try to reach out for the walls to steady myself, but one of the doctors pushes my arms back onto the bed, and my left hand howls with pain, and I cry out. The doctor says,

"Sorry," but his eyes are cold, and his mouth is hidden behind his mask. There's a beep and a jolt and a rush of cool air, and then I'm moving again. I see a sliver of sky, as blue as the wall in my dream, before I'm lifted and rolled into another metal box, although this one has shelves full of boxes and bottles and machines I don't recognize. There's a rumble beneath me as an engine starts up somewhere close by, and it sounds a bit like the red pickup that Amos used to drive, but it's much louder, and it sounds angry…

…a woman with a kind face wearing a white uniform helps me up from the bed I've been lying on ever since I woke up and gently lowers me onto a different one in a square white room with a window set high up in one wall. She tells me to press the orange button next to the door if I need anything, and a lump fills my throat. I ask her not to leave me, and she hugs me, and I start crying again. The voice in the back of my head gets really angry because I haven't cried this much since I was a little girl, but I can't help it. The woman with the kind face shushes me and strokes my hair and tells me it's okay, everything is going to be okay, she'll be right there if I need her, then gently slides out of my arms and gives me a smile before she walks out of the room, closing the door behind her. I lie down on the bed and I hear a heavy metallic thud as a lock slides into place…

…I drift…

A F T E R

I'm sitting on a dark-red sofa. My legs won't stop shaking, and my hand really hurts. I'm trying not to be scared, but I can't help it because I don't know what's going to happen to me.

I don't even know where I am.

The room I'm sitting in is bigger than my room at the Base, but it's still pretty small. The walls are pale gray, and the floor is dark gray carpet, and it contains the dark red sofa and a wide table with two chairs tucked under the far side, facing toward me. Everything is smooth and clean, and there's a machine sitting on the table and a camera above the door. The woman in the white uniform with the kind face—*Nurse Harrow*, whispers the voice in the back of my head, *she told you her name was Nurse Harrow*—brought me here five minutes ago, and I saw the words INTERVIEW ROOM 1 printed on the door as she pushed it open.

She asked me if I wanted anything before she left. I didn't have any idea how to answer her.

I hear a lock turn, and I hold my breath. The door opens, and a man walks into the room. He's small, with a thick beard and thinning hair and deep lines on either side of a pair of friendly eyes. He's wearing a white shirt and a tie, and he has a leather bag over his shoulder. He pulls out one of the chairs and sits down, then takes a stack of notebooks and pens out of his bag and arranges them carefully on the table in front of him. When everything is laid out how he wants it, he presses a button on the machine, waits until a small green light appears, then smiles at me.

"Hello," he says.

I don't say anything.

I know I asked the man in the suit a question, before, when I was lying on the bed with my mind drifting. But I'm thinking more clearly now, and some things are so deeply rooted in the fabric of who I am that I can't remember a time they weren't there, and it's hard to reason my way around them, even after everything that happened.

You never talk to Outsiders. Never.

"My name is Doctor Robert Hernandez," he continues. "I'm the director of psychiatry at the University of Texas Children's Hospital at Austin. Do you know what that means?"

I don't respond.

"It means I specialize in the well-being of children," he says. "Particularly children who have experienced traumatic events. I listen to them, and I try to help them."

In my head, Father John screams that Outsiders only want to hurt me, want to torture and kill me.

"I understand this must be an extremely frightening situation," says Doctor Hernandez. "You've been through a terrible ordeal, and I know you're in a lot of pain. But I'm not your enemy, no matter what you may have been told, and I promise that I mean you no harm. I want to help you. But for that to happen, you're going to have to trust me. Just a little bit, to start with. Do you think you can do that?"

I stare at him. It's clear from the expectant look in his eyes that he doesn't have the slightest idea what he's asking.

"How about we start with something simple? Why don't you tell me your name?"

I don't respond. My eyes stay locked on his.

"That's okay," he says. "That's absolutely fine. How about this? I'll ask you a question, and you just nod or shake your head. You don't have to say a word."

I don't move a muscle. I try not to even blink.

Doctor Hernandez's smile fades, ever so slightly. "No? You don't want to give that a try?"

I blink, because my eyes are starting to hurt, but that's all. He nods and scribbles something in one of his notebooks.

I watch the pen scratch across the paper, and I want to know what he's writing about me, but I can't ask.

"Okay." He sets the pen down. "The last thing I want to do is make you feel pressured in any way. I can only imagine how overwhelming this must be, so I think the best thing at this point is for you to go back to your room, and we'll try this again tomorrow. You don't have to talk to me, and I guarantee that nobody, least of all me, is going to force you to. But if I didn't honestly believe it would be helpful for you to do so, I wouldn't be here."

I resist the urge to nod as Father John screams in my head, calling me a Heretic and telling me that he always knew I was False.

Doctor Hernandez nods again, gives me a big smile, and starts putting the notebooks and pens back into the leather bag. "All right then," he says. "Get some rest. I'll see you tomorrow."

Nurse Harrow escorts me back to my room. I don't say anything as we walk along the gray corridors, but she still gives me a smile as she closes my door and locks it.

I take a look around the room that I assume is now my home. It's far from big, but it isn't tiny either; there were lots of smaller rooms at the Base, and this one has a sink and a toilet and a desk and a chair.

The door locks from the outside, so I guess that's the same.

I found a pile of clothes next to a thick stack of paper and boxes of pencils, pens, and crayons on the desk after Nurse Harrow brought me in here last night. Gray pants, underwear and socks, T-shirts and sweaters, sneakers. Most still wrapped in plastic, all still with their price tags on. I'm wearing some of them now.

I'm pretty sure they're the first new clothes I've ever worn.

There's a digital clock on the wall above the door; the glowing numbers read 10:17. Nurse Harrow told me she would bring me breakfast every day at 9:00 and lunch at 12:30, but I have no idea what I'm supposed to do with the time in between.

I lie down on my bed and stare at the ceiling for a while, then get up and walk back and forth until the muscles in my legs start to ache and my hand starts to burn beneath the bandages. I sit at the desk.

Apart from the Bible, there were no books allowed inside the Base after the Purge, and almost no paper or pencils, but I had a plain sketch pad that Father Patrick gave me when I was a little girl. The Centurions must have known about it, because I didn't hide it, but they never took it away. I had drawn on every page dozens of times, until the paper was deeply grooved by pencil lines that had been erased and redrawn and erased again. It was in my room when the fire started, so I guess it burned.

I take a sheet of paper from the stack and run my fingers over its surface. It's smooth because it's never been used.

It has no history.

I stare at the white wall in front of me until my mind empties, then take a pencil out of the plastic jar and start to draw.

For a long time now, what I draw has seemed beyond my control. I can start out meaning to draw a dog or a spaceship or a desert island, but it always turns into the same thing in the end. It's as though the pencil comes alive in my fingers, like it knows my true intentions better than I do. I sort of understand what a psychiatrist is from back when we were still allowed to watch TV and read books, even though I didn't tell Doctor Hernandez that. He would likely say that the drawings are my subconscious asserting itself. He would probably be right, but I'm never going to show them to him so it doesn't really matter.

I sketch the first lines and—almost instantly—the familiar image starts to work its way out of my head and onto the page. I trade pencils for colored pens and let myself drift into the monotony of repetition, my hand working on autopilot while jumbled, fractured memories float through my head…

…my dad, even though I know it's not really him. It's a version of him that my brain has animated from an old photo. He's smiling at me, and I wonder if he really looked like that when he smiled; people look different when they're moving rather than frozen inside a frame…

…fire exploding through the windows of the Chapel and racing across the desert floor like a wild animal pursuing its prey, crackling with savage delight…

…Honey's face as she said no to Father John, as she looked him in the eye and knowingly spoke Heresy…

…my mom, the last time I saw her. Sitting in the back of the red pickup, her eyes locked on mine as she clutched her possessions in a single plastic bag…

…Nate looming over me in the darkness, his eyes wide, his voice full of worry, his hands full of forbidden things…

16

…the locked door in the basement of the Big House…

…Father John, after his prophecies had finally come true and the Servants of the Serpent were at our gates. I search the memory of his face for the certainty that sustained the Legion, that convinced my Brothers and Sisters—convinced *me*, for the longest time—that The Lord would keep them safe and bring them Glory, and find nothing…

…Alice, her insides spilling out…

…the tank as it rolled forward…

…blood…

…empty bullet casings…

…so much blood…

…my entire world, in the final moments before it ended…

I shiver as a chill runs up my spine, then look down at the piece of paper and see the same picture as always.

Water fills most of the page, pale blue flecked with white. I don't know exactly what it is—a lake, an ocean, a river—because the largest body of water I've ever seen with my eyes is the fountain in the Layfield town square. Whatever *this* is, I'm not drawing it from memory.

Jagged brown cliffs rise from the water's edge to a flat headland of lush green grass, so different to the baked orange dust of the desert. Set back from the edge of the cliff is a small house, with pale blue walls and a white roof and a chimney with a delicate plume of gray smoke spiraling up into a sky that is almost the same color as the water.

Standing next to the house are two tiny figures. They're barely more than stick people, but I know exactly who they are.

One is me.

The other is my mom.

AFTER

I wake up in sheets soaked with sweat, a scream rising in my throat.

Bad dreams. The fire and Luke and Father John. I look at the clock above the door.

8:57.

I haven't slept this late in as long as I can remember. Probably the only times I ever have are when I've been ill. There are three minutes until Nurse Harrow will arrive with my breakfast, if what she told me yesterday was the truth.

Of course it wasn't! bellows Father John, his vast, booming voice echoing through my head. *She's an Outsider! They lie! They only ever lie!*

Goose bumps break out along my arms. The power in The Prophet's voice still terrifies me, even after everything: the absolute certainty, the blazing authority that tolerated no argument of any kind. I squeeze my eyes shut, and I concentrate really hard on the water and the cliffs and the blue house, and eventually the voice fades away, although I know I'll never truly be rid of it.

I open my eyes and sit up on the edge of my bed. My hand hurts worse than ever. Horizon used to tell me that wounds are most painful when they're getting better, and I really hope he was right because it feels like someone is pressing a flame against my fingers and when I scratch them through the thick layers of bandages it feels like the end of the world.

I don't know what time I eventually fell asleep yesterday. After I finished drawing, I cried for a while until Nurse Harrow brought me a plastic tray with a plate of hot dogs and hash browns. She had that kind look on her face, so I cried a bit more when she left, the tears rolling down my cheeks as I ate my lunch.

I don't know when, but at some point after I finished eating, I lay down and closed my eyes. I do the math in my head. I must have slept, on and off, for almost eighteen hours. I don't feel rested though. I feel worn out and used up, like I've been stretched too thin and there isn't enough of what's left to go around.

I feel empty.

A key turns in the lock, and there's a knock before the door swings open. It seems a little pointless, because I'm pretty sure I couldn't stop whoever it is from coming in, but I guess it's polite.

Nurse Harrow appears with another tray in her hands. This one contains a steaming plate of scrambled eggs, bacon, fried potatoes, a fruit cup, and a plastic beaker of orange juice. My first thought—so quick to rise into my mind, so very quick—is that there's no way I can eat it, because even though the fruit is in a little bowl, it's clearly part of the same meal as the potatoes, and fruit and vegetables in the same meal are *absolutely* not allowed. The rules of the Legion, delivered via Father John directly from the mouth of The Lord, are carved into my brain.

I try not to squirm as my stomach rumbles, and I even manage a tiny smile as Nurse Harrow puts the tray down on the desk. She glances at the drawing I did yesterday, and my heart accelerates in my chest because I don't want her to look. It feels like she's seeing me naked.

"This is very good," she says, her smile widening. "Where is this house?"

"Don't touch it." It's the first thing I've said since I was brought here, wherever here is, and my voice is barely a croak. In my head, Father John tells me I'm *stupid and useless and weak.* "Please don't."

Nurse Harrow nods and steps back from the desk. "I won't," she says. "I'll be back in twenty minutes. I want to change your bandages before you go to Doctor Hernandez. Is that all right with you?"

I nod. She gives me another smile, then disappears through the door and locks it behind her. I wait until I'm sure she's really gone, then I grab the drawing and fold it in half and clutch it tightly against my chest as I look around the room for somewhere to hide it.

There isn't anywhere.

Of course there isn't. Rooms with heavy doors that lock and windows you can't reach don't have hiding places. I think about the loose board under my bed at the Base, about the dark space beneath it, but the floor I'm standing on now is made of smooth plastic tiles, and the walls around me are flat and featureless.

The easiest thing would be to destroy the sheet of paper. But I don't want to. I just *don't.* It's the only thing in this room that is really mine.

Instead, I untuck my pillowcase and shove the folded drawing inside, and turn the pillow over so the obvious rectangular shape is pressed against my mattress. It's pretty much the worst hiding place ever. Even though I don't think there are any cameras in my room—I can't *see* any, at least—it will take Nurse Harrow or anybody else about five seconds to find the drawing if they decide to look.

But it's the best I can do.

"I'm going to suggest something," says Doctor Hernandez. "If that's okay with you?"

I'm sitting on the sofa in Interview Room 1 again. The psychiatrist is behind the desk, his notebooks and pens neatly arranged in front of him, the green light glowing on the machine beside him. He asked how I'm feeling this morning as soon as he walked through the door. I didn't answer the question, even though I actually do feel a little better—physically, at least—after Nurse Harrow changed my dressing and smeared greasy white cream all over the burned skin on my hand.

I don't answer this one either.

"I'm going to take that as a yes," he says. "My suggestion is that we trade. You ask a question, and I answer it. Then I ask, and you answer. How does that sound?"

In my head, Father John warns me not to fall for such an obvious trick, not to be stupid and gullible and False. I do my best to ignore his voice, but it's really hard. It booms and growls and roars, and for years and years, it was the only voice that mattered, the only source of truth in a world full of lies. Still, I try, because although I'm scared to talk to Doctor Hernandez—or anybody else for that matter—and I really don't want to answer any questions, there are two things I need to know. Two things I don't think I can go much longer *without* knowing.

Be brave, whispers the voice in the back of my head. This one isn't Father John's; it sounds a lot like me, except it says things I would never dare to.

"Okay," I say. Doctor Hernandez smiles. I wonder if he had

21

started to think I was never going to speak again. "But only if I can go first."

"Of course. Ask away. Anything you like."

I take a deep breath. "Where's my mom?"

His smile fades at the edges, and I see pity on his face. I hate that he feels sorry for me, but I can't tell him that because his expression has made me so scared about what he's going to say that my chest has seized tight, trapping my breath inside me.

"I'm sorry," he says. "I'm afraid I don't have any information on your mother."

My chest relaxes. His answer—or *nonanswer*, to be accurate—is pretty much what I was expecting, even though it still hurts to hear the words out loud.

It could be worse, whispers the voice in the back of my head. *He could have told you she's dead.*

It's true. That would have been worse. But I'm not sure by how much. Not knowing is awful, even after all this time.

"I'm sorry," he repeats.

"She isn't here?" My voice is still a croak, low and small.

"No," he says. "She isn't here."

"Is she still alive?"

"I don't know."

I stare at him. "You don't know?"

"I'm afraid not," he says. "I wish I could give you the answer you want or tell you a lie that would make you feel better, but I believe honesty is the most important element of this process. In time, when you're ready, there are other people who would like to talk to you, and it's possible they may have more information on the subject than I do."

The subject. You're talking about my mother, you asshole.

I blush at the bad word, even though I'm the only one who heard it. Doctor Hernandez frowns.

22

"Are you okay?"

"When?" I ask.

"I'm sorry?"

"When would these other people like to talk to me?"

"When it's appropriate," he says.

"When will that be?"

"When you're ready."

"Who decides that?"

"I do," he says, "in consultation with my colleagues. I can't give you an exact schedule, not at this early stage, but for now, I'll make you a promise. After we conclude this session, I'll ask the other agencies involved in this case for any information they have on your mother and bring you their reply. Does that sound fair?"

I shrug. I know he wants me to say yes, but I'm not going to. Doctor Hernandez looks at me for a long moment, then writes a note in one of his books. There are four of them, all different sizes, as well as three loose pads of paper. I don't understand how he can possibly need them all.

"All right." He puts down his pen and smiles at me. "My turn to ask a question. If that's still okay?"

Fair's fair, whispers the voice in the back of my head. I shrug again.

"Okay," he says. "Great. What's your name?"

"Moonbeam," I say.

His smile widens. "That's a beautiful name."

I say nothing.

"Do you have any others?" he asks.

"Other what?"

"Names."

"No."

"Most people have at least two."

I shrug. "Some of my Brothers and Sisters had six or seven. I only have one."

"Fine," he says. "That's fine."

I stare at him. He clearly wants me to say something more, but I don't have the slightest idea what.

"If you're telling me you only have one name, I believe you," he says.

You don't. Clearly you don't. Although I don't know why you think I would lie about my name.

"Okay," I say.

"What about John Parson? What did he call you?"

"Father John called me Moonbeam."

"Did he—"

I shake my head. "I don't want to talk about him."

"No problem." He raises his open hands in a *stay calm* gesture that makes me want to slam his head against the desk. "No problem at all. We don't need to talk about him or about anything else that makes you uncomfortable—until you're ready. Okay?"

I give him the tiniest of nods.

He looks relieved. "Great," he says. "Your turn."

"What have you done with my letter?" I ask.

He frowns. "I'm sorry?"

"I had a letter in my pocket," I say. "During the fire. Where is it?"

"I'm afraid I don't know. Was it important?"

The most important thing in the world.

I study his face, hoping to catch him lying. I've always been pretty good at reading people, especially after what happened to my mom, but all I see on Doctor Hernandez's face is concern, so I shake my head. "It doesn't matter."

He nods, although he doesn't seem at all convinced. "Okay. Why don't you ask me something else? That one didn't really count."

"I don't have any more questions."

"None at all?"

You didn't answer the one I had. "No."

"Why don't I give you a little information about what's happening then? You might want to ask me about some of it, and it might make you feel more comfortable with your new surroundings."

I doubt that very much, but I shrug. "Okay."

"Great." I'm starting to notice he says that a *lot*. "So this place, this building we're sitting in, is called the George W. Bush Municipal Center. It's in Odessa, about fifty miles from where you used to live. Do you know who George W. Bush is?"

I shake my head.

"He was president of the United States," says Doctor Hernandez. "Do you know what that means?"

"He was the head of the Government."

"That's exactly right," he says. "George W. Bush was president for eight years, until 2009, and this building was named for him when he left office. This section of the center, where we are now, is part of something called a secure unit. It's a place where people can be looked after, where they can be safe. Do you know where you were before you were brought here?"

"Hospital."

"Right again. You were in Mercy Memorial Hospital, six miles west of here. You were there for four days."

My head swims.

Four days? Is that really all it was? Can that be right?

"I know someone talked to you while you were there," continues Doctor Hernandez. "I know they asked you questions when you were in no fit state to answer them, and I'm very sorry they did. That shouldn't have happened. From now on, nobody will ask you anything unless I'm there to make sure you're okay with it. I promise."

I nod for about the hundredth time. It feels like nodding isn't enough, like he must be expecting more of a response, but I don't know what else to do. I guess I could try to smile, but I don't think it would be very convincing.

"You're not a prisoner here," he says, "and it's important that you don't see yourself as one. I understand there are locks on the doors and that you're being told what to do and where to go, and it's perfectly natural for you to find your situation frustrating. But you have to believe me when I tell you that everything is being done with your safety and well-being as the first priority. You're not in any trouble."

I very nearly laugh out loud.

You have no idea, I think. *Absolutely no idea at all.*

"So I can leave?" I ask.

"There you go," he says, his smile returning. "You *did* have another question."

I stare at him.

"The answer is yes," he says, when he realizes I'm not going to respond to what I'm pretty sure was a joke. "The entire purpose of my being here is to help you get on with your life as quickly as possible."

"But I can't leave now?"

He frowns. "Well, no. Not right this minute."

"So how am I not a prisoner?"

He appears to consider this for a second or two. "It's more about how you perceive your situation," he says eventually. "Look at this as a process that you and I are going to work through together and accept that we need certain boundaries in place for that to happen. We need to work in a space where you feel safe, where we can explore some of the things you've been through and take positive action to address them. When that process is complete, and I'm satisfied that you're safe and well and ready, you'll be free to go."

I don't believe that, not for a second. But I see no point in saying so out loud.

"When will that be?" I ask.

"The sooner we get started, the sooner we'll be done."

"Okay."

"Great," says Doctor Hernandez. He opens one of his notebooks. "How old are you, Moonbeam?"

Fair's fair.

"Seventeen."

"When's your birthday?"

"I'll be eighteen in November. On the twenty-first."

"I'll send you a card," he says.

Another joke. I stare at him again.

He looks down and scribbles something. I wait. Eventually his gaze returns to mine. "Is there anything you would like to talk about in this session?" he asks. "It can be anything, absolutely anything at all."

"No."

"Are you sure?"

"I'm not a liar," I lie.

"Of course you aren't," he says, and makes the *stay calm* gesture with his hands again. This time I want to snap his wrists, because I think I'm being *incredibly* calm, given the circumstances. "In which case, why don't you tell me something? It doesn't matter what, it doesn't have to be anything important. Just something about your life."

"Like what?" I ask.

"Completely up to you," he says. "Whatever comes into your head."

I consider this. I know what he *wants* me to talk about—the same thing the woman in the uniform in the hospital asked me about. But I'm not going to, not with him or anybody else. Not ever. Because I don't want to spend the rest of my life in a cell if I can possibly help it.

I'm not stupid. Maybe he thinks I am, but I'm not.

I know he'll never let me out of here unless I tell him *something*.

You need to look at this as a process, whispers the voice in the back of my head.

I take a deep breath and start to talk.

BEFORE

The cloud of dust rising from the dirt road outside the Front Gate of the Base is too small to be an approaching car, but all four Centurions head toward it, rifles in hand. We don't get a lot of visitors, and most of the ones we do get are unwelcome.

There are Private Property signs hung along the length of the fence, but that isn't always enough to put people off. For several years, we had trouble every fall, when college freshmen from Midland and Odessa were ordered to steal something from inside the Base and take it back to their fraternity brothers. I don't think any of them were actually successful in their mission. The Centurions usually ran them off before they reached the fence and sent them stumbling back into the desert, laughing and hollering. But on at least two occasions, a drunken, half-naked teenager had to be physically cut down from the coils of barbed wire along the top of the fence. We wrapped blankets around the boys—who were crying and bleeding and white with shock—and Amos drove them into Layfield in the back of the red pickup so they could get help. Eventually, it stopped happening. I guess people got bored of doing the same thing every year. I don't know.

I doubt this visitor is anything to be concerned about though, because it's the middle of the day, and whoever is kicking up the cloud of dust is walking right down the middle of the road. The college boys usually came through the desert to the west, from the bend in the highway where Horizon reckoned they parked their cars. Unsurprisingly, they only ever made the journey at night.

I walk toward the fence with a gathering crowd of my Brothers and Sisters: Iris, Alice, Luke, Martin, Agavé, and half a dozen others. I get a little flutter of excitement in my stomach as we approach the gate, where the Centurions have stopped and lined up, Horizon slightly in front of the others. I don't think there's going to be any trouble, but this has the potential to be unusual in a day that has so far been totally unremarkable.

The Centurions unlocked my bedroom door just after dawn, and I ate the same breakfast in Legionnaires' Hall that I always eat: two grapefruit halves, two hard-boiled eggs—eggs aren't a vegetable, so that wasn't breaking any rules—and a bowl of muesli with raisins. I worked in the vegetable gardens for a few hours, up behind the Big House, and was about to take my tools back to the sheds when Iris noticed the cloud of dust and called for the nearest Centurion.

I squeeze in between the broad shoulders of Bear and Horizon and peer through the metal bars of the Front Gate. And all of a sudden my skin feels really hot, like I've been out in the sun for too long.

Walking down the dirt road is a man. The desert breeze is blowing his long blond hair across his face, and his T-shirt looks like it has been sprayed over muscles so pronounced I'm pretty sure I could count them, even from a distance. He's wearing faded jeans and dusty boots, and there's a duffel bag slung over his shoulder and a smile on his face that makes my knees feel like they're going to give way beneath me.

"My word," breathes Alice. "Lead me not into temptation, Lord."

This makes me angry so suddenly that it takes me aback. Alice is twenty—five years older than me, with two daughters of her own—and some childish part of myself that I didn't know existed until five seconds ago wants to shout, "*I saw him first!*" But of course I don't, because that would be ridiculous. Instead I stare, my heart thudding in my chest, as the man stops a decent distance away from the Centurions and their guns and raises his hands in a gesture of peace.

"Easy now," he says. "I come in peace."

The deep drawl of his voice fills me with the urgent desire to wrench open the gate, sprint down the road, and hurl myself against him, even though he's an Outsider and he looks a lot older than me and the Third Proclamation makes it clear that I'm not supposed to think that kind of thing.

"I reckon we'll be the judge of that," Horizon says to the man. His voice is firm, but not completely unfriendly. "What's your business here?"

"I've got some questions I've been asking myself," says the man. "I heard this might be the place to find the answers."

"It might," says Horizon. "And then again, it might not. What's your name, friend?"

"Nate," says the man. "Nate Childress."

"Where you from, Nate Childress?"

"Lubbock," replies the man—*Nate, he said his name was Nate*—and jerks his head back toward the road he just walked down. "Originally, that is. Abilene most recently."

"Who told you there might be answers for you here?" asks Horizon.

"A waitress in the diner down in Layfield," says Nate. "Bethany, her name was. We talked a little, and she told me this was somewhere I ought to check out."

Thank you, Bethany. Thank you so much.

"That don't seem likely," says Horizon. "We don't have many dealings with the townsfolk."

"So she said," says Nate. "She told me she used to talk to kids from here, back when she was one herself. Said it was a shame when they stopped coming."

Horizon nods. The other three Centurions stand silently, having clearly decided to let Horizon do all the talking.

"All right," he says. "If you're looking for answers, there's a man here you ought to talk to. But I'll warn you now, while we're speaking as friends, that if your heart is False, he will see it. There's no lying to him, and definitely ain't no deceiving him, so if that's what you have in mind, you might as well turn around now and head back the way you came."

"Thanks for the warning," says Nate. "I reckon I'll take my chances."

"So be it then," says Horizon, and twists open the padlock attached to the Front Gate. "Welcome to the Holy Church of the Lord's Legion. If you have found the True Path, I hope your stay is long and fruitful. Although that won't be for me to decide."

The rest of us back up as he swings the gate open. Nate walks through it slowly, nodding at my Brothers and Sisters in turn. When he reaches me he smiles, and I feel the skin on my face turn as red and hot as the surface of the sun. I want to say something clever and funny and *amazing*, but my mind is a total blank, so I just stare at him as he passes by.

"I'll escort you to the Chapel," says Horizon, handing the padlock to Bear to reattach. "You can wait there for Father John."

Nate nods. "Lead the way."

Horizon slings his rifle over his shoulder, and he and Nate walk toward the building that stands tall at the center of the Base. The rest of us fall in behind them until we reach the blacktop of the yard, where Amos peels off and heads for the Big House, glancing back over his shoulder as he goes. Horizon leads Nate up the steps and into the Chapel and shuts the door, leaving the rest of us outside.

"Oh my," says Alice, with a look so full of lust I almost take a step back. "Be still my beating heart. If The Prophet doesn't let him stay, I'm going with him when he leaves."

"Watch your tongue, Alice," says Jacob.

"Why wouldn't Father John let him stay?" I ask, ignoring him.

"Why should he?" asks Luke. "People don't just wander in here out of the blue. He's likely a troublemaker."

"Hush, Luke," says Alice. "You don't know what you're talking about."

Luke shrugs. "We'll see."

"You're right," says Alice. "We will."

At the north end of the yard, Father John emerges onto the porch of the Big House and starts heading toward us, Amos close behind him. A hush falls across the gathered crowd as he makes his way down the stairs, his long dark hair fluttering above his shoulders. He wears a gray shirt and dusty blue jeans, and his face is stern and serious, but he still takes a moment to nod in our direction as he strides toward the Chapel before disappearing inside. Amos joins the rest of us, a frown on his weathered face.

"What did The Prophet say?" asks Luke.

"Father John don't explain himself to the likes of me," says

Amos. "He'll talk to the new fella, then him and The Lord will speak on the matter, and he'll tell us what's been decided."

"I think we should let him stay," says Alice.

"Uh-huh," says Amos. "I reckon I know what part of you came up with that opinion."

Alice narrows her eyes. "Don't speak to me like that, Amos. There's no need for it."

Amos shrugs and turns his back on her. The rest of us stand, unmoving and silent, waiting for Father John to deliver The Lord's judgment on Nate Childress. Minutes tick past as the sun beats down overhead, and my Brothers and Sisters and I strain our ears for any hint of what's happening inside the Chapel.

Eventually, what seems like hours later, the tall wooden door opens, and Father John steps out, his face impassive and unreadable. Horizon and Nate follow him down the steps and onto the yard. When The Prophet stops and faces the crowd, they do likewise.

"A man has been delivered into our midst," says Father John. His voice soars and rolls on the gentle breeze, full of thundering bass and effortless conviction. "It remains to be seen whether he has the potential to be a True Brother of the Lord's Legion or should be cast out as a Servant of the Serpent. *It remains to be seen*, and the truth shall not be revealed by anyone gathered here. Therefore, this man may stay the night inside our walls, while each and every one of us prays on this matter. Come the morning, I have no doubt The Lord will have made His wishes known. The Lord is Good."

"The Lord is Good," repeats every single person in the yard, myself included.

Father John nods at Nate, then turns to Horizon. "There's an empty bed in Building Twelve. Give him a blanket and make sure he gets something to eat."

"Yes, Father," says Horizon.

The Prophet nods, then strides back toward the Big House without another word. Nate surveys the crowd with a smile on his face, one that—to me, at least—looks more than a little uneasy.

"You heard Father John," says Horizon. "Who will show this man—"

"I will," I say. "I'll take him to Building Twelve."

Horizon smiles at me and nods. Nate raises an eyebrow in my direction as I feel Alice's glare scorch the back of my neck.

"All right then," says Horizon. "Nate, Moonbeam will show you where to put your belongings. The long building east of the Chapel is Legionnaires' Hall. Join us there in thirty minutes for lunch."

The crowd begins to disperse, muttering excitedly to each other. I'm not surprised; it's been more than two years since someone joined the Legion by any means other than being born. Nate swings his bag over his shoulder and walks across to me, a wide smile on his face.

"Moonbeam," he says. "That's a pretty name."

Oh Lord, let me die. Let me Ascend now, because nothing is ever going to be better than this moment.

"Thanks," I manage. All of a sudden, I'm incredibly aware that my voice is *ridiculous*, high and wavering and screechy like a cat's. I can't understand why nobody has told me that before now, and I'm genuinely considering never speaking ever again when the voice in the back of my head begs me to calm down. I take a deep breath and point north. "It's this way."

"Lead on," he says. "It's got a hot tub, right?"

I frown at him. "It's a wooden box," I say. "It's got a bed. Maybe some shelves."

He laughs, and my insides turn to lava. "You and me are going to be friends," he says. "I can already tell."

AFTER

"When did Nate Childress arrive at the Legion compound?" asks Doctor Hernandez.

I grimace. "I don't like that word."

"Compound?"

I nod.

"I'm sorry," he says. "I won't use it anymore."

"Thank you."

He writes something in one of his notebooks. "So when did Nate arrive?"

"Two summers ago."

He makes another note, then sits back in his chair and smiles at me. "Why did you tell me that, Moonbeam?"

"I thought it didn't matter what I told you?"

"It doesn't matter," he says. "I just wondered if it's a happy memory? The day Nate arrived?"

I consider his question. Everything is tainted by what happened later, my memories blackened and twisted and spoiled, but I try to remember how I felt the day Nate arrived, how I *really* felt, and how pleased I was when Father John announced that he would be allowed to stay.

"Yes," I say eventually. "It's a happy memory."

"Why?" he asks.

"Because Nate was my friend."

We sit in silence for a long while. He looks at me, a half smile on his face, and I have no idea whether I told him a story he wanted to hear, whether that's going to be good enough—for now, at least. Father John is ranting and raving in my head, cursing me for saying anything at all to an Outsider, to a *psychiatrist* of all people. Doctor Hernandez's gaze is steady, and his smile looks genuine. I'm finding it really hard to get a read on him, which I guess is deliberate on his part, but it's really frustrating. Eventually, after what feels like hours of a silence that is not comfortable, but not completely uncomfortable either, he looks at his watch.

"It's a little early, but I think I'd like to end this session here," he says. "As long as that's all right with you?"

I try not to let the relief that surges through me show on my face. "That's fine."

"Before we finish, there's something I need to ask you," he says. "Can you tell me where you lived inside the com—inside the Legion property?"

"Why?"

"We recovered a number of personal possessions from the buildings after the fire was extinguished," he says. "We want to return as many of them as possible."

My heart thumps in my chest. "What did you find?"

"Are you thinking about something specific?"

"No," I lie.

"So can you tell me where you lived?"

"Building Nine," I say. "It was the square building in the southwest corner. My room was the one at the western end, nearest the fence."

Doctor Hernandez nods and makes a note. When he looks up, his smile has returned. "I'm pleased with our progress," he says. "I think it's been a great start, and I think you should be very proud of how you engaged this morning. You were able to ask questions and answer them. That's a very important part of this process as we continue to move forward. How do you feel about that?"

"I don't feel anything," I say, which is the truth.

"I understand," he says, and I'm sure he thinks he does, even though there's no way he really can. "Where possible, I'd like these sessions to last the full hour, but I don't think we need to worry about that today. I am going to ask you to join me every morning, however. How does that sound?"

"Do I have a choice?" I ask.

He smiles. "Of course you do. But I think routine is going to be very important, and…what?"

I'm smiling. I can't help it. "Nothing," I say.

He tilts his head slightly to one side. "Are you sure?"

"I'm sure."

"Okay," he says, although it's obvious he doesn't believe me. "Like I said, I think routine is going to be very important in terms of making progress, and I know we both want to get you out of here as soon as possible."

Amen to that.

I nod.

"Great," he says. "Is there anything else you want to ask me before we finish up?"

I think for a second or two, and I realize there is. "Are you talking to my Brothers and Sisters as well?"

"I'm personally working with you and two other survivors," he says. "My colleagues are working with the other sixteen."

"Who?" I ask.

"I'm sorry?"

"Who are you talking to apart from me?"

"I'm afraid that's confidential," he says. "Although the other session I'm going to ask you to take part in should make it pretty easy for you to find out."

I frown. "What other session?"

"You and I will meet at ten each morning, after you've had breakfast," says Doctor Hernandez. "Your lunch is set for twelve thirty. Afterward, I'm going to ask you to participate in something called supervised social interaction, or SSI."

"What's that?"

"It's a type of group therapy. It allows me and my colleagues to monitor the interactions of people who have survived traumatic experiences, and it creates a space for those interactions to develop organically in a controlled environment."

I stare at him. There were a *lot* of words I didn't understand in what he just said. "So it'll be me and you and the rest of your colleagues?"

He smiles and shakes his head. "Not exactly."

At precisely twelve thirty, Nurse Harrow appears with my lunch. Today it's meat loaf and mashed potatoes smothered in a bright red sauce that's so sweet it tastes like caramel, but I'm really hungry so I sit at the desk and eat it while I think about Doctor Hernandez.

I don't trust him. Even though some eager, desperate part of me wants to, I *can't* trust him. I guess that almost goes without saying, although not because he's an Outsider—though that's still the first thought that enters my mind when I think about him.

39

The reason I can't trust him is because—right now—I don't really know what he wants.

I *want* to believe that he has no agenda, apart from helping me get better so I can leave this place, but I can't quite let myself believe that. So many people are dead—sixty-seven people, if the list of survivors the man read to me in the hospital was accurate— and I know things, *did* things, that either Doctor Hernandez or the other people he mentioned are going to want me to talk about. And those are things I can never tell anyone.

Sixty-seven people, whispers the voice in the back of my head.
All dead.

A lump leaps into my throat.

But eighteen are still alive, continues the voice. *Nineteen, including you. That has to count for something.*

I squeeze my eyes shut. I can't think about this now. About any of this. Doctor Hernandez's face appears, floating in the darkness beside me, and I'm surprised, but I force myself to focus on it, *on him*, until the lump in my throat recedes, and my head clears, and I feel something close to okay again.

Two things surprised me as the session in Interview Room 1 progressed. Firstly, that I found myself wanting to talk to Doctor Hernandez; and secondly, that it felt like it might be okay if I did. I'm aware of the idea of psychiatry, even though Father John made it very clear after the Purge that all methods of healing other than prayer are instruments of The Serpent. My mom talked about it during the rare moments when she actually spoke to me about my dad, even though she wasn't supposed to. Apparently he talked to someone every week until they moved to the Base. My mom called the person he talked to a therapist, but I'm pretty sure it's the same thing. Mom told me that a therapist's job is to put people at ease, to get them to open up and talk about things that are hard, or painful, or both.

INTERROGATING THEM! screams Father John. *CLAWING INTO THEIR SOULS, RIPPING AND TEARING! VIOLATING! DAMNING THEM TO HELL!*

His voice echoes through my skull, sending a shiver up my spine. I silently scream at him to shut up because I *want* to believe that Doctor Hernandez was telling the truth when he said he isn't my enemy, that he genuinely means me no harm. I really *want* to believe him. I just can't.

Not yet.

I finish eating and lie down on my bed. Through the small window, deliberately set too high up the wall for anyone to reach it, I can see a narrow rectangle of sky. I think back to the skies at the Base, the vast empty blue of the days, so bright you could barely look at it, and the infinite darkness of the nights, when the stars reached all the way from the ground to Heaven, a trillion points of glowing light. Tears rise in the corners of my eyes and spill down my cheeks. The quieter voice in the back of my head whispers that I have to be strong. I know it's right, but knowing doesn't make the tears stop, because being strong doesn't mean I'm not allowed to miss my Brothers and Sisters and the sky and the sun and the desert. I can do both, because nothing is ever only good and nothing is ever only bad. Everything is somewhere in the middle.

When I hear the already familiar sound of a lock turning, I sit up and look at the clock. The glowing numbers tell me that it's 1:55. The door swings open, and Nurse Harrow asks me if Doctor Hernandez told me about SSI. I nod, and she tells me it's time.

I get up and follow her down a long corridor, past door after identical door, until we reach one with a sign that says GROUP THERAPY on the wall next to it. Nurse Harrow unlocks it and stands aside. For seconds that stretch on and on, I don't move. I stand in the gray corridor, listening.

I can hear voices inside the room, but they don't sound like they belong to adults; they sound like the high, hectic voices of children.

I recognize one, and then another, and another, and my heart surges in my chest. I run past the smiling Nurse Harrow and through the door. I have just long enough to see the faces of my younger Brothers and Sisters before Luke appears in front of me, demanding to know what I've been telling the Outsiders.

The lie comes automatically. "Nothing. I haven't told them a thing."

"You better not have," says Luke. "You better be keeping your mouth shut."

I look at him. He looks as angry as I've ever seen him, which is saying something. His skin is flushed, his eyes blazing, his hands balled at his sides. Behind him, Honey, Lucy, Rainbow, Jeremiah, and all the others stand near the back wall of the room, which is much bigger than the interview room where I talk to Doctor Hernandez and full of chairs and tables and boxes of toys and games. They stare at me with glorious smiles on their faces, and my heart swells with joy and relief, but the voice in the back of my head is warning me to be careful.

Very careful.

"I said I haven't told them anything," I say. "Back off, Luke." He grabs my upper arm and squeezes. His knuckles turn white with effort, and it *really* hurts, but I refuse to let the pain show on my face. I keep my eyes locked on his.

"Let her go, Luke," says Honey. "You've got no right to question anyone. Nobody put you in charge."

Luke spins toward her. "You shut up!" he shouts. "You ought to be in Hell for what you did, so shut your damn mouth! Nobody wants to hear your Heresy!"

"You might well be right," says Honey. "But I'm not in Hell.

I'm right here. So why don't you let her go, Luke? You're not impressing anyone."

"They should never have let you out of that box, you little whore," spits Luke. "They should have let you die in there."

My stomach lurches, but Honey stares at Luke, her eyes clear, her skin pale. She's only fourteen, but she's the bravest person I know. Much braver than me.

"That's enough, Luke," I say, forcing calm I don't feel into my voice. "I haven't said anything. Just calm down."

He turns back to face me, and I see—so horribly clear now—the churning madness in his eyes that I didn't recognize until it was far too late. "The Lord is testing us." His voice rises and trembles. "He's listening to every word we say. *He's in this room with us now.*"

"I believe you," I tell him. "Can you let go of my arm, please? I'd like to hug our Brothers and Sisters."

He digs his fingers into my flesh, hard, then releases his grip. I step away from him, then turn and stride across the room and sweep Honey into my arms. As the others come running, I whisper into her ear, so quietly that nobody else can hear me.

"I know you must have questions. About the fire. Just remember what the first *S* stands for."

I let her go. She meets my eyes and nods as the rest of our Brothers and Sisters crash into us, almost piling on top of each other as they hug me with their little arms and tell me they're pleased to see me because they thought I had Ascended with the others, but they're really glad I didn't. I see the thick purple and black ridges on Lucy's face, and I feel tears spill from my eyes for the second time today. Not because I gave her the bruises, although I might as well have, but because this—a group of frightened children locked inside a building full of strangers—is not anything *good*, is not anything *True*, is not anything that should have been allowed to happen.

It should never, ever have come to this.

"What have they been asking you?" asks Aurora, one of Alice's daughters. My head fills with an image of blood soaking into the desert dirt, and I'm suddenly aware—*truly* aware, although I guess I already knew—that she and her sister, Winter, are orphans now.

Jesus.

They're six and five years old, and they're orphans.

Jesus.

"Nothing." I pry myself out of dozens of small grips and stand up. "Honestly. I was in the hospital until two days ago."

Aurora points at the bandages wrapped around my hand. "Did you get burned?"

I nod.

"Does it hurt?" she asks.

I give her my bravest smile. "It's not too bad," I lie. "But being in the hospital meant I didn't talk to anybody here until yesterday morning. What have they been asking you?"

"About my life," says Aurora. "What we used to do every day, what we ate. That kind of thing."

"Is it Doctor Hernandez you're talking to?" I ask.

She shakes her head. "Doctor Kelly. She's nice, for an Outsider. She keeps telling me to draw things."

"What things?" asks Luke.

I glance over and see a frown creasing his forehead.

"She said it didn't matter," says Aurora. "Whatever came into my mind."

"So what did you draw?" I ask.

"A unicorn."

I smile. "Anything else?"

"I drew Father John," she says. "I drew him on a golden horse, trampling the Servants of the Serpent."

44

Luke breaks into a wide smile as mine fades. "What did the Outsider say to that?" he asks.

"She didn't say anything," says Aurora. "She just put it in a folder and asked me about schooling."

"Good girl," says Luke. "You tell them *nothing*. You stay on the True Path, no matter what she says. The Lord is Good."

"The Lord is Good," says Aurora, her eyes shining. Most of the others—although not all of them—echo her, and Luke stares at me until I mutter the words too.

"Outsiders lie," he says, turning back to face the children. "Listen to me when I tell you so. *Outsiders lie*. A sickness infects their hearts, a darkness that The Serpent himself placed there and nurtured. A miracle took place before their very eyes—the Ascension of The Prophet and our Brothers and Sisters to their rightful place beside The Lord. But did they see? Did they throw themselves to their knees and renounce their Heresy? Did they plead for forgiveness? They did not because their poisoned minds would not allow them to accept the truth of what they witnessed. Pity them if you must, but never forget what they are and who they serve. They will try to break our connection with The Lord, to steer us from the path that we alone were True enough to walk, but we will not let them. *We will not let them*, because ours is the Glory everlasting, and each and every one of you knows that to be the truth. Our Faith is being tested, but this hardship will pass provided we remain strong with The Lord. Our time will come soon enough."

Luke pauses. I stare at him with horror churning my stomach, silently pleading with Honey, whose face is curdled with a disgust she clearly can't—or *won't*—hide, not to say a word. I have to assume that Doctor Hernandez and his colleagues are watching this, that they wouldn't let anything bad happen, but right now this feels a really long way from the safe place he told me that

SSI would be, and I don't like to consider what Luke might do if Honey speaks against him.

He stares into the rapt faces of our younger Brothers and Sisters, then turns and looks up into the nearest corner of the room. I follow his gaze and see a camera pointing down toward us.

"And to the Servants of the Serpent, I say this," he says. "You can try to corrupt us, to tear down our Faith, and drag us into the dirt. We welcome it because we are True and we are not afraid. Here we stand, before you. *We stand*, and when The Lord sees fit, we will Ascend to His side while you crawl on your bellies through the fires of Hell for all eternity."

Luke stares at the camera for long, silent seconds, then turns his back on it and kneels down. "Pray with me."

The children go to him willingly, taking each other's hands and forming a circle. Honey keeps as much distance between herself and Luke as possible, but she joins the circle, and I'm glad she does, for both our sakes. I hope she understood what I whispered to her. There are things she ought to know, things that only I can tell her, but I can't when I know other people are listening.

I kneel down. Aurora gently holds my bandaged hand, and Rainbow tightly grips my other. Before he closes his eyes and lowers his head, Luke gives me a long, cold look, and I get the message loud and clear.

I'm watching you.

I don't blame him. I really don't. He was suspicious of me for a long time before the fire, and he was right to be. He *is* right to be. Because here's what nobody knows, what I can never tell Doctor Hernandez or anyone else.

It's because of me that Aurora and Winter and so many of their Brothers and Sisters are orphans, and that so many people are dead.

It's all my fault.

A
F
T
E
R

I had nightmares again. Not as bad as last time, but bad. Fire and blood.

When I got back to my room yesterday after SSI, there was a bag lying on the desk. I stared at it for a long time before opening it with trembling fingers, because through the clear plastic I could see things I last saw in my room inside the Base. The knives with the engraved handles weren't there, and the photo of my grandparents and the page of my dad's diary are gone, presumably reduced to ash along with almost everything else. My letter wasn't in the bag. I'm not surprised. The seashell survived though, and so did the stopped watch. My dad's watch.

I ran my fingers over its glass face when I woke up, my head still full of the remnants of bad dreams. Then I put everything back in the bag and waited for Nurse Harrow to arrive with my breakfast.

I didn't eat very much.

When Nurse Harrow came back to take me to today's session with Doctor Hernandez, she asked if I was feeling all right, and I lied and said yes. I don't think she totally believed me, but she didn't press me about it as she escorted me to Interview Room 1, and for that I was grateful.

"How are you doing this morning, Moonbeam?" asks Doctor Hernandez.

I shuffle on the sofa and shrug my shoulders.

"Did you sleep okay?"

I shake my head.

"Did you—"

"Were you watching?" I interrupt. "Yesterday, I mean. When we were all together."

He nods. "SSI is always monitored."

"So is that how it was supposed to go?" I ask. "You thought that was okay?"

"It isn't supposed to go any specific way," he says. "It's an organic interaction. It goes in whatever direction the participants dictate."

"But it's supposed to help," I say. "Right?"

"That's certainly the intention," he replies. "Can I ask what's troubling you, Moonbeam? Is it what Luke said?"

Obviously.

"I guess I don't see how it's helpful for the others to hear that kind of stuff."

"I understand that," he says. "I really do. But Luke's process is different to yours, Moonbeam, and so is Honey's and

48

Rainbow's and everyone else's. People deal with trauma in different ways."

"You don't think letting him talk like that is dangerous?"

He leans back in his chair. "Do you genuinely think what Luke said is dangerous, or is it hard for you to hear because you don't believe it?"

I stare at him as Father John screams in my head, telling me only a Heretic would even come close to falling into such an obvious trap, only someone who was stupid and useless and False.

"If I thought what Luke did was dangerous," he says eventually, "I wouldn't have allowed the session to continue. I promised you a safe environment, and that is our first priority. SSI often involves vigorous debate, even disagreement, and it can lead to some challenging discussion, but the environment is controlled and monitored at all times. There is nothing for you to worry about."

"Okay." I don't believe him, not for a second, but I don't see any point in telling him so. I just have to hope that he's right and I'm wrong.

"Would you like to keep talking about SSI?" he asks. "It's absolutely fine if you do."

I shake my head.

He nods. "Okay. Great. I'd like to—"

"Do you have any children?" I ask. The question occurred to me last night when I was waiting to fall asleep, and if I don't ask it now, I'll have forgotten by the time we finish talking about whatever he wants to move on to.

Doctor Hernandez frowns. "Why do you ask?"

"You told me your job is helping children," I say. "I wondered if you have any of your own."

"Fair enough," he says. "It's a perfectly valid question. The answer is no, I don't have any children. Does that concern you?"

His answer deflates me a little. I thought the question might annoy him, that he wouldn't like *me* asking *him* personal questions rather than the other way around, but it doesn't seem to have bothered him at all.

"Moonbeam?" he says.

He asked you a question, whispers the voice in the back of my head. *Does it concern you? Tell the truth.*

"I don't think it matters," I say. I'd considered both potential answers for a while before I fell asleep. "I think you can probably be a good vet without owning any animals."

He lets out a bark of laughter, looks horrified for a millisecond or two, then gives in and laughs long and loud, his face turning bright red. I smile, even though it's obvious he's laughing at me, because it's a nice sound to hear.

"I'm sorry," he gasps, once he's pulled himself together. "I promise I'm not laughing at you. That's just the best validation of what I do for a living I've ever heard. I'm going to remember to use it in the future."

"Glad to be of service," I say. I'm still smiling. "How come you don't have any children?"

"My wife got ill when she was a teenager," he says, and my smile disappears. "She's fine. She recovered, but it left her unable to have children."

"I'm sorry."

He nods. "It's okay," he says. "But thank you."

"Have you been married a long time?"

"You're very inquisitive this morning."

"You told me questions were a good thing."

He smiles. "So I did. I met my wife in college. We've been married for sixteen years."

"What's her name?"

"Marion."

"Is she pretty?"

50

"She's the most beautiful woman in the world."

I smile. "That seems unlikely. No offense."

"None taken," he says, and from the look on his face, it's clear that he means it. "Love changes how you see everything. It blinds you, but in a good way. I look at Marion, and my brain can tell me objectively that she probably *isn't* the most beautiful woman in the world, but it doesn't matter in the slightest. She is to me."

My smile widens. It must be nice to have someone think that way about you, to know that, of all the people on the planet, there's nobody they would rather be with. I think back to how Father John looked at Esme and Bella and Agavé and all the others, and my smile disappears.

Doctor Hernandez notices. "Moonbeam? Are you all right?"

"I'm fine."

"Is there anything else you want to ask before we get started?"

I nod. "Two more things."

"I think I can guess the first of them," he says. "Your mother?"

I nod again.

"I put in a request to the head of the task force conducting the investigation into the Lord's Legion for any and all information regarding your mother," he says. "He acknowledged receipt, but I haven't heard anything since. I'll let you know as soon as I do."

"Thank you." I don't know what a task force is, but I'm grateful to him for asking. "I appreciate it."

"I told you I would," he says. "I meant it when I said I won't lie to you."

There isn't really any way to respond to that, because people always say they won't lie, but then they always do. And if I know that, then he should know it too, because he's much older than me, and he's spent his whole life outside in the world.

"What was your other question?" he asks.

I take a deep breath. "What's going to happen to me?"

He frowns. "We're going to work through this process together, like we talked about yesterday. Then we're—"

"I don't mean that," I say. "I don't mean here, in this room. I mean everything else."

"I don't—"

"You said there were other people who wanted to talk to me. What's going to happen when you let them?"

We stare at each other in silence for what feels like a really long time. I fight the urge to twist and squirm on the sofa, forcing myself to stay still and hold his gaze, waiting for him to answer.

"I don't know," he says eventually. "I know that's not helpful, and I'm sorry, but my focus is on working with you through everything that has happened to you and trying to prepare you to live the rest of your life, whatever it may hold. Everything else is out of my hands."

"Will I be going to prison?"

Prison is too good for you! howls Father John, his voice reverberating through my head. *You belong in Hell for what you did!*

Doctor Hernandez frowns. "Why on earth would you go to prison?"

Panic rolls through me like a tidal wave. "No reason," I say, trying to keep my voice level. "It doesn't matter."

He looks at me and doesn't say anything. I can see him trying to decide whether to continue with what I said or let it slide and move on.

"People don't go to prison unless they've committed a crime," he says. "Is there something you need to tell me, Moonbeam?"

Yes.

I shake my head.

"Are you sure?"

"Can we talk about something else?" I ask, hating the pleading tone that has crept into my voice. "Please?"

He stares at me, then writes a long note in one of his books. "Of course we can talk about something else," he says when he finally raises his head. "I think that's a great idea. So here's something I've been thinking about since yesterday's session. I noticed a reaction when I talked about routine being important. Would that be a fair observation?"

No shit.

I nod.

Doctor Hernandez sits back in his chair. "Why don't you tell me why?"

BEFORE

Amos is the only person allowed to go Outside.

Every Friday morning, he disappears in the red pickup that Dezra left behind after he was Gone, and he returns five or six hours later with the truck's bed piled high with diesel and tinned fruit and flour and dried pasta and beans and heavy sacks of seeds. Amos isn't a Centurion, but he and The Prophet were Called to the True Path together, which is why the task of gathering supplies—a necessary evil, Horizon calls it—was given to him. The Lord told Father John that Amos is least likely to be tainted by the world beyond the fences of the Base.

Father John obviously can't go himself—the Servants of the Serpent would murder him if they were given the slightest chance. The Outside is dangerous for *all* Legionnaires, even the very Truest; it corrupts and seduces, and its darkness seeps into the purest heart. So as soon as Amos gets back, while my Brothers and Sisters are unloading the supplies, Father John always takes him straight into the Chapel to cleanse him and bless him and make sure his feet are firmly on the True Path.

Amos came to the desert with The Prophet, years and years ago now, and he likes to say that all he ever found Outside was despair. He has told me more times than I can remember how Father John saved his soul from certain damnation, and that he would lay down his life for him without thinking twice.

I always tell him I hope that won't be necessary.

Today has been no different than any other Friday. Everyone waved Amos off not long after breakfast, then got on with the endless jobs and chores that keep the Base running smoothly and keep our Family healthy and happy. I spent the afternoon with Honey working on a barren patch of ground on the edge of the eastern gardens, hacking heavy stones out of the stubborn earth and hauling them into a pile behind the Chapel. It's hard work, and I'm tired and running with sweat. As a result, even though the sky has started to darken, it doesn't occur to me that Amos isn't back until I'm walking to my room, and Nate wonders aloud what might be taking him so long.

There's a long moment of silence. Most of my Brothers and Sisters have gathered in the yard, as they usually do at the end of the working day before the bell rings for dinner, and I see several of them frown and glance in the direction of the Front Gate.

"It's after six," says Bear. "D'you reckon I ought to tell Father John?"

The second he finishes his question, we hear something in the distance. The dirt road that leads from the gate to the highway is the best part of a mile long, so the rattle of the pickup's engine reaches our ears long before we see the glow of its headlights.

Lonestar jogs across the yard and opens the Front Gate. Barely thirty seconds later, Amos drives through it, so fast that Lonestar has to leap out of the way to avoid getting swiped. There's a squeal of brakes and a choking cloud of dust as the pickup skids to a halt in the center of the yard, and when Amos gets out, his eyes are wide, and his shirt is spotted with blood.

"Jumped," he gasps. "Outside the hardware store. Three of 'em jumped me."

Nate strides forward, a frown on his handsome face. He's always so calm, so good whenever anything bad happens.

"Are you hurt?" he asks.

Amos shakes his head and takes a deep, wheezing breath. "I'm fine. Took a couple of licks before I made it back to the truck, but nothing worse. They chased me, Nate. Can you believe that? Two trucks of 'em, chased me almost through to Lubbock before they got bored and quit."

"What started it?" asks Nate. I stare at him as he speaks, at the firm line of his jaw and the spots of red that have appeared high on his cheeks, like they always do when he's angry. I know I should be paying attention to Amos, because he's hurt and something horrible has clearly happened, but I'm staring at Nate instead.

I stare at him *a lot*.

"I didn't do nothing," says Amos. "I was unloading my cart, and this fella asked me where I was from. He wasn't really asking though, you know? He already knew."

"What did he say?" asks Nate.

"He asked me if I was one of those God's Legion faggots," says Amos, his face flushing crimson at the memory. "Then he asked if I'd fucked my daughter today."

A chorus of outrage rises from the crowd that has gathered around the pickup. There are shouts of *Heresy* and *Serpent*, and several of my Brothers and Sisters momentarily close their eyes in prayer.

"What did you say to that?" asks Nate.

Amos smiles grimly. "I told him I don't have a daughter."

Nate's laugh echoes across the yard. "Good answer. I'm going to guess that's when he jumped you?"

Amos nods. "Him and his buddies."

"Did you retaliate?"

The question, delivered in a familiar low rumble, doesn't come from Nate. As one, the crowd turns toward the Big House. Father John stands on the porch, his long hair fluttering in the cool evening air. He's wearing the same gray shirt, jeans, and boots he always wears, and his piercing eyes are fixed on the man standing beside the pickup.

"No, Father," says Amos. "I got myself loose, then I ran."

Father John nods. "Well done," he says, and favors Amos with a tight smile. "You have served our Lord as truly as I would expect."

Out of the corner of my eye, I see Luke frown. He's seventeen, a month or so older than me—at least, as far as anyone knows for sure—and has spent every day of his life inside the Base. Father John tells us every single Sunday morning that only good people, loyal people, the very *best* people who are Faithful and True are allowed to serve in the Legion, because The Lord does not make mistakes, and it is blatant Heresy to suggest otherwise. But I'm not sure Luke qualifies.

Not remotely sure.

When we were both twelve, I caught him hurting an opossum with a knife behind the maintenance sheds, hurting it so badly that Amos had to put the poor thing out of its misery with his rifle. Father John reminds us over and over that even the least of The Lord's creatures deserves our respect, with the obvious exception of Outsiders, and Luke got in trouble for what he'd done, but I don't think he has ever forgiven me for telling on him. I sometimes catch him looking at me in a way I really don't like.

"Servants of the Serpent attacked one of our Brothers!" Luke shouts. "Jumped him and bloodied him and ran him halfway across the county! We should go down to Layfield first thing in the morning and show them just what The Lord's vengeance looks like!"

A low murmur travels through the crowd. Most of the voices I can make out disagree with Luke's suggestion, but not all of them.

Nowhere close to all of them.

"That is what you would do, Luke?" asks Father John. His voice has dropped to a low rumble, but its tone is almost friendly, and I shiver as the crowd falls silent once more.

"Yes, Father," says Luke, his eyes shining brightly. "I would. I *will*, if you give the order."

"You would obey my order?"

"Of course, Father," says Luke.

"Without question?"

"Yes, Father."

"Yet when I commend Brother Amos for turning the other cheek, you call instead for vengeance?" asks Father John, his voice steadily rising. "In front of your Brothers and Sisters, in this place that we have built together, you presume to know the mind of The Lord better than I? You would be so arrogant?"

Luke winces, but he doesn't look away from the face of The Prophet.

"Do you doubt me, Luke?"

Luke doesn't respond. The Prophet steps forward to the edge of the porch, his face pale, his eyes clear.

"I asked you a question, Luke," he says, his voice like crashing boulders, the volume rising and rising. "I asked you a question, and in The Lord's most Holy name, YOU WILL ANSWER ME OR YOU WILL STARE AT THE INSIDE OF A BOX UNTIL THE FINAL BATTLE BEGINS!"

Father John's voice is so loud it's almost otherworldly; it booms and rolls and slams into your ears like thunder. Luke recoils, fear rising in his eyes, as several of my Brothers and Sisters take a step back from the ferocity of The Prophet's sudden fury.

"ANSWER!" roars Father John.

Luke swallows hard. "No, Father," he says, his voice barely more than a whisper. "I do not doubt you. I'm sorry."

"Do you admit your arrogance?" asks Father John. His voice has returned to its normal volume, as quickly and suddenly as it exploded into a bellowing roar.

Luke drops his eyes to the ground. "Yes, Father."

"Do you understand that questioning the will of The Lord is Heresy?"

"Yes, Father."

Father John nods. "Do not let this happen again, Luke. The Lord is far less forgiving than I am."

Luke doesn't say a word. He just stares at the ground, his face ashen.

"Men and women of the Lord's Legion," says Father John, turning his gaze to the rest of us. "My Family, who I love most on this cursed, sinful planet. You are Faithful and you are True, and your resilience in the face of Heresy humbles me each and every day. I thank The Lord for having brought us together, for His wisdom and His benevolence and His perfect shining example. Brothers and Sisters, we have known for many years that the final days are upon us, and The Lord has seen fit to remind us that time is growing short. Those of us who are blessed to walk the True Path will soon find ourselves in battle against those who serve The Serpent, and when that time comes, the vengeance of The Lord will indeed be a sight to behold. It will be a sight to behold, Brothers and Sisters, a wonderful and terrible sight. But the moment of that glorious final reckoning will not be chosen by mortal man, not by me and not by anybody here. The moment will be chosen by The Lord Himself. Do you doubt me?"

A deafening chorus of "NO!" rings out, but Luke's lips don't move. I know because I'm watching him.

Father John smiles. "The Lord is Good," he says. "Julia, attend to Amos's wounds and have Becky draw him a bath. Centurions, please gather in the Big House and wait for me there. Nate, make sure the supplies are unloaded and my personal items are brought to my study. The rest of you may carry on."

A low murmur of chatter fills the yard as the crowd begins to disperse. I see Julia head for the house behind the Chapel that she shares with Becky, where they keep the medical supplies, and I see Bear and Horizon and the others make for the Big House. On the porch, Father John stays absolutely still, and the voice in the back of my head whispers to me.

This isn't finished.

I grimace because I'm looking at Father John and he's staring at Luke with narrowed eyes and I know the voice is right.

"Luke?" says The Prophet.

Everyone stops dead. Luke, who had been making his way toward the pickup, turns back toward the Big House.

"Yes, Father?" he asks.

"Join me in the Chapel," says Father John. "I will pray with you."

Luke lowers his head again and trudges in the direction of the Chapel. He knows exactly what awaits him inside, and everyone else knows it too. My Brothers and Sisters quickly scatter, as though all suddenly gripped by the urgent need to be somewhere else.

Amos lets Becky take him by the hand and lead him away as Nate drops the pickup's tailgate and starts sorting through bags and boxes. I walk over as he lifts down a case of tinned tomatoes, the muscles in his arms gleaming in the rapidly fading light.

"Need a hand?" I ask.

He gives me a wide smile, and I welcome the familiar simultaneous sensations of my stomach turning to water and my skin bursting into flames. "I'm good," he says. "You carry on."

I nod, but I don't do as he suggests. Instead, I stand beside him as he sets the tomatoes aside and reaches into the truck's bed for the next box.

"Luke didn't look very happy," I say.

Nate shrugs. "He's a man of strong Faith. Or a boy, maybe. Could be that a little instruction on how to channel that Faith might do him good, but spiritual matters aren't my department."

"Everything is a spiritual matter," I say, quoting one of Father John's favorite phrases. "Every single thing we do is of concern to The Lord."

"You'll get no argument from me," says Nate. "You really want to help?"

More than anything.

"Sure."

"Here then," he says, and he pulls down two boxes wrapped in blue-and-red tape. "Take these on up to the Big House."

I take them from him. They're really heavy—almost too heavy for me to carry—but there's not even the tiniest chance I'm going to admit that to Nate.

"You got them?" he asks, as though he can read my mind.

"No problem."

"You're sure?"

"Didn't I just say no problem?"

He smiles at me again, and my insides fizz. The heat in my face intensifies to something very close to the temperature of the sun.

"All right then," he says. "I appreciate the assist."

"You're welcome," I say, and turn toward the Big House, holding the heavy boxes as tightly as I can. As I stagger across the yard, each step more tiring than the last, I glance down at the shipping labels and see one of the many names that Father John's personal items arrive addressed to.

James Carmel.

AFTER

"Did that seem strange to you?" asks Doctor Hernandez. He's sitting forward in his chair, and he's filled four pages in one of his notebooks while I've been talking. "The name on the labels?"

I nod.

"At the time?" he asks. "Or now, after everything that happened later?"

I consider his question for a moment. "At the time, I guess. Everyone understood the reason for it, but...yes. It seemed strange. It's not like the Base was hidden away."

"Do you know what was in those boxes?"

"No."

He scribbles new lines into his notebook. I wait patiently. I don't say anything, but I really don't like him writing about me while I'm sitting six feet away. It feels like he's talking behind my back. When he's finished, he puts his pen down and gives me an encouraging smile.

"We've still got twenty minutes left in this session," he says. "Are you—"

"I'm fine."

BEFORE

Luke has belt marks across his shoulders for about a week.

Nobody is surprised by their presence or by the fact that he makes absolutely no attempt to hide them. He wears them like badges of honor, striding around the Base in vests or nothing at all from the waist up, making completely sure that everyone sees the evidence of his penance as the marks gradually turn blue then purple then black.

When Friday comes around, Amos is all fired up to do the supply run into Layfield.

"Ain't nobody getting the jump on me twice," he tells anybody willing to listen. "I'll be ready for 'em this time. See if I ain't ready."

But as it turns out, his readiness—or lack of it—isn't put to the test, because Father John announces that there are to be no exceptions to the ban on going Outside until further notice. Amos's disappointment is clear, but he doesn't say a word. He would no more speak against Father John than he would criticize The Lord Himself. This stoic acceptance earns him credit with the majority of our Brothers and Sisters, who sympathize with his disappointment at not being able to carry out a task that benefits his whole Family. They take it as evidence—as if any more were needed—of the depth of Amos's Faith and devotion to his Brothers and Sisters.

I don't agree.

I suspect—I'm *sure*—that a significant amount of Amos's disappointment comes from the simple truth that—despite endless claims to the contrary—he *likes* going Outside, and actively looks forward to driving the pickup through the Front Gate on Friday mornings. I've never spoken my suspicions out loud, not even to Nate or Honey, because they are technically Heresy. The First Proclamation makes it clear that the Earthbound Realm is divided into the Holy domain of the Lord's Legion and the Outside; those who walk the True Path and the Servants of the Serpent. There are no gray areas, no in-betweens. But if I'm right about Amos, and I'm pretty sure I am, then I don't really blame him. Because— and this is *definitely* Heresy—I miss Outside too.

When I was little, before the Purge, we used to go Outside all the time. Only we didn't call it Outside then; we called it Town, or we called it Layfield, which was—and still is—its actual name.

Layfield, Texas. Established 1895. Population 2,147.

Father Patrick, whose name I'm not supposed to think, let alone say out loud, used to lead three cars full of my Brothers and Sisters into Town every morning apart from Sundays. I always rode in the back of the second car with Lizzie and Benjamin, who were my two best friends in the whole world until they were Gone. Lizzie's mom would park outside the law office where she worked as a receptionist, and before she went inside, she would give each of us a kiss on the forehead and tell us to be good. We always promised her that we would. For the next three hours or so we would walk back and forth along Layfield's main street, handing out fliers that invited people to hear the Word of The Lord and gratefully accepting any donations people were kind enough to make. Sometimes we sold the things we made during the long, hot afternoons at the Base: dream catchers twisted together from twigs and ribbon, dried flowers pressed into silver photo frames, handwritten psalms illustrated with every imaginable color of felt-tip pen.

Plenty of people ignored us, especially the men and women who worked and lived in Town and saw us every day. Occasionally someone would say something mean, but most of the time people were nice. The residents of Layfield were—and still are, I have no doubt—God-fearing folk, in their own way, and were generally respectful of our Faith, even though it differed from theirs. After the Purge, when Father John announced that it wasn't safe to go Outside anymore, I cried myself to sleep, and I know for certain that I wasn't the only one. The staff at the law firm made Lizzie's mom a cake and told her they were going to miss her after she handed in her notice.

It wasn't much of a surprise to anyone who was paying attention that she and Lizzie were Gone two weeks later.

The Prophet told us that even though the townspeople might *seem* nice and kind and friendly, it was a favorite strategy of The Serpent to send wolves in sheep's clothing among the True servants of The Lord, to better exploit their good nature.

I wonder if any of the men who attacked Amos last Friday were the same ones who used to press dollar bills into my hand or tell me how pretty my dress was.

I'm sure Father John would tell me they were.

With the supply run canceled, Friday is a lot less exciting than usual.

One of the most important rules of the Lord's Legion is that the storerooms must always—*always*—contain enough food to last all of us three months, in case the Servants of the Serpent ever lay siege to the Base and try to starve us out. Nobody is going to go hungry if Amos doesn't go into Town for a few weeks, but under normal circumstances, Friday is about more than the practicalities of survival.

Alongside the essentials like fuel and flour and tinned fruit, Amos almost always brings a few bags of treats—loaves of bread or cookies or doughnuts or brightly wrapped candy—and every month or so he fills a couple of sacks with clothes from the thrift store on the outskirts of Layfield. They tend to be full of oil-stained boots and jeans and shirts, all of which have seen much better days, but anything new to us is always exciting.

It's safe to assume that Father John doesn't officially approve of this practice. But supplying your Brothers and Sisters with a chocolate bar or an apple Danish doesn't feature in any of the Proclamations and isn't the subject of any specific rule, and allowing his Family occasional treats only makes them love him even more.

And the men and women of the Lord's Legion do love Father John. They really, *really* love him.

Nobody knows very much about his life before The Lord told him to come to the desert. Most of the men and women who were part of the Legion when he first arrived left during the Purge, and although they said a great many things—vicious, Heretical things—about him and his life in those last, frantic days before they packed their belongings and left the Base forever, they had already been shown to be liars whose hearts were False, so nobody listened to them.

Those who stayed, who resisted the seductions of the Servants of the Serpent and remained True, have known Father John for the better part of eight years now, and are generally more devoted to him than to themselves. The most Faithful of my Brothers and

Sisters consider The Prophet's life before he was called irrelevant, and would no more publicly speculate about it than they would douse themselves in gas and light a match.

Nevertheless, there *is* gossip, although always infrequent and always whispered. I've heard it said that Father John was a musician before he came to the Base, in Los Angeles or maybe San Francisco; that he was a traveling preacher who dedicated his life to the search for the True Path and was finally rewarded for his endless Faith; that he was a drunk—or possibly even a *criminal*—who was brought low by The Serpent before being Saved. Once I was old enough to understand that adults will say things in the presence of children that they won't say around other adults, I kept my ears open. I heard all these stories and dozens of others, and reached a simple, undeniable conclusion.

Nobody knows who Father John was before he became Father John.

He just *is*, and that's all that matters.

After we find out that Amos isn't going into town, I wander back across the yard. I'm supposed to be working in the gardens again today, but I'm not in any hurry to get started, so I slow my pace as I walk through the center of the only home I've ever known.

The Base—as it has been called since long before the Purge—is made up of more than two dozen buildings, including the Chapel, which is a slightly understated name for a church capable of seating two hundred people; the Big House, where Father John lives with his wives and their children; two neat squares of L-shaped houses; two long rows of wooden barracks; Legionnaires' Hall; the kitchen and the storerooms; and a low cluster of outbuildings that range from little more than sheds to towering structures the size of barns.

Over on the far side of the yard, I see Nate strolling toward the gardens and break into a jog to catch up to him. The voice in the back of my head tells me I'm pathetic for literally chasing him across the yard, but I tell it to shut up, because I'm not doing anything wrong, and I don't care what it thinks.

The truth is this: nothing has ever happened between me and Nate, and I know it never will.

I've *always* known that, ever since he arrived, not least because it's now less than a year until I marry Father John. I'm not stupid. But at the same time, how I feel about Nate is jumbled up, like a jigsaw puzzle with no edge pieces. He looks at me like I'm a little sister—not like some of my other older Brothers—and I'm sad about that, but I'm glad too, most of the time. He's never snuck in to see me after lights-out, and I know he never would, even though I sometimes lie awake until the dawn starts to creep into the eastern sky, tingling with guilt and hoping I'm wrong.

It's not just Nate; nobody else comes to see me after lights-out, not like they do Alice and Star and Liza and some of my other Sisters, the ones who are prettier than me. Nighttime visits are not allowed—the Third Proclamation is absolutely clear, as is the punishment for breaking it—but they *do* happen, and the Centurions are the only ones who have keys to the barracks, and they would never unlock the bedrooms of my Sisters for anyone without The Prophet's permission.

My door always stays locked until dawn. I guess Father John would be furious if he found out that anyone had touched one of his Future Wives, and that's what keeps my Brothers away. That's what I tell myself at least, that it's because of rules. My mom used to tell me to be careful around my older Brothers because men have a switch in their heads that gets flipped around pretty girls and makes them stupid and unpredictable.

I asked her once if my dad had it, and she told me he didn't

70

have a switch—he was just stupid and unpredictable all the time. It hurt my heart to hear her speak about him like that, but she knew him really well, and I hardly ever knew him at all, so I guess I have to take her word for what he was like. And it was nice to hear her call me pretty, even if she did it in a roundabout sort of way.

Anyway.

Nate hears me coming up behind him and turns around with a smile on his face, the one that always makes my heart beat double-time.

"Hey, Moonbeam," he says. "I knew it was you."

I smile back at him. "How come?"

"You have very distinctive footsteps," he says. "They always sound serious. Kind of earnest."

My smile twists into a frown. "What are you talking about?"

"I don't know," he says, and shrugs. "Take a listen sometime."

"I probably won't," I say.

He grunts with laughter and nods. "Fair enough. You feel like helping me pick a few cucumbers?"

"Sure," I say, and fall into step beside him as we head toward the western fence. The sun is beating down directly above our heads, bathing the entire Base in light so bright that it makes everything look brand new, and one of the hardest truths of them all appears in my mind like a punch to the gut.

I was happy here.

For a long time, I really was.

The Base isn't paradise, no matter what Father John likes to say; it's actually nowhere close, and never has been. There was a time, when I was a lot younger than I am now, that I was happy to believe almost anything if someone promised me it was the truth. For me, unlike most—maybe *all*—of my Brothers and Sisters, that time didn't last forever.

It wasn't Father John's fault; not then, at least. As he often says, he is merely a human being, as fallible and proud as any other, and even though we were all made in the image of our Creator, we are nowhere close to Holy. That state of perfect grace is reserved for The Lord Himself. As a result, I kind of always understood that The Prophet's words couldn't be accepted as irrevocable truth, and that understanding became clearer and clearer as I got older.

I know *without any doubt* that there is simply no way every single human being in the whole world who lives beyond the walls of the Base is bad, just like I know for *absolutely certain* that not every one of my Brothers and Sisters is good. Bad and good, False and True: they're the opposite ends of a spectrum of behavior, not the *only* two things a person can be. Because life isn't that simple. *People* aren't that simple, even though I'm sure things would be a lot more straightforward if they were.

I think Father John understands this, even if he would never say so. I think that's why he only claims to be the messenger, rather than the message itself. But for a long time the difference didn't matter to me. When he spoke, even if I doubted the actual words, I still *believed*.

I had questions, and I had thoughts that I never told anyone because I knew they would be called Heresy, but I still had *Faith* in him and my Brothers and Sisters and in the Legion. Right up until what he did to my mom.

"Penny for them?" asks Nate, as we reach the chicken-wire fence that surrounds the gardens.

"Bad deal for you," I say.

He smiles. "I know when there's something on your mind, Moonbeam. Spill."

I nod because he's right. There *is* something on my mind, beyond the bittersweet memory of happier times. Something that's been eating at me since last Friday and that I wouldn't dream of bringing up with anyone else.

"It's Luke," I say.

"What about that little shit?" asks Nate, and I actually gasp out loud, because *nobody* talks that way about one of their Brothers or Sisters. Not *ever*.

"You can't say that," I say, hating how I must sound like a shocked little girl.

"I can if it's the truth," says Nate, his smile widening. "Membership in the Lord's Legion doesn't automatically disqualify you from being an asshole. Sadly."

I giggle. I can't help myself.

"Anyway," he continues, "I don't think you're going to tattle on me to a Centurion. So what about Luke?"

"He questioned Father John. Right in front of everyone."

Nate shrugs. "And got a whipping for it. Do you have a problem with that?"

"No."

"So what then?"

I take a deep breath because I want this to come out right. "He causes trouble," I say. "Luke, I mean. And sometimes…sometimes it feels like he does it on purpose."

"He's seventeen," says Nate. "Of course he does it on purpose. He's trying to work out where he fits in the world, what his place is, so he acts out from time to time. Why does it bother you?"

"You weren't here last time," I say. "It feels familiar. That's all."

"Are you talking about the Purge?" he asks.

"I don't know," I say. "I think so. Yeah."

"Are you worried?"

I shake my head. "I guess not. I just don't trust Luke, Nate. I'm sorry. I didn't mean to make this into some big thing."

Nate smiles. "It's okay. And you don't need to worry. Luke is an objectionable little shit who could have done with being taken down a peg or two before now, but if I thought he was actually dangerous, to Father John or anyone else, I'd already have done something about it."

"What would you have done?"

His smile disappears, as suddenly as if it was never there. "I'd have strangled him while he slept," he says. "Now come on. Those cucumbers aren't going to pick themselves."

I force a smile as a chill creeps over me. He turns away, and I let him take a few steps before I follow him into the gardens.

AFTER

Doctor Hernandez has stopped taking notes; his eyes locked on me as I talked.

"Do you think Nate would have done what he said?" he asks.

I shake my head. "No."

"What makes you so sure?"

I shrug. I'm *not* sure, not a hundred percent. I know—without any doubt, because I saw it with my own eyes—that Nate was perfectly willing to hurt Luke, although I'm not going to say that. But I genuinely don't think he would have actually *killed* him, so I'm not technically lying.

"Were people punished for speaking heresy?"

"No," I say. That *is* a lie, such a big one that I worry I might burst into flames for telling it.

"For breaking the rules?"

"No."

"So people weren't afraid?"

I don't respond.

Doctor Hernandez narrows his eyes. "Moonbeam? Were the members of the Lord's Legion afraid of Father John?"

"What did you say?" demands Luke, his voice the low hiss of a snake. "What did you tell the Outsider?"

His face is barely an inch away from mine, and my back is pressed against the wall, while the rest of our Brothers and Sisters watch in silence, their faces stricken. I think about what Doctor Hernandez said about SSI being a controlled environment, and I wonder how long this would have to go on before someone came into the group therapy room and stopped it.

"I didn't say anything," I lie. "I tried to tell him about Father John, about how The Prophet was ten times the man he could ever hope to be, but he didn't want to hear that so he sent me back to my room. That's all, Luke. I swear."

He takes a half step back. I don't have any idea how long he stares at me, but he eventually breaks into a smile and runs his knuckles down my cheek. I try not to shudder.

"Good," he says. "You did good. They're trying to turn us against each other, right when it's most important that we stay strong. But we're not going to let them. Are we?"

I shake my head. The madness still gleams in his eyes, a dancing light that makes me want to puke. It's the same light I saw in Father John's eyes at the very end, as everything around him burned.

"That's right," he says, and turns to face the others. "We are *not* going to let them. The Prophet has Ascended, just as we were promised he would. Our Brothers and Sisters have Ascended, *as we were promised.* You saw them rise up to Heaven with your own eyes, and if you believe that we were left behind by accident, then you are lying to yourself, and you have proven yourself False. Each and every one of us is being tested, being challenged to prove our Faith and show we deserve to sit in the presence of The Lord with our Family. Do you understand what I am telling you?"

There's a murmur of agreement, but only a murmur.

He frowns. "I can't hear you," he says. "*Do you understand the truth that I am telling you?*"

Another murmur, barely louder than the first. The enthusiasm that briefly filled my Brothers and Sisters the last time Luke spoke about Ascension is gone. Maybe his words, so similar to those used by Father John over the years, have lost their power to inspire in the face of the reality of this room and this place, or maybe the last of the fight has finally drained out of them. Under the bright fluorescent lights of the wide room, they look exactly like what they are: frightened children, a long way from home. I stare at them, my heart aching in my chest. I glance at Luke, and I know he sees the same thing. He takes a step forward, his fists clenched, and tries again.

"I know you're in pain," he says. "I know you're scared, and I know you miss your parents. It's only natural, even though we all know in our hearts that this sinful world is only temporary. But this is *not* the time to lose heart, my Brothers and Sisters. This, right now, right here in this room, is the moment for us to hold more tightly to our Faith than ever before, to be True to the words of The Prophet and prove that we deserve to Ascend alongside him. Trust in him, as we always have. Trust in him, and I promise he will not let us down."

Willow starts to cry. I don't blame her, not for a single second. She's only ten years old, and she was standing in her mother's shadow when a bullet ripped off the top of her head. I imagine she might be having trouble holding tightly to her Faith at this particular moment, no matter what Luke says.

He walks over and kneels down in front of her, shushing her as best he can. Gentleness has never come naturally to Luke, but he tries, which I grudgingly have to accept is something. Willow stops crying after a minute or two, but her face remains a mask of utter misery. How can she be expected to understand the things she saw? How can anyone even begin to try and help her get over them?

Luke takes her hands. "There are things Father John taught me," he says, his voice low. "Abilities. *Powers*. Things that the Servants of the Serpent will not be able to comprehend. If our Ascension doesn't come soon, I won't hesitate. I'll use what I was taught, and I'll free us all from this place, and we'll start again somewhere new while we wait for The Prophet to Call us home."

Willow nods and manages a tiny smile.

"You're so full of shit, Luke," says Honey. "Don't lie to her."

Willow's smile disappears, and she looks up at Luke with eyes that are suddenly wide and full of uncertainty. He doesn't even glance down at her though; his gaze is fixed on Honey.

"You'll see," he says. "Oh, you'll see soon enough. You have no idea what I'm capable of."

"You're wrong," says Honey. "I know exactly what you are."

Luke gives her a smile that doesn't contain the slightest trace of humor, then turns his attention back to Willow. "Don't listen to her. Everything is going to be okay. There's nothing to be afraid of."

I stare at him.

I stare at him, and I don't say a word.

I don't say a single word because I think he's wrong.

Even now, after the fire and the bullets and the blood, there *is* still something to be scared of.

And I'm pretty sure I'm looking at him.

A
F
T
E
R

Doctor Hernandez opens the door of Interview Room 1 at two minutes past ten, but he doesn't step through it and head toward the desk like usual. Instead, he stands half in and half out of the room and gives me a wide smile that doesn't look totally convincing.

"Good morning, Moonbeam," he says. "How are you doing today?"

"I'm fine," I say. I can feel my forehead furrowing into a frown. "Aren't you coming in?"

His smile remains fixed in place. "Of course. But if it's all right with you, this morning's session is going to be a little bit different. Do you remember me telling you that there were other people who wanted to talk to you?"

Unease flutters in my stomach. "I remember."

"Great," he says. "Okay. So. One of them would like to talk to you now. How do you feel about that?"

"Who is it?" I ask.

"His name is Agent Andrew Carlyle. He works for the FBI. Do you know what that is?"

GOVERNMENT! screams Father John, his voice thundering through my head. *GOVERNMENT! DON'T TELL HIM ANYTHING! RUN! RUN FOR YOUR LIFE!*

I shake my head. I don't need him to know that Father John denounced the FBI and all the other Government agencies as Servants of the Serpent almost every Sunday morning.

"It stands for the Federal Bureau of Investigation," says Doctor Hernandez. "They work on very serious crimes, crimes that are bigger or more complicated than local police forces can handle on their own. It's important to say right up front that him wanting to talk to you doesn't mean you're in any kind of trouble, and that nobody is going to make you answer questions you don't want to. But it would really help the investigation into what happened to your brothers and sisters if you were willing to talk to him and listen to his questions. And I honestly think you might find it useful."

"Why does he want to talk to me?" I ask. "I don't know anything."

"He just wants to ask you about what you saw," he says. "What happened during the fire and before it. So what do you say? Will you talk to him?"

"Do I have a choice?"

"Always," says Doctor Hernandez. "But it will make the work that you and I are doing a lot easier if you cooperate with him. I'm sure that must sound like negotiation, and maybe it is, but it's also the truth."

"Quid pro quo," I whisper.

He frowns. "Exactly. Where did you learn that?"

From Horizon. When I was little, and we were still allowed to learn things.

I shake my head. "I don't know. I must have heard it somewhere once."

"You'll talk to him then? Agent Carlyle?"

I shrug. "I guess."

His smile reappears, as wide and unconvincing as before, and he ducks back through the door and pulls it shut. I stare at it, trying to slow my accelerating heart.

Stay calm. You're the only one who knows the truth, and they can't make you tell them. They don't know anything. So stay calm.

Doctor Hernandez walks back into the room, followed by a man carrying a plastic chair. He's taller than the psychiatrist, with dark hair parted neatly on one side and blue eyes that stand out against skin that looks like it's spent a lot of time outdoors. He's wearing a dark gray suit over a white shirt, and he nods at me as he sets the chair down.

"Moonbeam," says Doctor Hernandez. "This is Agent Carlyle."

"It's a pleasure to meet you," says the—*Servant of the Serpent*—newcomer. "How're you doing this morning?"

"I'm okay," I say, trying to keep my voice steady as I look up at him. "You?"

"I'm good," he says. "Thanks for asking. And for letting me sit in."

Like I had a choice.

"No problem," I say.

Doctor Hernandez starts unloading his notebooks and pens as Agent Carlyle slides off his jacket and drapes it over the back of his chair. When he turns back toward me, I see an angular black shape nestled in his armpit and my insides seize as I realize what it is. For a second I just stare, and then I scramble up the back of the red sofa, my eyes widening. My bandaged hand slams against the wall, and the pain is *awful*, but I barely notice it as a scream rises in my throat, a scream it takes every last bit of my strength to hold in.

"Moonbeam?" asks Doctor Hernandez, his voice full of urgency. "What is it? What's wrong?"

I shake my head. If I open my mouth to tell him, I know the scream will get out, because all I can see is Agent Carlyle's gun and all I can hear is the thunder of automatic fire and the whine of bullets and the screams of my Brothers and Sisters. The bitter scent of burning fills my head, and everything swims. I'm sure I'm going to faint.

Doctor Hernandez turns his head, searching for what I'm seeing, for what has caused me to back away from them. Then his eyes spring wide, and he jumps to his feet and hauls Agent Carlyle out of his chair by his shoulders.

"What the hell?" the agent shouts, his face flushing red. He tries to wrench himself free, but the psychiatrist grips him tightly and shoves him toward the door. Carlyle struggles, twisting and protesting, until Doctor Hernandez snarls, "The gun, you idiot."

Agent Carlyle freezes, his face turning ghostly pale, then lets himself be pushed out of the room. Doctor Hernandez slams the door behind them, but it doesn't catch and stands open a crack. I stare at the narrow gap while my heart pounds in my chest. It's been a *really* long time since I last took a breath.

My insides feel like they've turned to concrete. I focus on the sliver of gray corridor I can see through the narrow gap and tell myself to calm down and after a long, silent moment, I manage to force a thin whistling stream of air down my throat, and I relax, ever so slightly. Maybe I'm not going to faint after all. I take a deep breath, then another, and the pressure in my chest and the buzzing in my head clears and I hear voices coming from the corridor outside.

"What in God's name were you thinking?" asks Doctor Hernandez, his voice sharp and cold. "Do I need to tell you why wearing a gun into a therapy session is inappropriate? Please tell me I don't need to explain that to you."

"I didn't think," says Agent Carlyle. "It's habit, okay? I put it on in the morning, and I take it off at night. I'm sorry."

"You're sorry," says Doctor Hernandez. "Okay. Great. Can I ask you something?"

"Sure."

"Do you have any idea what that girl has been through? I mean, you read the reports, right? You understand the things she saw?"

I grimace in the empty room. Part of me hates hearing them talk about me like I'm some specimen in a laboratory, but another part likes hearing Doctor Hernandez being angry on my behalf. It's been a long time since it felt like anyone was on my side.

"All right, all right," says Agent Carlyle. "I'm taking it off. What do you want me to do with it?"

"Unload it," says Doctor Hernandez. "My briefcase locks, so you keep the ammo, and we'll put the gun in there."

"Okay," says Agent Carlyle. I hear the familiar metallic noise of a magazine sliding out of the pistol grip. "Fine. Here you go."

"Make sure it's off before you come in next time," says Doctor Hernandez. "I'm going to be perfectly straight with you, Agent Carlyle. If you do *anything* that I believe jeopardizes Moonbeam's progress in any way, I won't hesitate to file a report with your section chief. I'm entirely serious."

There's a long silence. I perch on the edge of the sofa, straining my ears.

"You're right," says Agent Carlyle. "I'm sorry. It won't happen again."

"Thank you," says Doctor Hernandez. Some of the usual

warmth has returned to his voice. "Just remember where you are and where she's been, okay? She's stronger than I had any right to hope she'd be, but don't underestimate the gravity of her situation. She's in an extremely fragile state."

"PTSD?"

"I haven't finished my initial assessment yet," says Doctor Hernandez. "I haven't ruled anything in or out, including PTSD. So tread lightly, okay?"

"Got it," says Agent Carlyle. I hear him let out a deep sigh. "She's the same age as my daughter, give or take six months."

"Get your head around it," says Doctor Hernandez sharply. "Deal with it. Bringing your personal baggage in there isn't going to help you or her."

"I've been in the FBI for eighteen years," says Agent Carlyle. It almost sounds like he's smiling. "I've led more than seven hundred interviews during that time."

"What's your point?"

"No point. I thought it might be of interest. Are we going back in?"

There's a long pause, and I wonder what's happening on the other side of the door. Are they staring at each other? Is Doctor Hernandez making Agent Carlyle wait for an answer because he's actually considering his question or because he wants to make it clear who's in charge? Silence can be a weapon when it's used properly—it makes people nervous, makes them say things they shouldn't say to break the tension. Father John understood that *really* well.

"Fine," says Doctor Hernandez eventually. "Let's go back in." I scramble back into my usual position—curled up in the corner of the sofa with my knees pulled against my chest. My mind races with questions.

What's PTSD? And what did he mean by "extremely fragile state"? Am I going to break?

84

The door swings open. Doctor Hernandez frowns at the handle, then over at me. I meet his eyes with what I hope is an expression of total innocence. He holds my gaze for a second, then sits down. Agent Carlyle does the same, the shoulder holster now nowhere to be seen, and looks right at me.

"I'm really sorry," he says. "I wasn't thinking. I guess you've seen enough guns to last a lifetime, huh?"

I nod.

"It won't happen again," he says.

"It's okay," I say. "I just wasn't expecting it."

"Of course you weren't," says Doctor Hernandez. "Your response was completely legitimate."

Agent Carlyle puts the pistol into the briefcase. Doctor Hernandez makes a big show of closing it and locking it, then puts it back on the floor by his chair.

"I'm sorry," repeats Agent Carlyle.

"Don't worry about it," I say. "Glock twenty-two, right?"

His eyes widen. "Come again?"

"In your holster," I say. "It looked like a Glock twenty-two."

"That's right," he says.

Doctor Hernandez frowns. "I don't think this is a productive line of—"

Agent Carlyle sits forward. "You know a lot about guns?"

You have no idea.

BEFORE

On Monday, Wednesday, and Friday mornings and Saturday afternoons, we have training.

It's one of two Legion activities—the other being Father John's Sunday morning sermon—for which attendance is *absolutely* compulsory. It overrides anything else that might need doing around the Base, no matter how important, and even any illness a Brother or Sister might be suffering. I've seen people in the feverish grip of the flu collapse halfway through a session only to stagger back to their feet and carry on once they've been revived, their faces full of terrified determination. Training always begins with a lecture from Father John, in which he reminds us about the evil that lurks Outside, the monstrous horror of the enemies that we are destined to face.

When the End Times arrive, we have been told to expect

demonic creatures with scales and wings and mouths full of teeth that will rise from the earth and take on the forms of those we love; grotesque animals with a dozen heads that breathe fire and scorch the ground beneath their hooves. When the Final Battle begins, The Lord will fill those who are True with the power needed to defeat the forces of darkness, and once the day is won, we will Ascend on pillars of light to sit at His side.

But until that Glorious day arrives, there is another enemy we must protect ourselves against—a human enemy, corrupted and twisted by sin, who Father John only ever speaks about in a tone of pure venom.

The Government.

It goes without saying that all agents of the Government are Servants of the Serpent, but to hear Father John tell it, they are *almost* as bad as their master. They are rats in human bodies, soulless abominations who hate The Lord and will do everything in their power to drive good men and women from the True Path. They will not think twice about murdering me and every one of my Brothers and Sisters if they get the slightest chance, and would love nothing more than to lock us away and torture us for the rest of eternity. The Government comes in many forms—the FBI, the ATF, the CIA, the sheriff's department, the police, the IRS, the Department of Homeland Security—but it is all one many-headed hydra, a sprawling monster with a single ambition: the victory of The Serpent on Earth.

I walk across the yard toward the shooting range behind the Big House. I don't hurry, even though I can see most of my Family already gathered, and arriving late to training is guaranteed to result in punishment. But it feels like everyone is already watching me—that everyone is whispering rumors about me, thanks to Nate and my mom—and right now, at this particular moment, I don't care if I give them another reason to look at me sideways.

I stride over and join the back of the crowd. Honey glances in my direction and gives me a smile, a gesture that I appreciate more than she could ever guess, but nobody else seems to notice my tardiness. In the clearing in front of the range, Father John has already started his lecture, his face tight and his eyes narrow as he explains exactly what the Government will do to us if we let our guard down for even a single second.

The Government has helicopters that will drop burning gasoline on you if they catch you Outside, beyond the reach of Father John's protection.

The Government will murder our youngest Brothers and Sisters, then roast their bodies over a pit of Hellfire and eat their flesh.

The Government will impregnate the Sisters of the Legion with parasitic creatures that will devour them from the inside.

The Government will cut off your arms and legs and sew up your mouth, then laugh as you starve to death.

By the time Father John is finished, several of my youngest Brothers and Sisters are in tears; they weep quietly as their parents stand beside them, nervous looks on their faces. Weakness is not tolerated inside the Lord's Legion. I glance at Honey out of the corner of my eye. She stares straight at The Prophet, her expression absolutely unreadable.

Once the lecture is over, it's time to shoot.

The range is as far from the Front Gate as possible, hidden from prying eyes by the Big House and the gardens and a row of maintenance sheds. It is absolutely vital—Father John constantly reminds us—that our enemies don't know how prepared we are until it's too late.

The Centurions are armed at all times, but the rest of the Lord's Legion are not allowed to have weapons of our own. In Father Patrick's time, most people kept a rifle in their rooms, but that changed after the Purge, along with almost everything else. So during training we use guns that are brought up from the locked room in the basement of the Big House by Amos, who carefully counts each weapon out at the start of every session and back in at the end.

We shoot for almost an hour, our sights trained on trees painted with crude likenesses of men and women with *FBI* written on their chests, on archery target discs, on cans and bottles and plastic jugs and pretty much anything else that can be hurled down the range. The noise is deafening, and the smoke that fills the air is thick and bitter and catches in your throat.

We fire Glock 17s and 22s, Desert Eagles, MP5s, Smith & Wesson .45s, Colt AR-15s, SIG Sauer P226s, AK-47s, M4s, M16s, Remington double barrels, Beretta 9 millimeters, and dozens and dozens of other guns. Children younger than eight are not allowed to shoot, but *everyone*—regardless of age—is required to be present. Most of my younger Brothers and Sisters could list twenty-six different models of firearms before they could recite the twenty-six letters of the alphabet.

I sight down the barrel of an M4, a rifle I remember barely being able to lift the first time it was handed to me, and squeeze the trigger. I'm braced for the recoil, my weight over my front foot, the stock pressed into my shoulder, and my arm barely jerks before I pull the trigger again and again. The shots are metallic drumbeats, each one followed by chunks of tree bark exploding into the air.

I empty the magazine, and as I reload, I glance in Father John's direction. He stands beneath the white oak tree at the edge of the western garden, watching his Family with benevolent pride on his face, and all of a sudden, I'm incredibly aware of the gun in my hands and what it can do. A thought flashes through my mind that is *so far beyond* Heresy that I instantly push it away in case it shows on my face.

When the shooting comes to an end, Amos gathers up the guns and carries them into the Big House while the rest of us get ready for combat training. The whole Legion separates into pairs of Father John's choosing, then fight for three minutes with everything they've got and anything they can find: hands, feet, fingernails, teeth, rocks, lumps of wood.

Like all training, it isn't optional. But unlike shooting, it's impossible to fake. If someone was watching really closely, they might notice if your bullets were failing to hit their targets, but you can pretty much get away with not really trying if you don't feel like it.

Combat is completely different. If you take it easy on whomever you've been paired with and a Centurion notices, they'll drag you out in front of everyone and make an example of you. There is no room for mercy inside the Lord's Legion—along with weakness and disobedience, it's the transgression that is punished most harshly, which is something you learn quickly if you've got any sense.

Father John whispers names to the Centurions, then watches as we're separated into two long lines that face each other. Standing opposite me today is Lucy, one of the kindest, sweetest girls in the entire Legion.

There's no way it's a coincidence.

And I would have to be stupid not to understand what's really going on: Father John is testing—*publicly testing*—whether I will still hurt someone I care about simply because he has told me to. Whether I will still obey orders. Whether I am still to be trusted. It feels like being on trial without ever having been told the charges, even though I know what they would relate to.

My mom.

Nate.

Lucy is only twelve, a full foot shorter than me, and probably eighty pounds soaking wet. I could take her down in about five seconds, and I know that's exactly what I *should* do—get this horrible business over with as quickly as possible, causing her the absolute minimum amount of pain in the process. But I don't want to do that.

I *won't* do it.

I'm trying to hide it—and I honestly think I'm succeeding, most of the time, at least—but I'm furious with Nate and with my mom and with myself. The anger is hot and sharp, and my head is full of thoughts that make me feel sick, thoughts that I was raised to believe would damn me to the eternal fires of Hell, and even though I know things changed—that *I've* changed—part of me is still the person I used to be, and that person still fervently believes that I should be punished for what I thought when I was holding the M4 and looking at Father John, and for all the other thoughts that keep me awake long into the night and poison my dreams.

That's bullshit, whispers the voice in the back of my head. *You haven't—*

I tell it to shut up. Because I *do* deserve to be punished, even if nobody knows it but me. I'm scared and angry and all alone, and I don't know what's going to happen.

But right now, I just want to feel *something*.

So when Bear shouts, "Go!" and Lucy shuffles forward and throws a tentative punch in my general direction, I don't move a muscle. Instead, I let her small fist collide with my nose and relish the pain that spurts through my head.

My eyes fill with water, and I taste coppery blood in the back of my throat. Through my tears, I see a panicked look appear on Lucy's face, but she has nothing to worry about, because I'm not going to retaliate. I wait, as still as a statue, for her to understand the situation, then let her hit me again and again.

Her third punch, much harder than the previous two, sends

me stumbling backward. My feet tangle, and I hit the ground on my back. Lucy stands over me, her usually gentle face twisted by the visceral thrill of violence, the primal pleasure that comes from inflicting pain on another living creature. I stare up at her and give her a smile, but it must look horrible with my mouth full of blood, because her eyes widen, and for a split second, she looks like herself—until Jacob Reynolds shoves her aside and stares down at me with eyes blazing with anger.

"Get up," he spits.

Everybody else has stopped fighting. Beneath the white oak, Father John is staring at me, but he doesn't look angry; his expression seems to be mostly curiosity. As I slowly get to my feet, I'm aware that I've become the center of attention.

"Pull that crap when the End Times arrive and you'll be dead," says Jacob. "Are you listening to me? You won't Ascend. You won't sit at the hand of The Lord. You'll just be dead, and your soul will be in Hell. Is that what you want?"

I stare at him, then give my head the tiniest of shakes.

He points at Lucy, whose eyes are full of apology. I want to tell her that it's not her fault, that she didn't do anything wrong, but I know that would only make the situation worse.

"You think you're doing her a favor by not fighting back?" asks Jacob. "You think you're protecting her? You're not. If she doesn't learn how to fight and get hurt and stand up and fight again, The Lord won't guide her through the Final Battle and she'll end up right beside you in Hell. You're *failing* her."

I spit blood onto the ground, and when I look back at Jacob, it's like I'm seeing him—*really seeing him*—for the very first time. He's fat and ugly and mean, and I don't know why I've ever listened to a single word that came out of his mouth.

"Hit her," he says.

"No."

There is an audible gasp from my Brothers and Sisters, because nobody ever speaks to a Centurion like that.

Nobody.

He takes a step toward me, his eyes narrowing. "You hit her, or I will."

"Moonbeam," says Lucy, her voice a trembling whisper. "It's okay. Just do it."

"I will not!" I shout.

Jacob flinches. He glances around, his face flushing with embarrassment and anger, then turns back to me. "Last chance," he growls.

"Go to Hell," I say.

The silence that settles over the crowd is total and terrible.

For a seemingly endless moment, Jacob doesn't respond; he just stares at me, his face crimson, his chest rising and falling beneath his denim shirt. Then—far more quickly than I would have thought possible for someone so fat and out of shape—he spins to his left and clubs Lucy across the face with his clenched fist, lifting her off the ground. She flies through the air, her limbs loose and trailing behind her, then hits the ground in a heap and starts to shriek.

"*No!*" The scream leaves my mouth as I dive forward, ready to sink my fingers into the soft jelly of Jacob's eyeballs and rip them out of his head.

I *almost* make it. Almost.

Lonestar tackles me in midair, slamming me to the ground and driving all the oxygen from my lungs with a noise like a bursting balloon. My head slaps the desert floor, and I see whole constellations of stars as he drags me to my feet and wrenches my arms behind my back. Bear sprints over and between them they lift me off the ground, holding my wrists and ankles tight. I swear and curse and scream for them to let me go, *let me go for The Lord's sake*, but they carry me across the shooting range without a word.

My Brothers and Sisters almost fall over themselves to get out of the way, each and every one of them making very sure not to meet my eyes as I spit and yell and howl. From beneath the white oak, Father John regards me with profound disappointment.

As I'm carried around the corner of the Big House, terrible thuds and screams drift through the warm air as Jacob sets about teaching Lucy the lesson I refused to.

A
F
T
E
R

The two men sitting behind the desk are pale when I finish talking.

I'm not surprised, even though I'm sure it was exactly what Agent Carlyle—and some guilty part of Doctor Hernandez—wanted to hear: the violence and punishments and guns. Blood rarely makes for happy endings, but it almost always makes for better stories.

"When did that happen to your friend?" asks Agent Carlyle. His voice is low and tight.

"Three days before the fire," I say.

"So that was the last training session the Lord's Legion ever had?"

A shiver races up my spine because I hadn't thought about it like that. "Yeah," I say. "I guess it was."

"You told me people weren't punished for breaking the rules," says Doctor Hernandez. His voice sounds almost childish, like a teenager trying not to sulk, and it makes me want to laugh out loud. "You told me that the men and women of the Lord's Legion weren't afraid. Why did you say that?"

I shrug. I could tell the truth—that I didn't trust him when he asked me and that I still don't entirely trust him now—but what good would that do me?

He glances at Agent Carlyle with an expression that looks weirdly like jealousy, then scribbles in one of his notebooks for a long time. When he finally returns his attention to me, his neutral mask of professionalism is firmly back in place.

"What happened to you?" he asks. "Afterward, I mean."

"Bear and Lonestar locked me in my room," I say. "I thought I'd be taken to the Big House as soon as training was finished, but that didn't happen. Bear let me out when the bell rang for dinner."

"Why do you think you weren't punished?"

I shrug. "Maybe Father John thought it would look bad, me being one of his Future Wives. Or maybe he was still deciding what to do with me when everything else started to happen. I don't know."

Doctor Hernandez makes a note, then nods. "You've mentioned the Centurions several times. Can you tell us about them?"

I nod. "It was the name Father John gave the four most trusted members of the Legion."

"He had a strange way of showing how much he trusted them," says Agent Carlyle. "In the end, I mean. But I guess you know that better than anyone."

My heart leaps in my chest. "What are you talking about?"

"I'm talking about what happened in the Big House," he says. "During the fire. What you saw."

Doctor Hernandez frowns. "Okay, I think we should—"

"I didn't go into the Big House during the fire," I say.

96

Agent Carlyle narrows his eyes. "You're sure about that?"

"I'm sure."

He stares at me. I force myself not to look away.

Stay calm, whispers the voice in the back of my head. *He doesn't know. There's no possible way he can know. So stay calm.*

"Fine," he says eventually. "If you say so, then I believe you."

"Be careful," says Doctor Hernandez, his voice low.

Agent Carlyle nods, then smiles at me. "Your father was a Centurion. Correct?"

I frown. "Who told you that?"

"That doesn't matter right now."

"It matters to me."

"Why?"

"Because the thought of people talking to you about my family makes me nervous."

"Are you—"

Anger bubbles through me. "I'm not stupid. Maybe you think I am, but I'm not. The only people who could have told you anything about my dad after he joined the Legion are the ones who left during the Purge. Everyone else is dead."

Agent Carlyle nods. "Apart from your younger brothers and sisters," he says. "And you."

I stare at him for a long moment, because that was a really shitty thing to do. He knows more than he's saying, *both* of them do, and that's pretty much okay because I know a *lot* more than I'm telling *them*. But to throw the memory of my dad at me like that—if they know he was a Centurion, it's a safe bet they also know he's dead—is just cruel.

"Nobody can tell me anything about my mom, but you want to talk about my dad?" I say. "That doesn't seem fair."

"No," he says. "I can see how it wouldn't."

"I told you I don't have any information on your mother,

Moonbeam," says Doctor Hernandez. "Don't you believe I was telling you the truth?"

I shrug.

"Okay," says Agent Carlyle. "So are you saying your father *wasn't* a Centurion?"

"You clearly already know." I'm trying to keep the frustration that is barreling through me out of my voice, but I'm not at all sure I'm succeeding. "Why do you need me to say it?"

"I'm more interested in why you won't," he says.

"Okay," says Doctor Hernandez. "I'm going to ask you both to take this down a couple of notches. A robust discussion can be healthy, but being combative isn't going to help anyone."

"Sorry," says Agent Carlyle, but I'm staring into his eyes and I know he doesn't mean it.

"My dad died fourteen years ago," I say.

He nods. "I know he did. I'm very sorry."

"So why do you care whether he was a Centurion or not?"

"I'm interested in whether or not it changes how you think about them."

"It doesn't," I say. "My dad was one of the original Centurions, when Father Patrick first established them. They were different then."

"Different to what they were like after Father John took over?"

I nod. "They changed after the Purge."

"You said the Centurions were just Father John's most trusted servants," says Agent Carlyle. "Even though they were the only ones allowed to carry guns, and they watched Jacob Reynolds assault your friend Lucy without doing anything about it, and physically dragged you to your room and locked you in when you hadn't done anything wrong."

I shake my head slowly. The frustration is spreading through me like a forest fire, threatening to burn out of control. "Why don't you tell me what you want me to say? It would be so much quicker and easier."

"That's not what anybody wants," says Doctor Hernandez, "and I'm sorry if that's the impression you're getting from this session. We want you to tell us what you remember, Moonbeam, what you think and what you feel. We'd like you to tell the truth, as often as you feel able to, but the last thing we want to do is put words in your mouth."

I'm suddenly on the verge of tears.

Doctor Hernandez's expression is so gentle and sympathetic that it makes me want to scream, and Agent Carlyle is looking at me like I'm not really an actual person, like all I am is a human-shaped folder full of information he needs to extract, and everything inside me is roaring and raging, and I hate them, I hate them both, and I hate everyone else in the whole entire world.

Including myself.

So you should! screams Father John. *You're no good! YOU'RE FALSE!*

"Can you tell us about the Centurions?" asks Doctor Hernandez.

"I already have." My voice is trembling.

"It's okay if you don't want to," he says. "But you haven't told us about them. Not really."

"I don't want to," I say.

A flicker of disappointment crosses Doctor Hernandez's face. "That's fine. That's absolutely all right. We'll pick this up tomorrow."

Agent Carlyle frowns—I guess he doesn't usually stop asking questions because the interview subject doesn't want to answer them—but he doesn't say anything.

Doctor Hernandez lifts his bag onto the desk and carefully puts his pens and notebooks back into it. Once everything is how he wants it, he stands up. "See you tomorrow morning," he says. "I hope SSI goes well this afternoon. I'll be watching."

I can't help myself. The fire inside me is almost out, but the last few embers are still smoldering.

"Just like a Centurion," I say.

He stops where he's standing and frowns at me. "Why did you say that?"

I don't respond.

He sits back down next to Agent Carlyle, who hasn't moved. "If the Centurions were simply the most trusted members of the Lord's Legion, why did you try to insult me by calling me one?"

"Because I know you think they were bad."

He nods, the frown still furrowing his brow. "You're right," he says. "That's exactly what I think they were."

"What happened to Lucy was right at the end," I say. "When everything was coming apart. It wasn't always like that. *They* weren't always like that."

Pathetic, whispers the voice in the back of my head. *You're lying to yourself. Who are you trying to protect? Them or you?*

"I believe that, Moonbeam," says Doctor Hernandez. "I genuinely do. So why don't you tell us what they were really like?"

BEFORE

You have to have rules. That's what Father John always says. Without rules, things fall apart.

But it's not enough to *have* rules; you need to make sure people follow them. You can explain how the rules benefit everyone, how they make everyone feel safe and secure, and lots of people— probably *most* of them—will follow them because they're decent souls who understand the way a society has to work. But that isn't always enough. Some people are less decent, less inclined to be selfless. Those people need an incentive to follow the rules, and because you can't reward someone every time they do the right thing, you have to turn it around the other way. You have to make sure there are consequences for *not* following the rules.

That's how it works inside the Lord's Legion.

There are four Centurions at any one time, and there have

only ever been six of them, because the title and the responsibilities that go with it are a lifelong commitment. They don't wear uniforms or badges, but everyone knows who they are—and not just because of the guns hanging from their belts or slung over their shoulders. In the years after the Purge, when new Brothers and Sisters still arrived at the Base pretty regularly, the first thing they learned was that Father John's word is final. The second was that the Centurions are the reason why.

I've heard people—usually when they're angry because they've been punished for doing something they shouldn't have been doing—compare the Centurions to the police on the Outside. My only understanding of them comes from TV shows, back when we were still allowed to watch TV, but they don't really seem like the same thing. The Centurions don't spy on people, or interrogate them, or try to trick them or set them up, and they're always humble; they never try to set themselves apart. But if something *does* go wrong, if someone strays from the True Path, even for a moment, they appear as if by magic. And when they do, they dispense The Lord's justice.

As interpreted by Father John, of course.

When I was twelve, one of my Brothers by the name of Shanti beat his four-year-old daughter Echo with a broom handle after he found her on the kitchen floor about to drink a bottle of bleach. The resulting noise reached every corner of the Base: the *crack-crack-crack* of the broom handle, Echo's high-pitched screams, Shanti's furious bellowing, and his wife Lena's desperate, terrified pleas for him to stop, to *stop for the sake of The Lord*.

I saw Horizon and Bear sprint across the yard, their guns drawn, and disappear into the kitchen. The bellowing and screaming intensified, then the two Centurions dragged Shanti out into the yard and hauled him toward one of the three metal container boxes that stand in the northeast corner of the compound. Shanti

102

kicked and fought and howled every inch of the way, but Bear and Horizon were relentless; they shoved Shanti into the box, slammed and bolted its door, and ran straight back to the kitchen to check on Echo and Lena, who eventually emerged into the sunlight with pale faces and bloody clothes.

Shanti was left inside the metal box for ten days and nights, with only half a loaf of bread and a two-liter bottle of water each day.

During the day, when the desert sun is beating down, the boxes get so hot that you can't touch them with bare fingers. By night, after the heat has bled out of the air with the setting of the sun, they get so cold that you can find frost on their roofs as late as May or even June.

For the first day, Shanti ranted and sobbed and hammered on the walls of the box, a relentless reminder of what justice inside the Lord's Legion looks—and sounds—like. By lunchtime of the second day, the noise had been reduced to a weak rattling burst every hour or so. By the third day, the box was silent.

On the fifth evening, Father John ordered the box opened, took a long look inside, and asked Lena if she wanted him to grant her husband mercy. Lena put her arms around Echo, hugged her tight, and told The Prophet that mercy was for the weak. Father John kissed her forehead, told her The Lord is Good, and ordered the Centurions to lock the box.

When it was finally opened for good, after almost two hundred and fifty hours, the man who was dragged out into the bright morning was not the same man who had gone in. Shanti couldn't walk without assistance, his skin was ghostly white and hanging off his bones like the flesh of a veal calf, and his eyes were sunken and lifeless. He could not meet the gaze of the Brothers and Sisters who had gathered to see him released.

It took three months for Julia and Becky—under the watchful

eyes of the Centurions—to nurse him back to a state approaching health. He spent three months lying in a bed, being spoon-fed thin soup. Three months in which Lena and Echo didn't pay him a single visit. As soon as he was strong enough to sit upright behind the wheel of a car and work the pedals, Shanti was Gone in a cloud of dust.

His wife and daughter didn't even say goodbye to him. Less than a month later, Father John announced that The Lord had chosen Lena to join him in marriage, and she and Echo moved their things into the Big House.

Most people never got into such serious trouble though, or received such severe punishments. The worst I ever got was a three-day fast. I was on evening guard duty for the first time and had left my post at the Front Gate when I heard a noise in the desert that turned out to be a stray cat.

The three-day fast was tough, but I deserved it; Horizon talked to me about it for a long time, explaining in his low, gentle voice how the Servants of the Serpent could have walked right through the Front Gate and into the Big House and murdered The Prophet and it would have been all my fault.

He was right. And the punishment worked.

Whenever it was my turn to do guard duty after that, I never left my post for a single second.

AFTER

"They starved you for seventy-two hours because you left some arbitrary post for a couple of minutes?" asks Agent Carlyle.

"They didn't starve me," I say. "It was *punishment*. It was for my own good."

Don't do that, warns the voice in the back of my head. *Don't make excuses for them.*

Doctor Hernandez writes something in one of his notebooks, then gives me the look I hate most, the one that makes it so very clear he feels sorry for me. "What other punishments were handed out by the Centurions?"

I don't respond.

Stay calm.

He puts down his pen. "Moonbeam? Don't you want to answer that?"

I shake my head.

Stay calm.

"Why not?"

"Because none of this is real to you!" The sudden loudness of my voice surprises me, but I refuse to be embarrassed. Instead, I enjoy the shock that springs onto Doctor Hernandez's face, the furrowing of his brow and the widening of his eyes. "None of it! You sit there with all your pens and your notebooks, and you write about me while I'm sitting here in front of you, and it's like you think I can't see what you're doing or that I don't know what you're writing about. And you're always so calm and all your questions sound so *reasonable* and everything is a puzzle that needs solving, even me, and you don't get it! I'm not telling you these things to entertain you or because I think they're what you want to hear. I lived through them! This was my *actual life*! Why can't you understand that?"

Agent Carlyle stares at me with his bright blue eyes, but I ignore him; all the energy I have left is focused on Doctor Hernandez.

"I'm sorry," he says after what feels like hours have passed. "I know that it's impossible for me to ever truly understand what you've been through, and I'll be the first to admit that I'm not perfect. But *this*, all of this, is a process for the both of us. There are things that you can't be expected to understand about the world you grew up in and the rest of the world outside the fences, and some of those things need to be challenged and exposed for what they really were. I'm trying to ease you into these discoveries as gently as I possibly can, although I have no doubt it doesn't always feel like that to you. Those feelings are totally valid, and I'm not trying to diminish them, or derail you in any way. Okay?"

My heart pounds in my chest, and my skin feels really hot, and my hand suddenly hurts more beneath its bandages than it has all day, but I hear sincerity in his voice, and I don't believe—or maybe don't *want* to believe—that he's faking it.

I take a deep breath. "Okay. I'm sorry."

"I'm sorry too," he says. "But now that we're having this conversation and we're being emotionally open with each other, let me ask you something. Would it surprise you to know that in the vast majority of the world, an adult could be sent to prison for denying a child food for three days?"

I stare at him. "Why?"

"The charge would likely be child neglect, or child abuse, or something similar," he says. "Do you know what neglect is?"

I shake my head. The word means nothing to me.

"Neglect is when a person fails to adequately care for someone who is their responsibility," he explains. "From the perspective of a parent or a guardian, it could mean failing to ensure that a child has clean clothes or goes to school when they're supposed to. Not feeding them for three days would *definitely* qualify."

"It was a *punishment*," I say, because it was. I broke the rules, and I was punished. That's how things work.

You don't believe that though, says the voice in the back of my head. *Maybe you did once, but not now. Not anymore.*

"Shut up," I whisper.

Doctor Hernandez frowns. "Moonbeam?"

I shake my head. "My mom was there. When Father John announced I was being given the fast. She *agreed* with him."

Neither man says a word.

"Can we stop?" I ask, and I'm ashamed by the pleading in my voice. "Please?"

Doctor Hernandez nods. "Of course we can," he says. "I think that's a good idea."

Nurse Harrow gives me a smile before she pulls my door closed and locks it. I try to smile back at her, but I don't think I really pull it off.

I stand in the middle of the room for a second or two, then lie down on my bed and stare at the ceiling, trying to banish the memory of Shanti's expression when he was finally allowed out of the box, the look of awful, desperate *relief* on his face.

I don't want to see it. And I don't want to see anything else that's horrible today either. I really don't think I can take it.

Instead, I try to picture my dad.

He died when I was barely three years old, so I shouldn't have any memories of him. But the weird thing is, *I do*. I can see him so clearly, from angles that make me think I must have been sitting on his lap or playing at his feet and gazing up at him. I know they can't be real because I was three. They have to be images that I've created in the years since he died, that I invented and buried so deep that my brain can no longer tell the difference between them and the truth.

It's unsettling, not being able to fully trust your own mind. There have been times, more than a few of them, when I actually wondered whether my dad existed or whether he was a comforting fiction my mom made up. But I don't—*can't*—believe that she would lie to me about something so fundamental, about how I even came to exist. The only photo I had of him was burned to ash along with almost everything else inside the Base, but I still have his watch, and I used to have his knives, even if I don't know where they are now, and they are real. They are actual physical things that used to belong to an actual physical person.

It's harder to accept the reality that he *did* exist and then he died, far younger than he should have.

Harder and more painful. But it's the truth.

BEFORE

"You're doing it wrong," says my mom. "Give it here."

I hold out the string and the jar of beads and watch as she starts threading them, alternating blue and white and pale yellow, letting them clatter together where she has twisted the string around her thumb.

I've never been much good at making things. When I was little, before the Purge, Alice and some of the girls made bracelets and necklaces to sell in Town, beautiful little things that gleamed and glittered and made the women of Layfield coo and purr and tell my Sisters how clever they were.

It used to make me feel jealous, watching them collect dollar after dollar in exchange for their jewelry while I paced back and forth along the hot sidewalk with a sweaty bunch of leaflets in my hand, trying to find someone who wanted to talk about the Word of The Lord. Most people didn't, although they normally weren't rude about it. We were kids, and adults try a bit harder to be nice when they're dealing with children. The majority just muttered "No thanks" and kept right on walking, barely even looking at me as they passed.

On those rare occasions when someone *did* stop, it was a totally different story. I might have been no good at threading beads, pressing flowers, and supergluing rhinestones, but I was good at talking to people. Most of them engaged me out of boredom or because they saw some sport in winning an argument with a little girl, but once I had their attention, the conversation usually didn't go how they were expecting.

I always started with a loaded question, one I knew they would say yes to. "Do you worry about Hell?" or "Do you believe in the power of The Lord?" always worked well, because almost everyone in Layfield claimed they believed in God, even if most of them were a long way from the True Path. And once they said yes to my opening question, I simply talked to them.

I told them about The Serpent and his Servants, about the End Times and the Final Battle, and I pressed leaflet after leaflet into their hands before inviting them to come out to the Base and make up their own minds. It seems crazy now, after Father John's First Proclamation banned almost all contact between the Lord's Legion and the Outside. In Father Patrick's time, not only was the Sunday morning service in the Chapel open to anyone who wanted to come, but people from the local towns actually came, pretty regularly. Some made the trip out of genuine curiosity, some because they had nothing better to do, but most weeks we would see a handful of unfamiliar faces sitting in the back row of pews. And more often than not, they would be people I had spoken to.

Father Patrick used to call me his little evangelist. Hearing it made me smile from ear to ear.

My mom strings a final bead, attaches the clasps, and holds the necklace out to me. "There you go," she says. "It's not difficult, Moon. It just takes a little practice."

I nod, because there's really nothing you can say to someone who doesn't understand why you can't do something they find easy, and fasten the necklace around my neck. The beads are smooth and heavy against my skin, and I smile.

"It's great, Mom," I say. "Thanks."

"Okay," she says, which I like to think is her way of saying "you're welcome" without actually saying it.

We're sitting on a bench near the western edge of the Base, underneath the ash tree that got struck by lightning two summers ago. Its dead branches point toward the sky like broken fingers, and there's a ring of dirt around the base of its trunk where nothing has grown since, not even weeds. Overhead, the sky is bright blue and absolutely enormous, without a single cloud to be seen, and the sun beats down, making the skin on my arms tingle. Lunch finished an hour ago, and normally we'd already be back at work, but today is Sunday, and we don't work on Sundays. Father John likes us to rest, to reflect on another week spent on the True Path and give thanks to The Lord for the blessings He has bestowed upon us. I glance at my mom. She's staring into the distance, a familiar emptiness in her eyes, and I feel a guilty twist of annoyance in the pit of my stomach.

Don't get me wrong, I love my mom. I really genuinely do.

I love her because she's clever and pretty, and she looks after me and tries really hard to keep me on the True Path. But the truth is—and it feels terrible admitting this, even to myself—a lot of the time, I don't actually *like* her very much. And it often seems as though the feeling is mutual.

She's never unkind to me, at least not intentionally. Some of our Brothers and Sisters are so awful to their children that I struggle to understand why they ever had them in the first place. They shout at them and insult them and—once they've gotten permission from the Centurions—punish them harshly for the slightest little thing they do wrong. My mom isn't like that at all, and I'm grateful.

It's sort of hard to explain what she *is* like. I think the closest I can get is that—more often than not—it feels like she isn't really there. It's as if the person I see every day is more like an echo than an actual person, as though all the life and energy has been stripped out of her and what's left is someone who walks and talks and laughs, but doesn't seem to actually *feel* anything.

This isn't a new development. For a long time, I thought her distance was because of grief over my dad, but he's been dead for more than a decade, and it seems like there has to be a limit on how long anything is allowed to make you feel sad, because otherwise how do people manage to live their lives? Surely there has to come a day when you wake up and it doesn't hurt anymore, like when I was seven and fell off the roof of one of the cars and broke my arm. If not, I honestly don't understand why anyone would ever fall in love or get married or have children, because all you're doing is guaranteeing that one day you'll get hurt so badly that you'll never recover, and that doesn't sound like a very good deal.

"Penny for them?" I ask.

She looks around at me. "What?"

"Your thoughts, Mom," I say. "Penny for them?"

"Oh," she says, and gives me a small smile. "Sorry. I was miles away."

Like usual. Like always.

"It's okay," I say. "What were you thinking about?"

"Your father." I stiffen. She hardly ever talks about him, even when I ask her to. "I was thinking about how much he loved this place."

"Why did he love it?"

"Because he was an idiot," she says. Then she sees the frown that has appeared on my brow and grimaces. "I'm sorry. I didn't mean that. I just mean he was easily impressed."

"By what?" I ask.

She shrugs. "By everything. People, art, music, books, places. *Especially* places. He grew up in Chicago, a city boy through and through, and when we moved to Santa Cruz, he used to tell me how amazing the Pacific was at least once a day, like every morning he was seeing it for the first time. But how he felt about the ocean was nothing compared to how much he loved this desert. He used to tell me it was undeniable proof of God's existence, that only The Lord could have created something so completely incredible and also made our brains powerful enough to take it for granted. He used to say this desert was the holiest place he ever saw."

"What do you think, Mom?"

She shrugs again. "It's a desert. As hot and empty as any other. It's pretty enough in the mornings and evenings, and I guess there's something to be said for the peace and quiet, but it's only a desert. Places are only places, Moon. People make them into more than they are."

"Didn't you want to come here?" I've never asked her that question—or any others like it—before, but it seems like she's in an unusual mood, like she wants to *really* talk to me, and I don't want to let it go to waste.

She frowns. "That's a very dangerous question, my little Moon," she says. "Are you implying Heresy on my part? Are you suggesting that I didn't welcome the Call of the True Path?"

My stomach drops like a stone. "No, Mom. I'm sorry. I wasn't—"

Her frown disappears, replaced by a gentle smile. "I'm teasing you," she says. "Although I want you to promise me that you'll never ask anyone else that question."

I shake my head. "I won't."

"Promise me, Moon."

"I promise, Mom."

"Good girl," she says. "And no, I didn't want to come here, to tell the truth. I loved our house in Santa Cruz, and I loved the ocean too, even if I didn't mention it as often as your father did. You were only eighteen months old, and you weren't exactly the easiest baby, so I wasn't with your father when he heard Horizon speak in the mission hall near the boardwalk. I had just put you to bed when he came home and announced that he had met a True messenger of The Lord, and that we needed to go to Texas."

"What did you say?"

She laughs. It's a lovely sound, one I don't hear very often. "I told him not to be so ridiculous. I told him that I wasn't going to uproot our family and move to the middle of nowhere because some traveling preacher said so."

"So how did we end up here?"

Her eyes go dim. "Your father could be very…persuasive." She pauses. "He knew that he would get nowhere by trying to convince me to change my mind, so he made it seem like he had let it go. But he kept mentioning what Horizon had said, things that I had to admit made a certain amount of sense, and when he eventually suggested that we come down here for a long weekend, to see what it was like, no pressure, I said yes."

"What happened?"

"We came," she says, "and we never left. On that Sunday afternoon, I moved you and me into Building Nine, and your father drove back to Santa Cruz to pack up our things."

"So what changed your mind?" I ask.

"I heard Father Patrick and some of the others speak," she says. "I talked to some of our Brothers and Sisters. And as I said, your father could be very persuasive."

A
F
T
E
R

The ceiling of my room is made of square gray panels, each one maybe two feet long.

Four of them meet right above me, at a point I've been staring at for I don't know how long. There's a stain across the corners of two of them, a smear of pale orange that fades as it bleeds into whatever the panels are made of. I guess there must be a leak above the ceiling, water dripping and spreading a tiny fraction farther every day.

It's weird to be allowed to think about my mother without worrying that someone is somehow going to peer inside my head and report me to a Centurion. After she was Gone, she joined the long list of people whose names were never to be spoken out loud, who had been relegated to the status of nonpersons, as though they had never actually existed at all. But she did exist, and there's nobody to stop me from thinking about her now.

I stare at my room's tiny window and wonder if she's out there, living a life that doesn't include me. I wonder if part of her was relieved when she was Banished—whether it gave her a chance to get away from everything, including her daughter and the ghost of her husband. For the longest time, I believed with all my heart that she would come back for me, that one day I would hear her call my name and she would be standing outside the Front Gate and I would climb over it and run to her and she would take me away and we would never look back.

But that didn't happen.

I thought a lot about what her never coming back actually meant in the darkness of my room in Building Nine, after the door was locked and the lights were out. Did it mean that she was scared of Father John, of what he might do to her, or to me? Or— and this would be much, *much* worse—did it mean that she simply never loved me, and my worst fears, the ones that crept into my head at my weakest moments, were true all along?

The worst part was that there was nobody I could ask about her, nobody I could talk to—even the Brothers and Sisters I felt closest to would have reported me straightaway. They might not have enjoyed doing so, but they would have done it without thinking twice.

Now though? Now there *is* someone I can talk to. But I still have no idea whether I can trust Doctor Hernandez or not. He may well be telling me the truth, that he doesn't know anything about my mom, about where she is, or whether she's even still alive. He may well have asked his colleagues whether they know anything, and if they do, he might even tell me, like he promised he would. Or…

Maybe he knows where she is but isn't telling me because I'm more likely to cooperate so long as there's something I want from him.

Maybe she's dead, and he knows, but he doesn't want to upset me because of my *fragile* state.

Maybe.

Tears well in the corners of my eyes as I hear footsteps come to a halt outside my room. I wipe them away because I really don't want Nurse Harrow to see me crying when she brings in my lunch. But the tears keep coming. It's like something inside me has sprung a leak that isn't going to stop.

Because a single thought is filling my head as I swing my legs off the bed, a thought that is both deeply profound and completely obvious, a thought that I have so rarely allowed myself to acknowledge.

I miss my mom.

I really, *really* miss her.

Two hours later, I walk into the group therapy room. I'm looking for Luke before the door has even closed behind me.

Part of me, the same part that spent the last few months before the fire looking over its shoulder, is convinced that he's going to jump out and attack me. I know it's stupid, if only because I have to believe that Doctor Hernandez and his other colleagues who are watching wouldn't let Luke hurt me, but I can't fully shake the thought. I quickly check left and right, like a child about to cross a road, but I see no sign of him. I relax, just a little.

"Hey, Moonbeam," says Rainbow. She's sitting cross-legged in the middle of the floor next to Lucy and Winter, and the three of them are scribbling determinedly with thick crayons on a big sheet of paper. I haven't the slightest idea what their drawing is supposed to be—from where I'm standing it looks like some sort of giant Satanic octopus—but it's good to see them playing together, even though the sight of Lucy's bruised face hurts my heart.

"Hey, Rainbow," I say. "Hey, everyone."

Most of my Brothers and Sisters look in my direction and smile or say hello or both. I give them my best smile back while I scan the room for Luke. I'm starting to think he isn't here, when Jeremiah gets up and races across the room with a paper airplane in his hand, making a gurgling noise he must think sounds like an engine, and I see him.

Luke is on the floor in the far corner of the room, his legs pulled up against his chest, his arms wrapped around his knees. His head is up, and I freeze because it seems like he's staring right at me, but then I look closer, and I don't think his eyes are actually focused on anything. They're sunken and hollow, as though he hasn't slept for days.

"He's been like that since I came in."

I find Honey standing next to me, her eyes fixed on Luke.

"Has he said anything?" I ask.

She shakes her head. "Not a word."

I grimace. Laughter and excited chatter fills the room as Aurora chases Jeremiah with what looks like a Play-Doh snake, and Sunset and Violet sit at one of the tables, singing a song that sounds sort of familiar but that I can't quite place. Then they stop singing, and Sunset writes urgently on a piece of paper, and I realize they're making it up as they go along.

None of them are paying any attention to Luke, which makes me feel more than a little conflicted. On the one hand, I'm pleased to see them getting on with the business of playing and singing and acting like normal children; but on the other, the fact that they don't seem to care that someone they've known all their lives is very clearly suffering makes me feel uneasy.

They're just kids, whispers the voice in the back of my head. *They don't know what's serious and what isn't. Just be glad they're okay.*

"Are you okay?" asks Honey, as though she can read my mind.

"I'm fine," I say. "Why?"

"You look like you've been crying."

The tears finally stopped about fifteen minutes before Nurse Harrow came to collect me for SSI, but there was nothing I could do about my eyes, which are red and swollen and feel as dry as the desert.

"I'm fine," I repeat.

She nods. It looks like she wants to say something else, but she doesn't.

I nod in Luke's direction. "I'm going to talk to him."

Honey frowns. "Why?"

"Someone needs to."

"Someone *is* talking to him," says Honey. "Ten o'clock every morning, just like you and me and everyone else. He's not your responsibility."

I want to tell her she's wrong because he wouldn't be here if it wasn't for me—*nobody would be here if it wasn't for me*—but I can't.

I can't tell anyone.

"I'm going to try," I say.

She shrugs. "Do what you have to do."

I nod, but I don't move. I don't *want* to talk to Luke. In fact, it's pretty close to the last thing I want to do.

But I can't leave him staring into space in the corner of the room.

I take a deep breath and force myself to walk toward him. If Luke sees me coming, he shows no sign of it; he doesn't move a muscle, and his eyes don't so much as twitch in my direction. I keep a *very* close eye on him as I turn my back to the wall and slowly slide down beside him.

"Hey," I say.

No response.

"Luke? Are you okay?"

Nothing.

"I'm just going to sit here for a little while, okay?" I say. "You don't have to talk to me if you don't want to."

His head doesn't turn, but there's a flicker of movement in his eyes. I stay absolutely still and silent, until he eventually mutters something inaudible.

I tilt my head toward him. "Say again, Luke? I didn't hear you."

"Why are we still here?" he asks, his voice little more than a low croak. "Why hasn't The Prophet come back for us?"

"I don't know, Luke," I say, because the only answer I have is one I know he doesn't want to hear.

"I didn't deserve to Ascend," he whispers. "That's all it can be. That's the only explanation. My Faith wasn't strong enough."

"Luke…"

"I wasn't good enough."

"Don't, Luke," I say. "Please. You can't think like that."

Ever so slowly, he turns his head. "We left the True Path," he says, his eyes fixed on mine. "I don't know how, but we must have. Somewhere along the way we got lost."

I stare helplessly at him. Despite everything he did, despite all the good reasons I have to hate him, my heart is aching, because this isn't the Luke who could have been, the person he had the potential to become. I'm looking at Father John's greatest creation—a broken thing, filled to the brim with lies and fear.

"Pray with me," he whispers. "Pray with me, Moonbeam. It still might not be too late."

I shake my head. "I'm not going to do that, Luke."

His mouth twists into maybe the most unsettling smile I've ever seen. "You were never really one of us, were you?" he whispers. "You never had Faith. You were never True."

"You're wrong," I say. "I did have Faith. I had it for a very long time."

"And now?"

I don't respond. He can draw whatever conclusion he likes from my silence.

For long, empty seconds we stare at each other. Then his eyes suddenly narrow, and his smile disappears. "This is your doing," he whispers.

A tremor of fear rolls up my spine.

Does he know what I did? Can he possibly?

He doesn't know anything, says the voice in the back of my head instantly. *But you need to be careful. You need to be very careful right now.*

I'm suddenly extremely aware of how little distance there is between us, and that there's no way I can move away from him without making it obvious what I'm doing.

"I didn't do anything, Luke." My voice is still mostly steady.

His eyes slowly widen, as though he's looking at something wondrous. "It is," he whispers. "It's you. How did I not see it until now?"

"I'm going to go now," I say, trying to stay calm. "I just wanted to check you were okay."

He reaches out and grabs hold of my arm.

Calm. Stay calm.

"Let go," I say.

He tightens his grip.

"Luke," I say. "Let go of my arm."

He doesn't move. He stares at me. The wild light of madness has returned to his eyes, and I can't look at it any longer. I wrench my arm free and leap to my feet as he uncurls like a striking diamondback, his face darkening to furious red.

"You!" he shouts.

The room falls silent as our Brothers and Sisters stop what they're doing and turn to us. Out of the corner of my eye, I see Honey take a step toward me, a deep frown on her face.

"I didn't do anything, Luke," I say. "There's no reason to get upset."

My words seem to momentarily confuse him, as though he can't quite believe what he heard—because *of course* there's reason to get upset, there's every reason to get upset—but he rallies quickly enough.

"Your mother was a Heretic!" he bellows, the words hitting me like a punch to the stomach. "She was a Heretic, and your best friend was an Outsider spy, and that makes you a Servant of the Serpent! *That's* why they won't come back for us! Because *you're* here! This is *your* fault! *YOU DID THIS TO US!*"

I take a step back from the roaring heat of his anger, but I don't protest, don't try to argue with him, because what could I possibly say? He's telling the truth.

The door opens, and two male nurses I haven't seen before step into the room.

"Luke," says one of them. "We need you to calm down."

He spins around, his eyes blazing. "You can go to Hell! Can't you see, Outsider? Can't you see The Serpent standing before you?"

"I can see that you're upset," says the nurse. "Do you think you can calm down and continue this session, or do you need us to take you back to your room?"

Luke stares at the nurse, his face twisted with crimson hatred, then spits on the floor. "I don't want to be anywhere near her," he growls. "Her stink makes me want to puke."

He strides across the room and out into the corridor without a backward glance. The nurses follow him, and the door swings shut.

I stand on my own in the middle of the room. My Brothers and Sisters are all staring at me, but I can't meet their eyes. I want to tell them that it's okay, that everything's all right, but I can't, because it *isn't*.

Nothing is okay, and *nothing* is all right. And I don't know if it ever will be.

AFTER

Agent Carlyle is here again. He followed Doctor Hernandez into Interview Room 1 as the clock above the door reached ten and gave me a smile as he sat down.

I didn't sleep well last night, although I can't pretend I'm surprised. Luke's face hung in the darkness above me, twisted with fury as he realized—or convinced himself—that I'm the reason he hasn't Ascended to sit at the right hand of The Lord. As a result, I'm tired, and my brain feels warm and sluggish, and I can't quite decide whether I'm glad Agent Carlyle is here or not.

Based on yesterday's session, it feels like he wants more straightforward answers from me than Doctor Hernandez, more *what happened and who did what when* and less discussion of what I feel or think. But more straightforward or not, who he is still makes me nervous. Doctor Hernandez works for a hospital and has a wife and seems pretty much like a normal person. Whatever else he may be, Agent Carlyle is still part of the Government.

I know that shouldn't matter anymore. Or at least, it shouldn't matter as much as Father John always told us it did. But some things go deeper than rationality; some ideas are sewn into the fabric of my soul, far beyond the reach of Doctor Hernandez and his colleagues and his process.

I don't know if there is any real chance of me getting out of this place. I want to believe there is, that Doctor Hernandez told me the truth and that one day I'll get to walk outside and feel the sun on my face and start a new life somewhere far from here. But even if that's a possibility, I don't know how long it might be until that happens, and I don't know who actually makes the decision to let me go. I'm starting to suspect that Agent Carlyle will have a good deal of say in the matter.

You need to tread carefully, whispers the voice in the back of my head. *You're not the only one who knows more than they're saying. He's smart, and he sees you better than you think. They both do.*

"Good morning, Moonbeam," says Doctor Hernandez, as he arranges his pens and notebooks. "How are—"

"I don't want to talk about the Centurions," I interrupt, because I'm tired and my hand hurts and I've been thinking about what I want to say ever since I woke up. "Or Nate or my mom or anything else that's bad. So I honestly don't know if there's any point in doing this today."

"That's all right," says Doctor Hernandez. "That's completely understandable. I'm sorry if yesterday's sessions made you feel uncomfortable."

"It's okay," I say. "How's Luke doing?"

"We're working with him," he says. "I'm confident of a positive outcome."

I hope you're right.

"Good. So shall I go back to my room?"

Agent Carlyle glances at Doctor Hernandez, who keeps his gaze fixed on me. "Why don't we just talk?" he says. "No questions you don't want to answer, no agenda, no process. A simple conversation."

I narrow my eyes. "What about?"

"I know you think that we've already made our minds up about the Lord's Legion. That we believe everything about it was bad. So why don't you tell us about the other side of it?"

"What do you mean?" I ask.

"Tell us about a time you were happy," he says. "A normal day or a memory that makes you smile. Something good."

"Why?" I ask. "That isn't the stuff you care about."

Doctor Hernandez shakes his head. "That isn't true. Agent Carlyle represents the criminal investigation that you are part of, even though I know you wish you weren't, but I promise you that I am interested in every aspect of your life, the bad *and* the good."

"I can't think of anything good." It's not even a lie.

"I don't want to believe that, Moonbeam," he says. "Are you sure?"

I think back, searching my memory for what he's asking, but it's not easy.

Not easy at all.

How it all ended has tarnished everything that came before, as though the fire itself has spread through my memories, scouring and scorching and turning everything dark. It's like the present has poisoned the past.

I can think of happy *moments*, but most of them are fleeting and only of interest to me: a joke I shared with Honey, the Friday afternoon when Amos brought hot churros back from Town, Nate's face when the light of the setting sun caught him from a certain angle. Nothing worth telling anyone else.

What about before the Purge? whispers the voice in the back of my head. *Before Father John took over the Legion?*

I search back further, digging deep into my memories, until one rises up out of nowhere, and I smile, both at the memory itself and because it's something I can safely give Doctor Hernandez and Agent Carlyle, that they can get their teeth into without getting too close to the things I don't want to tell them.

Which seems like a fair deal. To me, at least.

BEFORE

The fairy lights strung from the trees and between the corners of the buildings twinkle red and white and blue as Father Patrick winds up and hurls the baseball.

Horizon frowns as it flies toward him, takes a swing so huge it almost spins him off his feet, and connects with nothing but air. The ball thuds against the wall of the Chapel behind him, and everyone cheers and boos and whoops and hollers as he picks it up and throws it back where it came from, a wide grin on his face.

"Nice pitch," he says.

Father Patrick tips an imaginary cap, his red hair bright in the glow of the Fourth of July decorations. I'm cross-legged on the warm blacktop of the yard, my mom on one side, Honey and Alice on the other. Honey is only four and not interested in baseball, but Alice is keeping an eye on her while she chases one of the spare balls back and forth. She seems happy enough. I don't know where Honey's mom is—probably in her room, in the grip of one of her headaches. She gets them a *lot*.

My mom is finishing one of the last burgers that came off the grill before the game got started. She's got mustard on her upper lip and ketchup on the end of her nose, but I haven't told her because she looks funny, and I'm wondering how long it will take her to notice.

I ate two burgers, I don't even know how many chicken wings, some potato salad, some rice, and a spoonful of a green dip that Bear made. It tasted weird, sort of like moss, but I ate it anyway because I like Bear and I didn't want him to feel bad if nobody ate his dip. My grown-up Brothers and Sisters are drinking bottles of Coke and glasses of lemonade. I'm not allowed to drink Coke, but Bella already let me have a sip of hers. I don't think anybody saw.

"Two strikes!" shouts my mom, holding up two fingers. "He's got your number, Horizon!"

The yard is nearly full. When the game is over, some people will go and sleep off their barbecue and some will go into Legionnaires' Hall and watch real baseball on TV, and some will go and listen to music on radios in the gardens, but for right now, almost everyone is together in one place. I look around as Father Patrick tosses the baseball in his hand, at the men and women and children sprawled out in a loose rectangle, at the people waiting patiently for their turn to bat or pitch, and I smile because it's warm and sunny and I'm with my Family.

Horizon shakes his head at my mom and mouths, "We'll see."

She waves her fingers at him, but she's got a big grin on her face, and it's really good to see it, because she doesn't smile as much as I wish she would. Most of the time she doesn't look very happy, but I don't ask her whether she's okay anymore because the last time I did she got really mad and told me that I would be the first to know if she wasn't. I don't think that's true though. I think she just wanted me to stop asking.

Father Patrick starts his windup again as Horizon takes his stance and raises his bat. But as his arm whips forward, an *enormous* burp rips across the yard and echoes into the desert. Father Patrick pulls out of the pitch and almost overbalances as Horizon and everyone else turn toward the source of the noise.

Luke makes absolutely no attempt to pretend it wasn't him. His grin is huge, his face pink, his eyes bright with happiness. There's a moment of stunned silence before Horizon bursts out laughing, a great booming noise that engulfs the whole yard and is impossible to resist. Luke doesn't move as everyone else joins in—he just sits where he is, his face beaming with pride, as his Brothers and Sisters clap him on the back and ruffle his hair and the younger children stare at him with wide-eyed admiration.

"I'm going to assume you got enough barbecue, Luke," says Father Patrick, a broad smile on his freckled face. "Any chance I can strike Horizon out without any further distractions?"

"Sure thing, Father," says Luke, his grin widening.

"Why thank you," says Father Patrick. "That's most kind of you."

The last of the laughter fades away as he starts his windup again. This time nobody burps and nobody makes any other noise as he takes a big step forward and pitches the ball toward Horizon, who moves almost too fast for my eyes to follow.

Crack.

The ball launches off the bat like a rocket and soars high into the cloudless sky. About a dozen of my younger Brothers and Sisters leap to their feet and give chase, churning up dust and screaming with excitement as the ball thuds to the ground near the maintenance sheds and skids toward the fence. Horizon holds his pose for a long moment, a huge grin on his face, then tosses the bat nonchalantly to Bear as we cheer and clap and shout his name.

Father Patrick shakes his head, but the smile on his face is wider than ever. "That's a monster," he says. "I thought you'd cleared the fence for a second there."

Horizon smiles. "The Lord is Good, Father."

There's a commotion out by the sheds as the ball is located and a wrestling match begins for it. Aja manages to wrap his stubby fingers around it and takes off running, holding the ball above his head as a dozen small, dusty figures give chase. He sprints back toward the yard, laughing uncontrollably, then throws the ball with all his strength. It barely reaches the blacktop, but it bounces and rolls right to Horizon's feet. It thuds against the heel of his boot, but he doesn't seem to notice. He's staring toward the Front Gate.

"Car," he says.

Most of the crowd, me included, get to their feet and look south.

The Front Gate sounds grand, but it's only three planks of wood in a wide Z-shape, with a fence that runs away from it on both sides made up of lengths of chicken wire strung between wooden posts. It's supposed to keep out coyotes and other critters, but I've seen enough of them wandering the Base after dark to know it doesn't do its job very well.

Parked on the dirt road beyond the gate, surrounded by low clouds of settling dust, is a white car. As if hearing some unspoken order, everyone starts to walk toward it, Horizon and Bear and Father Patrick at the front.

Well. *Almost* everyone starts to walk.

I glance around as the crowd moves and see John Parson and Amos Andrews standing on their own in front of the Chapel. They're talking in low voices, and I'm suddenly weirdly sure that I'll be in trouble if they catch me looking at them, so I turn away. I manage a handful of steps before curiosity gets the better of me and I glance toward the Chapel a second time.

John and Amos are gone. I don't see them anywhere.

I frown. It isn't really any of my business what John and Amos are doing, but I don't know why they aren't coming with the rest of us and there was something weird about the expression on their faces as they talked to each other. I'm about to say something to my mom when the door of the white car opens and a man gets out.

I instantly don't like him.

He's fat, and his face is red and covered in sweat, and his nose looks like a rat's, all pointed and twitchy. He smiles at Father Patrick and the Centurions as they reach the Front Gate.

"Evening," he says, then digs into the back pocket of his jeans and pulls out one of the leaflets that me and my Brothers and Sisters hand out every morning in Town, the one that has HAVE YOU HEARD THE GOOD NEWS? printed on the front. "I came across this a couple of weeks back and haven't been able to get it out of my head since. Decided I ought to talk to the man who wrote it."

"I wrote it," says Father Patrick, "and I'll be more than happy to discuss its contents with you. What's your name, friend?"

"Jacob Reynolds," says the man. "It's a pleasure to meet you all."

AFTER

Doctor Hernandez sits back in his chair. "I'm sorry," he says. "I'm a little confused."

"Me too," says Agent Carlyle.

"Okay," I say. "What's confusing?"

"Is that really a happy memory?" asks Doctor Hernandez. "The arrival of Jacob Reynolds?"

"That day is," I say. "Everything after Father John took over the Legion is tainted. So that Fourth of July is the last really happy day I could think of."

The two men glance at each other.

"I'm still struggling over here," says Agent Carlyle. "I feel like we're missing some context."

I suddenly understand what their problem is, and excitement

flutters through me as I realize they really *don't* know everything about everything.

"Father John made his move the day after Jacob arrived."

"You're talking about the purge?" asks Doctor Hernandez.

I nod. "They already knew Jacob. Father John and Amos, I mean. I don't know how, or from where, but it was all planned. It was a setup. Nobody realized it at the time, but looking back now it's obvious."

"Was Jacob Reynolds welcomed in?" asks Agent Carlyle.

"Of course," I say. "Father Patrick welcomed everyone."

"What did Father John actually do?" he asks. "The day after, I mean. How did he take control of the Lord's Legion?"

"It wasn't as dramatic as you're probably thinking," I say. "There was no fighting or shooting or anything like that. Father John got up on the steps of the Chapel and announced that The Lord had spoken to him in the night, had come to him in the darkness, and given him a message."

"I'm going to go out on a limb and guess it didn't contain good news for Father Patrick," says Agent Carlyle.

I smile. "Right. The Lord's message was that the Legion needed Father John to lead it. He stood up in front of everyone and said that Father Patrick was a Faithful servant of The Lord, a kind and gentle man, but that kind and gentle men didn't win wars, especially not the Final Battle with The Serpent that we all knew was coming. He asked everyone to search their hearts and stand with him if they believed he was speaking the truth. Guess who were the first two to step forward?"

"Amos and Jacob," says Doctor Hernandez.

I nod. "They walked straight up and stood on either side of Father John. They didn't say anything, not a single word, but—"

"They were both armed," says Agent Carlyle softly. "Weren't they?"

I nod.

"Didn't you say that guns were permitted in Father Patrick's time?" asks Doctor Hernandez.

I nod again. "They were. But people didn't carry them on their belts. They were in the bedrooms and barracks."

"What did the Centurions do?" asks Agent Carlyle.

"Bear and Angel and Lonestar were the next to stand with Father John," I say. "Horizon stayed where he was for a few seconds, then he went too."

"And where was Father Patrick while all this was happening?"

"Right there." I can see the look on his face as the Centurions turned their backs on him and stood with Father John. I can see it so clearly. It wasn't anger, or even disappointment; it looked like grief, like his heart was breaking in his chest.

"He didn't do anything?" asks Agent Carlyle.

I shake my head.

"Say anything?"

"Not a word," I say. "It was already too late for that. A lot of people saw which way the wind was blowing and went with it, but a good number went to stand beside Father John with smiles on their faces. They truly believed he was what he said he was."

"Which was what?" asks Doctor Hernandez.

"A conduit to The Lord," I say. "His Holy messenger on Earth."

There's a long silence as the two men take this in.

"How did Father John get people to go along with that?" asks Agent Carlyle after a moment. "How did he convince them to believe him?"

I CONVINCED THEM OF NOTHING! Father John's voice thunders through my head. *THEY SAW THE TRUTH WITH THEIR OWN EYES! THE LORD DOES NOT MAKE MISTAKES!*

I shrug as casually as I can. "It's hard to explain unless you saw it for yourself," I say. "Everyone loved Father Patrick, including me. I always believed he was a good man, and looking back, I believe it more than ever. He was kind and decent, and he cared more about other people than about himself. He devoted his life to serving The Lord."

"And Father John?" asks Doctor Hernandez.

I think about this for a while before I answer.

"There were times when he barely seemed like a man at all," I say. "He seemed more like a force of nature, wild and unpredictable. What you have to understand is that he had been a devoted member of the Legion for three years before he made his move, and my Brothers and Sisters loved him. He was charming and clever, and he knew the Bible even better than Father Patrick. Anyone who wanted to speak in the Chapel was allowed to do so, and Father John spoke most often, and that was absolutely fine with everyone, because he was never not worth listening to. He would walk up to the pulpit in his dusty denim shirt with his long hair and green eyes and a gentle smile on his face, and then he would scream and spit and howl and pound the lectern until his knuckles bled. He spoke about The Lord like most people talk about their oldest friends, like the two of them had literally just finished a conversation before he stood up to speak. He screamed about battles and war and time growing short, and he talked about the Outsiders, over and over again. He told us that we were all that stood between The Serpent and victory."

"Was that in line with Father Patrick's teachings?" asks Doctor Hernandez.

"More or less," I say. "Father Patrick believed in the Book of Revelations and in Armageddon. It was what led him to found the Legion. He taught us that an end was coming and that the Faithful needed to be ready for it. But Father John's vision was more..." I search for the right word. "Extreme."

"Didn't Father Patrick realize what was happening?" asks

Agent Carlyle. "If Father John was such a good speaker, and so well loved, and was preaching a more aggressive version of the Legion's teachings, didn't he see the potential threat to his authority?"

"I don't know," I say. "I think maybe some of the others did because a few people left in the months before the Purge. But by the time Father John made his move, it was already him that most people went to if they had questions or doubts, and it was his answers they listened to. He always publicly deferred to Father Patrick, always made himself out to be a loyal Legionnaire."

"Was there violence when he took over?" asks Agent Carlyle.

I shake my head.

"Nobody went and got their gun and said they weren't going to let this happen?"

I shake my head again.

"What happened to the people who stayed loyal to Father Patrick?" asks Doctor Hernandez. "After Father John replaced him?"

"Nothing," I say. "It all happened really fast. There was a lot of shouting, and some pushing and shoving when people were loading up their cars to leave, but nothing more serious than that."

"Why was there shouting?"

I shrug. "Father Patrick begged everyone to stay calm, but some of the people who went were leaving family members behind, so it all got pretty tense. People were crying and calling each other Heretics and praying and begging the ones who were going to change their minds."

"Father Patrick left then too?" asks Agent Carlyle.

I nod. "He led the others out."

"Did you ever wonder what happened to him?" asks Doctor Hernandez. "And the others?"

"No. It was forbidden to think about them."

"It's not forbidden now."

I picture Father Patrick's earnest, freckled face as people loaded cars and wept and shouted and argued, as everything he had built collapsed around him.

"I guess I feel sorry for him, if anything," I say. "He lost what he believed was his life's work. I don't think I understood how hard that must have been at the time."

"I know he's been interviewed as part of our investigation," says Agent Carlyle. "I can probably get an update on what happened after he left the Lord's Legion if you want?"

I shake my head. "It doesn't matter."

He nods. "If you change your mind, let me know."

"I will. Thanks."

He nods again. "What about John Parson? What did he do while people were leaving?"

"He sat on the porch of the Big House and watched them drive away. He didn't say a word."

"Why do you think that was?" asks Agent Carlyle.

"Because he knew he'd won."

He gives me a tight smile. "Did you figure that out then?"

"I'm not sure," I say. "Probably later on."

"Pretty sharp."

I shrug. "I pay attention. Most people don't."

"They don't," says Agent Carlyle. "They really don't. Did people talk about the purge after it happened?"

"Everyone did," I say. "Father John insisted. The whole Legion gathered in the Chapel the morning after Father Patrick and the others left and talked it through. Everyone was told to say whatever was on their mind, no matter what it was."

"And after that?"

I shake my head. "It was forbidden."

"So you never talked to your mother about it?" he asks. "Or to Nate Childress after he arrived?"

I stare at him. "What did I say?"

"Agent Carlyle," says Doctor Hernandez, his voice low. "Moonbeam was perfectly clear about the things she doesn't want to talk about today. Please respect her choices."

Agent Carlyle doesn't take his eyes off me, but he nods. "You're right," he says. "I'm sorry."

Go to Hell.

"It's okay," I say.

"I'd like to talk a little more about the period before the purge," says Doctor Hernandez. "If that's okay with you?"

"That's fine," I say.

"Under Father Patrick's leadership, members of the Lord's Legion were allowed to watch TV and listen to the radio and play games and read books and eat whatever they wanted. Is that right?"

I nod.

"And after the purge, all that stopped?"

I nod again.

"And that didn't make people reconsider their loyalty to Father John?"

"It didn't seem to," I say. "I don't know for certain what anyone else was thinking, but Father John told us all that we had become too comfortable, too lazy, and indulgent. He told us we needed to be stronger, and most people agreed with him."

"Stronger for the final battle?" asks Agent Carlyle.

"Obviously."

"So your mom must have agreed then? Since the two of you were still there?"

"All right," says Doctor Hernandez. "That's enough. It's not appropriate for you to try and dictate this session, Agent Carlyle. I won't allow it."

He gives me a smile that I'm sure he thinks is supportive, an I'm-on-your-side smile, but I don't acknowledge it. Anger is bubbling inside me because I don't like people trying to manipulate me, especially when they think I don't know they're doing it. I don't like people thinking I'm stupid.

"I guess she must have," I say, my eyes fixed on Agent Carlyle. "Although maybe not, since she left in the end."

He narrows his eyes. "Left? Or was banished?"

The word cuts into me like a knife, and I feel myself go very still. "What did you say?"

"Three years ago," says Agent Carlyle, as though he didn't even hear my question. "On the twenty-second of this month. Does that sound about right?"

"Agent Carlyle," says Doctor Hernandez, his voice rising slightly. "I'm not going to tell you again."

"You don't know anything about my mom," I say. I'm wondering who they've talked to, who could have told them about the worst thing—before the fire—that ever happened to me, and I can hear the anger trembling in my voice. "Not a single thing."

Agent Carlyle doesn't respond; he just gives the man sitting beside him an extremely pointed look.

"I'm sorry," says Doctor Hernandez. "You made it clear that you don't want to talk about your mother today, and I think that's an absolutely valid choice."

Heat surges through me. "What if I've changed my mind?"

"This isn't an appropriate environment for that conversation," he says.

"Why?" I ask, and nod in Agent Carlyle's direction. "Because *he's* here?"

Doctor Hernandez nods. "That's one reason," he says. "There are others. The thing you need to remember is that this is a—"

"Please don't say process," I say. "I'll be happy if I never hear that word again. I've been here almost a week now, and the only thing I know for sure is that I'm not allowed to leave. So what's the deal here? Am I a prisoner? Are you going to charge me with a crime?"

"Hey now," says Agent Carlyle. "Nobody's accusing you of anything. Calm down."

But I can't calm down. I *won't*.

"Be straight with me," I say. "Tell me what I'm doing here and what's going to happen. Can you do that for me? Please?"

"I'm stopping this session," says Doctor Hernandez. "I'm sorry you're upset, Moonbeam, but please understand that I have your best interests at heart. Try to trust that."

"You've said that before." The anger has disappeared as quickly as it arrived, and I can feel tears welling in the corners of my eyes. I blink them back because I'm not going to cry in front of him, not again.

I'm.

Not.

Going.

To.

"And I meant it," says Doctor Hernandez. "You experienced a remarkably traumatic incident, Moonbeam, to say nothing of the years that preceded it, and I'm profoundly impressed by the strength and resilience you continue to display. I should probably have told you that more often than I have, and for that I apologize. But you have to understand that there are rules and schedules, and even though I know you find it hard to believe, they really are for your own good."

I laugh. I can't help it.

"*For my own good*," I say. "Do you know how often I've heard that?"

"No," says Doctor Hernandez. "I don't. But I want you to tell me. I really do. We just need to be careful. We need to take things slow."

140

"Let's call it a day," says Agent Carlyle. "It'll do everyone good to cool off a little." He stands, puts on his jacket, and looks at me. "You're not in any trouble, okay, kid? Get some rest and we'll talk tomorrow."

"What if I don't want to?" I ask, although I know it's a stupid question, because what I want isn't a consideration. It never has been.

"We'll talk tomorrow," repeats Agent Carlyle.

Doctor Hernandez stares at me as he sorts his pens and his notebooks back into his bag. It feels like there's something he wants to communicate to me, but I can't work out what it is.

Pity? Sympathy? Concern?

Whatever it is, it makes my skin itch with anger.

He gets up and follows Agent Carlyle out of the room, and I close my eyes and take a deep breath as I wait to be taken back to my room.

It's all right, whispers the voice in the back of my head. *You did well. It's all going to be all right.*

Nurse Harrow smiles at me as she closes my door. As soon as I hear the lock turn, I sit down at the desk and grab a sheet of paper and start drawing.

Water. Cliffs. The house with blue walls.

Me.

My mom.

In his Infinite and Perfect wisdom, The Lord has shown the True Path to those men and women whose Faith is strong, whose hearts are Pure and True. He has shown that the True Path is hard, and long, and has shown that Darkness lies on either side.

Certain revelations have been made to me, so that my Brothers and Sisters might better serve the Glory of The Lord.

THOSE WHO ARE GONE MUST BE FORGOTTEN. There cannot be space in the hearts of the True for Heretics. They must not be spoken of, nor allowed to enter the minds of the Faithful.

Outside is corruption and Godlessness, which will poison even those whose Faith is strongest.

THERE SHALL BE NO MORE DEALINGS WITH THE WORLD OF THE SERPENT, beyond that which is necessary as we wait to Ascend. No member of the Legion shall risk their Eternal Soul in the Outside, where monsters and demons roam and the True Word of The Lord is rejected by those whose eyes and hearts have been closed.

Those who are True must cast aside earthly concerns. All that is mortal is Godless, all that is human is Flawed.

The Lord is Good.

BEFORE

It's a hot day, even by Texan standards, when Amos finally goes back to Layfield.

The relief felt by the men and women of the Lord's Legion is palpable. We know that everyone beyond the fences of the Base hates us and wants to hurt us—it isn't something Father John ever allows us to forget—but living with that knowledge isn't always easy, and the idea that some kind of attack from Outside might be imminent weighed heavily on people during the lockdown.

As a result, when Amos gets into the red pickup and drives out through the Front Gate, there are actual cheers from some of my Brothers and Sisters who have gathered in the yard to watch him go. But as the long afternoon stretches out, and the time when he would normally be expected to return approaches, euphoria begins to be replaced by nervousness.

The sun has dipped below the slanted roof of the Chapel when I hear the distant rumble of an engine. I'm working on the shooting range behind the Big House, sweeping up the spent bullet casings and clearing out the rocks and fallen leaves, and I drop my tools and head for the yard. I never believed anything bad was going to happen to Amos—not *really*—but I'm surprised by how relieved I'll be to see him arrive home safely.

Most of my Brothers and Sisters have gathered on the blacktop by the time I get to the yard, their eyes trained on the Front Gate. Dust is rising beyond the low hill that hides the curve of the dirt road and the engine noise is getting louder. As I squint against the glare of the setting sun, the pickup appears, and the tightness in my chest that I hadn't really been aware of relaxes.

Luke and Bear unlock the gate, and Amos drives past them, bringing the pickup to a stop in the middle of the yard. A fresh chorus of cheers erupts at the sight of the mountain of boxes and sacks and bags in the bed, and within seconds, my Brothers and Sisters are swarming the truck; some are clapping Amos on the back and welcoming him home, others searching for sorely missed potato chips and candy.

"Vultures," says a low voice beside me, but there's no malice in it, and I grin as I turn toward its owner.

"Be nice," I say. "Everyone is happy to see him back in one piece."

Nate grins as he rolls his eyes. "Sure. I bet that's exactly what it is."

I give him the most convincing frown I can manage, one that's undermined by the wide smile beneath it. "I hope you're not suggesting that our Brothers and Sisters care more about Milk Duds and gummy bears than Amos's well-being?"

It goes without saying that Nate is the only person in the entire Legion I would say such a thing to. The only person I would even *think* about saying it to.

He snorts with laughter. "Of course not. That would be extremely wrong of me."

"It really would," I say, my smile widening into a grin.

"I'd have to tell the Centurions, and it would make me sad to see you get locked in a box."

"Then it's lucky for us both that I didn't say it."

He throws an arm around me. "Isn't it?"

And just like that, I can't breathe.

My insides have frozen solid at the feel of his callused fingers on the bare skin of my shoulder, the warmth of his arm across my back. I try to say something, *anything*, but nothing happens, because my brain has been reduced to mush and my vocal cords aren't responding. If Nate notices, he doesn't comment; he simply walks me forward, toward the pickup.

Of course he didn't notice, whispers the voice in the back of my head. *Why would he? You're his little Sister, and nobody thinks anything of putting an arm around their Sister.*

I tell the voice to shut up, even though it's right. I know that's how Nate sees me, how he thinks of me, and most of the time that's okay. But I can't help the thoughts that sometimes drift through my brain, the ones that make my face burn with heat and my stomach flip like an acrobat.

"Come on," he says. "Let's see if there's anything left worth having."

By the time we reach the pickup, all that's in the bed is a pyramid of brown and yellow UPS boxes addressed to James Carmel. Amos appears beside us as we stare at them, his lined face flushed with the humble pride of the returning hero, as though he has fought The Serpent himself single-handed rather than merely driven to Town and back.

"That lot are for the Big House," he says. "Get a move on, girl."

I roll my eyes and grab the nearest box, but it's heavy and I can barely lift it. Nate offers to help, but I give him an *I've got this* shake of my head as I wrestle the box into my arms and set off across the yard with it. Behind me, I hear Amos start to tell Nate the tale of his journey Outside, his epic, perilous quest to the Layton County Walmart.

I make it across the yard and up onto the porch of the Big House and kick the door with the toe of my boot. I hear voices and footsteps inside the house, and I wait with the box in my increasingly trembling arms until the door opens and Bella smiles at me.

"Moonbeam," she says. "Has Amos returned?"

I nod. "A couple of minutes ago."

Bella's smile widens. "The Lord is Good," she says, then drops her gaze to the box. "What's that you've got there?"

"Parcel for Father John," I say, like that isn't obvious.

"How kind of you to bring it," she says. "Why are our big, strong Brothers letting a little thing like you carry such a load?"

"I wanted to help." I didn't. I *wanted* to find a fresh doughnut or a candy bar, and when that didn't happen, I wanted to impress Nate. But the lie sounds better.

"Of course you did." She steps aside. "Come on in, Sister."

I thank her and stagger through the door. The downstairs of the Big House is one huge open room, with the fireplace and sofas and chairs at one end and the kitchen at the other—and, as always, it's full of people. Esme and Lena and Star all shout greetings, and about half a dozen of the children who are yelling and laughing and chasing back and forth pause what they're doing and look in my direction, before deciding I'm not that interesting and carrying on.

The walls of the room are hung with bright crayon drawings by the many children who call the Big House home, black-and-white photographs of the desert and the Base, framed extracts from the Bible, and the original handwritten versions of the

Proclamations, the ones that were transcribed by Jacob Reynolds. The floor is covered with rugs of every shape and color, many of them so threadbare that the wooden boards can be seen through them. Toys are everywhere, cars and puzzles and books and balls and airplanes—there are more things to play with in this one room than in the whole rest of the Base.

It's good to be one of Father John's children, whispers the voice in the back of my head. *Even if you really aren't.*

The sheer scale of my own Heresy almost makes me gasp out loud. I swallow hard, and something goes the wrong way, and I burst out coughing.

Bella frowns. "Moonbeam? Are you okay?"

"I'm fine," I splutter, as I try to suck air into my lungs. "Where do you want me to put this?"

"You said it was for Father John," says Bella.

Obviously.

I nod.

"You know where his study is," she says. "Go on up. He'll be glad to see you."

I nod again and pick my way carefully over to the stairs. I have no idea whether I'm going to be able to get this stupid box up them without toppling over backward and breaking my neck, but I know Bella and the others are watching me, so I take a deep breath and step onto the first stair.

Five steps later, less than halfway up, my legs are trembling so badly I don't know if they're going to hold me up. Six steps more, and I feel like I'm going to burst into tears of pain and frustration. By the time I put a shaking foot onto the upstairs landing, my arms feel like they have white-hot metal rods inside them.

I stagger over to a little side table, set the box down, and almost weep with relief. Pins and needles instantly stab at my flesh, but they feel wonderful compared to the agony they replaced. I let my arms hang straight down at my sides and look around while I wait for them to come back to life.

The upstairs of the Big House contains Father John's bedroom, his study, and the bedrooms that are occupied by his wives. There are six of them—for the time being, that is—and it's easy to work out where they stand in Father John's favor by where they sleep. One of them shares his bed, one has the room next door, and the other four make do with the two bedrooms farther down the corridor. The arrangements are not supposed to be discussed, but it's widely believed that the six women move rooms on a weekly—sometimes even *daily*—basis, depending on Father John's preferences.

You're going to know for sure, whispers the voice in the back of my head. *When you live here too. It's not that long now…*

I push the voice away. It's on a roll today as far as painful truths go, but I really don't want to hear it.

Up another set of stairs is the attic, where Father John's children sleep. I've never seen it with my own eyes, but I've been told it's split into two rooms, both full of bunk beds: a large space for the boys and a much smaller one for the girls.

There are eleven kids living up there, although it's not quite as straightforward as it sounds.

All of them were born after The Prophet arrived at the Base, and the official story is that each and every one of them is his, even the ones who arrived before he married their mothers. That's the *official* story.

But there are rumors, because people are still people even though the Third Proclamation is sacrosanct.

Rumors about some of my Brothers visiting the Big House after the doors are all supposed to be locked, supposedly with Father John's permission.

About the same men who visit Alice and Lena and some of my

younger Sisters after lights-out, who are let into their darkened rooms by the Centurions.

About things that aren't supposed to happen.

I can almost feel my arms again—they're still tingling, but I'm pretty sure they're actually there—so I take a deep breath and pick up the UPS box. My muscles scream in protest, but I grit my teeth and carry it across the landing to The Prophet's study. I give the door a kick, far gentler than I gave the one downstairs.

"Come in," calls Father John, and I'm amazed—as ever—by the booming *power* of his voice. It slices through all other noise, shutting it out and almost physically commanding you to listen.

To *obey*.

I bend my knees and try to reach the door handle. The tips of my fingers brush against it, but I can't get any kind of purchase without letting go of the box, which is wedged between me and the door, and I'm suddenly aware that my legs won't actually straighten anymore—they seem to have locked in their bent position.

"I said come in!" shouts Father John.

I freeze.

I can't turn the handle, and I can't let go of the box, and I don't have the slightest idea how I'm going to explain this ridiculous situation to The Prophet. I crouch where I am, my shoulder against the door frame, my legs trembling beneath me, until I eventually hear movement inside the study—the scrape of chair legs across floorboards, followed by the heavy stomp of footsteps.

The door is yanked open, and Father John fills the frame, his face flushed as he stares down at me. Then the crimson annoyance disappears as he recognizes my predicament, and he gives me a radiant smile full of utter benevolence; my insides lurch as I realize how desperately part of me still wants his approval, despite my mom and everything else.

Pathetic, whispers the voice in the back of my head. *Absolutely pathetic.*

"Moonbeam!" he exclaims, and snatches the parcel out of my hands as easily as if it was a box full of feathers. "Who told you to bring this to me? Who was too lazy to do it themselves? Tell me."

I shake my head. "Nobody, Father," I say. "I wanted to bring it."

"You're a good girl," he says. "A good, kind girl. Come in."

"Thank you, Father." A sharp ache in my lower back and a throbbing pressure in my head have joined the pain in my arms, but I manage to walk through the door without grimacing and try to catch my breath as The Prophet closes it behind me.

He walks around behind his desk, sets the box down next to the thick leather-bound Bible that he reads from on Sunday mornings, then frowns. "Are you all right, Moonbeam?" he asks. "Do you need to lie down?"

I shake my head. "I'm okay, Father." I'm pretty sure I sound at least vaguely convincing. "I'll be fine in a minute."

"Did this come back with Amos?" he asks, gesturing toward the box.

"Yes, Father," I say. "There're a few of them."

He nods. "The Lord is Good."

"The Lord is Good," I repeat.

Father John smiles and sits down in the battered leather armchair behind his desk. "Did you see the name on the shipping label?"

I hesitate because I'm not sure what the right answer is; one of the things you learn from talking to The Prophet, even once or twice, is that the right answer isn't often what you think it's going to be. His smile widens.

"Don't worry," he says. "You're not going to be in trouble. You saw the name on the parcel, didn't you?"

I nod.

"What is it?"

"James Carmel."

"Is that my name?"

"No, Father."

"Correct," he says. "Can you guess why the name on the label is false?"

I'm pretty sure I know the answer to this one.

"Because it wouldn't be safe."

He narrows his eyes. "What wouldn't be safe?"

"If the Outsiders saw your name on a parcel, they might steal it," I say. "Or put something bad in it before Amos collected it."

He stares at me for a long moment, his bright green eyes locked on mine. At the precise moment when I start to wonder if I've somehow said the wrong thing, he nods and breaks into a smile that—over the protests of the voice in the back of my head—fills my heart with guilty joy.

"That's right, Moonbeam," he says. "Those are *exactly* the kind of things the Servants of the Serpent would do. Well done. *Extremely* well done."

I flush with embarrassment. "Thank you, Father."

"You're a sharp girl," he says. "*Very* sharp. What a shame The Lord does not Call females to serve as Centurions. I suspect our Family could do worse than having you looking out for them. A lot worse."

I don't say a word because for me to even acknowledge the hypothetical idea of a female Centurion would be Heresy.

"You're no Heretic, Moonbeam," says Father John, as though he can read my mind. "Despite what some of our less kind Brothers and Sisters may think. You're no Heretic, and neither am I. It is not for me to interpret The Lord's wishes or look for ways around His commands. I merely pass them on, perfect as they are, because The Lord does not make mistakes. You understand that, don't you?"

"I understand, Father."

"There *will* be a new Centurion though," he says, sitting back in his chair. "That much has been made clear. The Lord will soon put an end to our Brother's earthly suffering and Call him to Ascend and, when it pleases Him to do so, He will tell me who should take his place. Who do you think The Lord will name?"

I shake my head. "I cannot speculate about such a thing, Father."

The Prophet smiles again, but his eyes have narrowed, and there is far less warmth in his expression than before. My stomach tightens, but I force myself not to look away.

"You can," he says. "Because I am telling you to. This is not a quiz, Moonbeam, with right answers and wrong ones. I am asking you to make a guess, and what you say will not leave this room. So answer my question and tell me who you think The Lord will choose as our new Centurion."

I rack my brain, because there is *always* a right answer, even when someone tells you there isn't. *Especially* when that's what they tell you.

"Luke?" I suggest.

Father John nods. "Interesting. Luke is a man of deep Faith, and his loyalty is beyond doubt. He lacks the wisdom that comes with experience, but he does possess a great deal of youthful vigor. If The Lord chose him, I would not be entirely surprised."

I breathe a silent sigh of relief and nod.

"What about Nate Childress?" he asks.

My stomach tightens another couple of notches. "What about him, Father?"

"Do you think he would make a good Centurion?"

I swallow hard. "I would not dare to presume—"

"You are a good girl, Moonbeam," he interrupts, his tone suddenly sharp. "You have shown yourself this very day to be both kind and loyal. Please do not disappoint me now by forcing me to ask you the same question twice."

Careful, whispers the voice in the back of my head. *Be very careful now.*

"I'm sorry, Father," I say. "Forgive me."

"Always," he says. "Now please answer the question."

"I think Nate would be good," I say carefully. "My older Brothers and Sisters would know better than me, but I think he would be fair, and I am sure his Faith is True."

Father John smiles. "You like him very much, don't you?"

"He is my Brother," I say. "I love him with all my heart."

His smile twists into something I don't like, something between a grin and a grimace.

"Of course you do," he says. "Which is exactly as it should be. But do you not think The Lord might believe that Nate joined this Legion too recently to be trusted with such a responsibility?"

My stomach twists again. It feels like the floorboards beneath my feet have turned to quicksand.

"I cannot begin to imagine the mind of The Lord, Father." His forehead starts to furrow, so I carry on quickly. "But you have always taught me that The Lord rewards those who are deserving, regardless of their circumstances. You have always taught me that He does not give anyone more than they can handle."

The half-formed frown on Father John's face shifts seamlessly into a broad grin full of pride. "How right you are," he says. "How *absolutely* right you are."

I lower my eyes to the floor and give what I hope looks like a nod of humble gratitude, because the only thing I want in the world is to be allowed to leave this room and go back outside and find a quiet place where it won't feel like I'm constantly teetering above the jaws of a trap.

Father John places his hand on the UPS box I brought him. "Do you want to know what's in here, Moonbeam?"

No. Yes.

"If you want to tell me, Father."

His grin fades. "Perhaps not. It may be that you are not ready for this particular truth."

"I'm sure you're right, Father," I say, because I'm not stupid enough to beg him to tell me a secret he could hold over me for as long as he sees fit.

Nowhere *near* stupid enough.

"Not ready," he repeats, seemingly to himself. His eyes have glazed over, as though he's looking in the far distance at something only he can see. Then they clear, and he gives me a small, tight smile. "Thank you for bringing the parcel, Moonbeam. It was kind of you, and I enjoyed our conversation. You can go now."

I nod. "Thank you, Father."

He waves a hand, then opens the Bible and begins to read. I wait for a second or two to make sure he doesn't change his mind about dismissing me, but he doesn't so much as glance in my direction. It's like I'm already gone, even though I'm still standing in front of him.

I take a deep breath and back slowly toward the door, relief creeping over me. I hold it in check as I make my way down the stairs and through the living room and out onto the porch, but it breaks loose in a roaring torrent as I step into the yard and run toward the small room I call home.

It's all right, whispers the voice in the back of my head. *Just breathe. You're safe. Everything's going to be all right.*

A
 F
  T
   E
    R

Doctor Hernandez and Agent Carlyle stare at me like I'm some kind of alien, but their expressions don't really bother me anymore; I'm used to them.

I started talking before they sat down, before Doctor Hernandez finished saying hello. I knew he would want to discuss yesterday's session, but I didn't want to do that, because I slept like crap and woke up drenched with sweat and my head felt heavy with worry about everything and everyone.

Luke wasn't at SSI yesterday afternoon. Honey and Lucy were clearly pleased, which is totally understandable, and I guess I can't blame the others for not seeming to care very much about his absence. He's not their responsibility. But he's mine, because of what I did. They all are. And as a result, I want—I *need*—to know what's going on with him. Which meant I had to give them something.

Quid pro quo, whispered the voice in the back of my head as Nurse Harrow escorted me along the corridor toward Interview Room 1.

Fair's fair.

"Thank you for trusting us enough to talk about Father John," says Doctor Hernandez. "I have no doubt it was hard for you."

I shrug. It was, but there are other subjects that would be harder. *Much* harder. "It's okay," I say. "Can I ask you something?"

"Of course," he says. "Anything you like."

"How's Luke doing?"

He nods. "We're looking after him."

I wait for him to say more, but it becomes clear he isn't going to. "Is that it?" I ask.

"That's all I can tell you right now," he says.

"He wasn't at SSI yesterday."

Doctor Hernandez nods again. "I know."

"But he's okay?" I can hear something close to desperation in my voice.

"We're looking after him," he repeats. "Do you mind if we go back to what you just told us?"

Why won't you talk about Luke? What aren't you telling me?

I don't say anything.

Doctor Hernandez sits forward. "Moonbeam? Are you happy to keep talking, or would you like to stop?"

Like it matters. If we stop now, we'll still be back here tomorrow and the next day and the day after that. Until you're done with me.

"Let's keep going."

He gives me a long look, like he doesn't know whether to believe me, then leans back in his chair and nods.

"All right then," says Agent Carlyle. "You said Father John had six wives at that time?"

I nod.

"That didn't seem strange to you?"

"Not really," I say. "I know you're going to tell me it is, but no. It seemed normal."

"Did anyone else have more than one wife?" he asks. "Or more than one husband?"

"No."

"Did Father Patrick have more than one wife?"

"Father Patrick wasn't married," I say.

"Was Father John? Before the purge, I mean?"

I shake my head.

"When did that change?"

I grimace at the memory. "I don't want to talk about this anymore."

Agent Carlyle tilts his head slightly to one side. "Why not?"

"Because I don't," I say. "Do I need to have a reason for everything?"

"It would help me if you did."

"Agent Carlyle," says Doctor Hernandez. "You're not interviewing a suspect. I'm going to ask you to moderate your tone."

"I'm sure you are," replies the FBI agent. "But I'd like to know why she doesn't want to talk about Father John's wives."

Don't, whispers the voice in the back of my head. *Don't you—*

"Why do you want to know so badly?" My voice is suddenly hot with anger. "Are you jealous of him? Would you like six wives yourself?"

Agent Carlyle recoils, as if I reached over the desk and slapped him across the face. We stare at each other for a long moment; out of the corner of my eye I see Doctor Hernandez watching, his face pale.

The faintest flicker of a smile appears on Agent Carlyle's face.

"That's a sharp tongue you've got there," he says. "You want to be careful you don't cut yourself."

I feel the anger bubbling through me subside. "There's no such thing as a sharp tongue. Technically speaking, that is."

His smile widens. "*Technically speaking*," he says. "Got you."

"Why was that funny?" I ask.

Doctor Hernandez frowns. "It wasn't. It was perfectly—"

"Most seventeen-year-olds don't use phrases like 'technically speaking' to qualify the things they say," says Agent Carlyle.

"Maybe the seventeen-year-olds you know aren't very smart," I say.

He snorts with laughter. "That might well be the case. In fact, that's a *distinct* possibility."

Doctor Hernandez glances back and forth between me and Agent Carlyle, his frown deepening. "I think we should try to—"

A knock on the door interrupts him. The handle turns, and a nurse I don't recognize pokes her head into the room.

"I'm very sorry to interrupt," she says. "Doctor Hernandez, there's a phone call for you from Austin."

"Take a message," he says.

"I tried that already," says the nurse. "Apparently it's urgent."

The psychiatrist rolls his eyes and stands up. "Fine." He looks at me. "I'll be back in two minutes."

"I thought I wouldn't have to talk to anyone without you here to make sure I'm okay?" I say.

That's mean, whispers the voice in the back of my head, and it sounds a lot like it's laughing. *That's really mean.*

Doctor Hernandez stops halfway to the door, frozen to the spot by his own promise.

"I'll step out too," says Agent Carlyle, and pushes his chair back from the desk.

"I wasn't serious," I say. "It's fine."

"Are you sure?" asks Doctor Hernandez. "You're absolutely right to object if you feel you need to."

"It's fine," I repeat.

Agent Carlyle slides his chair back to the desk with a half smile on his face.

"Okay," says Doctor Hernandez. "The two of you stay here. Agent Carlyle, I'd remind you that Moonbeam's care is my responsibility and ask that you not question her in my absence."

"No questions," says Agent Carlyle. "Got it."

"Okay," repeats Doctor Hernandez. It sounds like he's trying to convince himself. "I'll be back in two minutes."

He strides out of the room, and the nurse pulls the door shut behind him. Agent Carlyle gives me a smile, which I'm sure is meant to be reassuring, but it comes off as uneasy, like he's nervous about being left alone with me.

"So I guess we sit in silence," he says.

"Doctor Hernandez told *you* not to question *me*," I say. "He didn't say anything about the other way around."

His eyes narrow, but his smile suddenly seems a lot more genuine. "Is there something you want to ask me?"

"Am I going to prison?"

The smile disappears. "I already answered that."

"You told me no," I say.

He nods. "So why are you asking me again?"

"Because I don't believe you."

He stares at me. "I'm going to say this as plainly as I dare," he says. "I have to be very careful, because Doctor Hernandez is right about the work you and he are doing, and I don't want to screw it up in any way. That said, there's something you need to understand. You are *not* a criminal, Moonbeam. You are the *victim* of a crime. Of hundreds of crimes. Is that clear?"

I shake my head.

"Of course it isn't," he says, and lets out a deep sigh. "That's the goddamn worst thing about all of this. You don't even *know*."

I know so much more than you think.

"Know what?" I ask.

"It's not for me to…I mean, I can't…" He leans so his elbows are resting on the desk. "Look, you're not going to prison, okay? You're not going to prison because you haven't done anything wrong, at least as far as I know. I know there are things you aren't telling us, and that's fine for now. But even if you *had* committed crimes that I'm not aware of, a halfway competent public defender on their first day out of law school would make sure you never spent a single day in jail. Especially given that you're a minor."

"A minor?"

"A child."

"I'm not a child."

"You yourself?" he says. "As a person, with a brain and a heart? I couldn't agree more. But legally? Yeah. You are. You are considered a minor until you're eighteen."

"What happens then? Do I somehow turn into a different person than I was the day before, when I was still seventeen?"

Agent Carlyle frowns. "That's the age at which the law considers you to be an adult."

"Doesn't that seem a bit random?"

"No." He pauses. "I mean…yeah. I guess so. Maybe. But there has to be a line somewhere."

"Why?"

"Because the law treats children and adults differently," he says.

"So it's a rule because there has to be a rule?"

"If you want to put it like that."

"So it's no different to Father John's Proclamations then?"

He sits back in his chair and smiles. "You're too smart for me," he says. "I feel like I need to lie in a dark room for a while whenever we finish talking."

"I'm sorry," I say.

He shakes his head. "Don't be," he says. "I've been with the FBI for eighteen years, Moonbeam. Did you know that?"

I did because I heard him tell Doctor Hernandez when they thought the Interview Room 1 door was closed. But I don't want him to know that.

"No," I say.

"Eighteen years," he repeats. "In that time I've sat in rooms with rapists and murderers and terrorists and God knows what else, men and women who knew they were facing the rest of their lives in jail at best, execution at worst. And do you know something?"

I shake my head.

"*Every single one of them* was easier to read than you," he says, his smile returning. "I know that might not sound like much of a compliment, but it's meant as one."

"Thanks," I say, although he's right—it didn't sound like a compliment.

The door opens, and Doctor Hernandez steps back into the room. He glances at Agent Carlyle, then looks intently at me. "Everything okay in here?"

"Everything's fine," I say.

He narrows his eyes, then nods and sits down. "All right then. Where were we?"

"Moonbeam was refusing to talk about Father John's wives," says Agent Carlyle, and tips me a wink. It's barely more than a twitch of his left eyelid, but I see it and fight back a smile.

"Right," says Doctor Hernandez. "That's right. And that's a completely valid choice, so let's move on. I'd like to talk about how Father John exercised his authority over the Lord's Legion. Is that okay with you, Moonbeam?"

"Sure."

"Great. Thank you. So Father John set all the rules that the members of the Lord's Legion lived by?"

I shake my head. "Not *all* of them. Some were in place before the Purge."

"Like what?" asks Doctor Hernandez.

"There was a set daily routine when Father Patrick was in charge. Prayers before breakfast, then lessons until lunchtime, work and chores in the afternoon, then dinner and Bible study, and lights-out at ten o'clock. Most of it didn't change."

"But some things did?" he asks.

I nod. "Lessons were canceled. After the Purge, we started working in the morning and in the afternoon."

"Why?"

"Father John said everything worth learning was in the Bible."

Doctor Hernandez makes a note. "What else was different?"

"The TV got taken away. And the radios and all the books."

"People weren't allowed to read books anymore?"

I shake my head.

"Why not?"

"Because they came from Outside, like the TV programs and the songs on the radio. The First Proclamation banned them all."

"Specifically?"

"No. But it became clear really quickly."

"The First Proclamation is also what banned everyone except Amos Andrews from leaving the compound?"

I grimace. He knows I hate that word. "Yes."

"And that was the end of the Lord's Legion actively recruiting?"

"How do you mean?" I ask.

"You and your sisters going into Layfield to hand out leaflets," says Doctor Hernandez. "Men and women going out into the world and preaching, like your father saw Horizon do."

"Yes," I say. "That all stopped."

"Was it common? Before the purge?"

"Most people went out," I say. "Even Father Patrick would go

162

at least a couple of times a year. Father John did it a lot after he arrived."

"Was he good at it?"

"I've told you what he was like when he spoke," I say. "I never went with him, but I guess it worked on Outsiders as well. People would always arrive in the weeks after he'd been out preaching."

"Was that how he met Jacob Reynolds?" asks Agent Carlyle. "When he was spreading the word of the Lord?"

I shrug. "I guess so."

"So after the purge, there were no new members joining the Legion?" asks Doctor Hernandez.

"There were still a few," I say. "Father John told us that The Lord would show anyone who was worthy the True Path, and it would bring them to the Base."

"And it did?"

I nod. "People walked down the road to the Front Gate, like Nate did, having talked to somebody or heard about us somewhere. But not many of them. And Father John turned most away."

"And the gate itself was bigger? You said it was just planks of wood in Father Patrick's time?"

"It got built up after the Purge," I say. "Father John said it wasn't strong enough. He ordered the Centurions to start adding metal and barbed wire to it straightaway."

"So nobody was allowed out and nobody was encouraged to come in?"

I nod again.

"So your Brothers and Sisters who were born after the purge—"

"They don't know anything about the rest of the world. They've never seen Outside for themselves, and all they know is what they've been told. I can remember it, and I guess Luke and a couple of the others might be able to. But the younger children? No."

The two men glance at each other. I watch as they attempt to process what I'm saying, and I wonder what Doctor Hernandez was told when his phone rang in Austin and he was asked to come all the way out here—whether he really understood what he and his colleagues were going to be dealing with. He makes a long note in one of his books, then takes a deep breath.

"Okay," he says. "What else changed?"

"The doors being locked at night," I say. "That started with Father John."

"Was it in one of the proclamations?"

I shrug. "You tell me. You've obviously read them."

He nods. "I've read them."

"Then why are you asking me what's in them?"

"Because facts aren't the only things that are important," he says. "Because I'm interested in the answers you give, in what you feel comfortable talking and not talking about. I'm interested in where your boundaries are."

My boundaries?

"So you're just trying to catch me out?" I ask.

Easy, whispers the voice in the back of my head. *Take it easy.*

Doctor Hernandez's eyes widen, and his face fills with what is, at the very least, a convincing impression of surprise. "Not at all. Don't ever think that, please. I know there are aspects of what you went through that you don't want to talk about, and I respect that. Setting boundaries is a *good thing*. My job is to try and reach a place where you feel able to move those boundaries, where you are able to tell the truth about your experiences, even the ones you don't want to confront yet. *That* will be real progress."

I'm confused. It's like he's speaking a different language, one that I don't understand.

"So you don't care if I lie to you?"

"I'd like you to tell me as much of the truth as you feel able to," he says. "That's all I ask. I like to think I've been consistent on this."

Agent Carlyle puts his hand up, like a child who knows the answer to a question. "I'm all in favor of you telling the truth," he says, a grin on his face. "It makes my life a hell of a lot easier." Doctor Hernandez tries to give him a stern look, but he isn't able to hide a smile. I shake my head, in what I hope is a disapproving manner.

"Let's get on with it," I say. "If we're all finished being comedians, that is?"

Doctor Hernandez nods, the last traces of the smile still on his face. "Okay," he says. "So everyone was locked in their rooms at night? Because that isn't explicitly mentioned in any of the Proclamations, as far as I remember."

"Not every night," I say. "Lights-out was still at ten, unless Father John decided differently, and sometimes the Centurions locked the doors, and sometimes they didn't. But if they did, they didn't unlock them again till morning."

"Was there a pattern to whether the doors were locked or not?"

"What do you mean?"

"I mean, were they locked one week and then not the next? Or locked Monday to Friday and left unlocked over the weekend?"

I shake my head.

"So nobody knew from one night to the next whether their door was going to be locked?"

I shake my head again.

"Great way to keep everyone obedient," mutters Agent Carlyle. "Make it look like *not* locking them in their rooms is an act of kindness."

Doctor Hernandez nods and makes a quick note. "So the Centurions weren't ever locked in their rooms?"

I smile because that's really funny. "No."

"Father John?"

I resist the urge to laugh out loud. "Of course not."

"The rule didn't apply to him?" asks Doctor Hernandez.

I shake my head.

"Like most of the others," says Agent Carlyle.

I shrug. "I guess not."

"Were the rules written down somewhere?" asks Doctor Hernandez. "Could members of the Lord's Legion read them?"

"The Proclamations were written down."

"What about the smaller rules? The day-to-day stuff?"

"They didn't need to be written down," I say. "Everyone knew them by heart."

"So how did new rules get put in place?"

"Father John announced them," I say.

"On Sunday mornings? During his sermons?"

"Not always. Sometimes he just called everyone together."

"And announced that he was adding a new rule?"

"Yes."

"Because God told him to?"

"Yes."

"Did you believe that?"

I stare at him. The seconds stretch out, long and empty.

Tell the truth, whispers the voice in the back of my head. *Be brave.*

Doctor Hernandez breaks the silence. "Moonbeam?"

"I did."

"What about now?"

Images race through my head...

...my mom in the living room of the Big House, her face bleeding...

...Honey in the shadows cast by the maintenance shed, her eyes wide with fear...

…Nate in the darkness of my room, his hands full of objects that are forbidden…

Be brave, urges the voice in the back of my head. But I can't. I'm *not*.

I knew—I've always known—that the subject of my own Faith, in Father John and the Legion and everything else, would come up eventually. But in this room, at this moment, in front of these men, it feels like I might as well cut out my heart and hand it to them.

"I think I'm done talking for today."

While I wait for Nurse Harrow to arrive with my lunch, I lie on my bed and try to think—really think—about my situation.

Ever since I woke up in the hospital with my hand wrapped in bandages and my mind reeling with panic, I've been operating almost entirely on gut feeling, trying to get through one moment at a time, letting emotions flow through me unchecked…

…disorientation about where I am…

…fear about what's going to happen to me…

…paranoia about who I can trust…

…guilt about what I did…

You have to stay calm, says the voice in the back of my head. *You're stronger than you think. You have to keep going.*

But it's not that easy. I know the voice is right, but I've been running on adrenaline, and it feels like my reserves are almost spent.

I don't think I can go on like this for much longer.

Think. Just think.

I hate it when Doctor Hernandez tries to maneuver me, tries to lead me somewhere without telling me where or why, but—despite that—I do believe that he genuinely wants to help me get out of this place and have some kind of life.

I *have* to believe it because otherwise I might as well stop talking altogether and start getting used to the idea of spending the rest of my days staring at these four gray walls.

I have no idea what a life Outside would be like for me, and I doubt that Doctor Hernandez does either. He talks about a process, and he talks about *progress*, and I don't know if it's because of him or not, but one pretty major thing has changed since the fire that I really didn't expect: the thought of being Outside on my own doesn't fill me with the same stomach-churning dread as before. Not like it did after my mom was Banished and my head was filled with lies and I was scared all the time. When the Outside seemed almost as bad as the place where I had come to understand I was trapped.

All right, whispers the voice in the back of my head. *That's good. That's something.*

I stare at the ceiling and push Doctor Hernandez out of my mind and focus on the man who sits next to him every morning. I know I have information that Agent Carlyle wants, that he must believe that only I can tell him, and I know that's his main reason for talking to me. But I don't think it's his *only* reason for talking to me.

Not anymore.

It might be wishful thinking, but the wink he gave me after we talked when Doctor Hernandez was out of the room, the little smiles and nods when I reveal details he knows are hard for me, feel like they're meant to let me know he's on my side. Or make me believe so, at least. But there's no point in thinking like that because I can't ask him and he wouldn't tell me the truth if I did.

Either way, there are still two things I can't tell either of them: what happened in the Big House during the fire, and what happened the day before it.

And everything else? asks the voice in the back of my head.

I told myself I wouldn't talk about Father John. I told *them* that I wouldn't. But I did, and I didn't die. I'm still here, still breathing in and out.

So maybe…

Maybe Doctor Hernandez is right. Maybe it will do me good to talk about the rest of it, to tell as much of the truth as I can bear—about Luke, and Nate, and my mom, and everything else.

Maybe.

I know that I'm going to have to talk about the fire eventually. I know it's what Agent Carlyle wants to hear about, and for as much as I'm starting to believe—*hope*—that maybe I can trust him, I don't believe for a second that his patience is endless. But I can feel the heat of the flames, can hear the roar of the gunfire, and I don't want to go back there. I really, really don't. Maybe I can put it off a little bit longer.

There is a border between truth and lies, a border that Father John always described as a thick black line, solid and immovable. But I'm starting to think he was wrong, like he was about so many things. I think the line is so blurry that at times you don't even know which side you're on; like how you can tell the truth but not mention something important, or how you can tell a lie that has some truth in it.

For example, I told Doctor Hernandez and Agent Carlyle that there were always four Centurions, and that was the truth. But for the year or so before the fire, there were only really three, because one of them was very slowly dying.

I'll tell them about him tomorrow.

BEFORE

Honey and I stand in the yard with the Big House behind us, listening to the wet rattle of approaching death.

"It's not going to be long, is it?" says Honey.

I shake my head. "I don't think so."

"Good," she says. "Then he won't be in pain anymore."

"Let's hope not," I say, and I'm almost surprised by how much I mean it.

I really, *really* mean it.

Horizon has been a member of the Lord's Legion since the very beginning, long before the arrival of Father John and the Purge and everything that came after. I've known him for almost my entire life, and he was always a giant to me, in both body and spirit: a towering figure, with a broad back and mountainous shoulders, brown hair that sometimes reached all the way down to his belt, and a thick beard surrounding a mouth capable of unleashing the loudest, most infectious laugh I've ever heard. He always seemed larger than life, as though he was a character out of a fairy tale, full of warmth and wisdom and endless kindness.

The children who grew up inside the Legion *adored* him, and I was no exception. When I was little, my Brothers and Sisters and I used to follow him around the Base for hours on end, clinging to his tree-trunk legs and demanding to be lifted onto his shoulders, insisting he could *easily* carry us all at the same time and pleading with him to try.

He indulged us without a word of complaint, because he was a decent man, a *good* man. *He really was.* He was one of the original Centurions Called by Father Patrick, and he was one of the men who locked Shanti inside the box for ten days, but only because it was his duty; I know he took no pleasure in it. After Lena rejected Father John's offer of mercy for her husband, Alice told me she saw Horizon praying alone in the Chapel, tears running down his face. Julia and Becky nursed Shanti back to health afterward, but Horizon spent more time with him than anyone else; he spent hour after hour at Shanti's bedside, spooning soup into his mouth and reading the Bible to him.

Eighteen months ago, he started to cough.

At first, Horizon brushed it off when people asked if he was all right. "It's a cough," he told them. "It'll pass."

But it wasn't. And it didn't.

It got worse and worse, until half the Base was being kept awake by the racking noise echoing from the Centurion barracks at the western edge of the yard and a trash bag full of blood-soaked tissues was being brought out every morning.

In Father Patrick's time, people went down to the medical center in Layton for anything more serious than Julia and Becky could handle, like when I had my broken arm splinted and placed

171

in a sling. But that was one of the many changes after the Purge, after it was made clear that all doctors are Servants of the Serpent and all prescription drugs are Government weapons designed to destroy the minds of the True. Despite that, my Brothers and Sisters begged Father John to let Amos take Horizon to the doctor, and after two nights of prayer, The Prophet finally agreed. Amos drove Horizon through the Front Gate in the red pickup and returned forty-eight hours later, after an urgent detour to the big hospital in Midland, with news that broke the hearts of everyone who heard it.

Stage four lung cancer.

With intensive treatment, two years at the most. Without it, a year, if he was *very* lucky.

People prayed and wept and beat their chests and prayed some more and pleaded with Father John to do something, *anything* to help him, but Horizon merely smiled and thanked them for their concern and told them he was ready whenever The Lord saw fit to Call him Home. He had no regrets, he said; he had found the True Path before it was too late and had lived a life he was immensely proud of. When the time came, he would Ascend with a smile on his face.

And for a while, everything sort of went back to normal.

Horizon's booming cough became another feature of life inside the Base, as regular as the rumble of the generators and eventually so constant that it became background noise that you didn't notice unless you actually paused what you were doing and listened for it. His skin was ghostly pale, even when he'd been out in the sun, and maybe he moved a little slower than he once had, but he still set about each day with his familiar enthusiasm, his smile wide and warm.

He was dying though. And everyone knew it.

Following a request from Horizon himself, Father John

announced that it was forbidden to discuss the Centurion's illness within his earshot and ordered everybody to treat their Brother no differently than they always had. But the cancer loomed like a dark cloud, and as the months passed and Horizon began to shrink before our eyes, many of my Brothers and Sisters began to avoid him. It was too painful, they said, too hard to watch him fading away.

For me, that was the worst part of the whole horrible thing. Horizon never complained, never said a word to anyone, but the hurt was there in his eyes if you were brave enough to meet them. It was the kind of hurt that comes when the people you love turn their backs on you, even if they claim—and, I have no doubt, *believed*—that they're doing so because they love you too much to watch you suffer.

The cough rattles out of the Centurion barracks, thick and wet and heavy. Then it stops, and the whole Base falls quiet.

"Is that it?" asks Honey. "Is he gone?"

I don't answer. The Base is never completely silent, not even in the middle of the night, but for long seconds, all I can hear is the droning buzz of cicadas and the wind rustling through the trees. Then, like a stubborn car engine finally turning over, the awful, spluttering coughing begins again.

Honey takes hold of my hand. "Come on," she says. "Let's go."

"Where?"

She shrugs. "Somewhere that isn't here."

I give her the most convincing smile I can manage and let her lead me toward the gardens. The sun is beating down, and my skin is tingling, and my mind is full of the question Father John asked me in his study: when Horizon Ascends, who will take his place as Centurion?

From what I've overheard, most people seem to think there are three likely candidates. I guess Father John asking me about Nate makes him a potential fourth option, but I don't know whether

173

The Prophet was genuinely considering the possibility or merely interested in seeing what my reaction would be to the idea.

Joe Nelson, the first of the three names I keep hearing, was a Mormon before he joined the Lord's Legion, but we have never judged anybody on how they lived their life before they found the True Path and were Called. Joe used to own a small farm in northern Utah, and he has been in charge of growing food and tending the grounds of the Base for as long as anyone can remember. He took on the responsibility soon after he arrived, and within a year, he had expanded a vegetable patch that was mostly stones and weeds into a neat grid of six gardens, revived the almost-extinct orchard, built and stocked four henhouses, and grown the Legion's small herd of scrawny cows into fine producers of fresh milk.

Joe works incredibly hard, without a single word of complaint, and has built a reputation for being resourceful and driven, a man who does everything with the good of his Brothers and Sisters in mind. For much of the year, he is excused from the ten o'clock lockdown and is usually the first person awake in the entire Legion, leaving his cabin out near the maintenance sheds well before dawn and often not returning until the sun is long set. As a result, he has always been extremely popular.

The same can't really be said for Jacob Reynolds, who most people—those willing to discuss the subject out loud, that is—seem to believe is the most likely replacement for Horizon.

His arrival on the day before the Purge began has always been viewed as suspiciously convenient, even by those men and women who were overjoyed to see Father John take control of the Lord's Legion. There has always been a feeling that he was a latecomer who didn't earn the closeness to The Prophet that he enjoys, although that very closeness means that nobody would ever actually dare say so.

He is hugely fat, almost as wide as he is tall, with thinning hair

and a bright red face and a short temper and a profound intoler-
ance of those members of the Legion he considers to be Frivolous.
That's how he says it, like it has a capital letter. He lives alone in
a tumbledown shack on the western edge of the compound, as
far away from everyone else as it's possible to be, and you would
struggle to find a single one of my Brothers or Sisters who consider him a close friend. What he is, however, is a True believer, a
man who is deeply, *fanatically* Faithful to The Prophet.

It was Jacob who transcribed Father John's Proclamations,
spending long days and nights at his side as The Lord spoke to
and through him, and it's Jacob who gets the Chapel ready on
Sunday mornings for the weekly sermon. Father John has even
been known, on a handful of occasions when he has been particularly busy, to send someone who has come to him with a spiritual
matter to Jacob for advice—and that alone makes him a serious
candidate for the responsibility of being Centurion, a role that is
primarily about upholding the standards that are expected of every
member of the Lord's Legion.

So.

Joe Nelson. Jacob Reynolds.

That just leaves one other candidate, the same one I suggested
to Father John when he asked me.

A F T E R

"Had Luke made it clear that he wanted to be a Centurion?" asks Agent Carlyle.

I nod.

"How?"

I shrug and scratch at the fresh bandages covering my left hand. Nurse Harrow changed the dressing when she came to collect my breakfast tray. She smiled and told me it was looking much better, but I had to take her word for it. I didn't want to see for myself.

"It was obvious," I say. "He couldn't come right out and say it, because…well, you know why he couldn't."

"Because the Centurions were chosen by God," says Doctor Hernandez. "So it would have been heresy to put himself forward."

"Right. And Luke isn't stupid, so he never did. Instead, he

talked about responsibility, about how it was time for the next generation of the Lord's Legion to step up, and how he was the vanguard of his generation. Everyone knew what he really meant."

Agent Carlyle smiles. "Is that his description or yours?"

"His," I say pointedly. "I heard him say it more than once."

"*The vanguard of his generation*," says Agent Carlyle. "Pretty flowery for a boy who pushes girls up against walls and calls them whores. Why did he want to be a Centurion?"

I grimace. "That's not fair."

He frowns at me. "What isn't?"

"Using things that happen in SSI," I say. "I know you're watching and listening, and so does Honey, but most of the others don't. The illusion of being on our own matters to them."

Doctor Hernandez glances at Agent Carlyle.

"You're right," he says. "That wasn't fair, and I apologize. But I do need you to answer the question."

"I've forgotten what it was."

"Why did Luke want to be a Centurion?"

So he could tell people what to do. So he could punish them if they disobeyed. So he could hurt them.

"He was ambitious," I say instead.

"The Lord's Legion existed to serve the Lord," says Doctor Hernandez. "Not for personal glory. Isn't that right?"

"It is. But people are still people. They want the approval of others."

"Was Luke one of those people?"

"You've seen him in SSI," I say. "What do you think?"

"I think he's an extremely troubled young man," says Doctor Hernandez. "I think he wishes he hadn't survived the fire."

A heavy silence falls over the room. Agent Carlyle gives Doctor Hernandez a sideways glance, like he wasn't expecting him to actually answer my question. I wasn't expecting him to either, and part of me wonders if he meant to, because patches of pale pink have appeared high on his cheeks.

"Are you helping him?" I ask.

Doctor Hernandez nods. "We're doing everything we can."

"Why hasn't he been at SSI the last few days?"

He hesitates, clearly trying to decide whether to tell me or not. "He was extremely agitated after you and he discussed ascension," he says. "We were forced to sedate him, and that, as I'm sure you can imagine, fit very neatly with Father John's warnings about the outside world. Getting through to him afterward was...challenging."

"Is he going to be all right?" I ask.

"We're hopeful of a positive outcome."

I frown. "You've said that before."

"I know," he says. "I'm still hopeful. The intention is for him to rejoin SSI this afternoon."

"But you can't say for certain that he's going to be okay?"

Doctor Hernandez shakes his head. "No. I can't say that."

An image of Luke, kicking and screaming as the Governments carried him out of the Base while it burned down around him, fills my mind. I shudder.

"Thank you for telling me," I say.

"I probably shouldn't have," he says. "And it's very important that you don't discuss this with the others or let Luke know. I'm sorry to put you in this position, but it's for the good of everyone."

So I have to keep your secrets now, along with my own? Great. Thanks a lot.

"I won't say anything," I say.

He nods and attempts a tiny smile. "Thank you."

"Why do you lie to Luke when he asks you about talking to us?" asks Agent Carlyle. "Why don't you tell him the truth?"

"Because it's none of his business."

"Does he scare you?" he asks.

Yes.

"Not anymore. I feel sorry for him, if anything. But he used to scare me. I was scared of him for a long time."

"Why?" asks Agent Carlyle.

"I was worried he would hurt someone."

"Was he violent?"

Yes. "Sometimes."

"To you?"

I nod.

"What about your brothers and sisters?" asks Doctor Hernandez. "Was he violent to them?"

"Yes."

"But he wasn't a Centurion," says Agent Carlyle.

"No."

"So he had no authority."

"No."

"Did John Parson punish him for being violent?"

"Sometimes."

"But not always?"

"No."

Doctor Hernandez has filled half a page of one of his notebooks while Agent Carlyle and I were going back and forth. He puts his pen down and looks at me. "How was he viewed by the younger members of the Legion?"

"Luke?" I ask.

"Yes. Luke."

"What do you mean, how was he viewed?" I ask.

"Was he popular? Did they like him? Were they scared of him?"

"People felt differently about him at different times. Some days, some people liked him, other days the same people hated him, the same as anyone else. People are people."

179

"People are people," says Agent Carlyle. "That's right."

"What about you?" asks Doctor Hernandez.

"What about me?"

"Did *you* like Luke?"

"Now? I feel sorry for him, like I said."

"Not now," he says. "Inside the Legion. Before the fire."

I shrug. "He was my Brother. I loved him."

Doctor Hernandez smiles. "But you didn't like him?"

I hated him. I was scared of him, and I hated him so much.

"No," I say. "I didn't like him."

TRAITOR! bellows Father John, his voice raging into my head without warning. *HERETIC! YOU NEVER LOVED YOUR BROTHERS AND SISTERS! YOU WERE ALWAYS FALSE! YOUR FAITH WAS JUST FOR SHOW!*

I recoil because it's been a little while since I heard The Prophet's awful, booming voice. A tiny, desperately hopeful part of me had started to wonder if it was gone for good.

"You didn't like him?"

"No. And the feeling was mutual, believe me." I pause. "To be totally honest, saying he didn't like me isn't really enough. There were lots of times when I'm absolutely certain he hated me."

"Did you hate him back?"

"No," I lie.

"Why do you think he hated you?" asks Doctor Hernandez.

I shrug. "Why do people usually hate other people?"

"There can be any number of reasons," he says. "It can be the result of an incident, like if somebody has hurt them or someone they care about. Or it can be based on something arbitrary, like the color of someone's skin or their sexual orientation. And sometimes it can be for no clear reason at all."

"I think it was a little of all three."

"What makes you say that?"

I hesitate because getting into this is going to lead to some places I'm not sure I want to go. But the voice in the back of my head reminds me what I told myself last night as I was staring at the ceiling in my room.

Maybe it will do me good to tell as much truth as I can bear.

Doctor Hernandez frowns. "Moonbeam? Are you okay?"

"Luke was the Legion's first baby," I say, ignoring his question. "He was born in the Base, barely a year after Father Patrick started the Legion and before even the first foundation of the Chapel had been sunk into the ground. What you have to understand is that before the Third Proclamation, things were very different. People were…"

I trail off. I don't have the slightest idea how to talk about this with them.

"Sexual activity was less restricted?" suggests Doctor Hernandez.

I give him a profoundly grateful nod. "Thank you," I say. "That's exactly right. It was less restricted, so I don't know whether anybody ever knew who Luke's dad was, even at the time. Plenty of people must have known who his mom was, because she gave birth to him inside the Base, but nobody ever said anything about his father, including her."

"So she abandoned him after he was born?" asks Agent Carlyle.

"I don't know," I say. "She never acknowledged him, I can say that much. I know Luke asked about her, asked about them both, even after talking about the time before the Purge had been forbidden, but he never got any answers."

"What did people say when he asked?"

"They told him he was a child of The Lord. That he was raised by his Brothers and Sisters, and that *they* were his Family. But I heard rumors over the years. I guess everyone did. Names. Some women who were Gone, but some who were still there, who Luke talked to most days."

"Why do you think nobody told him the truth?" asks Doctor Hernandez. "There must have been people who could have identified his mother, as you said."

I shrug. "I guess she asked them not to."

"Imagine seeing your son in pain every day," says Agent Carlyle. "Seeing him and knowing you could help him but doing nothing, not even acknowledging him. What kind of person does that?"

"Don't judge her, whoever she was," says Doctor Hernandez. "We don't know what her experiences were. How hard her choices might have been."

Agent Carlyle makes a face, but doesn't say anything.

"Why do you think Luke's upbringing negatively affected how he thought about you?" asks Doctor Hernandez.

"I don't know for certain that it did. I'm just thinking out loud," I say. "But you already know I wasn't born inside the Legion, and that made us different, right from the start."

"Don't feel like you have to talk about your mother."

I shrug. "It's okay." I'm slightly surprised to find that it actually *is*. "My mom told me about their life before we moved to the Base. She was a schoolteacher until she had me, and my dad worked for a children's charity. You probably would have liked him."

Doctor Hernandez smiles.

"They were married eight years before I came along," I continue. "Mom used to call me her little miracle because her doctors had started to think she couldn't have children."

His smile fades. I remember what he told me about his wife, and my heart aches with sympathy for him. For *both* of them.

"Do you think that's what made your father open to what Horizon told him in Santa Cruz?" asks Agent Carlyle. "That he and your mother believed you were a gift from God?"

"I don't know. I never got the chance to ask him."

Agent Carlyle grimaces and nods.

"I guess you can't remember that far back?" asks Doctor Hernandez. "To when you first moved to the Base?"

I shake my head, even though I have a memory of the day we arrived that's so clear it could be yesterday. I can see the skeletal frame of the Chapel rising into a bright blue sky; the smiling faces of strangers as they welcomed my mom and dad and hovered over me, cooing and clucking and gently holding my tiny hands; the heat and the dryness of a world that felt totally, utterly alien. It feels like a memory, even though I know it can't be real because I was only eighteen months old. But it's happy, and it has my dad in it, so I'm keeping it.

"So Luke was first," says Agent Carlyle. "And you were second."

"There were children in the Legion when it was formed. The kids of the original members. But we were the first two to arrive once it existed. Once it was real."

"The first of many?"

"So many," I say. "In the early years, I remember people arriving every month. Not all of them stayed, but it seemed like there were new faces every time you turned around. You remember me telling you about Lizzie, my friend whose mom worked in Layfield?"

"They left after the purge," says Doctor Hernandez.

I nod. "That's right. She was probably five or six when they arrived. Honey was three, Alice was seven, Isaac was almost fourteen. Some of the others were older, some were younger. But, yeah. Luke and I were first and second."

"And you had your parents and he didn't," says Doctor Hernandez.

I nod.

"Were the two of you treated differently? By the rest of the Legion, I mean."

I think back to the days when Luke and I were little, when

Father Patrick was still in charge and the Lord's Legion was different. Lighter. Kinder. *Better.*

Was it though? whispers the voice in the back of my head. *Just because you want to believe something, doesn't make it the truth. You're smarter than that.*

I ignore the voice the best I can. "I guess so. But not the way you mean, like I was treated well and he was treated badly. Pretty much the entire Legion raised Luke, and cared for him, and looked out for him. They did the same for me, but I always knew I could go to my mom. It must have been confusing for Luke, especially once he was old enough to understand and ask questions. It must have been really hard wondering if his parents were right there every day, not acknowledging him, just—"

"Rejecting him over and over again?" says Doctor Hernandez.

I try to imagine what that must have been like: the frustration, the impotence, the endless disappointment. How easy it would be to assume there had to be a reason that your parents didn't want you, that it had to be your fault. How inevitably that would turn into anger, over time.

"I guess so," I say. "When I was little, I just thought he was mean, that he had taken against me for some reason or other. But looking back, I wonder how jealous he must have been of me and the other kids, how alone he must have felt. It makes me feel like I should have been a better friend to him. A better Sister."

"You were a child yourself," says Doctor Hernandez. "Luke's upbringing wasn't your fault."

I hesitate. "I guess not."

"You said there were times when you're certain he hated you," says Agent Carlyle. "Was that because his general attitude to you was different, or are you referring to specific incidents?"

The memory slices through me, cold and sharp. "There was… an incident."

"Do you want to tell us about it?" asks Doctor Hernandez.

That's a good question. A *very* good question. Do I want to tell them about the one time—before the fire, at least—when I genuinely thought I was going to die?

Tell them, whispers the voice in the back of my head.

Be brave.

"No," I say. "I don't want to tell you about it. But I will."

He nods. "Take it slow, and be aware of your feelings. We can stop whenever you need to."

I take a deep breath, let it out, and take another.

Doctor Hernandez narrows his eyes. "Moonbeam? Are you okay?"

I nod. "It was a Sunday…"

BEFORE

Father John's sermon—on the evils of addiction and how the Government uses drugs and alcohol to keep people away from the True Path—is still ringing in my ears as I follow Nate into the gardens.

I follow him *a lot*. I know I do. Often enough to make some of my Sisters giggle and whisper behind their hands.

I don't care though, because Nate is my friend and he's much older than me and I know he's never going to look at me the way I want him to so I'm not doing anything wrong and my Sisters can giggle all they want.

Joe Nelson gives us a bag of lettuce seeds, and I help Nate plant them, but he doesn't seem to be in a very good mood today. After about fifteen minutes of me trying to make conversation, he asks me to give him a break for a little while. He looks guilty as he says it, and I feel bad for him even as my face flushes with embarrassment and my heart breaks in my chest. I manage a tiny smile and tell him no problem, and walk out of the gardens and back through the yard. The sun is high overhead. It's *really* hot, and I can feel sweat running down my back. As I walk across the boiling blacktop, I realize that I have absolutely no idea what to do with myself. There's no such thing as finding yourself at a loose end inside the Lord's Legion—if you finish the job you've been given, a brand-new list of chores always appears, as if by magic. I know I should find one of the Centurions and ask him what needs doing, but right now the yard is empty and it's hot and quiet and it feels like the whole Base is asleep.

I walk past the Chapel, through the eastern row of barracks, and out into the desert, where the ground is dark orange and empty of life. Here it's nothing but dust and dirt and dead leaves. In the distance, shimmering in the rising heat, the fence runs to the north and south, barbed wire coiled unevenly along its top, signs reading PRIVATE PROPERTY hanging from it at irregular intervals. Between the fence and me stands a row of sheds and ramshackle shelters nailed together from wooden planks, where most of the tools and machines used to work Joe Nelson's gardens and fields are kept: lawnmowers, chainsaws, scythes, axes, hoes, shovels, and dozens and dozens of other implements. I head toward them, the look on Nate's face as he asked me to give him a break still filling my mind.

I'm not stupid, okay? I'm not some smitten little girl who believes in true love and happily ever after. I know—I've *always* known, ever since he first arrived—that Nate only sees me as a younger Sister, one who can't quite hide her crush on him, and I know that nothing is ever, ever going to happen between us.

The voice in the back of my head never misses the chance to remind me that he doesn't have those kind of feelings for me, but even if it was wrong—it isn't, but if it was—the Third Proclamation would still forbid him from acting on them. And even if he was inclined to break such a fundamental rule—if he was so wildly in love that he was willing to throw caution to the wind—he would be taking a much bigger risk by breaking it with me than with almost anybody else in the Legion. As Nate himself reminds me on a daily basis, I was chosen to be a Future Wife of The Prophet when I was ten.

There are five of us: Zara, Lily, Hanna, Hummingbird, and me. I'm the oldest, and Lily is the youngest. She's ten, although The Lord chose her for Father John when she was six. Being a Future Wife is a great honor, second only to being a Centurion, although it doesn't actually change anything. We don't go to live in the Big House until we're married, and that doesn't happen until we turn eighteen, so it's merely a thing that exists in the future that I've never really known how to feel about.

I can clearly remember my mom telling Father John over and over that I would make him a fine wife one day. Nate brings it up to people all the time too, even when it has nothing to do with whatever they're talking about. It's like he's trying to make sure nobody ever forgets my special status.

But me? I get that it's what The Lord wants for me, but that still doesn't make it feel like it is really, *actually* going to happen. Mainly because it's three years before I turn eighteen, and every single one of my Brothers and Sisters, including Father John himself, is absolutely certain that the Final Battle with The Serpent will begin long before then.

What if it doesn't though? whispers the voice in the back of my head. *What if you have to marry him, and move into the Big House, and into his room, and into his bed, and—*

I shove the voice away as hard as I can and keep walking, because I don't want to think about any of that right now. I've almost reached the first shed, which is little more than a sheet of rusting metal perched precariously on a frame of tree branches, when I hear a noise from somewhere behind the row of outbuildings. We have diamondbacks at the Base, what sometimes seems like dozens of them, and you learn pretty quickly to back up the way you came when you hear their rattle, even though you almost never actually see the snake.

This doesn't sound like a rattle; it's more of a grunt, like a deep breath being exhaled all at once. I stand still, and listen, and wait.

After a few seconds, I hear the sound again.

It's louder this time, and it's definitely coming from the other side of the large shed to my left. I walk forward, taking care not to snap a dry branch or rustle a clump of dead leaves. I edge my way along the side of the tumbledown building, and peek around the corner.

Embarrassed heat immediately roars into my cheeks, because Luke is standing in the shadows cast by the big shed and his jeans are undone and he's holding his thing in his hand. He's frowning, like he's concentrating really hard. As I watch, he slides his hand back and forth really fast and lets out the grunting noise I heard.

It isn't funny. It really isn't. I know that Luke will be absolutely furious if he catches me watching him. But despite that knowledge, I'm gripped by the insane desire to burst out laughing. He looks so *ridiculous*, so earnest and serious, and even though I understand that what he's doing is private, I can't make myself look away. I just can't.

Then there's movement on the other side of Luke, and the amusement that threatened to overwhelm me disappears as Honey steps out of the shadows. She looks confused, and it's obvious from her face that she doesn't want to be here.

"Touch it," says Luke.

Honey looks at him with wide eyes and doesn't move. "Go on," he says. "Do it. You're supposed to."

She stares at him for a long moment, then fixes her gaze on the ground. As she reaches out a trembling hand, I find myself moving, without having made the conscious decision to do so.

"Go back to the yard, Honey," I say, stepping out where they can see me.

Luke yelps with surprise and twists away from me, furiously buttoning up his jeans. "Get out of here!" he yells. "We're not doing anything wrong!"

Relief shines brightly in Honey's eyes, like she can't quite believe I'm actually here, that I'm really standing in front of her.

"Go on," I say. "It's all right. You're not in any trouble."

She doesn't waste another second; she runs, her footsteps thudding across the ground as she races away in the direction of the yard. Luke turns toward me, and I realize, maybe a second too late, that I should have run too, because the look on his face isn't the embarrassment I was expecting.

The look on his face is pure murder.

He lunges at me, grabs my shoulders, and drives me back against the wall of the shed. My heels scrape the dirt, and my head connects with metal. I see stars, whole galaxies of them. Luke's palm slams into the side of my face, beneath my eye, and an explosion of pain clears my vision.

I taste blood in my mouth, and I let out a scream, but a hand closes over my mouth and cuts it off as Luke presses himself against me, his eyes burning with hatred.

"Who in The Lord's name do you think you are?" he growls. "Spying on people? Meddling in what's none of your business?"

I search his eyes for some clue this is going to be okay, that he's only trying to scare me. I find nothing.

Absolutely nothing.

"Third…Proclamation…" I gasp, around the tight seal of his hand.

He laughs and lets his hand drop to my shoulder. "*You're* going to tell *me* about the Proclamations? Is that what's happening here? I know them better than anyone, apart from The Prophet himself."

"Then why were you about to break one of them?" I don't care about his answer, but I'm trying to buy time while my lungs refill with air so I can think my way out of this.

"I wasn't breaking anything," he says, and gives my shoulder a hard squeeze. "She's supposed to do what I tell her. Do you understand? It's her job to please me. *Your* job too."

His other hand slides up my thigh. I try to scream again, but he sees it coming and clamps my mouth shut even tighter than before.

"I know you're promised to Father John," he whispers, his eyes blazing with hatred. "I know you're being kept pure until then. But after he's done with you, I'm going to come and see you one night, and we're going to have some fun. A *lot* of fun. I'm going to—"

The hand on my shoulder and the one gripping my thigh come loose, and Luke goes stumbling backward, his eyes wide. His feet tangle, and he hits the ground as my legs give way beneath me. I slide down the wall, tears springing into my eyes. I wipe them away in time to see Nate stride forward and hammer the toe of his boot into Luke's ribs with a sound like a cleaver hitting a side of beef. Luke howls and tries to crawl away as Nate kicks him again, and again, and again, until Luke stops moving and lies still, his eyes full of pain and surprise. Nate raises his foot again, and I manage to find my voice.

"Don't! Nate, don't!"

His boot pauses in midair, and he looks at me with such naked fury that it freezes me solid. Then his face softens, and he slowly lowers his foot.

"Moonbeam," he says. "Are you all right? Did he hurt you?"

On the ground, Luke lets out a rattling gasp as I shake my head.

"Are you sure?"

"I'm okay," I say, even though it's not remotely true. "I promise, Nate."

He nods. "Go back to the yard."

"What are you going to do?"

Nate glances down at Luke, whose eyes are bulging with terror in a face that has turned a red so dark it's almost purple. "I'm going to take care of this," he says. "Now go. And don't talk to anybody else until I come and find you."

I get to my feet and half-run, half-stagger around the corner of the shed. I make it all the way to the edge of the yard before my legs won't hold me up any longer, and I sink to my knees and sob until I can't breathe.

AFTER

"Jesus," breathes Agent Carlyle. "Jesus goddamn Christ."

His eyes widened steadily as I talked, and he's staring at me with an expression so full of sympathy that I can't look at it because I'm pretty sure I'll start crying if I do.

"How old was Honey?" asks Doctor Hernandez quietly.

"Then?"

He nods.

"She was eleven."

Nobody says anything for a long time. My words hang between us like poison gas, souring the air. In the end, it's Agent Carlyle who regains his composure first.

"What happened to Luke?" he asks.

"Nothing. I don't know what Nate said to him or did to him after I ran, but Luke never mentioned it again. Neither did Honey."

"Did she go and find Nate? Is that why he came and helped you?"

I nod.

A tight smile rises on his face. "Brave girl."

You can't even begin to imagine.

"She really is," I say.

Doctor Hernandez rubs his eyes and takes a deep breath. He looks paler than usual, and his forehead furrows as he grimaces, as if the story I told has caused him actual physical pain. He closes his eyes for a second or two, then takes a folder out of his bag and opens it on the desk.

"I've got a copy of the Third Proclamation here," he says. "I assume it was transcribed by Jacob Reynolds?"

I nod. I can clearly remember the long, feverish summer night when Father John received the message that became the Third Proclamation from The Lord. His eyes rolled and his limbs twitched and his mouth foamed like a dog's. Jacob Reynolds was at his side throughout, his pen poised above a sheet of paper.

"'All has been shown to me,'" reads Doctor Hernandez. "'The Lord is the future, and the future is in me, and all is clearer than ever. There can be no wasted seed, no wasted womb, for we are too few and our enemies too many. A new generation of Legionnaires is needed, Faithful Warriors born with their feet on the True Path. Only the True can be allowed to enter this forsaken world, only those who carry the Light of The Lord, who have received it through me, His most loyal messenger. All else is Heresy.'"

A chill passes over me. The entire Legion gathered in front of the Big House as the sun rose the morning after Father John's conversation with The Lord and listened in silence as he stood on the porch and read those lines aloud for the first time. The Prophet looked exhausted, like a man who hadn't slept in years, but his booming voice was full of cast-iron certainty.

"What did this proclamation mean to you?" asks Doctor Hernandez.

"How do you mean?"

"What was your understanding of it?"

I shrug. "I'd have thought it was pretty clear. It meant that every man in the Base, with the exception of Father John, had to take a vow of celibacy. It said that the Legion needed a new generation of Brothers and Sisters who were descended only from him."

"What about married couples?" he asks. "Men and women who were in monogamous relationships?"

"It applied to them too."

"Because John Parson said so?" asks Agent Carlyle.

I BROUGHT THE WORD OF THE ALMIGHTY LORD TO MORTAL EARS! roars Father John, his voice an agonizing howl inside my head. *I GAVE WISDOM TO THOSE TRUE ENOUGH TO HEAR IT! I STEERED THEIR SOULS AWAY FROM THE SERPENT!*

I ignore The Prophet's voice and nod.

Of course. He said so. That was all it ever took.

"So the men of the Legion were ordered into celibacy," says Doctor Hernandez. "What about the women?"

"We were told to reject the advances of anyone other than Father John," I say.

"And *his* advances?"

"We were told to submit to them. For the good of the Legion."

Agent Carlyle clenches his fists and looks away. He hasn't quite managed to compose himself by the time he turns back to face me, and I recoil from the fury in his gaze.

"I'm sorry," I say. "I'm telling the truth. I promise."

He gives me the world's tiniest smile. "I know you are. You're doing incredibly well. I'm so proud of you."

I stare at him. I don't know how to thank him without saying the actual word, and that's not possible because a lump has lodged itself in my throat.

"What was the reaction to the Third Proclamation inside the Legion?" asks Doctor Hernandez.

I look away from Agent Carlyle and swallow hard. Nothing happens, so I swallow again, and again, until my throats clears and I can speak.

"Some people weren't happy," I say. "Especially given how things had been in the early days."

"It's our understanding that people left," says Doctor Hernandez. "Is that correct?"

I nod. "That's right."

"How many?" asks Agent Carlyle.

I think back to the day the Third Proclamation was issued, as men packed their cars and bundled their women into them and drove out through the Front Gate, their faces dark with anger.

"Thirty? Maybe thirty-five?"

"John Parson just let them go?" asks Agent Carlyle.

"Father John said The Lord was testing us," I say. "That the Third Proclamation had revealed those Brothers and Sisters who were False, whose Faith was just an act. He said the Legion would be stronger without them."

Agent Carlyle grimaces. "If by stronger you mean more obedient."

"Do you think that's what it was, Moonbeam?" asks Doctor Hernandez. "You told us Father John didn't react to people leaving after the purge because he knew he had asserted his authority, that he'd 'won,' as you put it. Was this the same?"

"I don't know. I don't think he wanted to lose people from the Legion, but I guess it was more important that it be full of people he believed were loyal."

"To him? Or to The Lord?" asks Agent Carlyle.

I shrug. "There was no difference."

"Do you really believe that?"

No. Yes.

"It doesn't matter what I thought," I say. "It matters what my Brothers and Sisters thought. And I've told you before. Most of them believed Father John was The Lord's messenger on Earth. It wasn't an act, or some bit of fun for people. They believed it with all their hearts."

"But what if—"

"I don't know what you want me to tell you," I interrupt. "I don't know what was inside Father John's head. I don't know whether he was glad people left because it proved their Faith wasn't strong enough, or because he wanted to get rid of people who wouldn't do what they were told, or both. I don't know if he was happy to see them go, or sad, or angry. All I know is that people left. They weren't prisoners."

"Right," says Agent Carlyle. "Even though Amos was the only man allowed to leave the compound, and nobody was allowed to use a phone or watch TV or read a book, and four armed men answered directly to a man who believed he spoke to God and handed out punishments that took months to recover from."

"I hate when you call the Base a compound," I say.

Agent Carlyle nods. "I know you do."

"People left," I say. "Father John never stopped them. I could have left."

"Do you really believe that, Moonbeam?" asks Doctor Hernandez.

I don't answer him right away. Not because I don't want to, but because I'm genuinely not sure how.

Be brave, whispers the voice in the back of my head. *Be honest with yourself, if nothing else. Be strong enough to confront the reality, not the lies you were told.*

I do what it tells me—I look back, and I think, and I try to be strong. It's painful, because there was a time, a *long* time, when I believed every single word Father John said. Before my mom was Banished, I believed in him and the Legion with all my heart. Part of me misses—will *always* miss—the certainty that came with that, the power and pride that came with being part of something that was right and True.

But then I think about my mom and Nate and the boxes and the locked door in the basement of the Big House. I think about my Sisters running toward the Governments with rifles in their hands and the five gunshots and what I found and what I did.

I think about blood and fire, and my stomach churns.

"I don't know," I say eventually. "I never tried to leave. So I guess I don't know for certain."

Doctor Hernandez makes a long note in one of his books, but it doesn't make me angry. Instead, I feel a weird sense of *relief*, because talking about all this, about Luke and Honey and Nate and the Third Proclamation, has made me unsteady, like the floor is rolling beneath my feet, and him writing about me, even though I'm sitting right in front of him, feels familiar.

"What happened after the people left?" asks Agent Carlyle.

"There was a celebration."

"Of what?"

"Marriage," I say. "Father John took his second and third wives that night."

"*That night?*" says Agent Carlyle. "The day he issued the Third Proclamation?"

I nod.

"Who were the lucky women?"

"Bella and Agavé."

"Were either of them already married?"

"Both of them were."

"And their husbands were still there?"

I nod again.

"How did they respond to Father John marrying their wives?" asks Doctor Hernandez. "What did they do?"

What do you think?

"They celebrated with the rest of us. Father John led Bella and Agavé from the Chapel to the Big House and everyone lit candles and followed them."

"What do you imagine their husbands were thinking at that moment?" he asks.

"I know exactly what they were thinking," I say, because I do know, without a shadow of a doubt. "They were praying their wives would serve Father John well."

The room falls silent for a long time as the reality I'm describing sinks in. As usual, it's Agent Carlyle who finds his voice first.

"It's going to take me a little while to get my head around all this," he says. "So if it's all right, I'd like to go back to Luke. Is that okay?"

I nod.

"You said there was no fallout whatsoever from what happened with you and him and Honey and Nate."

"That's right."

"I find that a little hard to believe, Moonbeam."

I frown. "I'm not lying to you."

He raises his hands in a *calm down* gesture that fills me with the urge to stab one of Doctor Hernandez's pens into his eye. "I didn't say you were," he says. "I'm not accusing you. I'm just wondering whether there might be more to what happened. Whether you might've left something out."

"Nate never told anyone, at least as far as I know. Neither did Luke or Honey. The Centurions never got involved, and nothing official ever happened."

Agent Carlyle nods. "I don't doubt that. And Nate didn't do anything himself?"

"No."

"Did you?"

I hesitate.

He narrows his eyes. "Moonbeam? Did you do something?"

Tell them, whispers the voice in the back of my head. *Be brave. Tell them what you did...*

BEFORE

I wait about a week.

I'm not stupid enough to believe that Luke will have forgotten about what happened. I doubt he *ever* will, not completely, and I'm absolutely *certain* he'll never forgive me for it. But circumstances have forced my hand, so I hope it's been long enough for what happened with Nate and Honey to no longer be at the front of his mind.

Long enough for him to have let his guard down.

We'd been living at the Base for only eighteen months when my dad died. He was patching up a section of fence near the northwest corner and just fell over. They rushed him down to the medical center in Layfield, but he was gone. The doctors examined his body and told my mom and Father Patrick that there had been something wrong with his heart, something that nobody could ever have known about. They said his death was instant, that he probably wouldn't have known it had happened.

I hope that was the truth.

When I was older, maybe six or seven, my mom gave me a box of things that had belonged to him, things that she thought he would have wanted me to have. Before she handed it over to me, she made me promise not to tell anyone I had it. I promised, even though I didn't understand why I had to.

The box contained two knives, a seashell from the beach in Santa Cruz, a seemingly random page from his diary, a black-and-white photo of his parents, and a watch he had stopped at the exact date and time I was born. I've read the page of his diary hundreds of times, and I look at the photo a lot because I've never met any of my grandparents. I don't even know if they're alive.

The knives have folding blades and flat wooden handles on which my dad carved and painted a pair of bright yellow and purple sunsets. They're small, their blades short and not very sharp, but I love the feel of them in my hands. My dad must have held them in his for hours, working slowly at the handles with chisels and brushes, and so holding them has always felt like a way for me to be close to him.

I try to clear my mind as I slip the knives into the pockets of my jeans and creep out of my room into the little corridor in the middle of Building Nine. It's empty apart from six plain wooden doors that lead into six identical bedrooms and a plastic glow-in-the-dark cross hung on the wall at the end. My mom used to live here too, in the room next to mine, and I feel her absence as I head toward the door. I'm not supposed to think about her because it's Heresy to do so, but the Centurions can't see inside my head and neither can Father John. Which is good, because I don't think he'd like a lot of what he saw.

I know the Centurions haven't locked us in tonight because

I've been lying awake for three hours since lights-out, and I would have heard the sound of the padlock clicking shut. Someone came to see Alice about an hour ago, and I wrapped my pillow around my head until they were finished. Sometimes they make an effort to be quiet, and sometimes they don't.

The door handle turns in my hand, and I step carefully onto the desert floor. There's no moon tonight, and when there's no moon in the desert, it's *really* dark, so dark that I can only make out the square outline of the yard in front of me. Like most of my Brothers and Sisters, I keep a little flashlight on my belt, but as I stand in the darkness next to Building Nine, shivering in the freezing night air, I decide not to use it. It would undoubtedly make things easier, but it would also massively increase the chances of someone seeing me.

And I don't want to be seen.

I head toward the southwest corner of the yard, navigating by the faint glow of the stars and my internal compass, taking each step slowly. The building I'm interested in is part of an identical row of four, and if I end up inside the wrong one, I'm going to spend the morning being questioned by the Centurions and the afternoon inside a box.

I creep around the yard, focusing on what Father John always tells us about the Final Battle: *You will be calm, and you will be careful, and you will trust in The Lord, and you will be triumphant.*

Calm. Careful. Triumphant.

What I've got planned isn't remotely what he meant his advice to be used for, but right now I'll take anything that stops my racing heart from leaping out of my chest.

Calm. Calm. Calm.

I reach the front of what I think—I *hope*—is Building Twelve and stand in the darkness beside the door. I take a moment or two to try and compose myself, even though it might well be a waste of time: if I've got this wrong, I'll know in a couple of seconds, and then how calm I am won't matter in the slightest.

I take a deep breath, hold it, and let it out. Then I take my dad's knives out of my pockets, open their blades, and slowly—*very slowly*—turn the door handle. I'm half expecting the door to be locked or to let out a screech of metal that wakes up the entire Base, but it slides open as smoothly and silently as if its hinges have just been oiled. I step into the darkness.

Buildings Eleven through Fourteen are barracks, long one-room buildings that each house three of my Brothers and are identical inside and out. So even though I can see the deep black silhouettes of three beds lined up against the rear wall, I still can't be sure I'm in the right place. I stare at the narrow bunks, trying to breathe silently as I wait for my eyes to adjust, and after a seemingly endless moment, I see what I'm looking for.

One of the three beds is empty.

Leo, the ten-year-old who should be asleep in it, came down with a fever yesterday morning and was moved into Julia and Becky's house next to the Chapel so they can keep an eye on him. Julia was a doctor and Becky was in medical school when they were Called onto the True Path, and they've saved at least a dozen lives between them in the decade since they joined the Lord's Legion.

Leo's empty bed is right where it should be. This is the place.

I tiptoe along the wall and stop beside the bed farthest from the door. I can see Luke's head resting on his pillow, can hear the low rumble of his snoring. I stare at him, steeling myself for what I'm about to do. Then I crouch down and press the knife in my left hand firmly against Luke's throat.

His eyelids flutter and slowly slide open. Then they spring wide, and his mouth opens, but before he makes a sound, I hiss into his ear.

"Don't make a sound and don't move a muscle. I'll cut your throat if you do."

He stares at me with utter incomprehension, and I wonder if part of him assumes he must be dreaming, because surely no girl would ever *dare* creep into his room in the middle of the night and threaten him with a knife. That simply does not happen to boys like him.

"You'll go in a box for this, you bitch," he whispers. "You'll—"

I slide the other knife beneath the covers and place it between his legs. His eyes bulge in their sockets, and he goes very, *very* still.

"Only if somebody finds out," I whisper. "And they aren't going to, are they?"

He stares at me, his body as rigid as steel.

"*Are they?*"

"No," he croaks, his voice barely audible. "I won't tell anyone. Just don't...please..."

"If you ever go near Honey again, if you even *look* at her or any of our Sisters in a way that I don't like, I'll come and see you again. And next time I'll leave you bleeding like a castrated bull. Do you hear me? Am I being *absolutely* clear with you?"

Tears brim in the corners of his eyes. Then slowly, and very carefully, he nods, the skin of his neck scraping against the blade of my dad's knife.

"Good," I whisper. "Sweet dreams, Luke. The Lord is Good."

I withdraw both knives at the same time, and I'm halfway across the room before he realizes they're gone. I hear a noise that is somewhere between a retch and a sob, but then I'm through the door and heading back around the yard the way I came, forcing myself to ignore the adrenaline surging through my body, to move slowly and keep quiet, and not undo all my good work.

A
F
T
E
R

"Luke kept his word," I say. "He never said anything to anyone, and he never went near Honey again."

"Did you worry he might come after you? That he would want revenge for what you did?" asks Agent Carlyle. He stares at me with an expression of such fierce pride that I can't help but smile.

I shrug. "I thought about it. After that, I never went anywhere without one of my dad's knives in my pocket. I figured it was better to be safe than sorry."

"That's right," says Agent Carlyle. "That's absolutely god-damn right."

"What would the Centurions have done to you if Luke had told them?" asks Doctor Hernandez.

"I'm not exactly sure," I say. "I know we'd both have been in trouble, him for trying to break the Third Proclamation with Honey and me for threatening one of my Brothers. But I don't know how bad it would have been or who would have gotten it worse."

"That's what you were counting on?" asks Agent Carlyle. "That he would be too scared of what might happen to him to report you?"

I nod. "I knew he wouldn't tell anyone."

"Bullies are cowards," he says. "Did anyone ever tell you that?"

I nod again.

"Who?"

"Nate," I say.

Doctor Hernandez narrows his eyes ever so slightly. "I think it would be best if we avoid using too many generalizations," he says. "Let's stick to what we can say with some degree of certainty, shall we?"

"You're the expert," says Agent Carlyle, but he gives me another wink as he speaks, and I try very hard not to let my smile expand into a grin.

"So you took precautions in case Luke came after you," says Doctor Hernandez. "Did he ever try anything?"

I shake my head.

"Why do you think that was?"

"Because he was a bullying little shit bird who pissed his pants when someone finally stood up to him."

Doctor Hernandez grimaces. "Please, Agent Carlyle. That really isn't helpful."

"Sorry," says Agent Carlyle, but he isn't, not in the slightest.

It's written all over his face.

Doctor Hernandez checks his watch. "We've gone over our time," he says. "I don't want to make a habit of doing so, but I think that was a highly productive session. I hope you agree, Moonbeam."

I frown and look at the clock above the door. 11:47.

I talked for almost two hours.

Holy crap.

"I'm sorry," I say. "I didn't realize."

"Don't apologize," says Doctor Hernandez. "We made a lot of progress this morning. Some issues were raised that I would like to explore further, but they can wait until tomorrow. For now, enjoy your lunch and try to get some rest before SSI."

"I'll definitely try," I say.

Nurse Harrow smiles at me as she puts down a tray full of lasagna and asks me how my hand is feeling. I tell her it's okay, and she nods before leaving the room and locking the door after her.

I eat at my desk, trying to work out whether I really do feel better because of the things I said during this morning's session. Am I *lighter*? Or is my mind playing tricks on me, like when you tell someone what they want to hear even if it isn't true? I'm still thinking it over when Nurse Harrow returns and tells me it's time for SSI.

As we walk down the corridor, I try to prepare myself for what I'm going to say and do if Luke isn't there and what I'm going to say and do if he is. I told Doctor Hernandez and Agent Carlyle the truth—I do feel genuinely sorry for him, for the life that was inflicted on him inside the Legion. But that doesn't mean I trust him or that I'm going to be stupid enough to turn my back on him.

Not even for a second.

Nurse Harrow holds open the door of the group therapy room, and I walk through it. I immediately see Luke standing on his own against the far wall and have to stifle a gasp because he doesn't look *anything* like himself. He looks like a corpse that's been propped upright.

His skin is gray, and his eyes are sunken and staring. I can see his hands shaking, even from across the room. He doesn't look at me as I enter or give any indication that there's life behind those empty eyes.

"He's not dead," says Honey, as though she can read my mind. "I checked. He just looks it."

"That's not funny."

She gives me a look that makes me feel about a foot tall. "I know that, Moonbeam. None of this is funny. Do you know what's going on with him?"

"No." I hate lying to her, but I think Doctor Hernandez is right—it won't do any good for the rest of them to think I'm being told more than they are.

"It doesn't look good, whatever it is," she says. "How are you doing?"

"Fine," I say. "You?"

"I'm good. Although it feels a bit like Doctor Kelly is losing interest in me. I don't have anything left to tell her that she doesn't already know. I think she's disappointed I'm not more damaged than I am."

"You can't really think that."

She smiles at me. "I don't. But she keeps sighing when I answer her questions. I think she's bored of me."

"That could be a good thing," I say. "If she thinks you're okay, maybe you're closer to getting out of here."

She shrugs. "Maybe, I guess."

"Do you think about it?"

"Getting out?"

I nod.

"I do," she says. "I don't know what it will be like, and sometimes it scares me. But it has to be better than this. And a *lot* better than where we were."

I nod again.

It scares me too.

We sit on the floor with our backs against the wall and look around the room. Most of our Brothers and Sisters sit in little groups, playing and giggling and chatting in low voices. None of them are paying any attention to Luke.

Jeremiah and Rainbow are on their hands and knees, racing toy cars back and forth across the floor. The others are building with Legos and coloring and drawing and tapping excitedly on little electronic pads that light up and make sounds. Honey told me that none of them played with any of the toys and games during the first couple of sessions, the ones that took place while I was still lying in a hospital bed. She said Luke warned them all not to touch anything that had come from Outside. So what's happening in the room feels like real progress. Jeremiah has a green car, and Rainbow has a bright red fire truck, and they make engine noises as they roll them in wide figure eights. Every so often, the little vehicles collide, and the two of them fall about laughing. The sound does my heart good.

Aurora closes a coloring book and wanders over to join them.

"Can I play?" she asks.

Jeremiah and Rainbow both nod. Aurora smiles, then digs through one of the plastic boxes, selects a red-and-white ambulance, and sits next to them. The three toy cars trundle back and forth, their wheels squeaking over the floor, the pretend engine noises like the high-pitched buzzing of bees.

I sit in silence next to Honey, watching the three children with a smile on my face.

Jeremiah moves his car into the middle of the circle. Behind him, Lucy and Winter start singing "All Things Bright and Beautiful," their voices low and soft and lovely, and he turns around to listen. Aurora wheels her ambulance in a wide arc, then slams it into the side of the green car, sending it skittering across the floor and into the wall near the door.

Jeremiah whirls back around, his face coloring red. "What did you do that for?"

Aurora recoils, her eyes widening. "We're playing," she says. "I'm sorry."

Jeremiah hops to his feet. "Go and fetch it!"

The color drains from Aurora's face. She looks like she's about to burst into tears, but she gets to her feet.

Honey sits forward, a frown on her face. "Jeremiah," she says. "She said she was sorry. Calm down."

"She did it on purpose!" says Jeremiah, his cheeks flushed pink. "She has to go get it!"

On the other side of the room, Luke's head turns toward the little drama playing out in the middle of the floor.

"Calm down," repeats Honey. "She'll get it. There's no need to shout at her."

"She needs to get it *now*!"

Aurora looks over at us, her face a mask of helpless misery. I get ready to stand up and defuse the situation, but Honey puts a hand on my shoulder and gets to her feet.

"It's okay," she says. "I'll get it."

"No," says Luke, his voice a low croak. "Aurora, do what Jeremiah tells you."

Honey stares at him. "Why should she do that, Luke? And why do you think this is any of your business?"

Luke turns to face her. He looks like a strong breeze would blow him over, but a faint version of the gleam I've come to dread has returned to his eyes. The room has fallen silent, and most of our Brothers and Sisters have nervous expressions on their faces.

"She did something wrong," he says. "She needs to make it right."

"They were playing, Luke," says Honey. "It's not a big deal."

211

"*Everything* is a big deal," whispers Luke. "Obedience is vital. Discipline. She needs to remember her place."

Honey narrows her eyes. "And where is that exactly?"

"She's a *girl*," he says, like it's the most obvious thing in the world. "She needs to do what she's told."

"Because you say so?"

Luke slowly shakes his head. "No. Because Father John said so."

"Father John is dead," says Honey.

"Watch your mouth," says Luke. His voice is rising, starting to sound more like it used to. "You watch your mouth. The Prophet Ascended, just like he always told us he would."

Honey rolls her eyes. "You're an idiot, Luke. You're too stupid to see the truth when it's right in front of you. To understand when you've been lied to."

Luke pushes himself from the wall and stands upright, swaying slightly from side to side. "And what does that make you?" he growls. "A Servant of the Serpent? Or a Heretic whore who needs to learn when to shut her mouth?"

"Luke," I say. "Please—"

He looks at me, and the hatred in his face freezes the words in my throat.

"You tell me which I am, Luke," says Honey. Her voice is steady and almost friendly, as though they're having a pleasant conversation. "In fact, why don't you tell everyone what happened when you tried to make me touch you?"

The faint color that has returned to Luke's face drains away. "Shut up."

"Tell everyone about when Moonbeam caught you trying to break the Third Proclamation with an eleven-year-old," says Honey. "Tell them how Nate Childress beat the crap out of you and left you crying on the ground."

"SHUT UP!" bellows Luke. "YOU SHUT YOUR FILTHY MOUTH!"

He rushes forward, his hands balled into fists. I leap up from the floor and tackle him at the waist, sending him tumbling to one side as Honey shrinks back against the wall. Luke hits the ground and rolls onto his back, the furious energy that galvanized him already gone. He stares up at the ceiling, his face twisted with terrible misery, and starts to cry. The sound is awful—thick choking sobs, like they're coming from the center of his soul—and as he puts his trembling hands over his face, the door opens and two male nurses walk into the room.

I hold my breath as they crouch next to Luke and prepare myself for another explosion. But it doesn't come. Instead, the nurses gently lift him to his feet and help him toward the door.

He doesn't remove his hands from his face, and he doesn't stop sobbing as they slowly walk him out into the corridor.

Broken, whispers the voice in the back of my head.

Nobody says anything.

I look at Honey, but she doesn't meet my eyes.

The door stands open, until Doctor Hernandez steps through it with a clipboard in his hand and looks around at us all.

"We're going to stop this session here," he says. "If anyone feels they need to talk about what just happened, my colleagues and I will be available for the rest of the day. The nursing staff will be along in a minute to take you back to your rooms."

I lie down on my bed and stare at the ceiling.

The voice in the back of my head is telling me not to cry, not to waste my tears on Luke, but there's a lump in my throat a mile wide, and salt water brims in the corners of my eyes, and I don't know whether I'm going to be able to obey it.

For the longest time, for the vast majority of my life, my response to something as horrible as what just happened would have been to pray, to ask The Lord to look after Luke and help him through his troubles. Part of me still wants to kneel down and clasp my hands together and shut my eyes, because I can remember how much better it used to make me feel.

But that time has passed.

I know praying won't help Luke, or me, or anyone else. It won't do a damn thing.

A
 F
   T
     E
       R

"We're looking after him," says Doctor Hernandez. His face is pale and his eyes are red, like he hasn't had enough sleep. "We're doing everything we can."

I shake my head. "There's nothing you can do."

"I don't believe that, Moonbeam. Nobody is beyond help."

"Luke is," I say. "It's not his fault, but it's the truth."

"Whose fault is it?"

"Father John's." I spit the words. "He dripped poison into Luke's ears, filling him with hate and horror and darkness. What chance did he have?"

THE CHANCE TO ASCEND TO THE RIGHT HAND OF THE LORD! screams Father John. *THE CHANCE TO—*

I shove his hateful voice away with every ounce of my strength and feel a surge of bitter pleasure as it falls silent.

"You were taught the same way," says Doctor Hernandez. "So was Honey and all the other Legion children."

"I know what we were taught," I say. "I was there."

"There's no disputing that Luke's life has been chaotic," he says. "But I believe he can be helped through this. I have to believe it."

"I hope you're right," I say. "I really do."

"But you don't think I am."

"No. I think he's broken."

I hold his gaze. I'm not going to back down on this because I'm right. I wish I wasn't, but I am.

I *know* I am.

Agent Carlyle glances between me and Doctor Hernandez. "All right then," he says. "You're doing everything you can, Doctor, you don't think it's going to help, Moonbeam, and everyone hopes Luke is okay. So how about we talk about something else?"

"Fine by me," I say.

Doctor Hernandez nods. "I think that's a good idea. Let's do that. We ended yesterday's session with you telling us that Luke never tried to get revenge against you for what you did to him."

I nod.

"And that was the truth?"

I hesitate, because I've already decided what I'm going to tell them this morning. I think it's the right thing to do, and I'm pretty sure that it's something I need to do, but the prospect still makes me nervous.

Be brave, whispers the voice in the back of my head.

"Moonbeam?" asks Agent Carlyle. "Did Luke try something?"

I shake my head. "He never got the chance. Things started to happen really quickly after that."

BEFORE

I saw funerals on television when we were still allowed to watch it, and some of my Brothers and Sisters have told me about ones they attended before they were Called to the True Path. They seem really sad, with black clothes and tears and people speaking in hushed voices.

Funerals inside the Lord's Legion are *nothing* like that.

There have been maybe half a dozen that I can remember. That's not very many, considering how long I've lived inside the Base and how many people have come and Gone in that time, but it's not really that surprising given that most people who find the True Path do so when they're young and healthy. Father John says The Lord only summons the useful—men and women who are strong and who will work hard for His Glory.

I asked Amos about funerals once when I was younger, after we buried Marcelo, the oldest of the original members of the Legion, and he explained that Outsider funerals are sad because Outsiders are selfish. They know they won't ever see the person who has died again—unless they end up occupying the same corner of Hell—and they weep and cry because it makes them think about the end of their own lives, so they're really just crying for themselves.

I don't think my mom would agree with him. I'll never know though, because I never asked her while I had the chance.

Anyway.

The death of the mortal body is *celebrated* inside the Legion, because we understand what has truly happened: our Brother or Sister has Ascended, to bask forever in the presence of The Lord. And if you believe that, if you *really* believe it, like I used to, then how could you possibly be sad? How could you be unhappy about someone you love having risen to a place of eternal joy?

It's a beautiful day when we finally bury Horizon; the air is warm, the breeze is gentle, and the sky is a bright, brilliant blue, as though The Lord has seen fit to acknowledge His Faithful servant's arrival by crafting a day of perfection for those left behind.

The Centurions locked the doors last night, and I'm already washed and dressed and waiting when I hear footsteps stop outside my door. There's a metallic clunk before it swings open and Bear peers in at me, his weathered face pale in the early morning light.

"Brother Horizon's gone," he says. "Did you hear?"

The six of us in Building Nine lay awake most of the night, listening to Horizon's coughing and spluttering getting weaker and weaker, aware that he was surely coming to the end of his path. Not long before dawn, a deep silence finally settled over the Base, and we knew.

"I heard him go," I say. "The Lord is Good."

"The Lord is Good," says Bear. "Come on. It's time to say goodbye to him."

I follow him outside. We waste no time burying our Brothers and Sisters, because what would be the point of waiting? The person we loved is gone, their souls and memories and everything they were; all that remains is the physical body they inhabited.

My Brothers and Sisters wander into the yard from every direction and gather in front of the Chapel, where a plain wooden table has been set up at the foot of the steps.

Lying on it, hands crossed over his chest, is Horizon.

His eyes are closed and his skin is waxy gray, but he looks so completely at peace that my heart races with happiness that his suffering has finally come to an end.

Father John emerges from the Big House and walks toward us. It's normally a nervous moment each morning when we see The Prophet for the first time, as his mood sets the tone for the day that is to come. If The Lord has given him bad tidings overnight, we know to expect extra hours of work and the most basic meals, whereas if The Lord has given him reason to rejoice, the day lights up and stretches out happily ahead of us. This morning, however, there is no uncertainty, and no nervousness; everyone, including Father John, is ready to say goodbye to our friend.

Bear, Angel, and Lonestar—the three remaining Centurions— stand in a row behind the wooden table. Horizon was one of them for more than a decade, and the pain on their faces is bright and clear. Because even though their Brother has Ascended, and even though they know—*they are absolutely certain*—that they will see him again when the End Times come, grief is not a choice that anyone makes, no matter what Amos told me: it's involuntary, rising up without your permission from a place you can't control.

Father John places a hand on each Centurion's shoulder in turn, then stands in front of them and looks out across the silent mass of the Lord's Legion.

"My Brothers and Sisters," he says, his voice low and vibrating with conviction. "My own Family, who I love most on this Earth. We are gathered on this beautiful morning, in the benevolent gaze of The Almighty Lord, to celebrate the Ascension of our Brother Horizon. I know that there is pain in our hearts, because we are all human and we are all flawed, but this is not the time for grief or for sadness. This is the time to rejoice in the Glory of a life spent on the True Path and give humble thanks to The Lord for Calling His Faithful servant Home. For Horizon, there will be no more pain. For our Ascended Brother, there will only be joy, absolute and everlasting. The Lord is Good."

The crowd echoes the words as one. I look around and see eyes glistening with tears, my Brothers and Sisters holding hands and leaning against each other.

"Horizon is gone from this world," continues Father John, "but we know, in time, that The Lord will Call each and every one of us to the place where we will see him again, where every Brother and Sister who has Ascended will be waiting to welcome us into Glory. The Lord permits no man to know when his time will come, but I trust in my heart that it will be soon for us all. *I pray it will be.* And until that glorious day when the End Times arrive and we vanquish The Serpent and every one of his Servants, we will follow the example of our Brother Horizon. We will keep our feet on the True Path, our hearts full of the Light of The Lord, and we will serve Him in all His Glory. Pray with me, my Brothers and Sisters."

Father John lowers his head and closes his eyes. Everyone in the crowd instantly does likewise, including me, but I only do it because I'm scared that someone will notice if I don't. I hear the low murmur of prayer all around me, a sound that I used to find comforting, as if it connected me to my Brothers and Sisters and proved that I wasn't alone.

It doesn't comfort me anymore though. Since what happened to my mom, all it does is make me angry.

The thing is, I no longer believe that all the men and women around me are praying because they genuinely want to speak to their Lord. Some of them, sure, but not all. What I believe now, what I'm *certain* of, is that some of them are praying simply because The Prophet told them to and because they're scared to death of disobeying him.

"The Lord is Good," says Father John. The crowd repeats the words I've come to hate more than any others and raise their heads. "There is a matter of great importance to attend to," he continues, gazing out at his people. "That of who will take our Brother's place as a Centurion of the Lord's Legion and assume the glorious responsibility of carrying out The Lord's Will here on Earth. I have prayed long and hard for instruction, as I know you all have, and I received that instruction this morning, at the precise moment of Horizon's Ascension. Proof, as if any more were ever needed, that The Lord sees all, and hears all, and gives no man more than he can handle. The Lord is Good."

"The Lord is Good," echoes the crowd. I keep my mouth firmly shut.

"I have never presumed to know the mind of The Almighty Lord," says Father John, his voice dropping to a devout rumble. "I have served Him to the best of my abilities, and I have done what He has asked of me without question or hesitation. His wisdom is infinite, His Will unquestionable, and *He does not make mistakes.*"

He pauses, letting the anticipation build. My stomach twists into knots, as the voice in the back of my head whispers to me.

You know who it's going to be. You know.

The voice is wrong—I don't know who the new Centurion is. I only know who I *don't* want it to be.

"The Lord does not make mistakes," repeats Father John. "It is therefore given to me to announce that The Lord has chosen

221

Nate Childress to serve as Centurion in His Legion, from now until such time as he Ascends. Where are you, Nate?"

Icy cold spreads through my bones.

He told you, whispers the voice in the back of my head. *He made it clear he was considering Nate. You didn't believe him.*

I shake my head because Nate can't become a Centurion. He *can't*. He's kind and gentle and good. He's my friend. It *isn't* fair. *It just isn't fair.*

Horizon was kind and gentle too. Would you rather the new Centurion was hard and cruel?

The words slice me open. I know the voice is right, that Nate will be a good Centurion, if there even is such a thing, but I don't care. *I don't.* Because this is going to change everything, and even though I'll still have Honey and Alice and Rainbow and the others, I won't have Nate anymore.

You never had him. You never did.

"Nate?" says Father John. "Show yourself, my Brother."

My chest flutters with panic at the thought of Father John sinking his claws deeper into Nate, drawing him into the dark heart of the Legion. I see Nate locking people into boxes and beating them with birch branches and putting them on punishment rations and I want to throw up.

I want to scream for him to run, *now*, before it's too late, but I don't. Of course I don't. Because I'm a coward.

There's a commotion on the east side of the yard as the crowd parts to reveal Nate. He stands easily on the asphalt, his jaw set, his dark green eyes fixed on The Prophet.

"Brother Nate," says Father John. "Come stand with your fellow Centurions. Don't be afraid."

Nate doesn't move a muscle. I drag my gaze from him in time to see the first hint of a frown appear on Father John's forehead.

"Did you not hear me, Brother?" he asks. "The Lord has blessed you with a great honor. Surely you would not refuse Him?"

"I'm sorry, Father," says Nate. "That's exactly what I must do."

A chorus of outrage ripples through the crowd as eyes spring wide and hands are clapped over mouths that have dropped open in shock.

Father John's frown deepens. "I find myself confused. Are you not a Faithful Brother of the Lord's Legion? Do you not walk the True Path?"

"I am, Father," says Nate. "And I do. But there are other men here who are more deserving of the honor of being a Centurion. There are—"

"IT IS NOT YOUR DECISION TO MAKE!" bellows Father John, his eyes blazing with sudden fury as the crowd falls silent. "It is the Will of The Almighty Lord! It is what He demands of you, and you do not choose to say yes or no! You fall to your knees and give thanks and praise His everlasting Glory!"

Nate doesn't respond. He just stares at The Prophet.

"Or perhaps you are not True?" asks Father John. The rage that engulfed him has disappeared as quickly as it arrived. "Perhaps you are a Heretic, sent by The Serpent to sow discontent among the Faithful? Is that the truth of this? If so, confess your treachery now, as I can imagine no other reason for you to so grievously insult The Lord these men and women have dedicated their lives to serving."

"I am no Heretic, Father," says Nate, "and my Faith is the equal of any man or woman gathered in this yard. So I ask that I be allowed to pray on this matter. The Lord will guide me, as He always has."

"I have told you what The Lord asks of you," says Father John, his voice cold and crackling with danger. "Was it not clear? Or do you doubt the Truth of what I say?"

"No, Father," says Nate. "But I would rather hear it from Him."

Someone giggles.

I sense movement around me as people turn to see who it was, but I don't move a muscle, because my attention is locked on Father John. I've seen The Prophet angry more times than I could possibly count, but I have never, *ever* seen what has flickered into his eyes as he stares at Nate.

Doubt.

Fear.

And in that moment, something I've vaguely understood for a long time becomes clear.

Father John is a terrifyingly powerful speaker, a man possessed of enormous, almost hypnotic charisma. He is capable of great kindness and fearsome rage—often in the same breath—and his knowledge of Scripture is unequalled. The Centurions are utterly loyal to him, his authority is absolute, and my Brothers and Sisters both love him and fear him, often in equal measure.

But none of that is why they do what he says, why his orders are obeyed without question.

Father John's authority, his *power*, comes from the central belief that lies at the heart of the Legion: that his voice is essentially interchangeable with that of The Lord.

Without that belief, there would be no reason for The Prophet's rules to be obeyed.

Without that belief, the Centurions would be nothing more than bullies, beating and punishing the disobedient.

Without that belief, everything would unravel. And Nate just challenged it in front of everyone.

"You may pray on this matter for a day and a night," says Father John. He pauses, and in that pause, I see that he understands how *precarious* his influence has become. "In that time, I have no doubt that you will come to see the truth that I have told you. You and I both know that The Lord does not make mistakes, everyone gathered here knows that to be true, and so it will be proven yet again. But I would no more interfere with a Brother's relationship with his Creator than I would cast him over the fence for the Outsiders to feast on his flesh. If you need to be brought to understanding at a slower pace, then that is your burden, and yours alone. We will hear your answer at dawn tomorrow, although I have not the slightest doubt what it will be. The Lord is Good."

"The Lord is Good," agrees the crowd.

Father John nods. "Until tomorrow."

He walks forward, lays a hand on Horizon's chest, and closes his eyes. His lips move in a brief silent prayer, then he turns and strides back toward the Big House without another word.

For a long moment nobody moves. There's a weird collective tension filling the yard, as though everyone is holding their breath. The three remaining Centurions glance at each other, clearly unsure what they're supposed to do now. In the end, it is Amos who breaks the silence.

"All right," he shouts. "I reckon that's more than enough standing around for one morning. Horizon's burial is going to happen before lunch, so anyone who wants to take a moment to say a personal goodbye to him has got a couple of hours to do so. But for now, get on into the hall for breakfast, then get to work."

The crowd breaks up and starts to move in every direction. I see my Brothers and Sisters scatter out of the corners of my eyes, but I'm not looking at them.

Nate hasn't moved an inch; he's standing in the same spot near the edge of the yard, his face pale, his eyes lowered. Several people speak to him as they head toward Legionnaires' Hall, but he doesn't give any indication that he hears them. He looks deep in thought—or prayer, maybe—and he doesn't even glance at me as I approach.

"Nate?"

Nothing.

"Nate?" I repeat, and grab his arm. He recoils, his eyes wide and unfocused. Then he seems to recognize me and gives me a tiny smile.

"Moonbeam," he says. "Go to breakfast. You don't need to be seen talking to me right now."

"What are you doing, Nate?" I ask, keeping my voice low. "Why did you say those things?"

He shakes his head. "You don't need to know. Just trust me, if you can. Everything's going to be okay."

"When?" I ask. "*None* of this is okay, Nate. None of it."

"I know," he says, and the pain on his face makes my heart lurch in my chest. "I know, and I'm sorry. Go to breakfast, and if anyone talks to you about what I did, call me a Heretic or tell them you think I might be the Serpent himself. Don't defend me, Moonbeam. Please don't."

I feel tears rise into my eyes and blink them away. "What are you talking about?" I ask. "Why won't you tell me what's going on?"

"I'll find you later, if I can," he says, his voice barely more than a whisper. "But I need you to put all this out of your mind, for both our sakes."

"How am I supposed to do that?"

"Try. Try really hard. And if you can't do it, lie. Just please don't do anything stupid, okay? Please, Moonbeam."

I open my mouth, but Nate turns away before I can form a single syllable. He strides toward Building Seven, where he sleeps. I stand at the edge of the empty yard and watch him go, trying to ignore what the voice in the back of my head is telling me.

You're never going to see him again.

A F T E R

"I'm sorry," says Doctor Hernandez.

I frown. "For what?"

"About Horizon."

"Why?" I ask. "You never knew him."

"I understand that," he says. "I'm sorry for *you*, Moonbeam. I'm sorry you lost someone you cared about."

"Oh," I say. I feel gentle warmth in my face. "Thank you."

"You're welcome," he says. "There was something I meant to ask you yesterday, after you told us about when Horizon got sick. Who paid for him to be taken to hospital?"

"What do you mean?" I ask.

"It costs money to see doctors. It costs a lot more money to have them run the kind of tests that tell someone they have cancer."

"I don't know," I say. "Father John must have given Amos some money before he left."

"Did you ever see money inside the base? In the Big House, maybe?"

I shake my head.

"Did Amos take money with him to Layfield on Friday afternoons?"

"He must have."

"But you never saw it?"

"No."

Doctor Hernandez nods. "Okay. Let's move on. I need to ask you about something that you might find upsetting. Is that all right?"

Like it matters.

"It depends what it is."

He nods. "You told us yesterday that Horizon was a good man. You were very insistent about it. And you just referred to him as kind and gentle."

I frown again. "So what?"

"If he was such a good man, I'm wondering why he stayed after Father John took control of the Legion," says Doctor Hernandez.

"He loved the Legion," I say. "He loved his Brothers and Sisters, and they loved him back."

Doctor Hernandez nods. He doesn't say anything, and I know he's hoping that silence will make me keep talking. I don't want to give him what he wants, but anger threatens spill through me and I don't think I can help myself.

"What do you want me to say?" I ask. "That staying after the Purge makes him evil, makes him some kind of monster? I won't say that because it didn't. It doesn't."

"Why did he tell you it was right that you should be starved for three days after you left your patrol post?" he asks.

"It was his job."

"Like locking Shanti in a metal box until he was half dead was his job?"

"Yes."

"Okay."

The anger that was building inside me has turned into frustration, and I'm suddenly on the verge of tears. Horizon wasn't perfect, not even close, but he was kind and he played with us when we were kids and he never complained and everyone loved him. *I loved him.* I really did.

"Why are you doing this?" I ask. "Why do you want to make him into someone bad?"

Doctor Hernandez winces. "That's not my intention. I'm trying to challenge your assumptions, to get you to look at situations and people from a different angle. I don't doubt your feelings for Horizon, and I'm not trying to undermine them. I'm just trying to show you another perspective."

"I loved him," I say.

"I know you did."

I shake my head. "I don't think you do. If you did, you wouldn't be trying to spoil my memories of him. Was Horizon really a good man, deep down? I don't know. And it doesn't matter, not anymore. He's dead. So why can't you let me remember him the way I want to? How does it hurt anyone to let me have that?"

Agent Carlyle sits forward in his chair and looks at Doctor Hernandez, who stares at me for a long moment, then drops his gaze.

"You're right," he says. "I'm sorry."

So you should be.

I take a deep breath. "It's okay."

He shakes his head. "No, it isn't. It's not for me to impose my opinions of the Lord's Legion and its members. I'll try not to do it again."

Try hard.

"It's okay," I repeat. "Can we talk about something else?"

"Good idea," says Agent Carlyle. "Like what you saw on John Parson's face when Nate Childress said no to him."

"Sure."

"You've told us about people who left the Lord's Legion," he says. "After the Third Proclamation, for example."

"Right."

"And Parson let them go."

I nod.

"Why do you think this was different?" he asks. "People leaving because they didn't want to follow Father John's rules could be seen as a rejection of his authority. So why do you think Nate Childress refusing to be a Centurion would have scared him?"

I consider this for a long time. "They weren't the same," I say. "When people left, Father John could tell the rest of us that they were leaving because their Faith wasn't strong enough, that they weren't really True and didn't deserve to be part of the Legion. That made the people who stayed feel special, like they were stronger than the people who were Gone."

"So why was what Nate did different?"

"Because it made Father John look—" I pause, and search for the right word. "Weak. No, not weak. *Fallible.* It made him look fallible."

"How so?" asks Agent Carlyle.

"Most of the Legion believed that Father John was a genuine Prophet," I say. "They truly believed he had a direct connection to The Lord, that they spoke with one voice. So when Father John announced that Nate had been selected to be the new Centurion, and Nate refused, that only left two options. Either The Lord was wrong—"

"Or Father John was," says Doctor Hernandez.

I nod, as Agent Carlyle smiles at me. "There were some people—Amos, Jacob, Luke, and probably a few others—who would have been more likely to believe that it was The Lord who had got it wrong. But not everyone. Not by any means."

"So you think he saw the possibility of people questioning him in the future?" asks Doctor Hernandez.

"I think so," I say. "And I think it made him realize that he had a problem in Nate."

"How do you mean?" asks Agent Carlyle.

"Because if Nate didn't stand up in front of everyone the next morning and say that he had changed his mind and Father John was right and he was proud to accept the honor of being a Centurion, it was going to look really bad."

"I think you're absolutely right," Agent Carlyle says. "So what happened?"

BEFORE

I'm dreaming about water, blue and warm and inviting, when something shakes me awake. The dream comes apart and drifts away. I open my eyes, and I'm lying on my bed. Someone is leaning over me in the darkness, their hand gripping my shoulder.

"Mom?" I ask, because my brain is still in that hazy place between being asleep and awake.

"It's Nate," whispers a voice. "Keep your voice down."

"Nate?" I whisper. "What are you doing here?"

"There's no time," he says. "They're going to come for me, and I have to be gone before they do."

I sit bolt upright, my mind clearing like a bucket of cold water has been thrown over me. I can just about see the outline of Nate perched on the edge of my bed.

"Gone?" I ask. "Where? What are you talking about?"

He shakes his head. "It doesn't matter. You're going to hear some things about me, Moonbeam. Things they're going to say I did. But you mustn't believe them, okay? Will you do that for me?"

Goose bumps break out along my arms. "What things?" I ask, and the desperate pleading in my voice makes my stomach churn. "What is this, Nate? *What's happening?*"

"I'm not who you think I am," he says. His voice is low and slightly choked, like the words are causing him pain. "But I never lied more than was necessary. Remember that, okay? Promise me you'll remember that."

I shake my head. "I don't...what..."

He takes hold of my shoulders. "*Listen to me*," he whispers. "You're a remarkable girl, Moonbeam. You're strong and smart and brave, and I'm proud to have been your friend. But I'm not going to be able to protect you anymore. So stay close to Father John. Don't let him forget that you're promised to him. Don't let *anyone* ever forget that. And stay away from Luke. He's dangerous."

I stare into the darkness. What does he mean, he won't be able to protect me anymore? I've never asked him to protect me from anything.

"You're scaring me, Nate," I say.

"I know, and I'm sorry. But I need you to listen to me. There isn't much time."

My heart is racing in my chest, but I try to force it to slow down, to not let panic overwhelm me. "I'm listening."

"Good." He presses two objects into my hand. "Take these. Hide them somewhere nobody will find them."

I reach for the flashlight on my bedside table, but he grabs my hand and holds it tight.

"No lights. I don't think they know I've left my room, but I can't be sure."

He lets go of my hand, and I run my fingers over the objects.

One of them is smooth and small and rectangular, the other feels like a plastic bag with something sharp inside.

"What are they?" I ask.

"In the bag is a skeleton key," says Nate. "It will open any door in the entire Base. *Any door*, Moonbeam. Do you understand what I'm telling you?"

An image fills my mind: the metal door in the basement of the Big House, behind which the guns are kept.

"I understand," I say.

"The other thing is a cell phone," says Nate, and I gasp in the darkness. I didn't mean to, and he urgently shushes me, but I couldn't help it. Phones are *completely forbidden*. The only one in the entire Base, at least as far as I know, is locked inside a box in the Big House, and it has been used only twice that I can remember: once to call an ambulance after Amber was bitten by a diamondback, and once to get the power restored after some vicious Servant of the Serpent cut the electricity cable out near the highway.

"Nate, why are you—"

"*Listen*," he says. "It's turned off, and you need to keep it that way unless things gets bad. I mean *really* bad. But if they do, press the green button to turn it on and hold down one. There's a number stored in its memory."

"What number?"

He shakes his head. "Don't use it unless you absolutely have to. There are things happening outside that I don't want to jeopardize, but I won't leave you on your own with no way of calling for help. I *can't*."

"Nate..."

"I have to go." Then his hands are holding my face. Under normal circumstances this would either freeze me as solid as a statue or reduce me to a dribble of putty, but these aren't normal circumstances. I'm shaking with rising panic, and my mind is flooded with questions. A single, desperate thought pounds the inside of my head.

Please don't leave me. Not you too. Please.

"I know you have doubts," he whispers. "You hide them well, but I know they're there. Listen to them, Moonbeam. Put your Faith in yourself, in your own eyes and your own mind. Don't trust anyone."

"Nate…"

He hauls me into a tight hug. "It's going to be okay," he says. "I promise."

My head rests against his chest, my body stiff, my arms hanging uselessly at my sides. There are a million things I want to say to him, but I can think of only a single one.

"Don't go," I whisper.

He squeezes me tightly, and his lips brush my forehead. Then his arms unwrap from around me. I hear the faint creak of my door opening and closing, the metallic click of the padlock being fixed into place, and I'm in the dark once again.

Alone.

AFTER

"Was he gone in the morning?" asks Agent Carlyle.

I nod. "He was. The Centurions woke us at dawn and told us all to gather in the yard. By the time we got there, Father John was already waiting on the Chapel steps. He looked furious."

"What did he say?"

"He told us Nate was an Outsider spy," I say. "That he had been working against the Legion since the day he arrived. He told us we were all idiots, that we had smiled and laughed and joked with a Servant of the Serpent who had been planning to murder us all in our beds while we slept. He said that he had seen through Nate immediately and had been waiting for us to do the same, waiting for a single one of us to have the brains and the Faith to see the truth, but that he had been forced to take action himself because we were all too blind and weak and stupid. He told us we had failed the Legion, had failed The Lord Himself, and that he was disgusted and disappointed with every single one of us."

RIGHTLY SO! I TOLD NOTHI—

I push Father John's voice away, hard, and it falls silent. Some distant part of me marvels at how much easier it has become to shut him up.

"Did you believe him?" asks Doctor Hernandez.

"I'm not sure," I say. "He clearly suspected something when Nate refused to be a Centurion, but whether or not he really had doubts about him before then, I don't know. Why would he have chosen Nate to be a Centurion if he didn't think he was True?"

"It might have been a test," says Doctor Hernandez. "A way to find out for sure about Nate, one way or the other."

"I guess. It made him look really bad though, Nate refusing his order in front of everyone. I don't know if that would have been worth finding out whether he was loyal or not."

"So what do you think was the truth?" asks Agent Carlyle. "Why do you think Nate did what he did?"

I shrug. "I don't know. I thought about it a lot in the days after he disappeared. For a while, I thought it was the idea of being a Centurion that spooked him, that he didn't want the responsibility. But when I thought about what he said to me in my room on the night he left, about things happening outside that he didn't want to jeopardize, and the cell phone and the key, I ended up thinking that maybe Father John was right. He pretty much had to make Nate sound as bad and False and dangerous as possible once he was Gone, and even though I don't believe Nate meant to hurt anyone, not for a second, that doesn't mean he wasn't a spy. But if he *was*, I don't know why he didn't just say yes to being a Centurion. It would have got him as close to Father John as anybody."

"Maybe he thought that closeness would mean a higher chance of being discovered," says Agent Carlyle. "Or maybe he couldn't face what he would have had to do if he said yes. Punishing people, hurting them, locking them in boxes. Maybe that was too much for him."

"I don't suppose you know who he really was?" I ask.

He shakes his head. "I don't know anything about Nate Childress. I'm sorry."

"Would you tell me if you did?" I ask, even though I already know the answer.

"No," he says. "Not if I wasn't allowed to."

"I guess that's honest, at least. Does that mean I shouldn't believe you don't know anything about my mother?"

Agent Carlyle's smile falters. "That's not what I—"

"It's fine," I say. "Forget it."

Doctor Hernandez glances back and forth between us, a frown of concern on his face. Agent Carlyle stares at me, then nods. I don't know what his gesture is supposed to mean. That I'm right not to believe anything they say? Or that I'm wrong, and he's telling me that I *can* trust him?

"So there was no sign of Nate?" asks Agent Carlyle. "The next morning, I mean?"

I shake my head. "They found a pair of bolt cutters by the southwest corner of the fence. There was a hole in the wire, and he was Gone. Amos went out looking for him in the pickup, in case he was hitchhiking down the highway, but nobody was surprised when he got home and told us he hadn't found him. I guess it's pretty easy to disappear in the desert."

Agent Carlyle nods. "It is."

"So that was that," I say. "The whole Legion got called into the Chapel, and Father John screamed at us for hours, telling us we had lost sight of the True Path, that our Faith was bullshit, that we were weak and stupid and that none of us deserved to Ascend. Lots of people were in tears by the time he was done."

"But not you."

I smile. "No. I thought about what Nate told me, about what my mom said when they Banished her, and I watched Father John scream and rant and froth at the mouth, and I saw him for what he was. What he *always* was."

"And what was that?" asks Doctor Hernandez.

"A man," I say. "A little cleverer than most, maybe, and blessed with a way with words. Not The Lord Himself, not even his messenger. Just a man, as vain and greedy and angry as any other."

He smiles at me. "I've never heard you talk about Father John like that before."

"It's hard," I say. "It feels wrong, even now. For a long time I was sure that even thinking a bad thought about him would see me spend eternity in Hell."

"But you don't believe that anymore?"

I shake my head. "I don't believe that anymore."

There you go, says the voice in the back of my head. *Well done. Tell the truth and shame the Devil.*

The truth.

It felt weird to say all that about Father John out loud, but that's what it is.

The truth.

And just like that, I feel lighter. It's like a weight has been lifted from my shoulders, like at least *some* of Father John's poison has been drawn out of my soul, making me feel better than I have in as long as I can remember.

"Did you stop believing when Nate left?" asks Doctor Hernandez.

I shake my head. "That was the final straw. But it goes back a lot further than that."

"To what happened to your mother?" he asks. "I'm sorry. I know you don't like to—"

"It's fine," I say. "I wasn't allowed to talk about her for a long time. I wasn't even supposed to think about her. But now, it's okay. And yeah, what happened to her was part of it. A big part. Although everything is sort of messed up with everything else, because it wasn't Father John I lost Faith in when my mom was Banished, not right away. I know it must sound bad, but I lost Faith in her. It made me understand that I could never automatically trust what any person said or did, no matter who they are or how much they mean to you. It made me realize that everyone is capable of being deceitful, even to the people they claim to love. It made me see that everyone lies."

"That's a hard lesson," says Agent Carlyle. "Finding out that your parents aren't perfect, that they're as flawed as anyone else."

"Agreed," says Doctor Hernandez. "That's never easy."

I nod.

"Most people don't learn it the same way you did, in all fairness," says Agent Carlyle. "Normally it's their mom getting a DUI or their dad having an affair with his secretary."

I frown. "An affair is when you have sex with someone who isn't the person you're supposed to have sex with?"

Agent Carlyle colors pale pink, and I realize he's not comfortable talking about this with me.

"Sorry," I say. "I didn't mean to embarrass you."

"It's okay," he says.

"It's absolutely fine," says Doctor Hernandez. "Although I don't think it's necessarily an appropriate topic for discussion."

"I'm not so sure about that," says Agent Carlyle. "It's a valid question, and she needs to start understanding the real world. Otherwise how is she going to cope when she gets out of here?"

"There's a process—"

Agent Carlyle and I groan in unison. For a millisecond, Doctor Hernandez looks absolutely furious, but the moment quickly passes, and he breaks into a smile.

"Fine," he says. "Go ahead and answer her question. Just be careful."

Stop talking about me like I'm not sitting here. I thought we were past that.

"I'm not a doll," I say. "I'm not going to break."

Agent Carlyle nods. "Having sex with someone other than a person you've committed to is called infidelity, although most people call it cheating," he says. "An affair is different. It's still cheating, but it's when someone has an ongoing relationship with someone who isn't the person they committed to and keeps it a secret."

"Is it worse?" I ask.

"Most people tend to think so," he says. "Plenty of people have forgiven their partner for having sex with someone else, but I don't know anyone who has forgiven an affair."

"Have you ever had one?"

Agent Carlyle's eyes widen, and the color in his cheeks darkens from pale pink to crimson. "*That* definitely takes us into inappropriate territory."

"Does it?" asks Doctor Hernandez, a mischievous grin on his face. "Thanks for letting us know where the line is. I'm sure Moonbeam and I are very grateful."

Agent Carlyle shakes his head, but there's a big smile on his face. "Let's get back on track, shall we?"

I meet their smiles with one of my own. "Sure."

"The day after Nate Childress left," he says, "what happened after you were all lectured in the chapel?"

"Everyone went to work," I say. "Father John ordered double shifts, and we got put on punishment rations for a week."

"What did that mean?"

"Two slices of bread."

"For each meal?"

I shake my head. "Each day."

"Each *day*?"

I nod.

He stares at me with narrowed eyes, like he's trying to work out whether I'm being serious. "Did Father John eat the same as the rest of you?"

What do you think? After everything I've told you about him, do you really still need to ask?

"Punishment rations didn't apply to him," I say. "Or to the Centurions."

"What about his wives?"

I nod.

"The children? *His* children?"

I nod again.

Agent Carlyle takes a deep breath.

"I'm sorry," I say. "I'm not trying to upset you. I'm just answering your questions."

He shakes his head. "It's not you, Moonbeam. I just can't...I mean, I just...Jesus. Okay. What did you do with the things Nate gave you?"

"I hid them."

"Where?"

"There was a loose floorboard under my bed. I put the phone and the key underneath it."

"Did anyone ever find them?"

"No."

"Did you ever use them?"

Careful, whispers the voice in the back of my head. "I used them both once," I say.

"Do you want to tell us about that?" asks Doctor Hernandez.

I shake my head. "Not right now," I say. "If that's okay?"

"That's fine," he says. "It feels like everyone could use some time to process the events of the last couple of days, so we've canceled this afternoon's SSI. Enjoy your lunch and get some rest."

"I don't sleep very well at night," I say. "Maybe I'll have better luck in the afternoon."

Doctor Hernandez smiles. "Fingers crossed."

Nurse Harrow gives me her usual smile before she pulls my door shut and locks it.

A shaft of late morning sunlight is blazing through my room's window. The sun is too high and the window is too small for it to reach all the way down to the floor, but if I stand on my tiptoes next to the door, I can angle my face up into the warm beam. I stand like that for a while, until the light moves out of my reach. I suppose I could stand on my chair, but that seems like it would be a weird thing to do.

Instead, I sit down at the desk, slide a sheet of paper off the pile, and pick up a thick blue crayon.

For it shall come to pass, when the End Times are upon us and The Lord Calls His Faithful Home, a Battle such as the human realm has never known. The Servants of the Serpent shall reveal themselves, and those men and women of Faith who walk the True Path shall be Called to serve the Glory of the Lord.

THOSE WHO ARE TRUE, WHO STAND IN THE FACE OF EVIL AND RAISE UP THEIR ARMS FOR THE LORD, SHALL ASCEND TO SIT AT HIS RIGHT HAND FOR ALL ETERNITY, to journey the Heavens in the blazing trails of comets, to bask forever in the Glorious Benevolence of The Lord.

THOSE WHO ARE FALSE, WHOSE FAITH IS A LIE, SHALL BE CAST INTO THE PITS OF HELL AND CRAWL THROUGH FIRE FOR ALL TIME, for they have proven themselves Heretics, unworthy of the favor of The Lord. We shall never speak of them again, nor allow them to enter our minds. They will be Gone, and they will not be mourned.

ON THE GLORIOUS FINAL DAY, ALL TRUTH WILL BE REVEALED, AND ALL MEN AND WOMEN WILL PROVE THE MEASURE OF THEIR FAITH. On that Glorious Final Day, those who are True will leave this dark realm and Ascend into the light. On that Glorious Final Day, those who walk the True Path will rejoice.

The Lord is Good.

AFTER

Nurse Harrow arrives with my breakfast at exactly nine o'clock—it's oatmeal this morning, with maple syrup and bananas and a plastic cup of bright pink grapefruit juice—and tells me that my session with Doctor Hernandez has been delayed. I ask her why, and she tells me she doesn't know. I ask her for how long, and she tells me she doesn't know, but that she'll come and get me when it's time.

She doesn't smile as she leaves. She *always* smiles.

I eat my breakfast more slowly than usual, then walk back and forth across my room for a little while because I'm not sure what I'm supposed to do. Doctor Hernandez made such a big deal about routine that I guess it must take something serious to make him change all the schedules.

Maybe the other sessions are carrying on as normal, whispers the voice in the back of my head. *Maybe it's only yours that has been postponed.*

Anxiety creeps into my chest, and I try my best to push it away. Whatever is going on might have absolutely nothing to do with me.

Then again, it might. It just might.

I grimace and keep pacing. From the door, around the desk toward the curtain hanging next to the toilet, along the short wall beneath the window, past my bed and back to the door, counting in my head as I go. It takes twelve seconds to walk around my room.

I look at the clock above the door. 9:48.

I sit down at my desk and try to draw, but nothing happens. Even my usual picture, the one I can literally draw without thinking, won't come. I cover two sheets of paper with jumbles of thick multicolored lines, the kind of scribbles a baby would do, then get up and start walking again. I try to lose myself in the laps, forcing myself not to count them, and after what feels like hours, I look at the clock again.

10:03.

A few days ago—I've no idea how many—I asked Nurse Harrow if I could have a TV in my room, to help fill the hours that stretch out in the afternoons after SSI. She said she would ask, but hasn't mentioned it since, so I guess that isn't happening. Usually, if I tell her that I want to go outside, she comes and gets me at a particular time and stands guard while I walk around a small paved courtyard. There's no wire on the tops of the walls, because I guess they don't want the place to look like a prison, but the walls are really high and smooth, and there's nothing in the courtyard except a small bench on one side. Sometimes I go out, but most days I don't. I draw and write and think and walk.

This is different. This is time that is allocated, that I *should* be somewhere, but I'm not. It feels all wrong.

I lie down on my bed and try to go back to sleep. I'm *always* tired, my bones heavy, my mind thick and sluggish, but I find no peace when I close my eyes; instead, my brain summons up images it knows I don't want to see.

Jacob Reynolds on his knees, his jeans soaked through.

Luke, with the hacksaw in his hand and terrible devotion in his eyes.

Nate and my mom and Father John. I open my eyes and check the clock. 10:11.

I check it again. 10:11.

Again.

10:12.

I've been staring at the clock for eighty-seven minutes when I hear the lock turn. I sit up as Nurse Harrow pushes open my door.

She still isn't smiling.

"They're ready for you, Moonbeam," she says.

I jump up off the bed. "Let's go."

We walk the familiar route down the corridors that leads to Interview Room 1. She knocks on the door before she opens it, and I frown, because she normally lets me in to wait for Doctor Hernandez and Agent Carlyle. As she steps out of the way, I see the two men are already in their usual chairs behind the desk.

They both turn their heads as I step into the room, and I instantly know that something is wrong. Agent Carlyle is mostly convincing in projecting his normal disposition, but Doctor Hernandez's eyes are red and sunken, as though he hasn't been to bed, and his face is pale gray.

I freeze. "What's going on? What's happened?"

"Come on in, Moonbeam," says Agent Carlyle. "Thank you, Nurse."

The door thuds shut behind me. I don't shift my gaze from the two faces in front of me.

"Take a seat, Moonbeam," says Doctor Hernandez.

I don't move.

"Take a seat," he repeats, and a sliver of fear lodges in my heart because it sounds like he's on the verge of tears.

I walk very slowly across the room and curl myself into my usual position at the end of the red sofa. "What's going on?"

The two men glance at each other. My stomach twists into a tight knot.

"Tell me," I say, the tremor in my voice clearly audible. "Please?"

Not her. Please don't let something have happened to her.

Doctor Hernandez nods. "There's something you need to know, Moonbeam." He pauses. "It's going to be upsetting for you to hear it, and I'm—"

"Is it my mom?" I ask.

"It's not your mother," says Doctor Hernandez. "We have no new information on her."

My stomach unclenches slightly. I stare at them. "Then what is it?"

"As I said, it's something that's going to be upsetting for you to hear," says Doctor Hernandez. "My colleagues and I have discussed it, and my—our—belief is that you're strong enough to handle it. What do you think?"

I don't say anything. How am I possibly supposed to answer that?

"I'm going to take that as a yes," says Doctor Hernandez. "Moonbeam, I need you to take a deep breath, and I need you to listen carefully to—"

"Luke's dead," says Agent Carlyle, his eyes fixed on mine. "He died last night. I'm sorry."

Doctor Hernandez gives him a furious glare, but Agent Carlyle doesn't even flinch; he simply stares at me, his expression steady. I focus on him as my mind temporarily struggles to form rational thought.

"I don't…" I manage. "I…what happened?"

"He committed suicide," says Doctor Hernandez softly. "In his room."

"How?" My voice is shaking.

"The details are—"

"Tell me what he did," I say.

"He bit his wrists open," says Agent Carlyle. He speaks very slowly. Deliberately. "He was taken to the infirmary, but he'd lost a lot of blood. They weren't able to revive him."

I stare at him. My head swims, and my stomach lurches, and my skin feels hot and prickly.

No.

What I told them yesterday rises into my mind, how I didn't think anything could be done to help Luke. I'd wanted to be wrong. I really had.

But I'd known I wasn't.

Broken, whispers the voice. *That's what you said he was. Broken.*

A lump appears in my throat. I was scared of Luke, and I hated him for such a long time, but I would never, *ever* have wished this on him, not this or anything close to it. My mind races into overdrive, conjuring a picture of Luke in the darkness of his room, tears streaming down his blood-smeared face as he digs his teeth into his own flesh.

"Can I have a glass of water?" I ask.

Agent Carlyle sits forward and fills a plastic cup from the jug that sits on the table. I take it with trembling hands and drink it in one go.

"I understand this must be extremely difficult," says Doctor Hernandez. "But you have to…Moonbeam? What is it?"

I'm not looking at him anymore. I'm looking at Agent Carlyle because his face has changed. The corners of his mouth have turned downward, and there's a dark shimmer in his eyes.

"There's something you're not telling me," I say. "Isn't there?"

Doctor Hernandez shakes his head. "I don't think—"

"Tell me," I insist. "I need to know."

"I don't think it's a suitable—"

"Luke wrote something on the floor before he lost consciousness," says Agent Carlyle. "Wrote it with his own blood."

My head swims. "What did he write?"

Agent Carlyle speaks quietly. "*I Ascend*. He wrote *I Ascend*."

Silence fills the room. The two men stare at me with obvious concern, but I'm not really looking at them anymore because I'm somewhere else.

I can smell salt and fresh paint and cut grass. I can feel a warm breeze on my face. I can hear her calling my name.

Stay with me, whispers the voice in the back of my head. *Stay right here. You can do this.*

I force myself to meet Doctor Hernandez's gaze. "Have you told my Brothers and Sisters?"

"Yes," he answers. "We had to move a lot of sessions around, but they all know what's happened. I'm sorry if you—"

"How did they react?"

He pauses. "We saw a range of responses."

"Like what?"

"Shock," he says. "Distress. Grief. Resignation."

"Happiness?" I ask.

He frowns. "In one or two cases," he says. "That doesn't surprise you?"

I shake my head.

"Why not?"

"Because lots of them hated him," I say. "Or were scared of him. Or both. And…"

Doctor Hernandez narrows his eyes. "And?"

"Because he's free."

"He's dead," says Agent Carlyle.

I shake my head again. "He *Ascended*. Try to see it from their perspective. Everything that Father John predicted has happened— the End Times, the Final Battle with the Government, the fire and blood and death. All of it. And now they're being held prisoner by the exact enemy he warned them about time and time again. So was Luke, but he got away. Some of them will think he's a hero."

Agent Carlyle shakes his head. "That's bullshit."

I wish it was.

I shrug. "Believe what you want."

"They don't know the details of Luke's death," says Doctor Hernandez. "We feel it would be too distressing for them. In all honesty, I had the same concern about telling you."

"I didn't," says Agent Carlyle. "I knew you could handle it."

Doctor Hernandez shoots him a sharp look. "With that in mind, I'm asking you to be very aware of what you say in front of the others. There's no such thing as too careful in a situation like this."

Amen to that.

"Are you canceling SSI again this afternoon?" I ask.

"That's the current plan."

"Don't."

"You don't think we should?"

"No," I say. "If you lock everyone in their rooms and stop them from talking about what happened to Luke, you're only going to reinforce their belief that they shouldn't trust anyone from Outside. You'll be doing Father John's work for him."

"We've considered that outcome," says Doctor Hernandez.

"It's something I'd like to talk to you about, as a matter of fact. It's partly why we decided to let you know about Luke last."

I frown. "Okay."

"You're now the oldest surviving member of the Lord's Legion," he says. "And I don't know whether you are aware of this or not, but your brothers and sisters look up to you. They trust you."

"They said that?" I ask.

"You're surprised?"

"I am," I say. "By the end, a lot of people were keeping their distance. I wouldn't have thought the children heard many nice things being said about me."

"Because of your friendship with Nate?" asks Agent Carlyle.

I nod. "And because of what happened with my mom. I wasn't exactly the most popular member of the Legion."

"I'm sure that was hard," says Doctor Hernandez. "Although I would argue it relates directly to what we're talking about. I would suggest that the isolation you felt in the last months before the fire, the sense of removal that came from being mistrusted and having nobody to talk to, allowed you to look at what was happening inside the Legion with an objectivity that your brothers and sisters, especially the younger ones, have never had."

"You're saying that I understood more than the others?"

"In a way, yes."

"I didn't know the fire was going to happen though."

"Not specifically," says Doctor Hernandez. "But you had started to consider the possibility of an existence outside the base, outside the Legion itself. You had progressed to the point where you were willing to question everything you had been told by Father John, to question the man himself, even though you were clever enough to do so silently. And I'll do you one better: I think he knew it."

"What?"

"I think Father John saw you as a threat," he says. "You said yourself that your mother being banished and your friendship with Nate put a target on your back, and you suspected that pairing you for combat training with Lucy was a test, a way to see where your loyalties really were. Like asking Nate to be a Centurion."

"Father John never did anything to me," I say. "If I was such a danger to him, why didn't he do anything about it?"

"Maybe he was planning to," he says. "Maybe he never got the chance."

"Because of the fire." Doctor Hernandez nods.

"I was nobody," I say. "I was an average member of the Legion. I'm nothing special."

He smiles. "I disagree. You have been through an ordeal that many people would never have been able to recover from, and I know it's been a struggle. That it's *still* a struggle. But you have displayed incredible resilience and courage, and you will have to trust me when I tell you that your brothers and sisters believe they can rely on you, and that you will look after them. Rainbow told one of my colleagues that she knows you won't let anything bad happen to her."

My heart swells with pride, and I blink back tears. "She said that?"

"She did," says Agent Carlyle. "I saw the tape."

I attempt a smile, but my insides are churning because I'm trying to hold it together, to not start crying on the red sofa, so I'm sure it comes out as a scowl that I'm glad I can't see.

"That's good," I say, my voice low and choked. "I never knew if…that's really good."

"They knew," says Doctor Hernandez.

"I always tried to—"

"Believe me," he says. "They knew."

I don't know what to say. I always did my best to look after my younger Brothers and Sisters, to try and show them a little kindness and a little love that didn't come with Father John's conditions attached to it, but I honestly never knew if they noticed.

I'm really glad they did.

"I want to ask for your help, Moonbeam," says Doctor Hernandez. "But I want to be entirely clear about what I mean, because we don't want to manipulate you or your fellow survivors in any way, and we have no intention of telling anybody how they should think or feel."

"They've all had more than enough of that," says Agent Carlyle.

"So what are you asking me to do?"

"Look after them," says Doctor Hernandez. "Your brothers and sisters. Be the person you are, the person they know and trust, and help them get through this. Help them survive. Can you do that?"

Yes, whispers the voice in the back of my head. *You can. And you must. It's too late for Luke, but you owe the rest of them that much.*

"I'll try," I say.

"Thank you," he says. "I wouldn't usually ask someone at this stage of their process to take on such a responsibility, but Luke's death has made it very clear that this remains an extremely volatile situation. I don't believe any of your brothers and sisters are at the same level of risk as he was, but—"

"There's no such thing as too careful," I say.

He nods.

"So what happens now?" I ask. "Do I go back to my room and wait for SSI?"

"That's up to you," says Doctor Hernandez. "Do you feel like talking this morning? I totally understand if you don't, but if you do, we're more than ready to listen."

I consider this. When I first arrived in this place, I would have jumped at the chance to go back to my room without having to talk about myself or the Legion or anything else. But I'm not sure that's still how I feel.

There has been no great epiphany, or at least, not one that I noticed. It's not like there was a moment when all my fears and doubts were hanging around my neck, dragging me down and filling my dreams with terror, and then another moment when all of that stuff was suddenly gone and my mind was light and clear. That stuff *isn't* gone—none of it. But if someone asked me and I was somehow compelled to tell the truth, I would have to admit that talking to Doctor Hernandez and Agent Carlyle about my life before the fire has made me feel better. Maybe only a little, and some days even less than that, but better nonetheless. And that isn't nothing.

It really isn't.

"What were we talking about yesterday?" I ask. "I honestly can't remember."

"About Nate," says Agent Carlyle. "About when he left."

I frown. "Right," I say. "Then the next part is mostly about Luke."

"That's fine," says Doctor Hernandez quickly. "You don't have to—"

"It's okay," I say. "It's the last story I have to tell about him. I guess it's sort of fitting."

Well, second to last. But I still haven't decided whether I'm going to tell you the other one.

"If you're sure?" he asks. "We can stop at any point, like always."

"I'm not sure," I say. "But I'll try."

BEFORE

It's been two days since Nate disappeared, and Father John's Sunday sermon is really, really angry.

They're always about the End Times and the Final Battle and the sacrifices and hardships we will have to endure to be victorious over the Servants of the Serpent, but this one *drips* with blood. He tells us how the Governments maintain their Satanic power by pulling unborn babies from the bellies of Faithful women and eating them; how they use alcohol and drugs to tear people away from the True Path, then lock them in underground rooms and pump gasoline into their stomachs until they burst. He tells us that these things—and others that are much, *much* worse—are what will happen to every single one of us if we don't fear the righteous wrath of The Lord and devote ourselves entirely to His Glory.

When he is finally finished, by which time most of my Brothers and Sisters are staring at him, ashen, and most of the children are quietly crying, he tells us that The Lord has given him the joyful news that Nate Childress—the Heretic, the Outsider spy, the lowest Servant of the Serpent—is dead. There are gasps inside the Chapel, along with a smattering of applause and a few exclamations of gratitude, as Father John smiles benevolently down at us all from the pulpit.

He *smiles*.

And I swear he looks right at me as he does.

I don't move a muscle. I stare straight back into those eyes I used to be afraid to meet, that I used to believe saw the True Path so clearly.

I don't believe that anymore.

And I don't believe that Nate is dead, not for a single second. I believe—I *know*—that he got away, that he escaped the Base and disappeared into the world Outside. Which is the one thing Father John can never, ever admit.

"Now that the ranks of our Legion have been purged and set firmly back on the True Path," he continues, "I can announce that The Lord has seen fit to reveal the real identity of His new Centurion, a man of undoubted Faith and devotion whose service will be loyal and True. It gives me no small pleasure to name Jacob Reynolds the Fourth Centurion of the Holy Church of the Lord's Legion. The Lord is Good."

"The Lord is Good," bellow my Brothers and Sisters, as they leap to their feet, clapping and cheering and hollering. Jacob stands, tears spilling down his permanently flushed cheeks, and bows his head toward the pulpit, where Father John dips his own in reply.

"Thank you, Father," he says, his voice cracking. "I will serve the Legion until my last breath."

"Do not thank me," says The Prophet. "Thank The Almighty

Lord, for it is Him who has Called you to His service. He does not make mistakes."

Jacob clasps his hands together and squeezes his eyes shut as his Brothers and Sisters surge down the aisle and along the pews to hug him and congratulate him and clap him on the back.

I watch and feel nothing. Not a thing.

I work in the gardens in the afternoon, hacking shallow trenches in the bone-dry ground that Joe Nelson will fill with seed. Sunday afternoons are usually a time for rest, but the entire Legion is still on punishment for not having seen through Nate before it was too late.

Across from me, Alice is watering the rows that were planted yesterday. She glances over at me every few minutes with what I'd like to think is concern, but might as easily be reproach. Either way, I don't meet her eye.

The sun beats down, and the hours pass, like they always do. I drink a bottle of water, refill it from the tap behind the Big House, and drink that as well, trying to stay cool but also trying to fill my stomach, which is growling with hunger. I ate one of my slices of bread for breakfast, and I'm keeping the other for dinner, which is so many hours from now that it might as well be next week.

I lose myself in the monotony of the task, in the steady drumbeat of the hoe's metal head on the hard ground. At some point, my brain shifts into neutral, and for the first time in days, I don't think about Nate or my mom or Luke or Father John.

I don't think about anything at all.

When the Chapel bell rings to signal the end of the working day, I carry the hoe over to the tap and scrub its metal head until it gleams. Putting tools away dirty is a punishable offense at the best of times; in the poisonous atmosphere that is currently suffocating the Base, it would probably be enough to get me a night or two in a box.

I head across the yard and toward the supply shed at the end of the row, where the hoe needs to be hung on exactly the right hook. Alice follows behind me with a half-full sack of seed in her arms, but she makes no effort to close the distance and walk alongside me. It would be nice to believe that she's too tired to speed up or too deep in her own thoughts, but I know she's avoiding me. Pretty much *everyone* is avoiding me, because I was close to Nate and he turned out to be a Heretic, just like my mom.

Part of me wants to turn around and scream at Alice until she understands that it's not fair to blame me for what other people did, that it's not fair for anyone to blame me, including Father John himself. But I don't.

Of course I don't.

A thud echoes out from somewhere up ahead, loud and heavy enough to rattle the walls and roofs of the ramshackle outbuildings. It's followed by a strangled scream that cuts off suddenly, as if whoever made that high-pitched noise has had the tongue cut from their mouth. Then me and Alice and everyone else who was trudging toward the sheds are running, our feet kicking up clouds of dust until we reach the big building in the middle of the row, the one where the tractor is kept, and every one of us stops.

On his knees in the middle of the shed is Jacob Reynolds, his eyes wide with terror, his crotch soaking wet. Standing behind him, pressing a hacksaw against the flabby flesh of his throat, is Luke. I barely recognize him: his face is dark crimson, his mouth is working silently—as though he's talking to himself or praying or both—and his eyes are wild and gleaming with fire. He sees us arrive and pushes the hacksaw deeper as he takes half a step back.

Jacob lets out a gasping sob that sounds like the last breath of a drowning man.

"Stay back!" bellows Luke, his eyes darting left and right like a cornered animal's. "I'll cut his throat. I swear it!"

"Luke," says Alice, her voice soft and soothing. "It's okay, Luke. Everything's okay. Just put down the saw."

I almost laugh out loud, because one look at Luke's face tells me that rational appeals to his better judgment are not going to work. For the time being, at least, he has completely lost his mind.

"Shut up," he growls. "Shut up, shut up, shut up, *shut up*! It's not fair, you hear me! *IT'S NOT FAIR!*"

"All right, Luke," says Alice, holding her empty hands toward him. "Just talk to me. What isn't fair? You can tell me."

Luke's face crumples as tears spill from his eyes. "I should be the Fourth Centurion," he says, his voice little more than a hoarse whisper. "It should be *me*. Nobody is more Faithful to the Legion than me, nobody more devoted to The Lord. But does The Prophet see it? No. He looks at me and sees nothing, and he picks this fat sack of trash instead."

Jacob whimpers, and I silently plead with him to stay quiet. Because I'm staring at Luke and I'm looking for something to make me believe that this is all for show, a bluff of violence that he wouldn't really carry out. But all I see is conviction, bright and shining.

All I see is *Faith*.

"Father John didn't appoint Jacob," says Alice. "The Lord Called him to serve. Or don't you believe that?"

"Don't you question me!" snarls Luke. "Don't you dare! You know what I'm talking about!"

"I don't know what you're talking about, Luke." Father John's voice rumbles like an earthquake as he walks into the shed, shaking the flimsy walls and silencing the small crowd that has gathered.

"So why don't you tell me? Do you doubt the Will of The Lord, or do you doubt that I am His messenger? Which is it?"

Luke's face pales, but the hacksaw doesn't move an inch. "Father," he says, his voice thick with misery. "How could you do this? How could you forsake me?"

Father John steps slowly through the crowd, his long hair fluttering in the breeze, his gaze steady.

"The fault here is yours, Luke," he says. "You have placed your own ambition above the Will of The Lord, which proves His wisdom in not choosing you for a Centurion of His Legion. Disappointment is a human weakness, my Brother, as is jealousy. And we are *all* human, you and I and everyone here, nothing more and nothing less. Your feelings can be understood, and they can even be forgiven, but this is not the way. This is not The Lord's justice, and this is not the True Path. If you search your heart, search it *honestly*, you will see that I speak the truth."

Luke stares at Father John with eyes full of tears, then lets out a huge, awful sob that shakes his entire body. He removes the hacksaw from Jacob's throat, takes an uncertain, staggering step backward, and sinks to his knees with his head lowered.

Jacob scrambles across the ground on his hands and knees until he reaches The Prophet's feet. "Thank you, Father," he gasps. "Oh, thank you. The Lord is Good."

Father John looks down at him, and disgust flickers across his face. "It's all right, Brother. Everything is going to be all right."

"I want him put in a box," splutters Jacob, his face reddening. "I want him locked away until he forgets what daylight looks like."

Father John goes very still. "*You want?*" he growls. "You are a Centurion of the Lord's Legion who just pissed himself on his knees, and you would tell me of the things *you want*? Get out of my sight, and pray to The Lord for His mercy. Pray harder than you have ever prayed that He might forgive this terrible failure."

Jacob stares up at The Prophet, his eyes wide with shock. "Father, I—"

"*GO!*" roars Father John. "*NOW, WHILE YOU CAN STILL WALK!*"

Jacob stumbles to his feet, pushes through the crowd, and staggers out of the shed. Some of my Brothers and Sisters turn to watch him go, but I keep my eyes locked on Father John. His face is like thunder, dark and full of danger.

"Luke," he says. "Stand and face me."

Luke gets up, his face a mess of tear tracks and bubbling snot. He lets the hacksaw drop from his fingers and stares at the ground.

"The Lord is Good," says Father John. "Get yourself cleaned up and wait in the Chapel. You and I will speak on this tonight."

Luke raises his head, and the grateful adoration on his face makes me want to puke.

"Thank you, Father," he whispers. "The Lord is Good."

AFTER

Agent Carlyle and Doctor Hernandez stare silently at me.

"Luke stayed in the Chapel for two days," I say. "Father John spent most of the time in there with him. When he finally came out, things sort of went back to normal. But not really. And not for long."

"That poor boy," says Doctor Hernandez quietly.

"What did Jacob Reynolds do?" asks Agent Carlyle.

"He tried to pretend like nothing had happened," I say. "He got on with being a Centurion, marching around the Base and issuing orders and giving out punishments. But everyone knew what Luke had done to him, and nobody forgot."

"Do you think that's why he tried to make an example of you in the last training session?" asks Doctor Hernandez. "To try and regain some of the respect he had lost?"

I shrug. "Maybe. He was like that before Luke attacked him though."

"Like what?"

"A bully," I say. "A piece of shit."

Doctor Hernandez frowns as Agent Carlyle grins. My face flushes because I don't usually call people things like that. Not out loud, at least.

"Call them like you see them," says Agent Carlyle.

I smile at him and nod.

"So Father John sided with Luke," says Doctor Hernandez. "And he humiliated Jacob, but let him carry on as a Centurion. Why do you think that was?"

I shrug. "He appointed Nate, and everyone saw that go wrong. He couldn't afford to have that happen again, so he had to stick with Jacob, even though I'm sure he already regretted choosing him."

"You're saying Father John chose him?" he asks. "As opposed to The Lord?"

"Father John chose him."

"You're sure of that?"

I nod. "I am."

He smiles at me and makes a quick note in one of his books. "You said everything went back to normal after that?"

"I said *sort of* went back to normal," I reply. "But I guess it didn't, not really. Things weren't the same."

"In what way?"

"It was tense. People were uneasy. Nobody said anything out loud, because nobody ever did, but you could tell, just by walking around the Base. It seemed like people were looking over their shoulders the whole time. Like they were scared."

"Of what?"

I shrug. "Everything. We worked double shifts, and

punishment rations got extended for another month, even though the Legion was supposedly back on the True Path. The Centurions were on the warpath, hauling people up for stuff that would barely have been noticed before Nate escaped and Luke did what he did to Jacob. And the punishments got worse. A *lot* worse. People were being beaten and whipped in the yard most days, for barely any reason."

"Where was John Parson while all this was happening?" Agent Carlyle asks.

"He sat on the porch of the Big House," I say. "Watching. Nobody dared meet his eye, not even Amos."

"What about Luke?" asks Doctor Hernandez.

"He spent almost all his time in the Chapel."

"Was that unusual?"

"People weren't sure what to make of it," I say. "He wouldn't talk to anyone apart from Father John. If you tried, he would look through you like you weren't there. He stopped working, despite the double shifts and the punishments, but nobody said anything, and the Centurions just seemed to ignore it."

"Do you think they were scared of him?" he asks. "After what happened to Jacob?"

"Maybe. Or maybe they weren't sure what Father John would do if they tried to put Luke on punishment. Either way, he shut himself in the Chapel, praying for hours on end, and after a day or two, everyone just left him alone."

"Do you think this was what caused the behaviors we witnessed in SSI?" asks Doctor Hernandez. "That Luke saw himself as the heir to Father John?"

"Not being appointed Centurion hurt him," I say. "It really did. His loyalty to the Legion was real, as was his love for Father John. But I don't know what would have happened without the fire. I don't know how he saw his future."

"Do you think—"

"We need to stop," says Agent Carlyle, and taps his watch. "If you're going to reinstate SSI and you want Moonbeam to have time to get something to eat before it starts."

I look at the clock above the door. 12:56.

"Absolutely," says Doctor Hernandez. "Moonbeam, are you—"

"I'm fine," I say, anticipating his question. "It'll be fine."

There's a dull ache in my stomach because I ate my lunch too quickly, but that's not why I'm last to arrive at SSI.

When we reached the door, I asked Nurse Harrow if we could stop in the corridor for a moment. She frowned and asked if I was okay, and I told her I wasn't, not really, because I didn't want to lie to her, but when she asked if she could get me anything, I shook my head. I needed a few seconds to gather my thoughts, to try to get my head around this changed situation, and my place in it.

I know what's going to be waiting for me inside the group therapy room, what Jeremiah and Rainbow and the others are going to want to talk about. Before I go in there, and before I say whatever it is I have to say to do what Agent Carlyle and Doctor Hernandez asked me to do, I take a second to think about Luke. I can't let myself grieve for him, not now; I need to keep what strength I have left for what I'm about to do. But what happened to him wasn't fair, and he didn't deserve it.

He was seventeen years old, and now he's dead.

Like Alice, whispers the voice in the back of my head. *And Agavé and Joe Nelson and all the others. Everyone is dead.*

Nurse Harrow frowns at me as I shake my head.

I'm still alive, I tell the voice. *And so are Honey and Lucy and Rainbow and the others. I have to help make sure they stay that way.*

I know that asking for my help was a huge display of trust by

Doctor Hernandez and Agent Carlyle, and I know they wouldn't have made the decision lightly. I'm grateful for it because I have to believe it means they think I'm making decent progress through Doctor Hernandez's process. He often says nice things to me, and he tells me I'm doing well when he wants me to keep talking, but I never really know whether to believe him.

This feels more tangible. This feels real. But it scares me too.

What I've been given is a chance at penance. It's my fault that my Brothers and Sisters are waiting for me inside the group therapy room instead of at the Base with their families, and I'll do anything I can to help them. Anything. That's not what scares me. What scares me is the prospect of finding out there's nothing I can do, nothing *anyone* can do. That they're beyond help, all thanks to me.

I nod that I'm ready to Nurse Harrow. She gives me a smaller, sadder version of her usual smile and opens the door. I step through it, and seventeen pairs of eyes turn toward me at the same time. "Hey," I say, hoping you can project calm without actually feeling it. "How's everyone doing today?"

"Luke Ascended," says Jeremiah. His eyes are bright, and there's a big smile on his face. "The Prophet Called him into the presence of The Lord. It'll be our turn soon."

My stomach churns. "Okay. Do you want to talk about that?"

Jeremiah nods eagerly, as do most of our Brothers and Sisters. Near the back of the room, Honey and Rainbow and a couple of others stay absolutely still, looks of disgust on their faces.

"Luke was the best one of us," says Jeremiah. "He was the most True. That's why he went first."

I sit down cross-legged in the middle of the floor and gesture for the rest of them to join me. They come willingly, even Honey and Rainbow, and arrange themselves into a circle, their eyes fixed on me. Several of them automatically hold hands with the person beside them.

"Is that what you all think?" I ask.

Most of them nod, their small faces earnest and serious. A few don't respond at all, and maybe half a dozen shake their heads. Of the dissenters, only Aurora is brave enough to actually speak up.

"I don't think Luke was the best," she says, her voice steady. "I think he was mean, and I don't think he Ascended. I think he's in Hell."

A shiver dances up my spine. Her eyes are full of determination, and my heart surges at the sight of it.

"You don't know anything," says Jeremiah, his voice rising. "You're just a stupid girl. Why don't you shut up?"

"That's enough," I say. "Everyone is allowed their own opinion."

"That's not an *opinion*," says Jeremiah, his voice high and trembling. "That's *Heresy*. Luke was our Brother, and he was Called Home by Father John, and she can't say he's in Hell. She isn't *allowed*."

Broken, whispers the voice in the back of my head.

I ignore it and focus all my attention on Jeremiah. He was born on the Base, both his parents and his older brother—his *biological* brother—died in the fire, and I remind myself that he's grieving, that he's a little boy whose entire world has fallen down around him. I tell myself to be patient with him.

With *all* of them.

"Is it important to you that Luke Ascended, Jeremiah?" I ask.

He frowns, like I've asked him the stupidest question in the history of questions. "Of course it is," he says.

"Why?"

"Because he's gone to sit at the side of The Lord," he says. "Like Father John promised."

And if you can believe that's what has happened to Luke, you can believe that's what happened to your parents and your brother.

"What do you think he's doing?" I ask.

"He's looking down on us right now," he says. "They all are."

"What do you want them to see?"

"That we wish we were there with them," he says, and I see tears in the corners of his eyes. "That we didn't want to be left here on our own. That we want to come too."

"Luke didn't go anywhere, Jeremiah," says Honey, her voice low. "Neither did Father John or anyone else. They're just dead."

I grimace as Jeremiah turns on her, his face flushing a deep, angry pink.

"You're a liar!" he screams. "Take it back!"

Honey shakes her head. "I won't."

Jeremiah jumps to his feet, his hands balling into fists. "I'll make you take it back!" he shouts. "I'll—"

"You won't do anything," I say. "Calm down, Jeremiah."

He looks at me, his eyes wide with outrage. "Didn't you hear her? What she said about The Prophet?"

"I heard what she said. I can see you're upset, and that's okay. But violence isn't the answer."

"If the Centurions were here they would—"

"What would they do?" I ask.

"They would beat her," says Jeremiah. The fervor in his eyes churns my stomach. "They would put her in a box until she promised not to say Heresy."

"Do you think that would be fair?" I ask.

He nods. "Definitely."

"Why?"

"Because that's what The Lord wants."

"How do you know that's what He wants?" asks Honey, taking the words out of my mouth.

"Because He told Father John." Jeremiah speaks each word really slowly, as though he's talking to someone stupid. "*And Father John told us.*"

"How do you know The Lord told Father John anything?" asks Honey.

"Because—"

"Because he said so," said Honey. "Exactly. But what if he was lying, Jeremiah? What then?"

"Why would Father John do that?" The innocent Faith shining on his face makes me want to go back in time to the fire and do what I did in the Big House all over again. "We're his Family. Why would he lie to us?"

"People lie," says Honey, her voice noticeably softer than before. "I'm sorry, Jeremiah. I didn't mean to upset you. But people lie."

There's a moment of pregnant silence, in which I genuinely don't know whether Jeremiah is going to launch himself at Honey or burst into tears. The rest of our Brothers and Sisters stare at me like they're waiting for me to do something. I want to tell them there's nothing I can do, that these are the conversations we need to have if any of us are going to move forward, but I don't know how to tell them that, so I don't say anything at all.

"I don't lie," says Rainbow thoughtfully. "I don't think it's very nice."

I let out an involuntary snort of laughter. My face fills with guilty heat, but the carefully considered seriousness in her voice sucker punched me, and the laugh was the only way my body knew how to process it.

Rainbow frowns at me in that frustrated way children do when they don't think they're being taken seriously. I wave a hand in her direction, trying to reassure her that I wasn't laughing at her, because I honestly wasn't. But then Honey starts to laugh, and so does Winter, and that sets me off again, and something gives way inside me—because what else are you supposed to do when the world has burned to ash, but you're still alive, still breathing, and there's still the prospect of a future, no matter how fragile and uncertain?

Three people laughing is more than enough to infect anyone within earshot, and soon almost everyone has joined in. Some are holding their sides and pressing their hands over their mouths, their cheeks turning pink, their eyes suddenly full of a joy that had seemed unimaginable ten seconds ago. Rainbow is still frowning, as though she isn't totally convinced we aren't laughing at her, but even Jeremiah manages the faintest of smiles, although I can't help but think it's more the result of Honey apologizing to him than anything close to genuine happiness.

But that's okay. It's a start.

And a possibility, faint and flickering, occurs to me for the first time since the fire: maybe things will turn out all right, at least for some of them.

Maybe.

A
F
T
E
R

The blue house. The smoking chimney. The green grass. The cliffs. The wide expanse of water. The two figures.

I draw and set the paper aside and grab a fresh sheet and draw the same thing again. The image doesn't require any conscious thought, which is just as well, because my mind is full of Luke.

Of all the awful things that happened because of Father John, a list that is long and full of horror, Luke's death—at this particular moment—feels like the very worst of them. My grown-up Brothers and Sisters *chose* to follow The Prophet, to trust him and believe in him and dedicate their lives to him, for their own reasons: genuine Faith, or desperation, or maybe just the need to be part of *something*, to be able to believe that life was more than merely what they could see and touch.

But Luke?

He *never* had a choice. His was made for him, before he was even born.

A memory surfaces. Luke when he was maybe ten or eleven, gangly and awkward, probably eighteen months after Father John arrived at the Base. He was sat near the southern edge of the yard writing numbers on the asphalt with a piece of chalk, like he was marking out a hopscotch grid. I walked across the yard and stopped behind him, reading the numbers over his shoulder.

21:1

19:11

21:8

12:9

20:10

1:5

He glanced up at me, smiled, then carried on writing. I stared at the numbers for a long time until I realized what I was looking at.

They're passages from the Bible. From the Book of Revelation.

I reach for a new sheet of paper as tears fill my eyes. I don't blink them back or wipe them away. I let them come because they're the least Luke deserves. That *all of them* deserve.

What chance did he ever have? With no parents to care for him and Father John as his surrogate father, whispering the end of the world into his ear?

Horizon told me once that if you beat a dog from the day it's born, it'll whimper and hide and look scared and cowed. But he said that eventually—and you won't ever know when it's coming—that same dog will bite. It'll bite because you've never given it a reason not to.

I push another page aside. The drawing is getting looser and looser; the house is now little more than an *X* in a square with a triangle on top, above grass that is green stab marks and water that is zigzag lines of blue.

I think about Luke, and Honey and Rainbow and the others, and Doctor Hernandez and Agent Carlyle, and I tell myself that all I want to do is help, that all I want to do is make things better.

Liar, whispers the voice in the back of my head, although it doesn't sound unkind. It sounds gentle.

I lower my head as fresh tears roll down my cheeks because I know it's right. I *am* lying, to myself—if all I really wanted to do was help, then I would have told Doctor Hernandez everything in our very first session, and to Hell with the consequences. But I didn't, and I still *haven't*, because I don't know what will happen to me if I do, and I'm scared to find out.

But...

What if something I haven't told them could have saved Luke? Some small detail that would have made Doctor Hernandez and his colleagues watch him even more closely or put him somewhere he couldn't have hurt himself?

No. No, no, no, no.

I can't think like that.

Nobody will ever know exactly why Luke did what he did because nobody is ever going to be able to ask him, unless it turns out that Father John was right all along.

I shiver, because *that* is a prospect I can't bear to think about. Not for a single second.

I start to draw again, trying to force myself to slow down and be more careful, to create something that looks like it might actually exist in the real world, and I think again about what Doctor Hernandez and Agent Carlyle asked me to do.

I'm grateful to them. I *am*.

Like with everything else that has happened since I woke up inside this gray place, I have to assume there's more going on than

I know. It's possible that their request is a calculated move, that they understand the way my brain works and can anticipate my responses and are allowing me the *illusion* of free will.

I don't think so though.

Doctor Hernandez's eyes were full of concern as he explained what they want me to do and why, which means he was either genuinely affected by Luke's death and what it might mean for the rest of the survivors or he's a horribly good actor.

There's no way for me to know which is true, but it doesn't really matter either way. Because I can't let this be about me anymore, about what I know and what I did and what will happen to me if anyone finds out.

My Brothers and Sisters are what's important.

They're what matter.

A
 F
  T
   E
    R

They smile when I tell them what Rainbow said, even though I know at least one of them will have been watching when she spoke.

"You did very well," says Doctor Hernandez. "You stayed calm, you encouraged discussion, and you didn't shut Jeremiah down when he started acting out. It was exactly what we were hoping for."

"I'm glad you're pleased," I say. "But I'm not doing it for you or for me. I'm doing it for them."

Agent Carlyle smiles at me.

"Of course," says Doctor Hernandez. "Can you tell me why?"

"Because there's going to be a day when they leave this place. And they're going to *see* with their own eyes that everything they know is wrong and that everything they were told was a lie. The ones who were born after the Purge only know about the real world secondhand."

"They'll be looked after," he says. "We're not going to abandon them. We'll help them every step of the way."

"I believe you," I say, and I genuinely do. "But when people they don't know start telling them what they've been brought up to believe is wrong, it makes it look like Father John was right about Outsiders."

"So you think it has to come from you?"

I shake my head. "I'm not saying that. I can see the progress they've already made, and I know some of them are starting to trust you and your colleagues. Do I think hearing the same things from me, or from Honey, will help? Yes. I think it will. But I honestly don't know how much good it will do. Their scars go really deep."

"You're trying," he says. "That's all you can do."

He's right, whispers the voice in the back of my head. *And it matters. It's not nothing.*

I nod.

"Was it what happened to the kids that made you start to doubt the Legion?" asks Agent Carlyle. "The thing with Luke and Honey, and what Jacob Reynolds did to Lucy?"

I shrug. "The thing with Honey was definitely part of it," I say. "But Jacob beating Lucy after training was only a day or two before the fire. My Faith had failed long before then."

"Can you remember what first made you question Father John?" he asks. "Was it your mother getting banished?"

I nod.

"Are you ready to talk about that?" asks Doctor Hernandez.

"No."

"Will you?"

"Yes."

"Why?"

"Because I need to."

BEFORE

The sky is low and gray as the Centurions escort me to the Big House.

My legs are trembling as I walk up the steps and onto the porch. Bear knocks on the door, and he and Horizon stand either side of me while we wait for someone to answer it. I ask them what's going on for probably the fiftieth time in the last two minutes, but neither of them answers and neither of them will look at me.

"Please," I say. "Tell me what's happening. Please."

Nothing.

"You have to come with us," was what Bear said. I was working in the gardens, although I wasn't really working, I was mostly daydreaming, and that's what I thought they had noticed when they came toward me. "Your mother has been called before Father John to answer for her sins."

I frowned at him. "What are you talking about? What sins?"

"Heresy," said Bear, and I felt my stomach turn.

Bella opens the front door, and I walk into the Big House on legs made of Jell-O, and I see my mom standing in the middle of the big living room. I shout her name because I'm really scared and nobody will tell me what's happening. She spins at the sound of my voice and gives me a look that I know well, the same look I saw when I fell off the car and broke my arm—the one she gives me when she wants me to be brave. Panic explodes through me, and I rush forward, desperate to throw myself against her, but Horizon takes a single giant stride and lifts me off the ground. I kick and thrash and scream, but he presses my arms to my sides and holds me tight.

"Don't make it worse," he whispers. "The Lord is Good."

"It's all right!" shouts my mom. "It's all right, my little Moon. Don't cry."

Horizon puts me down. He keeps his hands on my shoulders, but I don't think I could make myself move again. The look of fury on my mom's face, her cheeks red and her eyes blazing as she stares at Father John, has frozen me to the spot. The Prophet sits in the big armchair beneath the window with Angel and Lonestar standing silently on either side of him. Bella and Star and Agavé are perched on the staircase, their faces pinched and pale.

Everybody apart from me belongs to Father John. There's nobody here for my mom. I'm the only witness to whatever is about to happen.

There's no fear on my mom's face. Her mouth is set in a thin line as she stares at Father John, her gaze locked on his. My heart thunders in my chest, and my insides have shriveled to the size of a walnut. I'm shaking with fear because I don't understand this at all. I woke up this morning and had breakfast and went to the gardens and everything was totally normal, and now it's all been turned upside down.

"Do you deny the charges that have been brought against you?" asks Father John. His voice is low and deep and full of threat.

My mom doesn't respond. Doesn't move a muscle. She just stares at him.

He stares back for a long moment, then gives her a wide smile. "Let me repeat them for you, so that everything is perfectly clear, and The Lord's justice may be served in full. The first charge is Apostasy. How do you plead?"

Plead? First charge? Is this a trial?

"Not guilty," she says, in a voice like breaking ice.

"We found your journal," says Father John. He turns to Lonestar, who holds up a leather-bound book I've never seen before. "You admit this belongs to you?"

My mom gives the tiniest nod of her head.

"Excellent," says Father John. "It describes, in great detail, your deviation from the True Path. I will not read the passages aloud, as to do so would be to carry out the work of The Serpent, but it is safe to say they constitute a grotesque treachery against The Almighty Lord. Your own handwriting condemns you, clearly and utterly, so I will give you one more chance to admit your guilt. What do you say?"

My mom narrows her eyes. "You misunderstand," she says. "I cannot be guilty of Apostasy because it's impossible to abandon a Faith you never had."

Bella gasps with shock, and Agavé puts a comforting hand on her knee.

"So you admit that you are False?" asks Father John.

"I have no Faith in you," says my mom. "I never have, not for a single moment. I'll gladly admit that."

The Prophet smiles. "And so we reach the truth at last," he says. "Perhaps—"

"Father Patrick was a fool," growls my mom. "A harmless

dreamer who tried to serve his God the best way he knew how. But you? You're a snake-oil salesman. A vulture, preying on the weak and the desperate. You're *nothing*."

I gasp with shock. I can't help it because I don't think I've ever heard anyone speak to Father John like that, not even the Heretics who left during the Purge.

The Prophet's smile disappears. "Centurion?"

Angel frowns and glances at me. "Perhaps Moonbeam ought to—"

"Do as I command, Centurion."

"Yes, Father," says Angel, then steps forward and slams his hand across my mom's face. It's a slap rather than a punch, thank The Lord, but it still knocks her flat. Her head bounces off the floor, and I hear myself scream, and I try to run to her, but Horizon's fingers dig painfully into my shoulders, and my mom's eyes meet mine, and the message in them is exactly the same one that was whispered in my ear.

Don't make it worse.

"Pick her up," says Father John.

Angel does as he's told. One side of my mom's face is bright white, and there's a smear of blood at the corner of her mouth and across her cheek. I'm suddenly full of the purest hate I've ever felt, hot and cold and sharp enough to slit Angel's throat and hack The Prophet's smiling face to bloody ribbons. My body is literally *trembling* with it, even as the word *Heresy* fills my head.

"On the charge of Apostasy, I find you guilty," says Father John. "Let us move onto the second charge, that of Corruption of a True Member of the Lord's Legion. How do you plead?"

My mom spits blood on the floor and doesn't say a word. I stare at her, and my sudden rush of hatred gives way to fear.

I had no idea she kept a journal, let alone one that was full of Heresy and Apostasy, and I can't believe what I heard her say to

281

Father John. I can't *believe* it. A good number of Legionnaires have strayed from the True Path, and it's always sad when it happens because we know their souls are forfeit once they pass through the Front Gate and into the Outside.

My mom though? That's ridiculous. *Ridiculous.*

She's been a member of the Lord's Legion for thirteen years, and after my dad died and left her alone with me, when nobody could have blamed her if her Faith had been shaken, she stayed. *She stayed*, and not only raised me on the True Path, but also actively encouraged Father John to choose me as one of his Future Wives, committing us both as deeply to the Legion as it's possible to be. Now she's saying that not only does she not believe, but that she has *never* believed?

It makes no sense. No sense at all.

"Let us review the evidence that supports this charge," says Father John. "I will not have it said by anyone that The Lord's Justice is not thorough, or that those accused are not treated fairly. This journal—*your* journal—describes repeated attempts to persuade Shanti, a known Servant of the Serpent, to take you and your daughter with him after he abandoned the True Path and left the Lord's Legion. It describes how you explored the possibility of breaking into the Big House, stealing the emergency telephone, and contacting the Government with the express intention of inventing lies about our Family and inviting them to make an attack on our home. Finally, it describes how you considered assaulting Brother Amos before his weekly supply run and fleeing in our communal vehicle, presumably with Moonbeam as your unwilling captive. So I ask you again: on the charge of Corruption of a True Member of the Lord's Legion, how do you plead?"

I stare at my mom, my head spinning.

She wanted to leave? She wanted us both to leave? Why?

She spits blood again. "Go to Hell."

Father John smiles at her. "That is your fate, not mine. It gives me no pleasure to find you guilty of this second charge. But in light of the seriousness of your crimes, of the scale of your treachery against The Lord, I see no other option than to Banish you from the Holy Church of the Lord's Legion, for all eternity. The Lord is Good."

"The Lord is Good," repeat the Centurions and the wives of The Prophet. My mom doesn't say the words, and—for the first time in my life—neither do I.

"You may take thirty minutes to gather your personal belongings," says Father John. "When that time has passed, Amos will drive you to Town, and we will be rid of your Heresy. You will not speak to, or in any other way communicate with, your former Brothers and Sisters before you leave. Is that clear? You are no longer welcome here."

"If you think I'm going anywhere without my daughter," says my mom, "then you're even crazier than I thought."

What?

Bella gasps again.

"Father," I say, my voice trembling. "What is—"

The Prophet smiles. "Brother Horizon, take Moonbeam outside and wait there with her. The rest of you Centurions are with me. Everyone else go upstairs."

Bella, Agavé, and Star scuttle up the stairs without a backward glance. My mom meets my eyes, and though they're still full of anger, I see something that makes my head swim and my stomach churn.

Uncertainty. *Fear.*

It rises onto her blood-smeared face, and I suddenly understand.

She was ready for this. She knew it was coming. But something has gone wrong. This isn't how she thought it would play out.

"Come on," says Horizon, and he turns me toward the front door of the house. I try to push back against him, but I might as well try to resist the rotation of the Earth. My mom turns and meets my gaze as he walks me away from her, and I start to cry. Part of me is furious with myself for being so weak, but I can't help it. I *can't*.

"Mom!" I shout. "Tell him you didn't do it, Mom! You have to tell him!"

Her face crumples, and she looks away from me.

"Mom!" I shriek, as Horizon opens the door and bundles me through it. "Father, *please*! Please don't! Mom!"

The door slams shut. Horizon wrestles me onto one of the benches that run along the back of the porch. I'm shrieking and crying and punching and kicking him, but he doesn't even seem to notice. He just holds me tightly in his arms and whispers softly into my ear.

"Hush now," he says. "Hush, girl. There's nothing to be done. The Lord does not make mistakes, and you know that's the truth. The Lord is Good."

I drift out of myself. I know that sounds weird, but it's the only way I can describe it. I'm still sitting on the bench with Horizon's huge arms holding me in place, but I'm also somewhere else at the same time. I'm running through the desert at the edge of the Base, the wind blowing my hair out behind me, and I'm floating through a perfect blue sky, and everything is still and quiet, and I'm lying in my bed in my room, and it's dark and safe, and nothing bad is going to happen. Nothing bad is going to happen *ever*.

My tears have dried and Horizon has loosened his grip on me when the door of the Big House opens. Angel walks through it, leading my mom by the arm. I'm about to shout her name when she looks at me and the word catches in my throat. She doesn't look like the same woman I saw standing in front of Father John, admitting Heresy and denying her Faith; she looks like she's shrunken in on herself. Her eyes are red and brimming with tears, and she can't look at me, not properly. Her shoulders sag, and it looks like Angel's hand is the only thing keeping her upright.

"Mom?" It comes out like a croak. "What's happening, Mom?"

Her face twists, and it looks like she's going to speak, although part of me doesn't want to hear it. But then Angel shoves her down the porch steps and drags her across the yard toward Building Nine and all I feel is cold, like my spine has been replaced with ice cubes.

What happened in there? What did they do to her?

"Bring Moonbeam to me, Horizon!" shouts Father John from inside the house. "I would speak with her."

"Can you walk in on your own?" asks Horizon, his voice low. "Or do you need me to carry you? It's okay if you do."

I stand because I don't want his help, don't want him to touch me, but my legs give way beneath me, and he scoops me up before I fall. He puts an arm around me and leads me gently back through the door and into the Big House. Father John is still in his chair with Bear and Lonestar next to him, and Bella, Agavé, and Star are standing off to one side, near the staircase. He must have told them to come back down because they wouldn't have dared without permission. The Prophet smiles at me as Horizon helps me into the room.

"I'm sorry you had to see this, Moonbeam," he says. "I truly am. It is hard when someone falls from the True Path. It's hard for all of us. It means we have failed, myself included. If your mother had come to me when she first felt The Serpent's poison beginning to spread through her, and I wish with all my heart that she had, I would have moved Heaven and Earth to help her. I would have cast out The Serpent and fought to my last breath for her eternal soul, as I would for any of my Brothers and Sisters, and as I know any of them would do for me. But that time has passed, although it breaks my heart to say so. We all know that Heretics cannot be tolerated, not once they have actively begun The Serpent's work. I know *you* understand that, Moonbeam, because you're a clever girl. A *good* girl."

I stand in the middle of the room. Horizon is behind me, close enough that he can grab me if I fall, but I'm barely aware of his presence, because my head is spinning. Everything The Prophet is saying makes sense, everything he's saying is *True*, but it isn't Father Patrick or some other Heretic he's talking about.

It's my *mom*.

He narrows his eyes. "You are a *good* girl, aren't you?"

I think so.

I nod.

"Then tell me you understand why this has to be done."

"I understand," I say, my voice little more than a whisper.

Father John smiles. "I never doubted it," he says. "Not for a moment. Heretics are insidious creatures that corrupt and spoil. The only solution is to be rid of them, before the damage they do gets too great to repair. They are unworthy of the favor of The Lord. They are unworthy of love."

I stare into his eyes. It feels like he wants me to say something, but I don't know what it is, and even if I did, I don't know if I could form the words.

"Don't you agree, Moonbeam?" he asks.

I nod.

"Of course you do," he says. "So say it."

Tears rise into my eyes. "Say what, Father?" I whisper.

He smiles. "Say that you don't love your mother. Say it now, with The Lord as your witness. Show me your Faith is True."

No. Please, no.

The tears spill down my cheeks. I look at Horizon, hoping he will tell me I don't have to do this, that I'm not as alone as I feel, but he meets my eyes, and all I see on his face is duty.

"Moonbeam," says Father John, his voice sharp. "Look at me."

I drag my gaze away from Horizon's blank face and look at The Prophet.

"This is hard for you," he says. "I understand that, and you have my sympathies. But if you will not renounce Heresy, here and now, The Lord will surely wonder why."

"I renounce Heresy," I whisper.

"Good," he says. "And your mother?"

"Please, Father," I say, my voice a barely audible croak. "Please don't make me say it. Please."

He narrows his eyes. "Say it."

"Please..."

"Say it now, Moonbeam."

"Father..."

Father John leaps to his feet. "SAY IT!" he roars, his face crimson with fury. "SAY IT NOW, OR YOU WILL SPEND THE REST OF YOUR LIFE INSIDE A BOX! SAY IT! *SAY IT!*"

My head spins, and gray is flickering at the edges of my vision. I feel like I'm going to be sick. Horizon steps closer behind me, his hands ready to catch me if I fall. I focus on Father John's face, on the hatred and cruelty I see there, and I shut my eyes.

"I don't love her," I whisper.

"Who?" he asks. "Who don't you love?"

"My mother." The words comes out like a sob. "I don't love my mother."

Horizon squeezes my shoulder. I lower my head and cry, my chest heaving up and down. Hands touch my face and slide around my waist, and I hear Bella's voice beside my ear. "Don't cry," she says. "It's all right, Moonbeam. It's for the best. The Lord is Good."

I open my eyes. Bella and Agavé are kneeling next to me, their faces full of concern. I look at them, and it's like I don't know them. It feels like I've never met them before in my life. Like they're strangers.

"She may cry if she wishes," says Father John. He is back in his chair beneath the window with a gentle smile on his face, the anger that overcame him gone. "Her mother has been proven False, and that would be upsetting to any child, no matter how strong their Faith. You may cry, Moonbeam, and for a day and a night you may grieve your mother's Heresy."

I nod. "Thank you, Father," I say, the words like acid in my mouth.

His smile widens. "And after that time, you will never speak of her again. You will not even think about her. Is that clear?"

His words punch me in the gut. My stomach churns and spins, but I shudder through a wave of nausea and manage a tiny nod.

"It's clear, Father," I whisper. "I understand."

He nods. "I never doubted it. You will stay here until it is time for the Heretic to be cast out. The Lord is Good."

"The Lord is Good," I say, as the voice in the back of my head tells me something very, *very* different.

I sit on the floor of the Big House on my own as the thirty minutes my mother was given to pack up her life pass in the blink of an eye.

Father John goes up to his study, claiming he needs to ask The Lord to give our Family the strength to get through this difficult time, but the three Centurions, Bella, Agavé, and Star all stay in the living room with me. None of them say anything, and they make an effort not to stare at me, but I can feel them watching. Horizon stays near the door, I guess to make sure I don't bolt outside and beg my mom to take me with her—although it would make absolutely no difference if I did, because I would never be allowed into the truck with her and Amos. I could stand in the yard and scream and shout and plead for somebody to help me, but nobody would.

I wish that weren't the truth, but it is.

So I sit on the floor and try not to think about what's happening. I know it's cowardly, that members of the Lord's Legion are supposed to face adversity and stand up and be True, but I don't care about any of that right now. I really don't.

I can't imagine my mom not being here. It doesn't make any sense. It can't be real, let alone something that's going to happen in a matter of minutes. I can't bear to think of her Outside, among the Heretics and the Governments and the Servants of the Serpent. I don't want her to go, and I can't bear the thought of her leaving me here, but at the same time, I feel guiltier than I've ever felt in my entire life because I don't want to go with her. I don't want to leave my home and my Family and go out into the darkness.

I want her to stay. I want everything to stay like it is.

I want Father John to change his mind. I want him to give her another chance, even if it's her last one, even if they put her in a box for a month to atone for her Heresy.

But I know he won't.

The Lord does not make mistakes.

Emotions are swirling out of control inside me, as chaotic as dust in a storm. I stare at the floor, and I refuse to look at Horizon or Bella or any of the others, and I can't stop crying, not completely, but I'm not just upset. I'm shocked by what my mom has done, but I'm absolutely *furious* with her for being stupid enough to get caught.

I'm sure they would never admit it, but every member of the Lord's Legion, with the possible exception of Father John, has moments of weakness and doubt, when their thoughts betray them and they struggle to keep themselves on the True Path. I *know* they do because all human beings are fallible, as Father John teaches. But writing those thoughts down, filling an *actual, physical book* with your plans to break the rules and commit Heresy, is suicidal. She didn't even beg for forgiveness when it was clear that she had been found out. She admitted her crimes like she was proud of them, then cursed Father John and denied her Faith.

Why? Why would she say that? Even if it's the truth, why would she say it?

My head pounds.

I don't think my brain is working properly.

Why didn't she talk to me about what she was feeling? Didn't she trust me to keep her secret? Didn't she love me enough to want to tell me the truth?

Guilt pulses through me because maybe she assumed I would go straight to the nearest Centurion if she told me what was in her head. It's what I've been taught to do, and can I really say that I wouldn't have?

Can I *honestly* tell myself that?

I have so many questions. *Too* many. Most of them I want to ask my mom, but I'm distantly starting to understand that I'm never going to get the chance. I don't know how I'm supposed to carry on after she's Gone, and I don't know what I'm supposed to think, how I'm supposed to *ever* be okay with this. The tears keep rolling down my cheeks, and I face away from everyone and stare at the floor until the front door of the Big House opens and Angel steps through it and says that it's time.

Father John appears at the top of the stairs. "Very good," he says. "Did she give you any trouble?"

Angel shakes his head. "Quiet as a mouse, Father."

"And did you tell our Family of the verdict that has been passed? The verdict and the sentence?"

"I did, Father," says Angel. "They're waiting for you in the yard."

Father John nods, then walks down the staircase and across to where I'm sitting. "Take my hand, Moonbeam." He reaches down toward me. I take his hand, my skin crawling at the feel of his skin on mine, and let him pull me to my feet. He walks me toward the door, the Centurions, Bella, Agavé, and the rest of The Prophet's wives following silently behind us.

The entire Legion has gathered in the yard in front of the Chapel. At the center of the crowd, my mom stands next to the red pickup. The truck's engine is running and behind its wheel is Amos, a solemn look on his lined face. Everyone is silent and looking in any direction apart from at my mom, until Father John's footsteps thud across the wooden porch and the whole crowd turns to look at him.

At *me*.

Father John leads me down the steps and onto the blacktop, but it might as well be happening to someone else because I can't think and I can't breathe. All I can do is stare at my mom. She's gripping a black trash bag tightly in her hands—a single plastic bag to hold the contents of her entire life. Her eyes find mine, and she gives me a watered-down version of the look I saw when I walked into the Big House between Bear and Horizon, what now feels like a million years ago.

Don't cry. Be brave.

The crowd parts to let me and Father John approach the truck, then closes in our wake, sealing us inside. The Prophet lets go of my hand and turns to face his Legion.

"The Lord is hard!" he shouts, his voice booming across the yard and echoing off the buildings. "But He is always fair, and He is always just. He does not give second chances, and He does not make mistakes. He deals in right and wrong, and He deals in Truth. The Lord is Good."

"*The Lord is Good*," echoes the crowd.

I don't say a word. My whole body is shaking, and my skin is really hot. I feel like I'm going to throw up, but I can't take my eyes off my mom. She still doesn't look anything like her usual self, but she doesn't look as utterly *defeated* as she did when Angel walked her out of the Big House—some of the life has returned to her eyes, some of the color to her face.

Father John looks at her. "Do you have anything to say for yourself before the sentence is carried out?"

My mom meets his gaze. "May I hug my daughter?" she asks, her voice steady. "Please?"

The Prophet narrows his eyes, then nods. "Be quick," he says. "The Lord's justice waits for nobody."

My mom drops her bag on the ground and walks slowly toward me. I stare up at her, my mind empty, my feet frozen to the spot. There are so many things I want to say, things I know I'm going to regret *not* saying later, when she's Gone and this is all actually real, but as her shadow falls over me, I can't find a single word.

She pulls me carefully against her, as though she thinks I might break. For several long seconds I hang stiffly in her arms. Fresh tears spill from my eyes, and I wrap my arms around her back, burying my face into her shoulder and squeezing her so tightly that she won't be able to get away.

She won't be able to leave me.

"It's all right, my little Moon," she says, her voice low and choked. "Everything's going to be all right. Be good, okay? You be good."

She squeezes me even tighter, and for the briefest of moments, her mouth is next to my ear as she whispers three words that only I could possibly hear.

"*Under your pillow.*"

I frown and pull my head away from her shoulder, but before

I get the chance to ask her what she's talking about, she lets go of me. She picks up her bag and climbs into the back of the pickup without another word, leaving me completely alone in the middle of everyone I know in the world. Father John lowers his head and closes his eyes as his mouth moves in a brief silent prayer. Then he looks up and nods at Amos.

The pickup's engine rumbles as it reverses in a slow arc toward the side of the Chapel. I watch, my mind reeling with utter impotence, as Amos puts the truck into drive and it rolls forward, crunching off the smooth asphalt of the yard and onto the rough desert ground as he accelerates toward the Front Gate.

My mom stares back at us as she is driven away, at the men and women she called her Family for the last decade and more. As the pickup reaches the Gate, her eyes settle on mine.

Then the truck is out on the dirt road. It rounds the first bend and disappears from view.

A
 F
   T
    E
     R

"What was under your pillow?" asks Doctor Hernandez.

"Nothing," I say.

He and Agent Carlyle stare at me, their faces pale. I'm so used to seeing their expressions of shock as I talk that I barely notice them anymore.

"I can't imagine what that must have been like," says Doctor Hernandez. "I'm so sorry that happened to you."

"Thank you."

"Nobody defended your mother?" asks Agent Carlyle. "Not a single one of them took her side?"

I shake my head. "Father John said she was a Heretic. There was no arguing with that. And I can't blame them, I guess, because I didn't do anything either. I watched it happen."

"You were a child," says Doctor Hernandez. "There was nothing you could have done."

I shrug.

Maybe. Maybe not.

"Do you think your mom was a heretic?" asks Agent Carlyle.

I consider this. "It depends on what you think that means," I say eventually. "By the Legion's rules, the rules that Father John claimed came from The Lord, she probably was. I never got to see her journal, but she didn't deny that it was hers, and she didn't deny its contents. You have to understand that people raised inside the Legion were taught to not think about themselves, even before the Purge. There was a clear hierarchy: The Lord, the Legion, then everything else. Individual needs don't matter. What you might *want* doesn't matter. So I didn't question whether what happened was fair, even though my heart broke when she was driven away and I couldn't imagine what my life was going to be like without her. Her Heresy was still Heresy, even though she was my mom. I couldn't pretend it didn't matter because I loved her. Does that make any sense?"

Doctor Hernandez nods. "It makes perfect sense, sadly. I've seen it dozens of times, although rarely in such extreme circumstances. It's a fairly standard method of control."

I frown. "What does that mean?"

He sits forward. "The intentional creation of a situation where people value something *other* more than they value themselves. Where people will allow themselves to be hurt, or even voluntarily hurt themselves, because they have been conditioned to believe that something else is more important than their own well-being. If you control that other thing, in this case the word of God, then you control the people. Father John ruled over the Lord's Legion like a dictator, dispensing approval and disapproval, and the rest of you were programmed not to argue or resist in any way."

"And even if you did," says Agent Carlyle softly, "the Centurions had the guns. And we all know who they were loyal to."

I try to tell myself that I don't recognize the world they're describing, but the voice in the back of my head is sharp.

Don't. Don't lie to yourself, not when you've come so far. You feel stupid and embarrassed for having been part of it for so long, but you know what he's saying is the truth. You just have to face it.

"Your mother told Father John that she couldn't be guilty of apostasy because she had no faith to abandon," says Doctor Hernandez. "Did that fit the woman you grew up with?"

I shake my head, as much in an attempt to clear it as to signal my disagreement. "I never doubted her. She was never a fanatic like Jacob or Amos or Luke, but I always thought she was True. I've told you that I suspected she wasn't very happy, but I always assumed that was because of my dad dying or that it was just who she was. But I honestly never doubted her Faith or her loyalty to the Legion. She persuaded Father John to choose me for a Future Wife, so it would never have occurred to me that she was secretly trying to leave."

"Maybe that's why she did it," says Agent Carlyle.

I frown. "I don't understand."

"Maybe she thought that if she put her own daughter forward to marry John Parson, then her loyalty would be proven beyond doubt. Maybe she thought it would put her above suspicion."

"So what would have been her plan for when I turned eighteen?" I ask. "When I was supposed to actually marry him?"

"I imagine she was counting on having escaped by then," says Doctor Hernandez. "The *two* of you having escaped. She didn't deny that she was looking for a way out for both of you."

"Pretty big gamble," I say.

He nods. "It was."

"Do you think she wanted to leave the whole time?" I ask. "Right from when we first got there?"

"Do you?" he asks.

"Maybe not the whole time," I say. I've thought about this a lot since she was Banished. "But for a long time, yeah. I think she wanted to go. Wanted *us* to go. I just didn't see it."

"You were a child," says Doctor Hernandez. "In an exceptionally guarded environment, where nobody felt safe to say what they really thought or what they were really feeling. You couldn't have known."

"She could have told me."

"No," says Agent Carlyle. "She couldn't. What if you had told a Centurion?"

That's exactly what you would have done, whispers the voice in the back of my head. *You know it is.*

I stare at them.

"We're not presenting any of this as fact," says Doctor Hernandez. "We don't know the truth, and we aren't pretending to. But there's something I'd like you to consider."

"What?"

"I have no doubt that grief over the loss of your father was a major part of why your mother seemed distant to you, why you often felt she was unhappy," he says. "I also have no doubt that your perception of her was influenced by the natural sense of parental disappointment that accompanies adolescence, and I need you to understand that I mean no criticism when I say that, none at all. But what if part of why she appeared to be unhappy was because she never wanted to come to Texas and join the Lord's Legion?"

"I'm listening."

"When the two of you *did* talk about it, she didn't tell you they came for a long weekend and she experienced some profound epiphany and became a true believer. She told you they stayed because your father was very persuasive. So try and imagine yourself in the position I'm describing, as a hypothetical. You've been forced to uproot your whole life, to go somewhere you didn't want to go and join something you didn't want to join, and then the person you did it for dies and leaves you stuck with your daughter in a place you never wanted to come to in the first place. How do you think you would feel about that?"

"I think I'd be angry," I say, as that exact emotion flickers to life deep inside me. "More than that, in fact. I think I'd be *furious*."

Doctor Hernandez nods. "You said she seemed happier before the purge?"

"That's how it felt."

"So maybe she was," he says. "Maybe she thought life was okay then, that the Legion was an okay place for the two of you while Patrick McIlhenny was in charge, and maybe that changed after the purge. When she denied apostasy, she told Father John she had no faith in him. Not that she had no faith in God or even in the Lord's Legion. In *him*."

I nod. I hear her speak the words in my head, her voice laced with venom.

"But maybe by then it was too late," he says. "You said yourself that security was tightened after the purge, that rooms started being locked at night, and the Centurions started carrying guns. Maybe she realized that she had waited too long. Maybe *that's* why she was unhappy."

"Why wouldn't she have just taken me and left before Father John took over?"

He shakes his head. "I have no idea. Maybe she was scared to go back out into the real world. Maybe she was scared of it being only you and her."

I stare at him.

"It's just something for you to think about," he says. "Like I said."

He's right, whispers the voice in the back of my head. *You know he is. You never tried to look at things from her perspective. You were only concerned about how her behavior affected you. How it made you feel.*

"That's not fair," I whisper.

Doctor Hernandez frowns. "Moonbeam?"

I hear him say my name, but I don't respond because I'm not really in the room anymore. I'm trying to imagine, if what he is saying is true, how my mother must have felt when Father John took Father Patrick's place—how trapped, how utterly *helpless*. So many weeks and months and years that were still to come. So much time spent inside a prison you hadn't even realized was a prison until it was too late to escape.

"Are you all right?" he asks. "Do you want to stop?"

Yes.

I shake my head.

"So that was the moment?" asks Agent Carlyle. "That was when your faith began to fail?"

"I guess so," I say. "It's not like some light bulb came on in my head or anything like that. I didn't understand that anything was changing until a lot later. But looking back now, I guess that was it. That was when I started to think differently about things."

"When you realized things were starting to go bad?"

I shake my head again. "I knew my mom getting Banished was going to make things worse for me," I say. "I didn't know they were going to turn bad for everyone until later."

"When?"

"When Nate left," I say. "When Luke wasn't chosen as a Centurion. And…"

When they gave out the guns. When Father John chose his final wife.

"Moonbeam?" he asks.

The last of my strength deserts me. My hand is throbbing with pain, more than it has in days, and my head feels light and drifting. "Can we stop?" I ask. "Please?"

Agent Carlyle narrows his eyes, ever so slightly. "I know this is hard. I get it, I really do, and I don't want to push you. But—"

"There are things you need to know." I sigh. "I know. I'm not trying to be difficult. I'm honestly not. I just can't talk anymore today. Please, can that be okay?"

Agent Carlyle gives me a small smile and glances at Doctor Hernandez, who nods. "Of course it's okay," he says. "We'll pick this up tomorrow."

Nurse Harrow shuts my door, and I wait for the familiar sound of the lock turning before I sit down on the edge of the bed.

My legs are trembling, and my heart is racing, and it took all my self-control to make it back along the gray corridor without bursting into tears or grabbing Nurse Harrow's arm to keep myself upright.

I lower my head between my knees and take a deep breath, then another, and another. My head swims, but I close my eyes and ignore it. I focus on breathing—in, out, in, out. The pressure in my chest start to fade, and after a while, I open my eyes and sit up straight.

I get slowly to my feet, then walk unsteadily across the room and sit down at the desk and start drawing. Waves of blue and white water appear on the page. I try to force my mind to go blank, to let it wander wherever it needs to, even though I'm pretty sure I'm not going to like the destination.

An image of my mom appears, her mouth curved downward with the constant disappointment that I'd grown to hate the sight of. It used to make me wonder why I so clearly wasn't enough to make her happy, why a living daughter wasn't enough to cancel out the grief of a dead husband.

Oh God.

I realize—so late, *too* late—how clearly she must have seen things.

How it must have turned her stomach to watch me skipping across the yard and singing hymns, holding hands with my Brothers and Sisters in the Chapel on Sunday mornings, and staring at Father John with blind, unquestioning devotion.

How it must have hurt her to know that she couldn't risk telling me the truth in case I sided with my Family against her, or said the wrong thing to the wrong person and brought everything crashing down.

Oh God.

I always believed that she urged Father John to accept me as a Future Wife because she wanted to hand over the responsibility of taking care of me, of *loving* me, to somebody else as quickly as she could.

Oh God.

But if she only pushed me toward The Prophet because she hoped it would keep her safe from suspicion while she looked for a way for us to escape, then I can pretty safely assume that the thought of me actually marrying him horrified her every bit as much as it did me. Otherwise she wouldn't have tried so desperately to find a way out before the time came.

Oh God.

How could I have known that though? I was a little girl, and she kept her plans private, carrying her burden on her own and never saying a word to anyone. She played dutiful and loyal and True while she schemed and plotted, and for the longest time, everyone believed she was exactly what she appeared to be.

Including me.

That's because you're stupid, says the voice in the back of my head. It doesn't sound kind or gentle or sympathetic; it sounds angry and hard. *You're stupid and weak and ungrateful, and you only ever thought about yourself.*

"Shut up," I whisper.

She was your mother, and she was trying to save you both, and all you did was resent her for it.

"Shut up." The pencil flies back and forth, gouging the dark brown lines of the cliffs onto the sheet of paper.

She understood what the Lord's Legion really was, but you believed what you were told and couldn't see what she needed you to see. If you hadn't been so blind, she could have told you the truth before it was too late.

The pencil tears through the paper and snaps in half.

It's your fault that she's out there on her own. Your fault that you're both alone.

"SHUT UP!" I scream. I sweep my arm across the surface of the desk, sending paper and pencils and crayons flying into the air. I slam my fists down. Agony explodes up my left arm from my injured hand, but I welcome the pain because I know I deserve it. "SHUT UP, SHUT UP, SHUT UP, SHUT UP!"

I hear the lock turn, but I don't see my door swing open because my eyes are squeezed shut and everything is deep black and blazing red. Footsteps hurry across the floor, then arms encircle my shoulders and Nurse Harrow is telling me it's okay, it's all right, *everything is going to be all right.* I let her pull me to her chest as a torrent of anger and frustration—what feels like years' and years' worth, buried deeper than I ever knew—boils out of me, leaving me spent and dangling limply in her arms. Tears spill down my cheeks as she shushes me and rocks me back and forth like a baby. The voice in the back of my head speaks again, softer than before.

Tomorrow, it whispers. *Tomorrow you tell them everything. Like you said you would.*

No more hiding.

BEFORE

"Here," says Amos. "Try not to shoot your own foot off with it."

I resist the urge to roll my eyes and take the rifle from his hands. It's a Colt AR-15—black, mostly plastic, and surprisingly light for such a powerful gun. Amos moves down the long line of my Brothers and Sisters as Jacob Reynolds appears in front of me, holding out a bundle of empty magazines and a plastic bag full of bullets.

"Fill them, check them, keep everything clean," he says.

I take the ammunition without a word, and he moves on without giving me so much as a second look.

It's Tuesday morning. The Centurions unlocked the doors before dawn and told us all to assemble in front of the Chapel. Once we were gathered, Father John emerged and told us The Lord had made it clear to him that time was growing short, and that it was no longer wise to keep the Legion's weapons locked away in the basement of the Big House. It was time to have them at hand, ready to be used against the Servants of the Serpent when they finally made their move against those who walk the True Path.

He ordered us all to line up in the yard and told us that he would have more news for us once we were properly armed against our enemies. Then he strode away toward the Big House as my Brothers and Sisters started arranging themselves into single file.

I look down at the gun in my hands and frown. There are scratches and file marks around the lower receiver and the ejection port, and dull metal plates have been screwed into the plastic above the trigger guard on both sides. It doesn't look like the rifles we usually use during training, the ones that Amos counts in and out and keeps scrupulously clean—this one looks like it has been snapped in half and put back together.

I raise it to my shoulder and sight down its long barrel. As it often does, the deadly power of what I'm holding in my hands makes me think dangerous thoughts, like when you stand on a high ledge and part of your brain urges you to jump off. I could turn to my right and pull the trigger again and again and again, and most of my Brothers and Sisters would be bleeding on the ground before the first scream rang out.

I don't do it though.

You could, whispers the voice in the back of my head. *You know you want to.*

But I don't.

And that's all that matters.

"Brothers and Sisters!"

Father John's voice booms out across the yard. Everyone turns toward the porch of the Big House, from where he gives us a wide, benevolent smile.

"Gather before me, my Family," he says, beckoning with his hands. "Gather and hear the good news The Lord has shared with me."

I walk with the rest of the crowd and stand below the porch, squinting up at Father John as the sun climbs into the bright morning sky. When everyone is waiting in silence, he spreads his arms and stares down at us.

"The Lord has seen fit to grant me wisdom," he says. "This very morning He spoke to me. The Lord is Good."

"The Lord is Good," echoes the congregation.

"There is to be a celebration," continues Father John. "There is to be great joy and rejoicing, because The Lord loves his Faithful servants, those men and women who walk the True Path. He has allowed me to understand that the time has come for His humble messenger to take a new wife, to further the line of His Holy Legion. He has given me a name, and it is not for me or any other mortal man or woman to question the judgment of The Lord."

A low murmur spreads through the crowd. On the porch, behind their husband, I see Agavé and Bella and the rest of The Prophet's wives clasp their hands together and nod and smile in dutiful joy. I look around the crowd and see my Sisters staring at each other, clearly wondering which of them is about to move into the Big House.

"Those of you who have been promised to me are no longer promised," says Father John, and I feel my heart stop dead in my chest. "You are True Sisters of the Lord's Legion, and there is no insult intended, no punishment meant. But time grows short, and The Lord has seen fit to grant me new understanding. He does not make mistakes."

I stare up at The Prophet. The first emotion that fills me— irrationally, *ludicrously*—is rejection, hot and bitter. I've always dreaded the decreasingly distant moment when I would have been forced to marry him, but now that I've been released from that obligation, my heart is throbbing with what feels very close to grief.

Why doesn't he want me anymore? Am I not pretty enough?

Wouldn't I bear Faithful children?

Reality comes rushing in before I have time to consider the panicky self-loathing my brain is spewing out.

I don't have to marry him. It's over.

And just like that, the fleeting sense of rejection is gone, swept away by a tsunami of glorious relief. I don't care why Father John has changed his mind—because I know it was *his* decision rather than The Lord's—and I don't care what it makes people think of me. A single thought pulses through my head.

I'm free.

"The Lord has made His choice," says Father John. "He has made His will clear, and He tolerates no argument. I announce that He has chosen Honey to join His humble messenger in Holy Matrimony."

My elation disappears instantly and completely. It's like I never actually felt it at all. My stomach drops into my boots as everyone turns and stares at Honey. She's about ten feet away from me, standing as still as a statue beside her mother. Astrid beams with wide-eyed delight, as though every single one of her dreams has just come true. Honey isn't smiling though. She's staring up at Father John, her face so pale it's almost translucent.

Please, no. Not Honey. Oh, please not her.

"There is to be no delay," continues Father John. "The Lord has made it clear that this is a matter of utmost importance, and that there is no time to waste. The marriage will take place this evening. The Lord is Good."

For a second or two, nobody responds. Silence hangs over the crowd, as though everyone is processing what has happened, adjusting to yet another shifting of the ground beneath their feet.

And for a moment, I see the same flicker across The Prophet's face that I saw when Nate refused to be a Centurion.

The same *fear*.

Then Jacob Reynolds bellows, "The Lord is Good," and the moment is gone. Everyone else follows suit, and then people are cheering and clapping and crowding around Honey, telling her how lucky she is and how wise The Lord is to have chosen her, how *wise* and *clever* and *wonderful*. Up on the porch, Father John smiles as his wives applaud along with the rest of the crowd. But I ignore them all, because I'm staring at Honey as she receives the congratulations of her Brothers and Sisters, taking in her wide eyes and stricken expression. She's only fourteen; Father John has never married anyone so young.

Never.

"Honey," says The Prophet, and the crowd falls silent. "Will you come and stand at my side?"

Anger spreads through me. He makes it sound like he is asking a question, rather than announcing a formality. The illusion of choice, of free will for anyone but him, makes my skin crawl.

The crowd turns expectantly toward Honey, who is still staring up at her newly announced fiancé with the same empty expression. She hasn't moved a muscle. Then her face crumples, and her mouth drops open, and my brave little Sister, who has always been so self-possessed, ever since she was a tiny girl, lets out a terrible screeching sob.

"No!" she wails. "No, I won't do it! Don't make me!"

Gasps echo across the yard. Astrid drops to her knees in front of her daughter and speaks to her in an urgent, frantic whisper, as most of the Legion shake their heads and mutter about Heresy. I can hear some of what Astrid is saying—*it's a wonderful honor, it's The Lord's Will*—and I'm almost overcome by the urge to beat her head against the asphalt until she shuts up.

"I don't care!" cries Honey, between sobs that hurt my heart. "I don't! Please!"

I glance up at Father John, searching his face for the fear that I saw minutes earlier, the same fear that made him back down when Nate defied him—but I see only cold, terrifying fury. His eyes narrow, and I understand, with a certainty that almost makes me gasp, the thought that is roaring inside his head.

I am not going to let this happen again.

I push my way forward, intending to grab Honey and run until I can't run anymore, but when Father John's voice thunders out again, I stop dead along with everyone else.

"*SILENCE!*" he bellows. "This is the daughter you have raised, Astrid? This Heretic, who would deny the Will of The Lord?"

Astrid's eyes are full of panic as she stands and faces The Prophet. "Forgive her, Father," she says, her voice trembling. "She is only a child. She doesn't know what she's saying."

"Is childhood an excuse for Heresy?" asks Father John, his voice as heavy and dangerous as a landslide. "Is that what you are telling me?"

"Father, I—"

"*THERE IS NO EXCUSE FOR HERESY!*" he screams. "You know that as well as I do, unless you are even stupider than you appear! *There never has been,* for our rules are set by The Lord Himself, and our standards are not negotiable! Now stand aside and let me see her."

Astrid looks like she is going to faint with terror, but she manages to shuffle to one side, leaving the red-faced, tear-streaked figure of Honey standing on her own. I want to scream at Astrid until my voice gives out because I don't understand—I *can't* understand—why the sight of her panicked, sobbing daughter is not enough to make her grow a backbone.

"Honey," says Father John, and although his volume is lower

and his tone is gentle, I can still hear the anger rumbling underneath. "The Lord has made His wishes clear, and you know as well as I that He does not mistakes. So think hard, child. Think harder than you ever have."

Honey stares at him, her bottom lip quivering, her eyes wide and red.

"Would you defy Him?" asks Father John. "Or will you join me in Holy Matrimony, as He has commanded? I would have your answer."

Honey stares. Around her, on all sides, my elder Sisters stare intently at the ground.

Do something, I silently scream. *Something, anything, one of you.*

Stop this.

"No," whispers Honey, then looks up at Astrid with huge, pleading eyes. "Mom…please…"

A flicker of horror crosses Astrid's face, and she retreats half a step from her only child.

"That is…regrettable," says Father John. "It truly is. Centurions?"

The four men step forward. Suddenly, I understand what's going to happen. I try to force my throat to work, to howl for Honey to run, *just run and don't look back*, but I'm frozen solid, and all I can do is watch.

"Lock her in a box until she learns humility before The Lord."

Cries of shock ring out, and Astrid belatedly makes a grab for her daughter. "Please, Father!" she screams. "Please no!"

Honey wraps her arms round her mother and holds on tightly as the Centurions elbow their way through the shouting, protesting crowd. My paralysis finally breaks, and as Lonestar rumbles past me, I throw myself after him, trying to grab his shoulder, to turn him around and plead with him not to do this, but my fingers barely brush the fabric of his shirt. He doesn't even slow down, let alone stop.

Jacob reaches Astrid first. She shrieks and turns away from him, trying to shield her daughter, but he wrenches her around and grabs hold of Honey's wrist. Honey screams as her mom tries to hold on to her, and I wade through the crowd of my shouting, crying Brothers and Sisters. I'm almost there when Luke appears behind Astrid and drags her back, an awful, empty smile on his face. She flails at him as people shout up at the porch, pleading for The Prophet to show mercy because Honey is just a child and she doesn't understand what she's doing, that he *must* show mercy because children don't go in the boxes, *children never go in the boxes*.

Father John doesn't even glance in their direction. His gaze stays fixed on Honey as Jacob scoops her up and carries her, kicking and screaming and sobbing, across the yard toward the shipping containers, their metal sides glowing in the hot Texas sun.

A
F
T
E
R

Lunch is hot dogs and french fries and a little cup of beans that taste like soap and a plastic glass of chocolate milk.

I eat quickly, then draw the house and the cliff and the water and the two little figures a couple of times while I wait for Nurse Harrow to escort me to SSI. The drawings are basic, little more than the scratchy scrawls of children, but that's okay. I'm not really concentrating on them. My mind is full of Agent Carlyle and Doctor Hernandez, of their faces when I finished telling them about Father John's announcement.

They were both as pale as ghosts.

Doctor Hernandez was trembling as he stared at me, as though it was taking actual physical strength to maintain his usual composure, and there were patches of red around Agent Carlyle's eyes, as bright as blood against his ashen skin. It looked like he had been crying, although I'm sure I would have noticed. I *think* I would have noticed. I guess he was thinking about his daughter while I talked, about what he would do if anyone ever tried to do to her what Father John did to Honey.

I think about all they must have seen in the years of doing their jobs—the horrible things they must have heard, the damaged men, women, and children they must have met—and it's weirdly reassuring that they clearly haven't been numbed by it all. That they haven't lost their ability to be shocked and upset when someone tells them something awful, that they still manage to keep going afterward, to keep getting up each morning and moving forward. It's a reminder that they're human, and it gives me hope that there might still be a future for me.

I don't have the slightest idea what it might look like, but I guess that doesn't really matter right now.

After they asked me a lot of questions—about the box, about how The Prophet's wives reacted, about how much my Brothers and Sisters protested—Agent Carlyle told me he was glad that Father John is dead. Doctor Hernandez told him it wasn't a helpful opinion, because I guess he doesn't want me thinking that violence solves problems, but Agent Carlyle told him he didn't care and said it again.

"I'm glad he's dead."

I didn't respond. What could I have possibly said?

Doctor Hernandez would have been disappointed if I'd replied "me too," but I know he would have been concerned if I'd disagreed. And when he's concerned about something, he wants to talk about it. So I said nothing. A memory crept into my mind, a pool of dark red spreading across the floor of the Big House, but I didn't say a single word.

There was no more time left in the session, so I promised them I would finish tomorrow morning. And I *will*, even though I know it means telling them one of the two things I swore I would never tell anyone.

Be brave, whispers the voice in the back of my head.

I'll try. I'll try my very hardest to be brave. But I'm terrified, and I can't pretend I'm not, no matter what the voice says.

I know I have to tell them what I did. I'm scared, because I don't know what the consequences are going to be, but I know I have to, and part of me—the deep part that I suspect is where the voice comes from—is ready for this to be over.

Part of me *wants* to tell them.

Because as I explained what Father John did to Honey, as I found myself back in the yard and felt the warmth of the sun and heard the voices of the men and women I used to call my Brothers and Sisters, I felt the weight around my shoulders—the one I've been carrying with me for what feels like forever lessen again, ever so slightly.

There's a knock on my door before it swings open, and Nurse Harrow, as kind and smiling as always, tells me it's time. I smile back, then get up and follow her out into the corridor.

The atmosphere in the group therapy room is different today.

Luke's absence still hangs over everyone, and I hear the word "Ascend" several times as my younger Brothers and Sisters talk in low voices over coloring books and toys, but the atmosphere in the room seems lighter. It feels like they're no longer checking over their shoulders or overthinking everything they say in case it gets them in trouble. Part of me wonders whether they ought to be more sad, that a matter of days shouldn't be long enough for them to have seemingly moved on from the death of someone they knew their entire lives, but I don't raise the issue, and neither does Honey—I think we're both happy to let them play.

The two of us are sitting at a plastic table in the corner of the room, watching Jeremiah and Aurora chase each other as three of the others count backward from fifteen, their voices rising to excited screams as they reach zero. The rules of the game are totally incomprehensible to me, but that's okay.

"Some of them will be all right," says Honey, as though she can see the question I was considering on my face. "Not all of them, maybe not even most of them. But some of them will be okay."

I shake my head. "Everyone they know is dead."

"Little kids are resilient," says Honey. "What happened will always be with them, but they'll move on. And I'll tell you something else, even though it sounds crazy right now—they'll forget about it, most of the time at least."

"Their heads are still full of what Father John taught them."

She shrugs. "They'll learn new things."

I look at her. I want to believe what she's saying, that Doctor Hernandez and his colleagues will pluck all the lies out of their heads and replace them with helpful, *truthful* ideas and patch over all the cracks. But I look at Jeremiah and Aurora and Rainbow and all the others, and I see nightmares that will never completely leave them and wounds that will never fully heal.

I see long roads ahead, for all of them.

"When did you stop believing in the Legion and Father John?" I ask Honey. "When did you see through it?"

She frowns. "I never believed. I realized it was all bullshit as soon as I was old enough to think for myself, same as you did."

I feel embarrassed heat rise into my cheeks.

Honey narrows her eyes. "*Not* the same as you did?"

I shake my head. "My Faith started to fail after they Banished my mom," I say. "Until then, I was a True believer. I thought you knew that."

"I didn't," she says. "I always thought we were the same."

"I'm sorry."

Her frown turns into a wide smile. "Don't say that. You saw the truth in the end. That's more than most people did."

"How come you saw it right away?"

She shrugs. "I don't know. It just seemed obvious to me that the only person really benefiting from the Lord's Legion was Father John."

I stare at her, my mind reeling.

It's so simple, when she puts it like that. So very clear. Why did it take me so long to see it? Why couldn't I be as clever as her?

"So what would you have done?" I ask. "If the fire hadn't happened?"

"Left," she says instantly. "As soon as I was old enough that they couldn't send me back to my mom. Wasn't that what you were going to do?"

"I think so," I say. "Until those last few days I was promised to Father John, so my plan was to leave before they made me marry him."

"And find your mom?"

"I guess so. I mean, yeah. If she's still out there."

"She's out there," says Honey.

"How do you know that?"

She smiles at me. "I have Faith."

I smile back. "What about your mom?"

Her grin fades, and grief flickers across her face. "What about her?"

"She wouldn't have gone with you, would she?"

"Not a chance," says Honey. "She was a Legionnaire to her bones. She didn't know how to be anything else."

"Do you miss her?"

She considers my question for a second or two. "I do," she says. "I really do. But I don't think she could have survived outside the Base, so part of me thinks it was a kindness. You know she was ill, right?"

I nod. Astrid's illnesses, which some unkind members of the Legion suggested got worse whenever she was asked to do something she didn't want to do, were well known.

"She believed she would Ascend when she died," says Honey. "She believed it with all her heart, so I guess she got what she wanted. If she had made it through the fire and been forced to sit in a room while Government agents tore holes in everything she believed in, it would have destroyed her. So I think maybe it was for the best."

I look at her. I don't know what to say.

"And who knows?" says Honey, giving me a grim smile. "Maybe they had it right all along. Maybe she's in Heaven, sitting at the side of The Lord."

I nod. "Maybe."

In the middle of the room, the frantic countdown reaches zero again. Jeremiah does a strange little dance, his arms and legs jerking back and forth as though he's getting an electric shock, then throws himself flat on the floor, where Aurora and Rainbow leap on top of him. Everyone cheers and screams and yells, and Honey smiles.

"Why did you do it?" I ask. "Why did you say no to marrying him?"

She keeps her eyes fixed on our Brothers and Sisters, but I see a frown furrow her forehead. "What was I supposed to say?"

"It would have been easier to say yes."

"You're right," she says. "It would have been easier."

We sit in silence for a little while, watching the children play.

"You really think they'll be okay?" I ask.

"I don't know," she says. "I hope so. And I know one thing for certain, Moonbeam. Despite everything that happened, despite the fire and the loss and the grief, they've got a better chance now than they did before. A *much* better chance."

I watch my Brothers and Sisters play and run and shout, their faces lit up with the simple pleasures of being alive and with their friends. Honey's belief in human resilience should make me feel a little better, given that it's my fault that these children are here in this gray place without their families.

But it doesn't.

At all.

BEFORE

I stride across the yard toward Building Nine, my mind full of Honey's face as they closed the door of the box.

I don't think I've ever felt this angry. *Ever*. When they Banished my mom, it felt like my heart was breaking, like it was actually physically breaking in my chest, but this is different. I want to scream and howl and burn this place down and dance on the ashes and salt the earth so nothing ever grows again.

Amos emerges from the shadows of the Chapel and blocks my way. "She's getting what she deserves," he says. "You get that, right?"

I stare at him. My head is full of fire, and the blood in my veins feels like ice water. I tell myself to stay calm, to *calm down*, because I won't be able to help Honey if I get myself locked inside the box right next to hers.

I take a deep breath and force a nod.

Amos narrows his eyes. "Let me hear it. Let me hear you say you understand."

"I understand." My voice sounds like the growl of an animal.

"I hope so," he says. "Because this ain't the time to do something stupid. Honey'll take her medicine and be out before you know it, so you go on and simmer down. The Lord is Good."

I stare at him. There's no way he could possibly guess what I'm going to do, but Amos is smarter than he looks, *a lot smarter*, so I have to be careful.

"Did you hear me?" he asks.

"Yes."

"And?"

"The Lord is Good," I spit.

His eyes narrow even more. The anger in my voice is clear and unmistakable, but I keep my gaze fixed on his, and I breathe slowly and deeply. I wait and I wait, and after what feels like hours but can have been only a few seconds, he steps to one side. I stride past him and across the yard without so much as a backward glance.

I open the door to my room and lie down on the bed. I force myself to wait. If Amos believes I'm going to be a problem, he'll go straight to Father John and voice his concerns. In which case, I've probably got a minute—maybe two, at the most—before a Centurion appears at my door. So I wait.

Five minutes, I tell myself. *Long enough to be sure.*

I stare at the door, waiting for Jacob Reynolds to push it open and tell me that Father John needs to talk to me. I force myself to settle down, to be rational and considered and careful, but all I can see is Honey's face and all I can hear is my mom calling Father John a snake-oil salesman, calling him a fraud and a liar to his face.

Calm, whispers the voice in the back of my head. *Stay calm.* But I can't. My insides feel like an electric current is being passed through them. It's mostly anger, but there's a little crackling ball of excitement there too. When something cruel or unfair happens to one of my Brothers or Sisters, my overriding feeling is usually impotence. But that's not the case now.

Not this time.

Nate was very clear. He told me I was only allowed to use the cell phone if things got *really bad*. I know he meant really bad for *me*, but I think he will forgive me for the choice I'm about to make. Because if locking a fourteen-year-old girl inside a metal box with no food or water in the height of the Texas summer doesn't qualify as *really bad*, then I can't imagine what would.

I check the clock on my little bedside table. Three minutes since I lay down. I can't hear anything unusual outside, no shouting and no thud of approaching footsteps, but I make myself wait just a little longer.

Two more minutes. Better safe than sorry.

The thought almost makes me laugh out loud. Because the great, shining truth that I'm furious took me so long to understand is that *nobody* inside the Legion is safe, except for Father John and maybe—*maybe*—his four Centurions. We've been told time and time again, in sermon after sermon and Proclamation after Proclamation, that we're safe inside the fences of the Base, because the monsters are all Outside. But the truth is exactly the opposite: the fences keep the real world out, and the monsters are inside with us.

I check the clock again.

Four minutes.

I watch the second hand complete its slow circuit, silently pleading with it to hurry. When it finally reaches twelve, I get off my bed and kneel down beside it, positioning myself so I'll be able to see the door if it opens. I reach under the bed, and my fingertips find the edges of the loose board without me even having to look.

I pry it up and set it carefully aside. Inside the little hollow are the things my dad left me and the two objects Nate gave me before he escaped. I leave the mementos and the skeleton key where they are and lift out the cell phone.

It seems to vibrate with danger in my hand. If anyone catches me with it, my punishment will make Honey's look like a gentle slap on the wrist.

I stand and examine the phone. It's a rectangle of black plastic, with a small screen on the front and fifteen oval buttons below. The one at the top left of the grid has a little green shape on it. I take a deep breath, trying to slow my racing heart, and press it with my thumb.

Nothing happens.

My heart sinks like a stone.

Maybe the battery is dead. Maybe the phone is broken. Or maybe it *never* worked, and this was all a cruel practical joke, and Nate is somewhere Outside, laughing himself silly at the stupid girl who actually believed that he would ever—

The screen lights up, and I almost drop the phone on the floor.

I hold it tightly in both hands and study it. There are rows of dashes on either side of the screen, and the word *Searching* glows at the top. Then it disappears and is replaced by *AT&T*. Next to this new word are five little circles. The one farthest to the left is colored black. The rest are empty.

The screen is really bright, much brighter than I was expecting, and I'm suddenly terrified that someone will see it through the walls of the building, so I stuff the phone into the pocket of my shorts. It makes a really obvious, straight-edged bulge that anyone who sees it will probably ask me about, but there's nowhere else to put it. I'll just have to make sure nobody sees it, because I don't dare use the phone here. It's quiet in my building now, but anyone could come in at any moment, and I might not hear them until it was too late.

I walk across my room and stop next to the door. I can't hear anything—*anyone*—in the corridor outside, but I still only open it about an inch and peer through the narrow crack.

Nothing. Just the pale wood of the walls and the glowing cross and the five other bedroom doors.

I slip out of my room and walk along to the front door. I press my ear to it, hear nothing out of the ordinary, and pull it open. There's no sign of Amos, or Father John, or any of the Centurions. Just the dark patch of the yard and the distant, shimmering shapes of my Brothers and Sisters going about their business.

I breathe a sigh of relief and step outside. It's barely ten in the morning, but the air is baking hot, the kind of heat that makes it feel like your insides are boiling. I think of Honey, sitting on the floor inside the box as its metal sides get hotter and hotter, and push the image away. I need a clear head for what I'm about to do, not one that's clouded by fury.

I walk round the yard, skirting the edge of the scorching blacktop, then cut east toward the maintenance sheds. It's not only a matter of finding somewhere inside the Base where I can't be overheard—I could stand at any corner of the fence and nobody would be able to hear a word I said. But if I did that, the likelihood of being seen standing on my own at the farthest corner of the Base with something pressed against my ear would be dangerously high. I might just as well walk into the Big House and use the cell phone in the middle of the living room.

What I need is somewhere remote enough that I can't be overheard and sheltered enough that I can't be seen. The sheds, where I stopped Luke from forcing Honey to do something horrible and where he *did* do something horrible to Jacob Reynolds, are the best solution I can think of.

The morning work is underway, so the tools and equipment that my Brothers and Sisters need for their chores should already

322

be out. They'll be returned when the Chapel bell rings for lunch, but that's at least two hours away, and that's if it isn't canceled—meals are usually the first things to go when Father John is unhappy with us, and the look on his face as Honey was carried away was far beyond angry. Somebody might realize they need a tool they hadn't anticipated and come and get it, and there's a chance that one of the Centurions might notice I'm not where I'm supposed to be and come looking for me, but it's pretty unlikely, and there's really nothing I can do about it.

It's quiet when I reach the row of sheds and shelters, but I still do a quick zigzag through them, making sure they are as empty as they seem. Scythes and forks and spades hang from rows of hooks above sacks of seed and fertilizer and weed killer and insect repellent. The tractor, a rusting hunk of green metal that always leaves a thick cloud of black smoke in its wake, is parked inside the biggest shelter, a small puddle of oil spreading beneath it.

I don't see anything. I don't hear anything. There's nobody around.

I check a second time, just to make absolutely sure, then stand in the warm shade on the far side of the largest shed, where nobody will be able to see me without me hearing them coming, and take the phone out of my pocket. For a long moment I hold it in my hand. It feels like I'm about to enter the unknown. Nate told me there was only one number in the phone's memory, but he didn't tell me whose number it was. I have to assume it's somebody who can help me, given his instructions about when to use it, but I don't even know that for certain. Then something else occurs to me: it's been the best part of a decade since I spoke to anyone outside the Lord's Legion, since the First Proclamation banned everyone but Amos from going into Town.

The best part of a decade spent with the same people. The best part of a decade shut away behind a fence.

I close my eyes, take a deep breath, and hold down the button with the number 1 on it. There's a deafeningly loud beep—my eyes spring open, and I dart my head around the corner of the shed, because I'm half expecting to see a Centurion sprinting across the desert toward me, ready to smash the phone on the ground and lock me in a box for the rest of my life.

But there's nothing. The Base is still and quiet.

The word *Dialing* appears on the screen, above a series of numbers. Then *Dialing* changes to *Connected*, and I hear a tinny voice emerge from the phone's speaker.

"Layton County Sheriff's Department."

I freeze. For several seconds, I stare at the phone, unable to say a word.

"Hello?" says the voice.

I summon an image of Honey, her skin reddening as the box heats up, her tongue hanging out of her mouth like a dog's, her eyes rolled back to white. A shudder rattles up my spine, my paralysis breaks, and I lift the phone to my ear.

"Hello?" I say.

"Layton County Sheriff's Department," repeats the voice. "How can I help you, ma'am?"

"I don't know," I say, which I know must sound stupid, but it's the truth. "I...I think I need help."

"Okay." It's a woman's voice, and it sounds steady and kind. I suddenly find myself fighting back tears. "Try to stay calm, ma'am. Tell me what's happening."

"I'm a member of the Lord's Legion." My stomach is churning, and I can hear my voice trembling. "Our Church is off State Highway 158, not far outside Layfield. Do you know where that is?"

"Sure," says the woman, but she doesn't sound kind anymore. She sounds annoyed. "The Lord's Legion. Right."

"My name is—"

I stop. I can't give this woman my name. If she does send help and Father John finds out I'm the reason it came, he'll kill me.

I think he'll actually kill me.

"Go on, ma'am," says the woman. "What's your name?"

"I can't tell you." Panic is starting to rise in my chest because I don't know how this is supposed to go and I'm sure I'm getting it wrong. "My friend Nate Childress gave me this number. Do you know him?"

"I'm afraid I don't know any Nate Childress, ma'am."

I frown. "Are you sure?" I ask, because that can't be right.

"Pretty sure," says the woman. "And you should be aware that making a false report to law enforcement is a crime in the state of Texas, so unless you have something real to tell me, I'm going to terminate this call."

"Don't," I say, and I'm shocked by how desperate my voice sounds. "Please. I don't...I don't know what else to do. I'm sorry."

"Are you all right, ma'am?" asks the woman, and some of the kindness has returned to her voice. "Do you need me to send someone to your location?"

"Yes," I say. "They locked Honey in a box, and it's really hot, and she's only fourteen, and she didn't do anything, not anything at all..."

My voice breaks, and I start to cry. Because it's not right what they did to Honey, it's *not fair*, and to Hell with anyone who thinks different.

"Can you repeat that, ma'am?" asks the woman. "Are you saying someone has been locked inside a box?"

I nod, then realize how dumb that is. "Yes. My friend. Her name is Honey."

"Who locked her in the box?"

"Father John did. He said she had to marry him, but she didn't want to. She's only fourteen."

"Okay," says the woman. Her voice is steady, and she's speaking more quickly, as though she's suddenly all business. "What about you, ma'am? Are you somewhere safe?"

"*No.*" Tears spill from my eyes and stream down my face. "It's *not* safe. I thought it was, but it isn't."

"Give me your location again."

"The Holy Church of the Lord's Legion," I say. "Outside Layfield, off Highway 158. I don't know the actual address."

"That's okay," says the woman. "Stay on the line while I—"

I hear the distant snap of a dry branch, and my nerve finally fails me. "I can't," I whisper. "Please help. I'm sorry."

I fumble the phone away from my ear with trembling hands and hold the green button down again until the screen goes blank. I shove it back into my pocket, take a futile couple of seconds to try and compose myself, then round the corner of the shed and head back toward the yard, my heart thudding against my ribs.

I try to walk normally—not too fast, not too slow—and I force a smile onto my face that I hope will make it clear to anyone who looks at me that everything is absolutely fine.

That I don't have a care in the world.

A
 F
  T
   E
    R

I started crying as I told Agent Carlyle and Doctor Hernandez what I did. I didn't want to, I really didn't want to, but I couldn't help it.

I didn't stop talking though. Once I'd started, once I was telling the truth and to Hell with the consequences, I just wanted to get it over and done with.

I stare at them, my tears drying on my cheeks, and wait for them to tell me how much trouble I'm in. While I wait, I search inside myself for the guilt that has been my constant companion ever since the tank appeared outside the Front Gate, but all I find is exhaustion and sweet, sickly relief.

"Moonbeam," says Doctor Hernandez, his voice low and thick. "I know that was extremely difficult for you. I want to thank you for finding the strength to be so brave."

I screw up my face so I don't start crying again and nod.

"There's something we need to tell you," says Agent Carlyle. "Something it never occurred to us you didn't know."

"What is it?"

His eyes lock on mine. "We knew you called the Layton County Sheriff's Department."

I stare at him. "What?"

"We knew you made the call," he says. "We've heard the recording."

No. That can't be right.

If they knew what I did all along, then why have they been so nice to me? Why didn't they call me a murderer and lock me up and tell me I'll never see the sun again?

If they didn't know, whispers the voice in the back of my head, *why would they say they did? What would they have to gain from being so cruel?*

"I'm going to take this slow," continues Agent Carlyle. "Because I need to make sure I'm understanding correctly. You thought a joint task force of the FBI and the ATF, comprising more than two hundred agents and a dozen vehicles with tactical support and remote surveillance, was mobilized and dispatched to the Lord's Legion compound because you made a call to the sheriff's department?"

I nod.

Obviously.

"And you now believe that making the call was a mistake, because you didn't realize what would happen when help arrived? That Father John would order your brothers and sisters to open fire on the authorities?"

I nod again.

"As far as you're concerned, you called them, they came, and then everything went to Hell."

I stare at him.

"So you think your brothers and sisters died because of what you did?"

My stomach lurches, and I don't respond.

"And you've carried that weight with you ever since?" His voice is trembling, as though he's on the verge of tears. "You believe that everything that happened to the Lord's Legion was your fault?"

"It was," I say, my voice a hoarse whisper. "It *was* my fault."

Agent Carlyle gives me the most gentle smile I've ever seen. "No. It wasn't. None of this is your fault, Moonbeam. Not any part of it."

My whole body feels numb, and my mind feels heavy.

Listen, urges the voice in the back of my head. *Listen to him.*

"What do you mean?" I manage.

"The Holy Church of the Lord's Legion had been under investigation by three separate federal agencies for more than two years," says Agent Carlyle. "The file was opened after a UPS employee in Lubbock intercepted a package containing firearm conversion kits and blasting caps that was headed to a post office box in Layfield. It was addressed to James Carmel."

I frown. "It contained what?"

"Firearm conversion kits let you change a gun from semi-automatic to fully automatic. I'm going to guess you understand the difference?"

All too well.

I nod.

"Automatic weapons are legal in Texas, but they have to be registered on a database when you buy them," he says. "Whereas you can buy a semiautomatic in a department store with a valid driver's license. Converting them yourself is illegal because it means you can amass an arsenal of automatic weapons that nobody knows you have. Does that sound familiar?"

My head fills with the smell of smoke and the deafening rattle of gunfire. Nausea rises through me, but I nod.

"I thought it might," he says. "Blasting caps are what they sound like. They're used to trigger explosives."

"To make bombs," I say.

Agent Carlyle nods. "Even before the package was intercepted in Lubbock, the Lord's Legion was under periodic surveillance as a potential domestic terrorism risk. The agencies had been building the case against John Parson and his closest associates for a long time, and the serving of the warrant that initiated the confrontation with the Legion members had been scheduled for more than a month. The fact that it took place the day after you made your call was nothing more than a coincidence. The Layton County Sheriff's Department entered the information you gave them into their system, and it was immediately flagged by the FBI. They were specifically told to take no action, as there was an active investigation underway. So absolutely *nothing* that happened that following day was your fault, Moonbeam. Do you understand what I'm saying to you?"

I stare at him. I don't know why he's lying to me after all this time. But he has to be, because if he knew I made the call, if they *both* knew, then why wouldn't they have told me so before now? Why would they have let me carry on believing everything that happened was my fault?

Because you never told them that's what you thought, whispers the voice in the back of my head. *You didn't trust them enough to tell them.*

"We knew you made the call," says Doctor Hernandez. "I didn't want to rush you into talking about it, because I knew it would be hard for you, and I wanted to let you reach that place of trust on your own terms. But if I had known you were blaming yourself for what happened, I would have told you the truth during our first session."

"I believe you," I say, and I'm slightly surprised to find that I do. I genuinely do.

The realization fills my head, but is quickly pushed aside. I know everyone is still dead so I shouldn't really be happy, but the thought filling my mind is *They didn't die because of me.* It wasn't my fault, and it's all I can do not to burst into tears of joy.

Agent Carlyle shakes his head. "I can't believe you've been tormenting yourself with that," he says. "You should have told us."

"I wanted to." My voice is high and unsteady. I don't know whether to laugh or cry. "I thought about it, but I couldn't make myself do it. I wasn't sure I was going to be able to go through with it today. You have to understand that every time I walked into SSI, I saw a group of children who were orphans because of me. *Because of what I did.*"

"I'm so sorry," says Doctor Hernandez.

I take a deep breath. "It wasn't my fault?" I need to hear him say it again. "It really wasn't?"

He smiles at me and shakes his head. "No, Moonbeam. It really wasn't."

I close my eyes. The wave of relief fills me to the tips of my fingers and toes, breaks, and rolls back. My mind starts to clear as it recedes, and something occurs to me. I open my eyes and frown at Agent Carlyle.

"How were you watching us?" I ask.

"I'm sorry?" he says.

"You said the Legion was under surveillance for a long time. How?"

"Lots of ways," says Agent Carlyle. "All mail in and out was being intercepted and opened, and we had long-range microphones that could hear what was being said inside the compound, cameras that could see what was happening."

What?

331

My frown deepens. "So you saw what the Centurions did to Honey? You saw Lucy get beaten senseless by a man ten times her size? And you didn't do anything?"

Agent Carlyle winces. "I wasn't part of the task force," he says. "I was brought in as part of a team to investigate what led to the fire. But I know they didn't see and hear everything. Not even close."

"So they didn't know what life was really like inside the Base?" I already know the answer. I just want to hear him admit it. "The cameras and microphones somehow missed all the bad stuff?"

"You have to understand how an investigation of this scale works," he says. "The priority was gathering the necessary evidence for federal firearms and conspiracy indictments. They were building cases of illegal imprisonment and assault and pursuing about a dozen other charges at the same time, but it was the automatic weapons and blasting caps that were going to put John Parson away for the rest of his life."

"So in the meantime, they just watched people get hurt? They just let it happen?"

He doesn't drop his gaze from mine. "Yes. I know how callous that must sound. But these investigations take time, and the agencies couldn't risk alerting John Parson to their surveillance. So they watched and listened and waited until they were ready to move."

A terrible thought fills my head. *Oh God.*

"Everything I've told you," I say. "Did you know it all already?"

Doctor Hernandez's eyes widen. "Absolutely not. Everything you have told us has been vitally useful."

I see no deception in his eyes. Only concern that this session has somehow started to go wrong.

"Doctor Hernandez is telling you the truth," says Agent Carlyle. "My role when I came into these sessions was to ask you to expand our understanding of life inside the Lord's Legion. To confirm what we suspected, yes, but to tell us details we *didn't* know. I promise."

"Okay," I say. "I believe you."

"Thank you," he says.

"I still don't get it," I say. "I don't understand how they could know people were being hurt and not do anything about it."

"If it makes you feel any better, they had a fail-safe inside the base," he says. "In case things ever got really out of—"

"Agent Carlyle," says Doctor Hernandez sharply.

I stare at the two men, a frown creasing my forehead. Father John was right about one thing, if nothing else.

"Nate," I say. "You're talking about Nate."

Agent Carlyle looks at me for a long moment, then nods.

BEFORE

Nate and I are walking the eastern perimeter of the Base.

The fence is almost twelve feet high—thick wooden posts driven into the ground with sheets of metal mesh strung between them and razor wire coiled along the top, its angular blades pointing out in a hundred different directions. It was strengthened and heightened after the Purge, and its maintenance is one of the most vital jobs on the work rotation. Animals dig underneath and fallen branches tear holes in the wire, which makes patching the fence a daily chore.

The sun is descending rapidly toward the western horizon, filling the sky with unearthly purple light. I was in the gardens all afternoon, pulling out weeds on my hands and knees, so I'm hot and tired and my forehead is coated with dust and sweat and my hair is glued to the back of my neck. All of which is obviously ideal on the day Nate invites me to go for a walk after the Chapel bell rings to signal the end of the working day.

We used to go walking pretty often, but everything has been weird lately. It's nearly a month since Amos was attacked in Town, but it feels like a lot of people are still on edge, as though they're worried it was a sign, maybe a signal of something *worse to come*. And even out here by the fence, about as far away from the building next to the Chapel as it's possible to be, I can still hear Horizon coughing.

Everyone is waiting for him to Ascend, because nobody still believes that he's going to get better, no matter how hard everyone prays. And although nobody would dream of saying so out loud, it's obvious that a lot of my Brothers and Sisters will be relieved when his time finally comes.

I guess I can understand that though. Listening to someone die is hard, especially when it's someone you love.

Nate stops and raps his knuckles against one of the wooden posts. He seems distracted, like he has a lot on his mind.

"Penny for them?" I ask.

He smiles because this is an old joke between the two of us. "Bad deal for you," he replies.

"Everything okay?" I ask. "You're pretty quiet."

He shrugs. "I'm fine. Yourself?"

"I'm all right."

"Do you miss your mom?" he asks.

I stare at him. I can feel my mouth hanging open, and I'm distantly aware that I must look ridiculous, but I can't seem to do anything about it. His question, so dangerous and so out of the blue, has sent my brain reeling in search of an appropriate response.

It's absolutely *forbidden* to mention former Brothers and Sisters who have been Banished from the Legion; we are supposed to act as though they literally never existed. If the question had come from anyone other than Nate, I would have assumed it was some clumsy attempt at a trap—that whoever was asking had every intention of reporting me to the Centurions if I admitted such a profound failing.

Nate wouldn't do that to me though. He wouldn't. So I have to take his question at face value, and that means thinking about my mom, which I don't do very often. Not because it's forbidden—I care a lot less about what's allowed and what isn't these days—but because it's still really painful to think about her; so much so that I've pretty much accepted that's the way it's always going to be.

"That's kind of a blunt question," I say.

"Sorry," says Nate. "You don't have to answer if you don't want to."

The silence stretches out. "Yeah," I say. "I miss her."

"It's a shame I never met her," he says. "I think I would have liked her."

I smile at him. I know he's trying to be nice, and I'm not going to disagree with him about something I can never know for certain, but I'm not sure he *would* have liked my mom. Not everyone did.

Including you, whispers the voice in the back of my head. *Some of the time, at least.*

I wince and silently tell it to shut up.

"She was Banished the summer before I got here," he says. "Right?"

I nod.

"So she's been Gone almost three years."

Dear Lord, has it been that long already?

"I guess so," I say.

"Do you buy what people say about her? That she was a Heretic?"

Heresy is the exclusive domain of Father John and even talking about it can be viewed as Heretical, if you say the wrong thing. But I trust Nate, and I *want* to talk about my mom. I haven't spoken about her out loud in a very long time.

"They found her journal," I say. "The things she wrote in it were Heretical. There's no pretending they weren't."

"So?" he asks.

"So I guess she was a Heretic. By Father John's definition, at least."

He nods. "And by yours?"

I frown. "My what?"

"*Your* definition of Heresy."

"I don't have one." I'm lying, even though I trust him, because some things go so deep that there's no easy way around them.

"Okay," he says. "That's fine. Maybe we should talk about something else."

He seems disappointed as he resumes walking. I take a deep breath and stay where I am. After a couple of steps, he turns back and frowns at me.

"Aren't you coming?"

"Ask me again," I say.

He narrows his eyes. "Ask you what?"

"About what she was."

"Okay," he says, and walks back to stand in front of me. "Do you think your mom was a Heretic?"

"Yes," I say. "I think she lost any Faith she ever had in the Lord's Legion a long time before they Banished her. Maybe after the Purge, or when my dad died, or maybe it was never there in the first place."

Nate doesn't say anything. He just looks at me with his bright green eyes, so I plunge on because when you open certain doors, the kind that are supposed to be kept shut, you have to go all the way through them and to Hell with the consequences.

"I know I'm not supposed to think about her. And I guess she deserved to be Banished, given the rules we all live by. But I don't think she did anything wrong, Nate. Not anymore. Is that bad of me?"

I'm close to tears. Part of it is rising panic, because if Nate isn't who I think he is, I've voluntarily handed him enough ammunition to have me locked in a box until the End Times. But part of it—*most of it*—is an unstoppable torrent of relief. I've wanted to say that for such a long time, so long that the unspoken words had started to feel physically heavy, like a weight around my neck.

Nate takes a step closer. "No," he says, his voice low. "I don't think that's bad of you. I don't think it's bad at all. But I need you to promise me you won't ever say what you just said to anyone else, okay? Do you promise?"

I nod. "I promise."

"Good," he says. "You can't trust our Brothers and Sisters, Moonbeam. You can't trust anyone who isn't me."

"Okay," I say, but his words, and the horrible truth in them, cut me like a scalpel. I can feel tears threatening to break loose from the corners of my eyes.

Nate sees them and gives me a fierce smile. "Don't cry. It's going to be all right."

"How?" I ask, my voice trembling. "How is *anything* going to be all right?"

"The Lord is Good," he says.

"I don't think I believe that, Nate."

Heresy, whispers the voice in the back of my head, but it doesn't sound like it's angry with me. It almost sounds *proud*.

Nate points at the razor wire coiled along the top of the fence. "Why is this here?"

"To keep our enemies out," I say automatically.

Nate's smile widens. "Spoken like a True Legionnaire. Why is it *really* here?"

"I don't know," I say, but I *do*. I just want him to be the one to say it because I'm afraid to.

"To keep us in," he says. "You, me, and everyone else."

I shake my head, because even though that's *exactly* what I've come to believe in the years since they Banished my mom, the certainty that has been pounded into me ever since the Purge is too strong to simply push to one side.

"People can leave whenever they want," I say. "Nobody is forced to stay."

"Only Amos is allowed to go into Layfield," says Nate. "The rest of us aren't allowed outside the Base. And when was the last time somebody left the Legion of their own free will?"

"After the Purge."

He nods. "People who were loyal to Father Patrick. Do you think Father John was sad to see them go?"

"What about after the Third Proclamation? Lots of people left then."

He nods. "People who had made it clear that they weren't going to obey the new rule and who would almost certainly have caused trouble if they'd stayed. If they hadn't made the decision to leave, Father John would have Banished them within a month. I guarantee it."

"My mom..."

"Your mom was a Heretic," he says, grimacing at the word. "She was found guilty of Apostasy, although that wasn't her real crime. You know that, don't you?"

I frown. "What do you mean?"

"Having to Banish someone for Apostasy is bad, because it means having to admit that Faith is something that can be lost," he says. "If Father John had believed there was any way to bring your mother back into line, he'd have done whatever it took."

"So why didn't he try?" I ask. "Because of what she said to him?"

Nate frowns. "What did she say to him?"

I stare at him. I've never told anyone what I saw in the Big House the day my mom was Banished. And very few people actually know the truth: The Prophet, the Centurions, Bella and Agavé and Star, and me.

That's all. That's everyone.

And my mom, of course. Wherever she is now.

"She told Father John she had never had any Faith in him. She called him a snake-oil salesman, who preyed on vulnerable people."

Nate shakes his head and lets out a low whistle. "Wow. I'm not surprised he got her out of here as quickly as he possibly could."

"He sent Angel to watch her while she packed her things," I say. "He told him to make sure she didn't speak to anyone."

Nate grimaces. "I bet he did. That proves the point I was trying to make. From Father John's perspective, she was dangerous. It was safer for him if she was Gone."

"Why was she dangerous?" I ask. "She had never caused any trouble."

"Because of you, Moonbeam," he says.

What?

I stare at him. "I don't…"

"Your mother hadn't just been looking for a way to leave the Lord's Legion," says Nate. "Father John said her journal made it clear she had been planning *to take you with her*. And you're promised to him, selected by The Lord to be his wife when the time comes. Can you imagine how it would have looked if your mom had succeeded with her plans? What it would have done to his standing with our Brothers and Sisters if she had managed to take you away from him?"

"But she *wanted* me to marry Father John," I say. "She suggested it to him, over and over again, and she celebrated when he announced that The Lord had chosen me as a Future Wife. Why would she have done all that if she was planning to take me away from here?"

"I don't know."

Bullshit. You know something you're not telling me.

"Why don't I believe you?" I ask.

"I'm telling you the truth, Moonbeam," he says. "There are things it's safer for you not to know, lots of them, but if I knew anything about your mom, I would tell you. I promise."

I frown. "What things? What isn't safe for me to know?"

He doesn't answer. He stares through the fence at the desert outside.

"Nate?" I ask. "What things?"

His eyes stay fixed on the distant horizon. "Why is Father John so scared of the Outside?"

"Because it isn't safe."

"Who says so?"

"Father John."

Nate grunts with laughter. "Of course," he says. "Why isn't it safe?"

"You mean why does he say it isn't?"

"Yes."

"Because it's where our enemies live."

Nate nods. "Right. The ones we've been told will torture us and abduct us and murder us if they get the slightest chance. But have you ever actually seen anyone out there, Moonbeam? Apart from college kids gawking through the fence, that is?"

"No," I say. "And I understand what you're getting at. But for the sake of argument, wouldn't they be hiding if they were out there?"

"Maybe," says Nate, and gives the fence a shake. "But according to Father John, the Servants of the Serpent have tanks and bombs and helicopters that spray gasoline. If that's the case, do you really think this chicken wire would keep them out?"

"I guess not." I pause. "So what are you saying? That our enemies aren't real?"

Nate shakes his head. "That's not what I'm saying. I'm not going to tell you that nobody out there hates us, and I'm not saying the Outside is some peaceful paradise. But Father John is preparing the Legion for a battle he believes is inevitable, and that kind of thinking has a tendency to be self-fulfilling."

I frown. "I don't understand."

He looks at me for a long moment, then breaks into a sad smile. "I'm sorry," he says. "I've been talking way too much. We should get back."

"It's okay." I don't want him to stop talking, and I don't want to go back to the rest of our Family; I want to stay here, where I don't have to be frightened about everything I say and where nobody looks at me like the daughter of a Heretic.

"It's okay?" he repeats. "I don't know if it is, Moonbeam. I really don't. But we're where we are, you and me, so I'll say one more thing before we go."

I wait for him to continue.

"There's a room in the basement of the Big House," says Nate. "It has a door that's always locked."

"Where Amos keeps the guns for training," I say. "I know that."

"There's more than guns inside that room," he says. "A *lot* more."

"Like what?"

He doesn't answer. He stares straight at me, his eyes slightly narrowed, as though he's waiting for me to do or say something.

"Like what?" I ask. "Tell me."

342

He shakes his head. "I think that's enough for today."

Anger blooms in my chest. "Don't do that. I'm not a kid, Nate. You don't get to decide what's enough for me and what isn't."

He smiles a wide, genuine smile that lights up his face. "I didn't mean for you. I'm going to walk back around to the gardens. Are you coming?"

I don't respond right away. I want him to tell me about the locked room. and I'm still deciding whether to be annoyed with him about the "that's enough" comment because he definitely wasn't talking about himself. But I can tell by the look on his face that he isn't going to tell me anything else right now, and I don't think I can actually be angry with him when it feels like he might be my only friend in the whole world.

"Sure," I say eventually. "Let's go."

He nods, and I fall into step beside him as we walk north along the fence.

He'll tell me about the room in the basement later, I think. *I'm sure he will. It's not like either of us is going anywhere.*

A
F
T
E
R

"I didn't know about Nate," says Agent Carlyle. "When you asked me about him before, I mean. I was telling you the truth."

"I guess I have to believe that, don't I?"

"I hope you can."

I shrug. "So who was he working for? The same people as you?"

Agent Carlyle shakes his head. "He was ATF. You know who they are, right?"

I nod. They were on Father John's list of evil Government agencies. "Alcohol, tobacco, and firearms."

"That's right. They sent him in after the package was intercepted in Lubbock. It seems only about five people knew he was there."

"Do they know if that included Father John?" I ask.

"Nate's case file is classified," says Agent Carlyle, "but I talked to one of the agents in his section, and they don't think John Parson knew. The current theory is that he asked Nate to be a Centurion in good faith and only accused him of being a spy to save face after Nate turned down the offer. They don't believe Parson would have given him a night to reconsider if he had suspected the truth."

I grimace. "They're probably right."

"I think so too," he says.

"So I never actually knew him then?" I ask. "The *real* him, I mean. The person I thought was my friend was a lie."

Agent Carlyle shakes his head. "That's not true. Undercover agents are trained to deviate from their actual personalities as little as possible. It's a lot easier to be convincing when you're not pretending to be someone else. So the person you knew was real."

"Was his name really Nate Childress?"

"It was."

"I don't suppose there's any way I can see him?"

Doctor Hernandez flinches. "I don't think we're at that stage in—"

"Forget it," I say, and look back at Agent Carlyle. "If you talk to your colleague again, ask him to thank Nate for everything he did for me. Tell him I'm grateful."

"I will," he says. "You can count on it."

"Thank you."

"Why do you think he told you those things about the Legion's enemies and the locked door in the basement?" asks Doctor Hernandez.

"I don't know," I say. "I've thought about it a lot, especially after he escaped. Maybe they were eating away at him, and he just couldn't keep in anymore. I like to think I was the only person he trusted enough to say them to. But I don't know."

"He took a big risk," says Agent Carlyle.

"He knew I wouldn't tell anyone," I say. "Or at least, I hope he did. I'd have gotten in trouble too."

"As much trouble?"

"No," I say. "But it wouldn't have been good for either of us."

"Do you think he trusted you because he could see you were struggling with your own faith?" asks Doctor Hernandez.

"That would make sense, I guess. But I don't know what he saw."

He writes a quick line in one of his notebooks. "Are you okay to keep going?" he asks. "We can stop if you'd like."

I shake my head. "I want to finish this."

Agent Carlyle smiles. "All right then. Can you tell us what happened the day after you made your call to the Layton County Sheriff's Department? The seventeenth?"

Be calm, whispers the voice in the back of my head. *It's all right. It's going to be okay.*

"The day of the fire," I say.

They both nod.

It's going to be okay.

I close my eyes and cast my mind back until I can feel the heat, and hear the gunfire, and smell the blood and the dust.

It's going to be okay.

I take a deep breath. I open my eyes.

I speak.

BEFORE

I'm walking across the yard when I hear a low noise in the distance.

While everyone else had been finishing breakfast in Legionnaires' Hall I went to talk to Honey, to let her know that I was thinking about her, that she hadn't been forgotten, but Amos appeared behind me before I managed more than a few words and dragged me away, his face as dark as thunder. I heard Honey say "Hello" before his hand landed on my shoulder, so I know she is still alive at least, even though her voice was weak and it sounded like her throat has been lined with sandpaper.

"Are you stupid, girl?" asked Amos. "Are you determined to make a bad situation worse?"

I shrugged off his hand. "I'm talking to my Sister," I said. "There's no rule against that."

"*Your Sister* is being punished for Heresy," said Amos. "You can talk to her after she's made herself right with The Lord. Not before."

"And that's okay with you?" I asked, my face filling with angry heat.

"The Lord is Good," growled Amos. "Now get the hell out of here, and be glad I don't reckon this is worth concerning The Prophet with."

I'd stared at him for long seconds, my head throbbing with fury, then turned on my heel and strode away toward the yard.

Now I stop, the rumbling noise low and distant.

The dirt road that runs from the Front Gate to the highway is almost two miles long, but when the wind is blowing in the right direction we can hear the occasional rumble of a far-off engine. We can't see the vehicles themselves, because the road snakes between two low hills that block the view to the south, so I like to guess what they are—the big trucks we used to see lumbering along the highway when we were still allowed to go into Town maybe, or yellow buses full of children, or families in cars and mobile homes, singing along with the radio at the tops of their voices.

My first thought is that it's one of those I'm hearing now.

I stop in the middle of the yard and look past the Front Gate, straining my ears. The noise is a low rumble that sounds like an engine, but after a few seconds, I realize something.

It's getting louder.

Around the yard, I see several of my Brothers and Sisters stop as well. No one says anything, and no one looks particularly concerned, but they're listening. They're *all* listening. On the porch of the Big House I see Bella cradling one of her children, and by the side of the Chapel, I see Jacob Reynolds staring south, his eyes narrow.

The rumbling gets steadily louder, until the ground starts to shake beneath my feet. Occasionally—*very* occasionally—some local drives up to the Front Gate so they can see the Lord's Legion weirdos for themselves, but this doesn't sound like a car or a pickup.

It sounds bigger. A *lot* bigger.

The hairs on my arms are standing up, and my stomach feels hollow, like I haven't eaten for days. My gaze is fixed on the first bend in the dirt road, maybe a hundred meters outside the Front Gate.

The early morning air is warm and absolutely still. It feels like everything has been put on pause, like the whole world has been told to take a ten-minute break. Then something huge and black rounds the bend, and everyone starts to run and shout at the same time.

It looks a lot like the tanks I saw on TV before the Purge, in the days when we were still allowed to watch movies—six giant wheels carrying an angular metal box with a long pole sticking out at the front and a circular turret on top. It's moving slowly down the dirt road, its engine roaring and belching smoke, but there's something horribly inevitable about its rumbling approach.

Jacob lumbers across the yard, bellowing at the top of his voice. People start to sprint in every direction. The front door of the Big House slams open, and Father John strides out onto the porch, a deep frown on his face. His eyes spring wide. Then his booming voice echoes out across the yard as he bellows for everyone to arm themselves before he disappears back inside.

Goose bumps break out across my skin.

Arm themselves.

I think about the AR-15 Amos gave me. It's lying on my bedside table, loaded and ready for use.

The tank stops outside the Front Gate, and I watch a line of vehicles follow behind it. There are black vans with the letters ATF printed on their sides and red-and-white ambulances and dark green jeeps and half a dozen black-and-white cars. One of the cars turns to one side as it stops, and what's printed on its door stops my heart dead in my chest.

Layton County Sheriff's Department.

I can't move. Can't breathe.

I stare at the words as my mind fills with a single terrible thought.

I did this.

Around me, people are running in every direction. I hear confused cries that sound like they're being made by children, but as I try to force myself to turn and look for them I see Luke come running out of Building Twelve with an AK-47 in his hands. The look of gleeful joy on his face shocks me out of my paralysis.

I run toward him, shouting for him to put down the gun, as the turret on the top of the tank opens and a dark shape—*a Government*—appears. It has a bullhorn in its hand, and I'm still far away from Luke when its amplified voice blasts out across the Base.

"Members of the Holy Church of the Lord's Legion," it says. "We are in possession of a federal arrest warrant for John Parson and a federal search and seizure warrant for these premises, both produced in accordance with the Federal Rules of Criminal Procedure and both signed by Judge Warren Hartford of Layton County. Please assemble in the central yard with your hands raised while we execute these warrants."

I'm still running toward Luke when he skids to a halt at the edge of the yard and raises the AK-47 to his shoulder. I hear someone yell, "Gun!" and I scream for him to put it down because I know who these people are and why they're here, and this isn't what I wanted, oh Lord, *this isn't what I wanted at all.*

Fire licks from the barrel of the AK-47 as Luke pulls the trigger. The shots are deafening in the still morning air, a drumbeat of metallic explosions. A short burst of gunfire rattles out from somewhere near the Front Gate, and dust erupts into the air as bullets hammer into the ground where Luke was standing. But he's already sprinting toward the Chapel and disappearing around its side. Screams of fear and howls of fury float across the yard, and as I stare at the bullet-shredded patch of ground where Luke was standing, gunshots ring out from what sounds like everywhere all at once and my world is suddenly full of flying lead.

I hurl myself to the ground and wrap my arms around my head. I hear bullets crunch into the blacktop around me and, in the distance, so far away that it might as well be the next county or even the next *state*, I hear the amplified voice of the Government shouting "Cease fire!" over and over again—but the roar of guns doesn't reduce in the slightest, let alone stop.

I scramble to my feet and frantically scan the wide expanse of the Base. Some of my Brothers and Sisters have taken cover behind buildings and trees and hunks of machinery. One or two are frozen where they stand, their eyes squeezed shut, their faces full of terror, but most of them are firing streams of bullets in the direction of the Front Gate. Screams float above the thunder of the gunfire, and I can't tell which are pain and which are violent euphoria at the Final Battle having begun at last.

I sprint off the yard, keeping as low as I can. I risk a look to the south as I reach the corner of Building Eight and see four Governments dragging a limp black shape through a hole in the fence, waving furiously at one of the ambulances. The Government in the turret is still shouting into the bullhorn, demanding that everyone cease firing, but nobody seems to be paying any attention. Everyone is yelling and shooting. The chaos is deafening. I run around the back of Building Eight, expecting to feel bullets punch me in the back at any moment, to see my own blood spray out onto the dirt.

I dart across the gap to Building Nine and drag open the door. I race along the corridor and throw myself into my room as bullets slam into the walls around me. The AR-15 is lying on my bedside table, but I don't even look at it as I crawl across the floor and slide under my bed. I wrench up the loose floorboard, grab the plastic bag with the skeleton key in it, and scramble to my feet. I run back down the corridor and throw open the front door, but a volley of bullets smashes into the frame, and I scream as I dive away and curl myself into a tight ball on the floor.

Splinters of wood rain down on me as I crawl back to the open door. The air outside is already heavy with smoke and the bitter, acrid smell of gunfire. The noise is relentless, an endless cacophony of gunpowder explosions and the crunching impact of bullets. I pull myself up into a crouch, take a deep breath, and burst through the door. I'm sprinting north as soon my feet reach the ground, heading for the row of metal boxes near the fence.

This is my doing, all of it. I set this nightmare in motion, and I'm sure there's nothing I can do to stop it. But there is *something* I can do.

I can make sure Honey doesn't die like an animal in a cage.

I'm halfway around the yard, ducking and weaving along the edge of the blacktop, when the door of the Big House opens and Father John appears again, his face blazing with righteous anger, an M4 rifle in his hands.

"CENTURIONS TO ME!" he bellows. "CHILDREN TO AGAVÉ! FIGHT, MY BROTHERS AND SISTERS! FIGHT TO THE LAST! THE FINAL BATTLE IS UPON US!"

A roar goes up across the Base, and the shooting somehow manages to intensify, to a level where the air feels like it is mostly bullets and my head feels like it's being squeezed in a vise. But a single thought manages to penetrate the punishing racket; it fills my mind as I run, as cold and certain as a winter storm.

We're dead.

You've killed us all.

A
F
T
E
R

"I've listened to every audio recording made that morning," says Agent Carlyle. "You can clearly hear John Parson order everyone to 'fight to the last.'"

My throat hurts, but I manage a nod as I pour myself a cup of water from the jug on the desk.

"Do you feel like you can keep going?" asks Doctor Hernandez. "It's absolutely fine if you need a break."

I drain the little plastic cup and shake my head. "I don't want a break," I say. "I want to finish this."

He looks at me for a long moment, then nods. "Take it slow," he says. "You're doing so well."

BEFORE

I'm about to sprint across open ground toward the box when Jacob Reynolds lurches out of the smoke in front of me, wild-eyed, clutching a rifle in his hands.

I skid to the right, my feet churning up orange dust, and run hard toward the back of the Chapel. Bullets hammer holes in the white wall as I reach the corner of the building, and I lose my footing as I throw myself around it. I land on my hip, sending a bolt of agony screaming down my right leg, and as I try to scramble up, it gives way beneath me. I fold back to the ground, howling in pain. I pound at my thigh with both hands, trying to punch feeling back into it, and I'm rewarded with a sensation that feels like someone has covered my entire leg with fire ants. The pain is so awful that for a horrible second I'm sure I'm going to puke, but when I stagger to my feet for the second time, my leg barely holds me up.

I limp along the rear wall of the Chapel, past the row of arched windows, until movement inside the building catches my eye. I stop and peer through the glass. Luke is backing along the aisle between the rows of wooden pews, pumping yellow liquid out of a red plastic barrel and spraying it across the floor and the benches. He reaches the door that opens onto the yard, tosses the barrel aside, and pulls a box of matches out of his jeans pocket.

Understanding slams into me. I hammer on the window with my fists, shouting his name as he strikes a match and applies the flame to the rest of the box. He looks at me, and my insides turn cold, because the smile on his face is the worst thing I've ever seen.

"THE LORD IS GOOD!" he bellows, his eyes locked on mine. Then he pitches the burning matchbox down the aisle and dives out through the door.

The whole world turns yellow.

There's a sound like a thousand thunderclaps, and I feel my feet leave the ground as the Chapel windows explode in a hailstorm of flying glass. Fire billows out through the empty spaces. The heat is unbelievable, and I roll back and forth on the dry ground because I'm sure I must be burning, I *must* be on fire, because everything is so unbearably *hot*.

I hear the gunfire dip as screams rise once more. I get to my feet, my ears ringing, the hair on my arms burned away. The Chapel roof splits open. Flames roar up and out, sending black smoke swirling into the sky. Burning chunks of wood crash down onto flat roofs, and before I've even had time to draw a breath, it seems like half the Base is on fire. I stagger back from the intense heat, coughing and spluttering and trying to clear my head. Someone grabs my shoulder and spins me around. I'm sure it's going to be Luke, that he's going to shoot me dead with his AK-47 and nobody will ever know—but it isn't. It's Star, her eyes bulging, her hands clutching an M16 that is almost bigger than she is.

"Why aren't you fighting?" she yells. "This is it, Moonbeam! The Final Battle!"

"Where are your daughters?" I ask, my voice a hoarse croak. "Where are your girls, Star?"

"Agavé took all the kids to the west barracks," she says. "They'll be safe there until the victory is won. Come with me, Moonbeam. We'll fight for The Lord together."

I shake my head and take a step back. She looks at me with complete incomprehension, then raises the M16 and aims it at my chest.

Everything stops.

The heat of the fire fades away. The noise of the shooting drops to nothing. Even the smoke seems to hang still in the air as my heart freezes solid in my chest. Because when I look into Star's eyes, I don't see the woman who has mostly been kind to me, who always seemed to genuinely adore her children and love her Brothers and Sisters. Instead, I see the animal stare of a person I don't recognize.

"Don't…" I say. "Star…please…"

She glares at me, the gun steady in her hands. I wait for my life to flash before my eyes, because that's what's supposed to happen when you're about to die, but I don't see anything. Nothing happens. Everything is still until Star jerks the gun away and disappears into the smoke without a word.

I stand rooted to the spot, until my brain produces an image of Honey lying dead on the floor of the box, and the voice in the back of my head screams for me to wake up. I take a couple of deep breaths, then turn north and run into the thickening smoke.

My leg is still screaming with pain, but it holds me up, and that's all that matters right now. The row of boxes looms in the distance, and I risk a glance over my shoulder as I head toward them.

Fire is spreading across the bone-dry ground like running

water, igniting everything it comes into contact with, and the swirling clouds of smoke are making it hard to see anything. I can see the black shapes of the Governments moving near the fence, but I can't tell whether they've moved into the Base itself. The gunfire is still endless—a constant thudding that makes my ears ring.

I reach the only occupied box and make my way to its front. I pull the plastic bag out of my pocket, rip it open, and grip the skeleton key tightly in my hand. I shout to Honey as I approach the door, telling her, "*It's okay. Everything's going to be all right.*"

I slide the key into the padlock and twist it. For a millisecond, it doesn't move, but then the lock springs apart and thuds to the ground. The door creaks open, and I stare into the darkness for a long moment because I don't know what else to do.

The box is empty.

I spin around and try to peer through the drifting smoke. The Chapel is a raging inferno. The blurry shapes of my Brothers and Sisters move back and forth, firing guns at targets that are invisible from where I'm standing.

I can't see Honey. There's no sign of her.

I hear approaching footsteps, and I'm suddenly very aware that I'm probably the only unarmed person for five miles in any direction, apart from the children in the west barracks. I turn in time to see Bella emerge out of the smoke, a black pistol in her hand.

"What are you doing, Moonbeam?" she asks. "Why are you—"

"Where's Honey?" I ask.

"That's none of your concern!" she shouts, her eyes flashing with anger. "Why aren't you fighting for your Family? Where's your—"

"Tell me where she is, Bella!" I yell. "Tell me right now!"

Her eyes widen, and she raises the pistol, but I'm already moving because I've had one gun pointed at me in the last five minutes and that was more than enough.

I slam my hand down on her wrist. The impact vibrates all the way up my arm, and Bella howls in pain as the gun tumbles to the ground. I step forward and push her chest with both hands. She staggers backward until her feet tangle, and she sprawls flat on her back. My hands are balled into fists as I stride toward her because I'm scared and I'm pulsing with adrenaline and I don't think I've ever felt so angry as I do right now, so completely fucking *outraged*. I snatch the pistol off the ground and point it at her heart.

"Where is she, Bella?" I growl. "I'm not going to ask you again."

"Amos let her out," she says. Her eyes are wide. There is fear in them as she looks at me. "I think he put her with the others."

"In the west barracks?"

She nods. I don't waste time saying anything else; I leave her lying on the ground and head back the way I came.

I sprint across the yard, my eyes streaming, my heart pounding in my chest.

The noise of the gunfire is still deafening, and I hear—I actually hear—bullets whizzing past me, their low whines like the speeded-up buzz of insects, but I don't slow down, and I don't change course. The Chapel is burning out of control, its roof engulfed by roaring fire and sending up a huge black plume of smoke, and the amplified voice of the Government booms across the compound, repeating its demand over and over again.

"Put down your weapons and come forward slowly with your hands in the air!"

Nobody is listening. Not the other Governments, and definitely not any of my Brothers and Sisters.

In the distance, back near the Front Gate, the tank rumbles forward, crushing the flimsy wire fence and churning the desert floor. Somewhere, over the engines and the endless rattle of gunfire, I can hear screams of pain and pleading shouts for help, but I force myself to ignore them and keep going: my gaze is fixed on the wooden cabins at the western edge of the Base.

I trip over something.

My feet tangle, and I go sprawling onto the cracked blacktop of the yard. Pain crunches through me as my shoulder hits the ground, but I grit my teeth and get back on my feet and look to see what I fell over.

Alice is lying on her back, her hands clutching her stomach.

Her shirt has turned red, and she's lying in a pool of blood that seems too big to have all come out of one person. She's still alive though. Her eyes are dim, but they find mine, and she looks at me with an expression I can't describe. There's pain there, a lot of pain, and shock, and fear, and something that looks like confusion, like she wants to know how things ever came to this.

I hold her gaze. I want to stay with her, to tell her it's all right and that she's going to be okay, but it isn't all right, nothing is, and I don't know very much about bullet wounds, but I don't think she is going to be okay.

I'm pretty sure she's going to die.

I stare at her, wasting seconds that the still-functional bit of my brain screams at me for wasting, then run toward the west barracks. Alice's eyes widen as I start to turn away, but I don't see anger in them. I think she understands what I have to do.

That's what I tell myself, at least.

A figure emerges from the swirling smoke, and I skid to a halt, my hands raised. But it isn't one of the Governments, with their black helmets and goggles and guns. It's Amos, his eyes red and puffy, one arm limp at his side, a pistol trembling in his good hand.

"Where's Father John?" he asks, his voice hoarse and torn. "Have you seen him?"

I shake my head and try to circle around him, but he grabs my arm and pulls me close.

"Where is he? Where is The Prophet?" he rasps.

"I don't know!" I scream, because the tank has reached the yard, and the gunfire is heavier than ever, and the fire is leaping from building to building faster than I can follow.

I push Amos as hard as I can, and he stumbles backward. He swings the pistol at me, but I'm already moving. I hear shots behind me, but none of them find their target before I plunge into the smoke.

It's instantly hard to breathe. I clamp one of my hands over my mouth and nose, but the thick, bitter smoke slips between my fingers, and I start to cough. I see my fallen Brothers and Sisters all around me as I run, dark shapes I stagger left and right to avoid. A few are moving, dragging themselves across the ground or twitching and spasming like they're having a fit, but most of them aren't.

Most of them are still.

The west barracks appear in front of me, their walls and flat roofs wreathed in acrid smoke. The gunfire is constant behind me, and with so many bullets flying through the air, it feels like a matter of time until the inevitable happens. As long as I unlock the cabins first, I don't care.

I really don't.

I stumble out of the worst of the smoke and toward the nearest cabin, fumbling the skeleton key out of my pocket. I grab the padlock hanging from the door, and there's a sizzling sound. I don't understand what has happened—until pain explodes through me, and I wrench my hand away. Most of my palm stays stuck to the metal lock. I fall to my knees, clutching my ruined left hand against my stomach, and a scream that doesn't sound human bursts out of my mouth.

It's overwhelming. The pain.

It feels like someone has pushed my hand into a jar of acid and is holding it there, and as my brain tries to process the agony, everything else fades away: the smell of the smoke, the heat of the fire, the noise of the guns. Gray creeps in from all sides, like the volume of my senses is being turned down. Then something shoves me from behind, and everything comes hurtling back as I tumble to the ground.

A Government is standing over me, its face hidden behind its mask, the gaping muzzle of its gun pointing between my eyes.

"Hands where I can see them!" It's a man's voice. "Show me your hands!"

They tremble as I hold them up. "Please," I say, my voice a raw croak. "Children. There are children in these cabins. Please."

"Shut up!" he yells. "Not another word!"

"Please," I repeat. "In the cabins. You have to help them."

The Government glances at the buildings. My head is spinning, and my stomach is churning, and I feel like I'm going to pass out from the pain screaming in my hand, but I force my eyes to stay open, force my reeling mind to focus on the dark figure above me.

"Padlocks," I whisper, and hold out the skeleton key. "Please…"

My strength fails me. The Government looks at the cabin. Looks down at me. Looks at the cabin.

"Shit!" he shouts, then grabs the key from my hand and spins toward the door. I watch him grip the padlock with his gloved hand and slide the key into the lock, and I wonder for an awful moment whether this is all going to have been a waste of time, whether there are some locks that even a skeleton key can't open. Then the cylinder turns, and the padlock springs loose. The Government hauls the door open, and my coughing, spluttering Brothers and Sisters come flooding out, their eyes red and streaming with tears.

"Go to the Front Gate," I manage to croak. "Stay together. Put your hands up…"

At the back of the crowd, I see Honey, and I feel something in my chest that overwhelms the pain in my hand. Her eyes are swollen and puffy, and her skin is pale, but her mouth and jaw are set in familiar lines of determination. She's breathing, if nothing else.

I wasn't sure she would be.

She helps the last few crying, panicking children out of the cabin and leads them south, toward the Front Gate. The Government races to the next cabin, shouting into his radio for backup. Something breaks loose inside me, a surge of relief so powerful it's almost physical. It breathes new life into my exhausted muscles, and I drag myself into a sitting position.

The children make their way across the yard, their little hands raised in surrender, until a rush of Governments come sprinting out of the smoke and scoop up my Brothers and Sisters and carry them out through the gaping holes in the fence. I can hear them crying and shrieking for their parents, and my heart breaks for them, but they're alive, they're still alive, and that's all that matters, that's the only thing that matters as the world burns.

I hear a scream, loud and high-pitched enough to cut through the gunfire and the roar of the inferno, and I turn my head toward it. Near the blazing ruins of the Chapel, two of the Governments have caught hold of Luke and lifted him off the ground by his arms and legs. He's thrashing in their grip, howling and bellowing for them to put him down, to let him go with the others, to let him Ascend.

His voice, full of fury and fervor and desperate, frantic panic, is the last thing I hear before everything goes dark.

A
F
T
E
R

The room is silent for a long time after I stop talking. I feel spent, like every last bit of me has been used up, but it's not a bad feeling; it's weird, and I don't know what I'm supposed to do now, but I imagine this is what free must feel like.

"I can't imagine what it was like to go through all that," says Doctor Hernandez. His voice is quiet, and he's staring at me so intently that it's making me a little uncomfortable. "I think you're a remarkable young woman, Moonbeam. What you just did, telling us that like you did, took a level of bravery that almost leaves me speechless."

"Almost?" I say. It's a small joke, but he smiles.

Agent Carlyle isn't smiling. "I think your bravery is beyond question. And I hate to have to do this, but I'm afraid we need to return to something that came up a long time ago. I didn't push you on it then, but this time I have to." He pauses and takes a breath. "Are you sticking to the story that you didn't go into the Big House during the fire?"

"It's not a story," I lie. "It's the truth."

He narrows his eyes, but I don't see anger in them; I see only disappointment. "Fine," he says. "Let's go through it. Did you know nearly two hundred hours of video were shot on the morning of the seventeenth?"

"No."

"The agents serving the warrant were wearing body cams," he says. "And every vehicle had at least one camera. Every single frame of footage has been analyzed, and we've been able to put together a clear visual record of the entire incident, from half a dozen different angles. Which is why I can say with absolute certainty that Honey didn't come out of the west barracks after Agent Jefferies used your key to open the doors. She walked through the front gate with her hands up four minutes earlier and was already being treated by the emergency services when the rest of the children were released."

"I saw her come out," I say.

"You didn't, Moonbeam. She wasn't in there."

"I *saw* her," I say. I feel like a child, sticking stubbornly to a lie even when you know you've been caught, but it's the only thing I can think to do. I've told them everything else, even though I never wanted to.

There's only one thing left, and I can't tell it to them. I *can't*.

Agent Carlyle doesn't say a word. He stares at me.

"I saw her," I repeat. "I don't care whether you believe me or not."

"All right," says Doctor Hernandez. "Let's try to stay calm. There's no need for this to become combative."

"I am calm," I say.

"Me too," says Agent Carlyle. "Did you know one of the cameras got a very clear shot of you pointing a pistol at Bella?"

"I told you about that."

"You did," he says. "You told us you left her lying on the ground and went to the western barracks to release the children who had been locked in there."

"That's what I did."

Agent Carlyle shakes his head. "No," he says. "It's not. You *did* go to the western barracks, but it's not what you did *next*. After you left Bella, we have a clear shot of you entering the Big House, where you stayed for almost six minutes."

"That's not true." My voice is starting to rise. "How many times do you need me to tell you?"

"Moonbeam," says Doctor Hernandez. His tone is gentle. "I understand the need for you to protect yourself. I really do. But I had hoped we'd reached a place of trust."

"I'm telling you the truth." My face feels hot, and I hope they can't see that my hands have started to shake. "But thanks for trying to make me feel guilty. I really appreciate it."

He winces, and his face colors what I guess is an embarrassed pink.

"I can bring a screen in here and show you the footage," says Agent Carlyle. "Do you think that might jog your memory?"

I shake my head. "I don't need to see any footage."

"So you won't tell us what happened inside the Big House?"

Stay calm, whispers the voice in the back of my head. *It's okay. If they knew what you did, they wouldn't be pressing you like this. They would have just said so.*

I take a deep breath. "I don't know what happened," I say. "Because I didn't go in there."

"I think you did," says Agent Carlyle. "In fact, I *know* you did. So I'm curious about what it is you don't want to tell us."

I shrug. There's nothing I can say to that. Nothing I *will* say to that.

Doctor Hernandez sits forward. "I think we should stop here. We know how hard this has been for you, Moonbeam, and I don't want you to think that we don't appreciate your honesty or your strength. I think a good night's rest and a little time to think things through will do us all good."

Agent Carlyle nods. "I think you're right. We can carry on in the morning. Maybe we'll all see things a little differently then."

"Fine," I say, although I don't really see the point, because I've been thinking about this a lot longer than they have, and a few hours isn't going to change anything.

Doctor Hernandez gathers up his belongings, and the two men head toward the door. Agent Carlyle looks over his shoulder at me before he unlocks it, and the expression on his face punches me squarely in the heart. It's not anger, and it's not even disappointment—it's sympathy.

He feels sorry for me.

The door closes, and I stare at the wall, trying to slow my racing heart.

They don't know, I tell myself. *It's okay. They don't know, and they won't ever know unless you tell them. You have to stay strong.*

Because this isn't like the phone call I made to the sheriff, where it turned out I was wrong about how much trouble I thought I was going to be in. If they find out what I did inside the Big House, I'll never get out of here.

Never.

I sit at my desk and make a conscious effort to draw something that *isn't* the cliffs and the water and the blue house. I try to draw Nate, the way I remember him.

366

It seems like hardly any time has passed since he woke me up in the middle of the night to give me the phone and the key and tell me he was leaving, but there must be something weird going on inside my head because I can't really remember what he looked like.

I was so sure I was never going to see him again that I wonder if my subconscious decided there was no point in holding on to him, that keeping him alive in my memories would be too painful. I scratch a pencil across a sheet of paper, trying to magic him out of thin air—the handsome lines of his face, the green of his eyes, the wide mouth that was usually curled into a smile that poured molten heat into my stomach.

My first attempt looks nothing like him, so I crumple the paper and throw it aside. The second and third are no better, and the first hot embers of frustration begin to grow inside me. But the fourth drawing captures *something*. It's little more than a jumble of lines, but at their center, if I look the right way, I can see the curve of Nate's chin, the hard angles of his jaw. I let the pencil slide up the page, trying to picture his eyes and the warmth I always saw when I looked into them, but my brain betrays me. It screams that he was a liar, a *professional* liar, who never cared about me in the slightest, and the drawing instantly loses whatever truth it briefly contained.

I ball up the paper and hurl it at the wall. It bounces to the floor beside the others as I sink back in my chair and try to think.

What must it be like to pretend to be something you aren't? What kind of person do you have to be to do that, and do it so convincingly for so long?

You should know, whispers the voice in the back of my head. *For how long after they Banished your mom did you pretend to be a True and Faithful Legionnaire? Three years? Until the very end?*

I tell the voice to shut up because that's not the same thing at all. It really isn't. Maybe I didn't tell my Brothers and Sisters that my Faith was starting to fail me, but I was still the person they'd always known. I was still *me*. Whereas Nate lived inside the Base for more than two years, and he was *never* who he claimed to be. People trusted him and liked him and welcomed him into their Family, and all that time he was watching and listening and lying and plotting.

You don't know that. You don't know whether he was really the person you thought he was or whether he was someone else. All you know for sure is that he was pretending to believe in Father John and the Legion. Just like you were.

I push the voice away again, harder this time, because I want to be angry with Nate, and I'm not remotely in the mood to be told what to do or how to think. Even if he didn't lie about the person he was, he lied about why he joined the Legion, and he lied every time he called someone Brother or Sister, because people don't spy on their Family. Not normally anyway.

Was he filing reports on us? I guess he must have been, because there would have been no point sending him in if he wasn't sending information back out.

Did he write reports about me? About the stupid little girl who followed him around like a puppy and was so pathetically grateful for his attention that she never saw what was right in front of her?

The thought stabs at my chest like a knife.

You can't believe that. Doctor Hernandez said he was mostly himself, and what would he gain by lying to you? You have to believe that he was your friend.

I think back to all the time I spent with Nate. Moments that were warm and happy now feel cold and empty, like dark clouds have settled over them. The color and light are gone, replaced by monochrome gray, and part of my brain marvels at its ability to undermine my memories, to so rapidly rewrite my own history.

To use the truth about Nate to hack and tear so viciously at the deepest parts of myself, at the fragile, precarious center of whoever I really am.

I have to believe he was my friend. I have *to.*

I get up from the desk and lie down on my bed.

Nurse Harrow will bring my lunch in a few minutes, and then it will be time for SSI, unless it's canceled again. Then the evening will stretch out, long and relentless, and then night will come and maybe my sleep will be free of bad dreams, and maybe it won't. And then it will be morning, and I'll be taken to Interview Room 1 again, and they'll ask me the same questions they ended today's session with, over and over and over.

And they won't stop because what happened inside the Big House is the last thing I know that they don't. And that's fine. I don't blame them, I really don't, but I'm not going to tell them what I did.

Not just because I'm scared of what will happen to me if I do.

But because it's the only thing I have left that's mine.

AFTER

Doctor Hernandez steps into Interview Room 1 and shuts the door behind him.

I'm scratching the new bandage that Nurse Harrow wrapped around my hand when she brought me my breakfast; the skin underneath is still a little shiny, but it looks almost normal now, and it's itching like the bandage is made of poison ivy. I frown as he sits and opens up his leather satchel.

"Where's Agent Carlyle?" I ask.

He smiles as he arranges his pens and notebooks. "He had to go to Dallas for the day. He'll be back tomorrow."

Bullshit.

"If you say so."

His eyes narrow, ever so slightly. "I'm telling you the truth, Moonbeam."

"I believe you," I say. "I just wonder if people are telling *you* the truth."

"What do you mean?"

"Agent Carlyle has been in all of our sessions apart from the first few," I say. "Then the two of you decide I'm lying about the fire, and the next day he gets called away to Dallas? Out of nowhere?"

"I have no law enforcement role, so I'm sure there are a great many things I'm being kept in the dark about," he says. "All I can tell you is that I watched Agent Carlyle get into his car this morning after he told me he'll be back tomorrow."

"Then I guess you have to trust him," I say. "And I have to trust you."

He frowns. "Is that a problem?"

"I don't know," I say. "It was, and then I started to think maybe it wasn't. But now I'm not sure."

"I'm going to be entirely honest with you," says Doctor Hernandez. "I'm *glad* Agent Carlyle isn't here this morning. I think we've seen a number of significant breakthroughs in the last few days, but the necessities of the investigation have meant we've had to deal with those breakthroughs in a way that wouldn't have been my first choice. I'm keen to get back to *you* and how *you're* doing."

"I'm fine."

He narrows his eyes. "That's dismissive."

"It's the truth."

He nods and writes something in one of his notebooks. As I wait for him to finish, two things become suddenly clear to me. The first is that my interrogation—*because that's what it was*—is over, and we're going back to Doctor Hernandez's process. The second is that Agent Carlyle clearly believes he's got everything he's going to get from me—everything useful, at least—and I'm still here.

I'm never getting out of this place.

"It's not true," I say. I know it's stupid to voluntarily bring up what we talked about yesterday, but some stubborn part of me wants to keep hammering the point, to somehow convince them to ignore their evidence and believe my lie.

"What Agent Carlyle said about me going into the Big House. It's not true."

Doctor Hernandez finishes his note and puts down his pen. "That interests me," he says.

"Why?"

"I've watched the footage Agent Carlyle was referring to," he says. "I've seen you walk into the Big House and come out six minutes later. So I *know* there's something you aren't telling us, even if I don't know what it is. And that's fine, Moonbeam. The details of what happened that morning are extremely important to Agent Carlyle and his colleagues, but I'm not an investigator. What *I'm* interested in is why you don't want to talk about whatever it is."

"So you're calling me a liar too," I say.

He smiles at me. "I think we both know you're not telling the whole truth," he says. "I don't believe you're delusional, and I don't think you're experiencing memory loss. I think you're making the choice to withhold information. If you want to explore that choice, then I'm more than happy to do so. But if you'd rather talk about something else, that's okay."

"Let's talk about something else," I say.

Honey and I sit at one of the tables in the group therapy room and watch quietly as our Brothers and Sisters amuse themselves. Jeremiah's eyes were red when I walked through the door, but he absolutely denied he'd been crying when I asked him. He and

Aurora are playing with Lego now, and he seems okay, although it's impossible to know what's really going on inside any of their heads.

"Rainbow's been having nightmares," says Honey quietly. "About the fire. She told me."

I grimace. "I'm not surprised."

"She said she was trapped in her room," says Honey. "In Building Twelve. The fire was getting closer and closer, but she was lying on her bed and she couldn't move. She was screaming for help, but nobody came."

I picture the way she looked as she and the other children made their way across the yard toward the Front Gate with their hands raised above their heads, as the fire roared and bullets flew in every direction, as dark shapes moved through the smoke, and men and women they'd known their whole lives—their brothers, sisters, *parents*—bled and died on the ground. The fact that they aren't all catatonic might seem like a miracle, if I still believed in such things.

The heavy guilt that dragged at my insides when I looked at them is gone, and I'm grateful for that. I really am. But I don't actually feel better as I watch them play and chat and laugh. If anything, I feel *worse*—because it's somehow harder now to admit that there's nothing I can do to make things right.

It's not your job to make things right, says the voice in the back of my head. *You know it's not.*

I know now the fire wasn't my fault. That this isn't my responsibility. I didn't put my Brothers and Sisters in this room, and I didn't fill their hearts with grief.

But...

Part of me—an increasingly large and hopeful part—had come to believe that if I could find a way to trust Agent Carlyle and Doctor Hernandez enough to tell them about the phone call I made, if I could unburden myself of the guilty secret I'd been carrying around with me, then I would be free. And in the end, I was able to do more than simply put down the guilt—I was able to see it washed away.

But as I look at my Brothers and Sisters, I understand that I'm not free.

Not even close.

I'm as trapped as they are.

A F T E R

It's the fourth morning in a row that Agent Carlyle isn't here. Doctor Hernandez doesn't bother trying to excuse his absence anymore. I guess he knows there's no point. Agent Carlyle got everything he could from me, and now he's gone.

The worst part is, I miss him.

My anger and disappointment at his sudden disappearance have worn off, and I actually miss him.

Because I liked talking to him. By the end, at least. I *liked* it, and I'd gotten used to him being there—to his winks and his deep laugh and the way his emotions lived just below the surface, always on the verge of getting the better of him. I told him things I had promised myself I'd never tell anyone, and I don't regret it. I understand he had a job to do, a job I ended up being a key part of. It's not like I thought we were actually friends, that when this was all over he was going to adopt me and take me home, and his daughter and I would be like sisters, and we'd all live happily ever after. I'm not an idiot.

I only wish he hadn't made it so clear how disposable I was.

You know what would bring him back, whispers the voice in the back of my head. *You know what you could promise to tell him. You know he would come running.*

I *do* know, and part of me wants to do exactly that. What happened inside the Big House has started to pull at me, to drag me down, and part of me wants to come clean, no matter the cost.

So do it, whispers the voice. *Finish this, once and for all.*

I can't, I tell it. *You know I can't. Because it's not about Agent Carlyle or Doctor Hernandez or even about me. It's about my Brothers and Sisters. It's about the people I used to call my Family. I can't tell them.*

It's all right, whispers the voice. *It really is. But maybe there's someone else you could tell.*

My heart stops cold in my chest.

I repeat the voice's words over and over in my head, wondering how it could possibly have taken so long for me to think of this. Because I know who it's referring to. There *is* someone I could tell.

I know exactly what I'm going to do.

"How are you this morning, Moonbeam?" asks Doctor Hernandez.

"I'm fine," I say. "I need to tell you something."

He sits back in his chair. "Of course," he says. "Tell me."

I take a deep breath. "I went into the Big House." My chest tightens as I say the words out loud. "During the fire. I did go in."

He nods. "Okay."

"I'm sorry I lied. I really am. I just…I felt like I needed to."

"Can you tell me why you felt like that?"

I shake my head. I probably *could* explain it to him, and I

376

suspect he might even understand, but it will take a long time, and I don't think it matters anymore.

"That's okay," he says. "That's absolutely fine. And whatever happened inside the Big House, if you saw something, or *did* something, I promise you it will be okay. You're not going to be in any trouble."

Father John's voice appears in my head, for the first time in what seems like years. *YOU WILL BURN IN HELL!* he howls. *THE LORD KNOWS WHAT YOU DID, AND HIS JUSTICE IS HARD! AN ETERNITY IN THE LAKE OF FIRE AWAITS YOU! HERETIC! WHORE! MUR—*

I stamp on his screeching voice as hard as I can. It falls silent, leaving the hateful echo of its words.

There's a chance that he is right—that The Lord *does* know what I did. But I don't believe anybody else does. Agent Carlyle may suspect something close to the truth, but I'm pretty sure Doctor Hernandez is just trying to reassure me, which is something he does a lot.

"It's not about getting into trouble," I say, although it still *is*, at least partly. "It's mixed up with a lot of stuff that doesn't have anything to do with you or Agent Carlyle. That's why I couldn't tell you. Why I *can't* tell you."

"Okay," he says. "What *does* it have to do with?"

"Me," I say. "The Lord's Legion. Father John."

He stares at me. I know he's trying to work out whether I'm actually telling the truth or trying to buy time with another lie. I meet his gaze and hold it.

"All right," he says eventually. "You can't tell me, and you can't tell Agent Carlyle, but you're willing to tell *someone*. Am I understanding this correctly?"

I nod.

"Okay," he says. "Why don't you tell me what you have in mind?"

Thank you.

I nod again. "Bring Nate here," I say. "I'll tell him what happened inside the Big House. After that, he can tell you and Agent Carlyle and anyone else who needs to know. After that, I don't care."

A
F
T
E
R

I have butterflies in my stomach as Nurse Harrow pulls the door to Interview Room 1 open.

I lay awake for most of the night, trying to imagine how I'd feel when I see Nate again.

I think I'm going to be angry with him for not trusting me enough to tell me the truth about who he really was, not even at the end, when the darkness was closing in. But mostly I'm excited at the thought of being able to talk to someone who really, *really* understands where I grew up and the life I was forced to lead and who I won't have to explain anything to.

I sit on the red sofa and wait impatiently. Doctor Hernandez steps into the room maybe a minute later, and I know Nate isn't here as soon as I see his face. He's wearing a wide smile, but it doesn't reach his eyes.

"Good morning, Moonbeam," he says. "How are—"

"He's not here," I say. "Is he?"

The smile disappears. "I'm afraid not. I submitted your request to the section chief in charge of the investigation yesterday morning, as soon as we ended our session. They told me they'll get back to me."

"Do you believe them?" I ask.

"Yes."

"I guess that makes one of us."

AFTER

For the fifth night in a row, I slept horribly. I don't remember if I dreamed, but I woke up covered in sweat with my heart lurching in my chest, so I suspect not being able to remember is probably for the best.

Doctor Hernandez walks into Interview Room 1 on the stroke of ten, and before the door is even shut, I ask him the same question I've started asking every morning.

"Any news?"

He gives me a small, sad smile and shakes his head.

AFTER

Agent Carlyle is back.

He follows Doctor Hernandez through the door and gives me a wide smile. I should be angry with him for so obviously ditching me once I had nothing useful left to tell him, but as the two of them take their usual seats behind the desk, I'm overcome by a weird rush of happiness, because everything is suddenly back to what I had started to think of as normal.

I smile at Agent Carlyle, surprised by how pleased I am to see him. I had resigned myself to the fact that Doctor Hernandez and Nurse Harrow and my Brothers and Sisters were going to be the only people I spoke to between now and whenever I get out of here.

If I ever do.

Honey told me they have to release me when I turn eighteen.

I don't know where she got that idea from, and I don't know if it's true or not, but even if it is, that's still months away. And I can't shake the feeling that they'll be able to keep me locked up for as long as they want, if Doctor Hernandez decides it's for the best. It's not like anyone is going to speak up on my behalf. I don't know why Nate hasn't come. Maybe it was only Agent Carlyle who actually cared about what happened inside the Big House, and maybe it was stupid of me to think otherwise. Maybe Nate's been sent spying somewhere else and they can't get him out. Or maybe Doctor Hernandez is the only person apart from my Brothers and Sisters who hasn't forgotten about me. That's what I was starting to believe, until about five seconds ago.

"Hey, Moonbeam," says Agent Carlyle. "Long time no see."

Whose fault is that?

"I've been right here," I say.

His smile fades. "Sure," he says. "Of course you have."

"How come you're back?" I ask.

The smile disappears entirely as he glances at Doctor Hernandez. I feel a familiar cold creep up my spine.

What now?

"I'm afraid Agent Carlyle has some bad news, Moonbeam," says Doctor Hernandez, and I fight back the urge to laugh, because what other kind is there? "We'll talk it through for as long as you need, but I want you to tell me immediately if you feel like you have to stop. Okay?"

Freezing cold spreads through me. "Is it my mom?"

"No," says Doctor Hernandez quickly. "It's not your mother."

My chest relaxes ever so slightly. "All right," I say. "Then what is it?"

"It's Nate Childress. I'm afraid…"

"He's dead, Moonbeam," says Agent Carlyle. "I'm really sorry."

I stare at him. My first, desperate thought is that this is some kind of test or maybe a trick, a horrible *mean* trick, but I look into his eyes and all I can see is pain.

"What..." The words fail me, and I try again. "I don't..."

Agent Carlyle puts me out of my misery. "His body was found a week ago," he says. "It was buried in a shallow grave, half a mile from the Lord's Legion compound. A murder investigation is ongoing, and the entire case was classified until last night. Only preliminary conclusions have been released, but the condition of the body suggests that he's been dead for several months. The theory is that he was murdered—"

"The night he escaped," I say, my voice barely a whisper.

Agent Carlyle grimaces. His face is full of concern, and his eyes stay fixed on me as Doctor Hernandez sits forward.

"Moonbeam?" he asks. "Are you all right?"

I look at him. I can't even begin to imagine what he wants me to say.

A deep frown creases his forehead. "Moonbeam? Talk to me."

I blink back tears from the corners of my eyes and try to speak around the lump that has formed in my throat. "What happened to him?"

"He was strangled," says Agent Carlyle. "I'm so—"

"By Father John?" I spit the words.

"It's impossible to say with any certainty. John Parson and the three men who were serving as Centurions at that time are certainly the primary suspects."

Lonestar. Bear. Angel. My Brothers.

Goose bumps break out along my arms. I focus on them because everything else is too big and too painful.

"It's not out of the question that forensics will turn up con-clusive evidence," continues Agent Carlyle. "But it's probably unlikely."

"So Nate didn't get away," I say. I'm trying to force myself to think, to process what he's telling me, but my mind feels numb. *Everything* feels numb. "They killed him."

He nods. "The working theory is that he was caught trying to escape."

Think. Calm down and think it through.

"Then why was Father John so angry the next morning?"

"You tell me," he says. "What would have been the reaction among the Legion if he had announced that he and his Centurions had murdered someone?"

I consider the question as carefully as my reeling brain will allow. A decent number of my late Brothers and Sisters would have had no problem with the murder of an alleged Servant of the Serpent—they would have seen it as The Lord's justice being served. But I'm pretty sure most of them, particularly those men and women who joined the Legion before the Purge, would have found it very difficult to accept.

What I do know, with absolute certainty, is that such an announcement would have caused utter panic inside the Base. People would have expected the Government to come looking for their missing spy, and once they…

"Why didn't anyone come?" I ask. "Nate disappeared almost two months before the fire. Didn't anyone notice he was missing?"

"He had no check-in schedule," says Agent Carlyle. "The restrictions inside the Legion compound didn't allow for regular contact. Several months without hearing from him was apparently normal, so his handlers didn't realize they had a problem until the preliminary investigation into the fire was complete. The ATF expected to see him walk out with the rest of the survivors, and when that didn't happen, they assumed one of the recovered bodies was going to be his."

The cold that has taken hold of my spine is spreading slowly through me. I know what I'm being told is horrible, and I'm distantly aware of what its implications might be, but right now I'm trying to feel something for Nate, feel *anything* for him, but I can't. All I feel is tired.

So very, very tired.

"Is there anything else you want to know?" asks Agent Carlyle. "The information I have is pretty limited, but I'll tell you anything I can."

"Did he have a family?" My voice is a thick croak. "Did he have people on the Outside waiting for him?"

"He had parents and a sister in Arizona," he says. "They've been informed. He wasn't married, and he had no children."

I nod because I don't have the slightest idea what to say.

More grief, more misery, more broken lives.

More pain.

"I'm so sorry, Moonbeam," he says. "I really am. There's nothing I would love more than to come in here one morning and give you news that actually made you happy. We debated telling you about Nate, but in the end, neither of us believed that keeping it from you was the right thing to do. I hope we made the right call."

No. Yes. I don't know.

"I'm going to end this session here," says Doctor Hernandez. "This is a lot to take in, and I want to make sure you have the time and space you need to process it. But I'll be here for the rest of the day, as usual. If you need me, tell one of the nurses, and I'll be there as soon as I possibly can."

I manage a tiny nod. "Thank you."

I sit on my bed as Nurse Harrow closes my door. The tears come as soon as I hear the lock slide into place, spilling from me with such force it feels like they might never stop.

I try to picture the Nate I knew, the kind, decent man who never treated me like a little girl and tolerated my crush on him and never took advantage of it. But the only image my poisonous, treacherous brain is either able or willing to conjure up is Nate with a pair of disembodied hands wrapped tight around his neck, his handsome face turning purple, his beautiful green eyes bulging as the life is squeezed out of him. I see the grave that awaits him, a shallow hole in the desert surrounded by an audience of coyotes and vultures, patiently waiting to fight over his insides.

I lurch from the bed, my stomach convulsing, and lean over the sink. I retch and spit and retch again, my body heaving uncontrollably, but nothing comes up. Tears drop steadily into the sink, and I can taste salt, and my skin is burning, and I don't want to look into the polished sheet of metal that serves as a mirror because I don't want to see my face.

When my stomach finally settles, I stagger to my desk and start drawing. The pencil carves deep grooves into the paper, black lines and jagged shapes, as I try to give a shape to the anger and grief that are filling me, to *get them out of me* and trap them on the page.

I believed Nate got away.

With all my heart, I believed it.

Even in those terrible final days, when I doubted everything and trusted nothing, I always believed that he escaped, that he was somewhere out in the world, the same as my mom. But if Nate is—

Don't, whispers the voice in the back of my head. *Don't go down that road. There's nothing good at the end of it.*

But I can't help it.

Because what did I really see, the day they Banished my mom? Amos drove her out of the Base in the pickup, then came back without her. Father John told me she was going to be taken into

A
F
T
E
R

Nurse Harrow puts my breakfast tray on the desk and tells me my morning session is canceled, but that Doctor Hernandez is on call if I need him.

I was excused from SSI yesterday afternoon. I didn't mind. I didn't want to talk to anyone, and I don't think I would have been a very positive influence on my younger Brothers and Sisters. Instead, I drew and paced back and forth and lay on my bed, and at some point after the small square of sky I can see through the high window had turned black, I fell asleep.

I can't remember my dreams, if I had any. It feels like a mercy.

Breakfast is yogurt and fruit and bacon and a tiny stack of pancakes and a plastic cup of orange juice, and it all looks good, but I'm not remotely hungry. I feel completely empty, but I don't think it's a physical sensation.

I know I should eat something so I force down half the

pancakes and a couple pieces of fruit, even though swallowing makes me really aware of my throat and that brings the image of Nate's bloated, strangled face back into my mind. I try to push it away, but focusing on it only makes it sharper and more detailed, and my mind is determined to fixate on the very worst of it: the broken blood vessels in his eyes, the burst capillaries under his skin, the spit and foam on his lips.

My stomach revolves, and I run to the door and press the Call button on the wall beside it. Instantly, as if by magic, Nurse Harrow opens the door and asks if I'm all right.

"No," I say, because I don't see any point in lying to her.

"Are you ill?" she asks. "Do you need me to get one of the doctors?"

I shake my head. "Can you ask Agent Carlyle to come and see me?"

She frowns. "I'll have to run that past Doctor Hernandez."

"That's fine," I say. "Please ask him not to come though. I only want to see Agent Carlyle."

"Okay, Moonbeam," she says, her frown fading but not quite disappearing. "I'll take your request to him now."

"Thank you."

Nurse Harrow gives me a small, unconvincing smile, then disappears down the corridor.

I try to draw while I wait for her to come back with Doctor Hernandez's response, but everything comes out ugly, so I crumple the paper and lie down on my bed and stare at the ceiling until I hear the familiar sound of a key turning in a lock. I swing my feet onto the floor and sit up, expecting to see Nurse Harrow's endlessly kind face, but when the door swings open, it's Agent Carlyle who walks into my room.

"So this is where they keep you," he says, and smiles at me. "Luxurious."

I return his smile with one of my own. "It's an upgrade on where I used to live, believe it or not."

He grunts with laughter. "I believe you."

"Thanks for coming," I say. "I didn't know if they'd let you. Or if you would."

"Doctor Hernandez caught me in the parking lot," he says. "I'm supposed to be on my way to Odessa."

"Will you get in trouble for not going?"

His smile widens as he shrugs. "I guess they'll have to manage without me," he says. He takes hold of the door, then stops. "I need to leave this open. Is that okay with you?"

"Why?"

"There are rules about unmonitored interactions. It's a safe-guarding issue."

I raise an eyebrow. "So I can call for help if you decide to attack me for some reason?"

"Correct."

The word "unmonitored" sticks in my mind. "So does that mean there really aren't any cameras in here?"

"Not as far as I know. So. What can I do for you, Moonbeam?"

I shuffle across the bed until my back is against the wall and wrap my arms around my knees. "It's been hard for you, hasn't it?" I ask. "Listening to me talk about the Legion?"

He nods without hesitation. "It has. I'm sorry if it's been obvi-ous, but...yeah. I've found it hard. Very hard, at times."

"Why?"

His eyes glaze over slightly as he considers my question. "I like to believe the world is fundamentally a fair place," he says after a moment. "I'm sure that sounds naive, especially to you, and I've seen plenty of horrible exceptions over the course of my career,

391

but I sleep easier at night when I can convince myself that people get what they deserve, by and large. Do you get what I mean?"

I nod. "I think so."

"Right," he says. "So here's the thing. I don't doubt for a second that there were plenty of people inside the Legion, maybe even a majority of them, who were living the way they had come to believe their Lord wanted them to. I *know* there were because you've told me about them. I think they were decent, and I don't think they meant any harm, but they still ended up dead on the ground with guns in their hands because John Parson scared them and twisted them up and fed them lies. I've seen their photos, the men and women who paid with their lives for putting their faith in the wrong person, and I look at them, and I don't think they were stupid or vicious or weak. I think they were misled, and I think what happened to them could happen to anybody, given the right set of circumstances. To people I know. People I love. And I try to imagine how that would make me feel, but I can't imagine where I would even start."

I'm pretty sure that's the most I've ever heard him say in one go. He looks a little paler than he did when he walked through the door, but his eyes remain locked on mine.

"Part of me hopes Father John was right all along," I say. "It would mean all my dead Brothers and Sisters are sitting beside The Lord right now, just like he promised them."

"But you don't think that's the case?"

I shake my head.

"Did anyone defy him?" he asks. "When he told everyone to fight to the last, did anyone refuse?"

The memories of that morning, which are never far below the surface, rush into my head—the flames, the smoke, the blood.

"Yes," I say. "I saw some people try to hide. It didn't save them though."

He sighs. "No. It didn't."

"They're not who you're asking about though, are they?"

He shakes his head again.

"You know, don't you?"

Agent Carlyle gives me a gentle smile. "Why don't you tell me what happened when you went into the Big House?"

I stare at him.

Go on, whispers the voice in the back of my head. *Tell him.*

Let it all go.

I take a deep breath.

BEFORE

Bella's eyes widen and she raises the pistol, but I'm already moving because I've had one gun pointed at me in the last five minutes and that was more than enough.

I slam my hand down on her wrist. The impact vibrates all the way up my arm, and Bella howls in pain as the gun tumbles to the ground. I step forward and push her in the chest. She staggers backward until her feet tangle and she sprawls flat on her back. My hands are balled into fists as I stride toward her because I'm scared and I'm pulsing with adrenaline and I don't think I've ever felt so angry as I do right now, so completely fucking *outraged*. I snatch the pistol off the ground and point it at her heart.

"Where is she, Bella?" I growl. "I'm not going to ask you again."

"I don't know," she says.

"I don't believe you," I say, and raise the pistol so it's pointing between her eyes. "Tell me where she is. Right now."

"She's safe," whispers Bella. "She's with The Prophet."

"Where?" I ask. "In the Big House?"

She nods. I turn without another word and sprint back the way I came.

Orange flames are licking the roof of the Big House as I approach it, sending a column of black smoke into the sky.

The air is thick and hot and I'm coughing behind my hand and my eyes are watering as I reach the steps. I stagger onto the porch when four gunshots ring out from inside the house, deafeningly loud and almost simultaneous. I hurl myself flat as terror explodes through me.

Not Honey. Oh please, not Honey. Please.

I stay down and listen, my face pressed against the hot wooden boards and my heart thumping against my ribs, but there's silence from inside the building. Behind me, out across the yard, the shooting seems to have died down, but I can't let myself think about what that might mean. Instead, I get to my feet and kick open the front door and step inside the Big House, Bella's pistol trembling in my hand.

The first thing I smell is gun smoke. The first thing I see is blood.

It's *everywhere*, splashed across the walls and running across the floor in glistening rivers. An awful coppery smell cuts through the acrid smoke and makes me gag. I take half a dozen deep breaths, squeeze my eyes shut for a brief, blissful moment, then force myself to look more closely at a room that now resembles a slaughterhouse.

Lying in a circle in front of the fireplace are four dead bodies. The backs of their heads are gone, but I recognize them all. Bear. Lonestar. Jacob. Angel. Father John's Centurions.

Three of them are holding pistols in their dead hands, and a gun lies on the floor beside the open fingers of the fourth. Gray smoke is drifting lazily out of their mouths. Their eyes are closed, their legs bent, knees together, and I fight back a wave of nausea as understanding slams into me.

They were kneeling. When they shot themselves, they were kneeling.

A sound that is somewhere between a sob and a gasp escapes my lips. Because this is *insane*, this is just completely—

There's a noise to my left.

I turn, the pistol shaking in my hand, in time to watch Father John step through the door beneath the stairs, the one that leads down to the basement. He stops as he sees me, his eyes narrowing.

"Moonbeam." His voice is still full of its rumbling fire. "Why aren't you fighting with your Brothers and Sisters? Did you not hear my order?"

"I heard it," I say, and I can hear the anger vibrating in my voice, can actually hear it. "Why aren't *you* fighting, Father? Why are you hiding in here?"

"Watch your mouth," he says, his face darkening. "The Lord has a plan for each of us. He does not make mistakes."

"No?" I ask. "What happened to the Centurions?"

He frowns, as if I've asked a stupid question. "They have Ascended."

"Did you tell them to do it?" I already know the answer. I want to hear him admit it.

"I explained what The Lord required of them," he says. "I didn't put the guns in their hands. I am merely His messenger."

"You're a murderer," I growl. "They trusted you and believed in you, and now they're dead, like half the people outside are dead. You killed them. *You* did."

"Your Brothers and Sisters are fighting bravely against the Servants of the Serpent," he says. "Which is more than can be said for you, Moonbeam. *They* understand what is at stake, and if

396

The Lord chooses this day to Call them Home, they will Ascend in Glory."

"Then why didn't you Ascend with the Centurions?" I ask.

"The Lord is not done with me yet," says Father John. "There is still work for me to do in this realm."

I stare at him as a new thought occurs to me. It's *awful*, but I instantly know it's the truth; I can feel it, deep in my bones.

"You told them you would," I say. "Didn't you? You *told* them you were going to die with them."

"How can I possibly know what they were thinking in their final moments? They Ascended with smiles on their faces and the Glory of The Lord in their hearts, so what does it matter?"

I raise the gun, almost without realizing I'm doing so, and point it at the center of Father John's chest. He goes very still.

"Don't be stupid, Moonbeam," he says. "Give me the gun."

I shake my head. "Where's Honey?"

He frowns. "I have no idea."

She means nothing to him. None of us mean anything to him.

"Bella said she was here."

"She was," he says. "I let her join her Brothers and Sisters."

"She's fourteen years old." Every inch of my body feels cold, like I've been dipped in ice water. "And you sent her out into the middle of a gunfight?"

"She asked to go," says Father John. "She wanted to fight with her Family. How could I deny her that opportunity?"

"Like you couldn't deny Bella?" I ask, my voice rising. "Or Star, or the rest of the women who called you their husband? They went out there with guns in their hands while you cowered back here. How could you do that to people you claim to love?"

"The Lord grants wisdom to those who can handle it," says Father John. "He does not make mistakes. Now give me the gun, Moonbeam. I won't ask you again."

The pistol starts to shake violently in my hand as he takes a step toward me.

"Give me the gun," he repeats, his voice low and gentle. "You're right, I should have led the Legion's charge myself. I should have stood with our Brothers and Sisters, but I am merely human, Moonbeam. *We* are merely human, and we are flawed, and The Lord understands our weakness. But we can Ascend together, you and I. We can go to Him, this very moment, and we can sit at His side for all eternity. Just give me the gun."

I take a step back. "Don't come any closer."

He smiles at me. "You're not going to shoot me, Moonbeam. You are a good girl, and you walk the True Path. You wouldn't shoot your Prophet."

"You are no Prophet of mine," I say, my voice trembling. "You're a coward and a fraud. My mother was right about you."

Fury explodes onto his face. "And you are nothing more than a Heretic *whore*," he snarls. "Like the Godless bitch that spawned—"

The gun goes off with a deafening bang.

For the briefest of moments, the living room is absolutely still and absolutely silent, as though the universe has been paused. Then Father John takes an uncertain step, his eyes widening, his hands groping for his chest, and everything happens really fast.

Blood gushes out between his fingers, soaking his shirt crimson. Smoke curls from the barrel of the gun in my hand.

He stares at me, and I watch as the light fades from his eyes. Then he topples backward and crashes onto the floorboards, his limbs splayed and limp.

My fingers open involuntarily, and the gun drops to the floor. My chest is locked tight, and my lungs are screaming, but all I can do is stare at the crumpled figure in front of me. Blood spreads across the floor beneath him, and he's lying completely still. I don't need to check his pulse because I know he's dead.

He's dead.

Because I shot him.

I killed him.

I drag a gasping breath down my throat as my stomach churns, doubling me over. I squeeze my eyes shut, because maybe when I open them there'll be no blood and nobody will be dead and I'll be lying in the darkness of my room in Building Nine and this will all have been a nightmare. But when I look again, nothing has changed. The smell of blood still fills my nostrils, and the pistol is still lying next to my feet, and Father John is still dead.

The voice in the back of my head appears, hard and full of urgency. It tells me to snap out of it, that there's nothing I can do here except die with everyone else, but even though I know the voice is right, I can't make my body move. I'm frozen to the spot, overwhelmed by the horror all around me.

By what I did.

Move! screams the voice. *You have to move! While there's still time!*

I manage to turn my head, and my eyes settle on the door beneath the stairs, the one that Father John emerged from. I feel the angular weight of the skeleton key in my pocket, and I hear Nate's voice telling me that there's more in the basement room than guns, *a lot more.*

I take an unsteady step toward the door, and another, and another, and then I'm holding the wooden frame and I'm looking down the stairs Father John walked up—*before you shot him*—barely a minute earlier. The lights are on, and I can see the basement landing. I start down the stairs, gripping the banister tightly because I'm not remotely confident that my legs are going to hold me up.

I stumble off the last step and stagger until I regain my balance. The metal door Nate mentioned stands in front of me, its surface gleaming dully. I take the skeleton key out of my pocket, slide it into the heavy lock, and twist it to the left. It turns easily, the mechanism smooth and silent. The door separates from its frame with a heavy *thunk*. I push it open and walk into one of the few rooms in the entire Base I've never been in before.

Lights flicker to life above my head, and my heart leaps into my mouth. The strip bulbs are blinding fluorescent white, and I scan every brightly lit corner of the room, but there's nobody here. The panic that leaped through me recedes, and I take a long, slow look around.

Two whole walls hold metal racks that reach almost to the ceiling. And even though dozens and dozens are being fired by my Brothers and Sisters at this very moment, the racks are still full of guns.

So many guns.

Shotguns and rifles and pistols, their barrels gleaming with oil, sit above shelves groaning with boxes of every type of ammunition, and as I try to take it all in my first thought is to wonder where they came from. Surely Amos didn't pick them all up on his Friday trips into town?

But then I think about how long the Lord's Legion has existed, how many times the red pickup has gone back and forth to Layfield, and how long Father John has been preaching the End Times. I think about it all, and I stare at the racks of guns, and I suddenly understand what Nate tried to tell me when we were walking next to the eastern fence. How carefully Father John has been planning for what is taking place outside right now.

How much he *wanted* the Final Battle to come.

Even though he knew people would die. But that didn't matter because he never intended to actually fight himself.

Anger flickers in my chest, but I don't push it away. I welcome it. It clears my head and fills my reeling body with strength. I let it settle over me and take a look around the rest of the room.

On a big table in the middle, a number of dismantled rifles lie in pieces next to plastic boxes full of screws and discarded cartons. Standing on its own in the center of the wall opposite is a gray filing cabinet.

I walk across to it, still clutching the skeleton key in my hand, but it's immediately clear that I'm not going to need it. The top drawer is open. I slide it out fully and peer inside.

Hanging on plastic rails are a bunch of cardboard files. They have no labels, but when I lift out the first one, the anger that was bubbling in my gut is replaced by cold, familiar unease. The file is full of drivers' licenses.

Dozens and dozens of them.

I pick up a handful and see faces I recognize beside names I've never heard before. The first one has a photo of Horizon that must be at least twenty years old—his thick beard is still there, but the lines around his eyes are nowhere to be seen—and lists his name as Michael Brantley, of Sioux Falls, South Dakota. The second looks like someone I vaguely remember from when I was little, maybe one of the people who left after the Purge, and the third is someone I don't recognize at all, which is weird.

The fourth makes me gasp out loud.

Bella may be lying dead on the ground outside for all I know, but in the photo I'm staring at, she looks barely older than me. Her long blond hair is parted in the middle, and she's smiling into the camera. The faded type on the plastic card tells me her name is Megan Joiner, and that she lives in Burlington, Vermont.

I flick through the rest of the licenses. The men and women my Brothers and Sisters used to be smile out at me, their faces frozen in time, as ice creeps under every inch of my skin and settles there. I put the cards back into the folder and pull out the next one. It's full of letters and certificates I don't have time to read, but I recognize some of the names at the tops of the pages.

Chase Manhattan. Citibank. Wells Fargo.

I slide the drawer shut and open the next one down. There's only one folder inside this one, and a lump climbs into my throat as I lift it out. It contains a thick sheaf of documents, held together by an elastic band, but I can see the words on the first page, and I know what they mean.

Last Will and Testament.

I put the documents down on the top of the filing cabinet, pull off the elastic band, and read the first page's single short paragraph.

I, Amos Nathaniel Andrews, being of sound mind and body, do hereby give notification that, upon the event of my death, I leave all my worldly possessions to John Parson, of Layton County, Texas, or to his descendants. I do this of my own free will, under the watchful gaze of The Lord.

The second document is almost identical, with only Amos's name changed.

As is the next one.

And the next. And the next.

I leaf through the rest of the bundle, maybe fifty or sixty pages, and find the same thing on every single one: men and women freely and willingly leaving everything they own to John Parson.

To Father John.

Freely and willingly, whispers the voice in the back of my head. *Right.*

Another part of what Nate told me that afternoon on the edge of the Base suddenly makes sense. He made it clear that the fence couldn't keep our enemies out, but he claimed it was capable of keeping people in. I didn't understand what he was saying until now. It isn't the *fence* that keeps people in, and it never has been—people stay unless Father John wants them to go because he has made sure they *can't* leave.

I guess Outsiders can get a new license if they need one because people must lose them all the time. But how do you build a new life when someone has taken over all your bank accounts and savings accounts and has a signed document saying that everything you own will one day belong to him? Drive through the Front Gate as fast as you can and go to the police? Hire a lawyer? Put your Faith in the Government and ask for their help?

Maybe.

But what if Father John was right all along? What if you go to the police and end up strapped to a table in a basement with gasoline being poured down your throat? Are you sure that won't happen? Are you *so sure* that you'll take the risk?

Paranoia. *Fear*. Behind it all, time and again, at the root of everything.

Fear and control.

I close the folder, my skin crawling at the feel of the pages, and open the third and final drawer. This one has no folders in it at all; instead it is piled high with dozens of objects that I don't recognize, but that I instinctively understand.

Wallets and bunches of keys. Photos of smiling men and women. Silver cigarette lighters and necklaces of multicolored beads. Gold and silver rings. Toy cars and cards with baseball players on them. Notebooks made of leather and paper. At least twenty cell phones.

Things that my Brothers and Sisters once held dear, that mattered to them in ways they probably couldn't have fully explained, taken away and put in a filing cabinet behind a locked door.

Mementos of the people they used to be. Keepsakes of lost lives.

Tears creep into the corners of my eyes because I'm thinking about my dad's knives and the page from his diary and the photo of my grandparents, and I'm trying to imagine how it would feel to give them up, to hand them over to somebody knowing I'd never see them again, and I just can't. Then I see a white envelope at the back of the drawer, and I pick it up, suddenly sure I'm going to faint.

There's a single word on the envelope. Eight letters, scrawled in handwriting I would recognize anywhere.

It's my mom's handwriting.

And written on the envelope is *Moonbeam*.

I don't know how long I stare at it. It's probably only a second or two, but my head is swimming, and my breath is stopped in my lungs, and it feels like hours, like days and weeks and months, like eons of time are wheeling past in the blink of an eye. The gunfire rattles endlessly outside, but I don't hear it. The roar of spreading fire crackles and spits, but I don't hear it either. The room is starting to get hot, but I don't feel it.

I don't hear anything, and I don't feel anything because I'm no longer here.

I'm somewhere else.

I'm standing on a bright green cliff top, and I'm looking out over water that is so blue it hurts my eyes. I don't turn around, but I know there's a house behind me, a house with cornflower-blue walls and a white picket fence and smoke curling up out of its chimney, and I know the footsteps I can hear belong to my mom, and I know she's smiling as she walks toward me, and any second now she's going to put her hands on my shoulders and tell me it's time to come inside because dinner is—

A deafening screech fills the basement, shocking me out of the place my mind has retreated to. I clap my hands over my ears because the sound is *awful*, so loud and so harsh that I don't think I can stand it, and I stagger across the room toward the open metal door.

Barely a second later most of the ceiling collapses, smashing the table to pieces and burying the floor beneath a smoldering heap of charred wood and broken glass. There are chairs and floorboards and bits of what looks like a bed frame in the pile of wreckage. I cough and gag on a billowing cloud of dust and ash. And when I look up, I can see swirling smoke and a blue sliver of sky above me.

The roof has fallen in.

The voice in the back of my head appears, urgent and insistent. *You have to go*, it says. *You have to go right now.*

I turn back toward the door, ready to do as I'm told, when panic grips me. I look down in what feels like slow motion, but the letter with my name on it is still in my hand, and I manage to take something close to a normal breath as I stagger out through the door and peer up the stairs. I can't see any damage, although I guess that doesn't really mean anything if the whole roof has come down. The door at the top could easily be blocked, which would leave clambering up through the hole in the ceiling as the only way out of the basement.

A quick glance over my shoulder is enough to confirm that the room is already on fire in half a dozen places. I stare at it for a moment, but then I remember the boxes of ammunition that are now buried by burning beams and rugs and splinters of plasterboard, and I turn and run up the stairs as fast as I'm able, coughing and spluttering, tripping and stumbling over every other step. I reach the top and turn the door handle and push it with all my strength.

The door swings open, and I stagger into the living room. The entire house is creaking and screeching, and there's an ominous bulge in the center of the ceiling, but it seems to be holding, for now at least.

I stuff the envelope into my pocket and head for the front door, past the bodies of Father John and the Centurions, past pools of blood that have merged into a gleaming crimson lake.

A
F
T
E
R

For a long time, Agent Carlyle just stares at me.

"That's the truth," I say, my voice barely more than a whisper. "That's all of it."

He keeps staring. His face is pale, his expression unreadable.

"Say something," I say. "Please?"

He stands and walks forward. Part of me breathes a sigh of relief when he leans across the bed, because this is surely the moment I always knew was coming, when the handcuffs snap around my wrists and he tells me I'm under arrest for murder. But that's not what happens. Instead, he takes hold of my shoulders and pulls me gently away from the wall and wraps his arms around me.

I start to cry, great sobs that fill my throat and rack my chest. He holds me close and tells me it's okay, and I want to tell him I'm not crying because I'm sad, I'm not even crying at the memory of what I did, but I can't form the words.

I'm crying because the last locked door inside myself is open. I'm crying because I had forgotten what it felt like to not have a heart full of secrets, to not be scared all the time. I'm crying because I don't know what happens next, and that's okay, that's really okay. Not knowing feels like being free.

"So many people dead," he says. His voice is low, his mouth close to my ear. "So many lives destroyed, and for what? So one man could be king of a patch of desert full of men and women who desperately wanted to believe in something."

He lets go of me and steps back. I shuffle to the edge of the bed, and we look at each other, and I don't have any idea what I'm supposed to do now.

I have nothing else to tell them. Nothing left to say. I'm empty.

Agent Carlyle leans against my desk. "The rest of what you told us was the truth? It happened like you said?"

I nod. "I went to the west barracks," I say. "I burned my hand on the padlock, and one of the agents used my key to let the kids out."

"Honey?"

I shake my head. "She wasn't there. Rainbow led the others across the yard, and the last thing I remember is Luke being carried toward the Front Gate."

"She said she looked for you," says Agent Carlyle. "Honey, I mean. She only went to the gate after she saw the roof of the Big House fall in."

"She should have gone right away," I say. "But she made it out in one piece. That's all that matters."

He nods. "And you saw Amos Andrews?"

"I saw him," I say. "I think he shot at me, but I'm not sure."

"Why do you think he wasn't summoned to the Big House with the Centurions? He was John Parson's oldest companion."

"I don't know. I guess that didn't mean very much to him at the end."

"I guess not," he says.

Ask him, says the voice in the back of my head. *Just ask him. It's okay.*

I take a deep breath. "Am I in trouble? For what I did?"

He frowns. "What you did to John Parson?"

I nod.

He shakes his head. "Absolutely not. I told you before that what you did would be the easiest case of self-defense any attorney ever put forward. But it's not going to come to that. The criminal investigation is now focused entirely on John Parson and the other senior members of the Lord's Legion. No other charges are being brought."

"They don't know what I did," I say. "Your colleagues, I mean. They might think differently if they did."

"I don't think they would," he says. "My understanding is that the investigation will conclude that one of the Centurions shot Parson before they killed themselves. I can tell them the truth though, if you really want me to."

I don't hesitate. "Tell them. I don't want any more secrets. I don't want to have to carry anything with me when I leave here."

"Are you sure?"

"I'm sure."

"You understand I can't guarantee how my colleagues will react to this?" he asks. "It would probably be safer for me to tell them you found Parsons dead when you entered the Big House."

"I'm sure you're right," I say. "I'm sure that would be safer. But I want you to tell them the truth. I'm tired of lies."

He nods. "All right. I'll tell them what happened. I should warn you that it might take a while for them to reach a conclusion."

"I think I can handle that."

He smiles at me. "I don't think there's much you can't handle, Moonbeam."

I wish I was as sure about that as you are. "Thank you."

He nods, and his gaze moves to the wall behind me. It looks like he's contemplating something, so I sit quietly and let him get wherever he's going. After a silent minute or two, he stands and pulls a small orange folder out of the inside pocket of his jacket.

"What's that?" I ask.

He holds it out. "Something that belongs to you."

I frown as I take the folder and open it. Then my heart stops dead, and my whole body goes numb because I'm holding the envelope I took from the filing cabinet in the basement of the Big House. It's crumpled and dirty, and it's obviously been opened, but my name is still clearly legible on the front.

"Have you read it?" My gaze is fixed on those eight scrawled letters. I didn't mean to ask him that—it was just the first thing that came out when I opened my mouth.

He nods. "I've read it."

"And you just happened to have it in your pocket?"

"It was released from evidence yesterday afternoon," he says. "Doctor Hernandez would have returned it this morning if your session hadn't been canceled. He told me to bring it when you asked to see me."

I stare at the envelope. Part of me, the same part that never wanted to tell anyone anything, wants to ask Agent Carlyle whether he would have given it to me if I hadn't told him what happened in the Big House, but nothing good would come from knowing the answer to that. Instead, I slide two sheets of paper out of the envelope with trembling fingers, unfold them, and start to read.

My dearest Moonbeam,

My journal is missing, which means it is only a matter of time before I get taken to Father John to answer for what's in it. I don't know what is going to happen then, so this is a worst-case-scenario letter. I don't think he'll kill me—although I wish I was more sure about that—but if he Banishes me, there are things you need to know. Because I know he won't let me take you with me. I know it.

The first thing is that THE LORD'S LEGION IS A LIE. It's a lie, and I will never forgive your father for bringing us here, and I'll never forgive myself for letting him. I'm so very sorry. The second thing is that Father John is far more dangerous than anyone understands. He believes the Final Battle is coming, believes it with all of his rotten heart, and HE WANTS IT TO COME. He will make it happen if it doesn't happen on its own, and people will get hurt, or worse. I can't see any other way for this to end, and my only hope has been that we wouldn't still be here when it does.

But I think you know this already—or suspect it, at least. You're much cleverer than me, Moonbeam. You always have been. So keep your eyes open, trust your instincts. Believe that I LOVE YOU and have always tried my best to protect you. Keep yourself safe. BE SAFE.

If they Banish me, you're going to hear things about me after I'm Gone that will be hard for you. I don't know what they will be, because most of them will be lies thought up by Father John, but at least one thing will be true—that for a long time I have been trying to find a way out of this place, for both of us.

I asked Shanti to hide us in his car when he left, but he was too scared to do it. I can't blame him for that, I suppose. I tried to leave after the Third Proclamation, but Father John stopped

411

me. He didn't care about me—he never has—but he cares about YOU, Moonbeam, and I know he watches you closely.

I should have left after the Purge. That was our best chance, I see that now. But I was scared, Moonbeam. I was scared of the world Outside, and I was scared of raising you on my own. By the time I realized what was happening, it was too late. I'm sorry I wasn't stronger. I'm sorry I let you down. So whatever they say about me after they Banish me, whatever they call me—a Heretic, a Servant of the Serpent, and God knows what else—just know that I tried to find a way out, and that I'll keep trying. I WILL NEVER STOP TRYING.

I know you resented me for persuading Father John to choose you as a Future Wife, and I've never blamed you for that. I understand it. I honestly do. But I did it because there are things about the Legion that I tried my best to keep from you, things that I hoped you might never have to find out if he had a vested interest in you.

The Third Proclamation isn't real. IT IS A LIE, LIKE EVERYTHING ELSE.

Most of the children born since it was issued are NOT Father John's, no matter what anyone says. The real fathers are men who crept into rooms that were unlocked by the Centurions and into the beds of girls who have never been ALLOWED to know that what's being done to them is wrong. In the real world beyond the fences, those men would spend years in prison if anyone ever found out. Inside the Legion, that behavior passes for normal.

Nobody talks about it, and the girls are warned never to tell anyone the truth. The only ones whose doors stay locked at night—WHO ARE OFF LIMITS, AND THEREFORE SAFE—are those girls who have been promised to Father John. Girls like you, Moonbeam.

I don't know if you'll ever forgive me for pushing you toward him, but try to understand that it was the only way I could keep you safe. Some of your Brothers started looking at you when you were still a little girl, and it scared me so badly, because I couldn't be with you every second. I couldn't sit next to your bed every night, watching your door. Getting you promised to Father John was the only way I could protect you until I found us a way out, and I didn't realize until it was far too late that all I'd done was make escaping so much harder.

I didn't understand that he would never let anyone take you away from him once you were promised. That he could never let you leave him.

I thought I was being so clever.

I'm SORRY, my little Moon. I'm more sorry than you'll ever know. I would have climbed the fence with you in my arms if I hadn't been sure they would have caught us before we reached the highway. But they would have, and our punishments would have been awful. I don't care what happens to me—I haven't for a very long time—but I couldn't put you in danger. I couldn't.

You are the only thing that still matters to me.

So here's what you have to do. If they Banish me—and I'm sure they will, because Father John won't take the risk of letting me stay once he's seen my journal—I want you to tell EVERYONE that I deserved it, and I want you to mean it with all your heart. I want you to MAKE THEM BELIEVE YOU. Stay close to Father John, NEVER, EVER stop looking for a way out, and stay safe until I can come back and get you.

I WILL COME BACK FOR YOU. I WILL COME BACK AND TAKE YOU AWAY FROM THIS TERRIBLE PLACE. I PROMISE.

This is your grandparents' address. If you make it out on

your own, get in touch with them. They will help you, and they will know how to find me.

Michael and Anne Dalton
364 Green Harbor Lane
St. James, WA
78046

I love you more than you could possibly know, my little Moon. I know I was hard on you, and I know you believed that I didn't care, but I was SO SCARED of drawing attention to us, of anyone ever suspecting what I was trying to do.

I'm sure there have been times when you didn't think I loved you—I don't blame you for that, and I hate myself for giving you reason for doubt. But love is dangerous inside the Legion. Father John demands absolute obedience and devotion, and he is jealous and he is cruel.

The truth is this: YOU ARE THE BEST THING THAT HAS EVER HAPPENED TO ME, and I will spend the rest of my life trying to make up for what your father and I did to you.

Be careful. Stay safe. And never stop looking for a way out. NEVER STOP TRYING.

I LOVE YOU.
Mom

I look up at Agent Carlyle and squeeze my eyes shut. The concern shining out of him is too much for me to handle.

I try to process my mom's letter, but my brain and my heart feel like they're broken. I summon the list of questions I've always wanted to ask her, a list that is never far below the surface of my mind, and realize, with something close to grief, that most of them have now been answered.

She *did* love me. She *did*.

She loved me, and she tried to find a way out, to leave Father John and the Lord's Legion far behind us. She tried so hard, even when she knew the trouble she would be in if anyone found out.

The coldness I always hated about her, that always made me feel like she didn't care about me at all? If I take her letter at face value—and I guess I have to, given that it's all I've got left of her— then the distance she kept between us was calculated rather than careless; a deliberate attempt to appear unremarkable while she worked on our escape behind the scenes. Even promising me to Father John—which she was right, I had never completely for- given her for—was done for reasons I couldn't have understood at the time, to keep the darkness at the heart of the Lord's Legion away from her daughter.

To protect me. To buy time. To buy us *both* time.

I open my eyes and look at the names and address she wrote down. Her mother and father. My real family, the one I've never known.

"We tried to contact your grandparents," says Agent Carlyle. "Your grandfather died seven years ago, and your grandmother eighteen months later. I'm sorry."

I nod, although I never met them, and two more dead people just feels like numbers at this point. I *feel* nothing. I don't know if I *can* feel anymore. I think I might be permanently numb.

"So they died before my mom was Banished," I say. "When she was still inside the Base."

"We sent a team up to the town where they lived," he says. "In case your mother had gone there asking about them after she left the Legion. None of your grandparents' neighbors remembered seeing her, and the county courthouse has no record of anyone attempting to access their estate."

"So she just disappeared into thin air?"

"There hasn't been a death certificate issued in her name," says Agent Carlyle. "But I'm afraid that's pretty much all we know for certain."

Something shrivels up inside me. I feel it shrink and disappear, and it takes me a second to understand what it was. When I do, I feel its departure like a punch to the gut.

The last flickering ember of my hope is gone.

"She never came back for me," I say. "The letter says she won't ever stop trying, but she's been Gone three years. She never came back."

Agent Carlyle stares at me, his eyes full of profound sympathy.

"Do you think she forgot about me?"

He shakes his head vehemently. "I don't believe that for a second. Not one second. And neither should you."

"Do you think she's dead?"

"Moonbeam…"

"Tell me the truth," I say. "Do you think she's dead?"

"I don't know," he replies, although his eyes tell a different story.

"Okay," I say.

"I'm sorry, Moonbeam. I truly am."

I feel nothing. I feel numb.

"I said it's okay."

"We have people searching," he says. "If she's out there, they'll find her."

They won't. But that's not your fault.

"I believe you."

"I approved the investigation team personally." He clearly wants to convince me there's still a chance. "They're the best at what they do. Don't give up."

Too late.

"I won't," I lie. "So what happens now that we're done? Where do you go next?"

"I'm not going anywhere," he says. "I'll be around whenever you need me. Just say the word."

My smile stays fixed in place. I really want to believe him, but I don't have any Faith left.

It's all used up.

A
F
T
E
R

There aren't as many of us as there used to be.

It's been more than a month since the fire, since my surviving Brothers and Sisters coughed and spluttered and staggered away from the only life any of them had ever known. The daily routine hasn't changed: I meet with Doctor Hernandez in the morning, and sometimes Agent Carlyle sticks his head through the door of Interview Room 1 and says hello. It's nice when someone makes an effort to see you even though there's nothing you can do for them.

It feels honest.

Rainbow was the first to leave. Doctor Hernandez told me her grandparents had been trying to persuade the Government to let them take her out of the Legion for years; with both her parents dead, it didn't take very long for a judge to sign her into their custody. I saw her right before they arrived to collect her, and it was like she couldn't decide whether to be scared or excited. Grief still hung over her like a cloud—I think it will be a long time until it breaks apart and drifts away for any of us, if it ever fully does—but the prospect of leaving the gray corridors of the George W. Bush Municipal Center, even with two people she had never met, filled her face with happiness. It was a joy to see it, even though it hurt my heart when she wrapped her little arms around me and hugged me and told me she loved me and said goodbye.

Since then, Aurora and Winter have gone to an aunt and uncle who live in Hawaii, and Lucy has gone to live with her grandmother on a farm in Iowa. We throw a little party in the group therapy room every time someone leaves, with chips and candy and jugs of orange drink, and some people cry, and everyone tells each other to be safe and look after themselves. One or two of the youngest kids still say "The Lord is Good," but it doesn't really feel like they mean it anymore; it feels like a reflex, like they've forgotten that they won't be in trouble if they don't say it.

Honey is still here, and so is Jeremiah, and ten others. Some of them will be leaving soon, to live with relatives that Agent Carlyle and his colleagues have tracked down. But some of them, including me, either have no living family or—and this is never said out loud—don't have anybody willing to take them in. I asked Doctor Hernandez what will happen to them, and he said they'll eventually go to foster families, men and women who take in children who aren't theirs and look after them.

It seems to me that the existence of those people is far better evidence that The Lord is Good than anything Father John ever told us.

"I want to talk about anger," says Doctor Hernandez. "Is that okay with you?"

I smile. "I feel like we've covered that once or twice."

He smiles back at me. "I didn't mean for that to sound as

ominous as it did. What I meant was, I'd like to talk about how we move on from anger. Move *past* it."

"All right," I say. "That sounds good to me."

He nods and sits back in his chair. There's no recording machine on the desk these days, and he's far more relaxed than when we first started talking to each other. He was so careful with me in those early days, as though he was afraid that one ill-judged comment might cause me to shatter into a million pieces. Then, when Agent Carlyle started to take the lead in questioning me, it felt like Doctor Hernandez saw me as a puzzle to be solved, as some kind of objective challenge to his professional skill and experience. Now he talks to me like we're friends, and even though I know we aren't, not really—I don't exactly see us hanging out if and when I finally leave this place—I like it a lot more this way.

"You have every right to be angry about what you experienced," he says. "You should be angry, and to be totally honest with you, I'd be worried if you weren't. We've worked through a lot, but I want to make sure you're processing your anger, that you're staying focused on keeping it manageable. I don't want it to consume you."

"It doesn't," I say.

"Are you angry, Moonbeam?"

"Yes." I don't lie to him anymore.

"With who?"

"With Father John."

He makes a quick note in one of his books, but even that doesn't bother me like it used to. "What about your mom?"

I shake my head. "I'm not angry with her."

"Amos Andrews? Jacob Reynolds?"

"No and no."

"Luke?"

I pause for a second, then shake my head.

He narrows his eyes. "Are you sure? You know you can tell me if you are. It's okay."

"I'm not angry with any of them," I say. "I *was*. For a long time, I was scared of Luke, and I was angry at my mom, and I hated Amos and Jacob. I'm not saying any of them were blameless for the things they did that made feel like that, not at all. But most of it wasn't their fault."

"Whose fault was it?" asks Doctor Hernandez.

I smile. "Are you going to make me say his name again?"

"No," he says. "I don't think that's necessary. I'm going to say it though, if that's all right with you?"

I shrug. "Say whatever you want."

He rolls his eyes, but there's a smile on his face. "What about Father John? Can you imagine a time when you might no longer be angry with him?"

"I don't know," I say. "I hope so."

"Can you ever imagine forgiving him for what he did?"

"No."

"Are you—"

"I'm sure."

A F
T
E
R

"He lives in a place called London," says Honey. "I have to take an airplane for ten hours to get there."

I smile. "I'm sure you'll be fine."

She nods. "When I talked to him on the phone, he told me he would sit next to me and hold my hand the whole way," she says. "I asked him how old he thought I was, and he got all embarrassed. I think I'm going to like him."

"He's your mom's brother?" I ask.

She nods again. "Apparently I've met him before. He says he came to see me in the hospital when I was born. My mom never mentioned him though."

We're sitting in the group therapy room, and I'm trying really hard to keep my smile convincing, because I'm happy for Honey that she's leaving, so happy I could burst, but I'm going to miss her so very much.

"I'll write to you," she says. "There are still some things I want to ask you, once we aren't being supervised."

I think back to what I whispered in her ear, during the first SSI session I took part in, and smile at her. She grins right back.

"And you can come and visit me," she continues. "When they let you out."

"I'd like that. You'll have to ask your uncle though."

She grins. "He'll say yes. I know he will. He sent me a picture of his house. It's *huge*."

"He must have done well for himself."

"I think he's rich," she says. "I didn't quite understand what he does for a living, something to do with hedges, I think, but whatever it is must pay him a lot of money."

"It's going to be great," I say. "I know you're going to be happy."

She nods, then her smile fades. "So are you, you know. When you get out of here you can go wherever you want. You can do anything."

I nod.

"We survived, Moonbeam," she says. "You have to remember to be happy about that."

I laugh. "So wise."

She narrows her eyes. "I'm serious. Promise me you'll remember."

"I promise," I say.

She leans forward and hugs me, her arms tight around my ribs, and I hug her back with all my strength, and I smile, because she's right. We *did* survive.

Both of us—*all of us*—left some of ourselves in the fire, but we made it out.

We're still here.

A
F
T
E
R

The door opens, and Agent Carlyle and Doctor Hernandez walk into Interview Room 1. They sit down in their usual chairs, and both men smile at me as Agent Carlyle sets a thick folder down on the desk in front of him.

"Good morning, Moonbeam," he says. "All good?"

I smile. "Maybe seventy percent good?"

"Not bad," he says. "How's the hand?"

The bandages finally got taken off yesterday afternoon. There are shiny ridges on my fingers and loops of white scar tissue on my palm, and the new skin is bright pink, like a baby's. Nurse Harrow seemed really pleased though and kept telling me it could have been worse, could have been *a lot worse*.

I guess she's probably right.

"It's fine," I say. "It feels like the skin has been stretched too far, but it's okay."

"I'm glad to hear it," he says. "Now, I've been authorized to provide you with some information, but only if you want to hear it. You're allowed to say no."

Cold trickles through me, a sensation that almost makes me feel nostalgic. "About my mom?"

Doctor Hernandez shakes his head. "I'm afraid not, Moonbeam. This is regarding Father John."

An involuntary shudder runs through me, and I grimace.

I hate the fact that even the mention of his *name* is still capable of provoking a physical reaction in me. It's probably been two or three days since I last thought about him, maybe even a week, because I've been making a conscious effort not to let him into my mind, but he loomed so large over the lives of the people I called my Family that I know I'll never be totally rid of him. At least his voice, which I thought for a while was going to torment me forever, has fallen silent.

"What about him?" I ask.

"I told you he was being investigated for a long time before the fire at the Lord's Legion compound," says Agent Carlyle. "That investigation is still ongoing, and it's likely to be at least another year before it's completed and submitted to the Justice Department. However, my Section Chief has authorized me to share the first draft of the headline summary with you, if you want to hear it."

"What does it say?" I ask.

"Most of the information won't be news to you," he says. "But it does describe some of what he did and who he was before he arrived in Layton County. You told us that everyone was forbidden from speculating about that period of his life, so I thought you might be interested in hearing the truth."

"I am," I say. "Tell me."

Agent Carlyle opens the folder. "John Parson. Born March

425

twenty-third, 1971, in Modesto, California, to Charles and Laurie Parson. They divorced in 1974, and as far as we can tell, Parson's mother raised him largely on her own. Pretty unremarkable childhood, average high school transcripts, a couple of misdemeanor cautions for underage drinking and DUI, no record of any college attendance. In 1990, he was cosignatory on an apartment lease in Echo Park in east Los Angeles. No tax returns have ever been filed that match his social security number, so we can't be certain how he made a living during his time in LA, but a number of Parson's known associates from that period told us he was at least an occasional musician, playing club gigs for cash. It was also around this time, according to their statements, that he started using and dealing heroin. Do you know—"

"I know what heroin is," I say.

"You told us that one of Father John's favorite sermon topics was the evils of addiction," says Doctor Hernandez.

I nod.

"And he believed prescription drugs were tools of The Serpent."

"That's right," I say.

He gives me a smile and writes quickly in one of his notebooks.

"Parson was arrested by the LAPD in the summer of 1992," says Agent Carlyle. "He pled guilty to possession with intent to distribute and was sentenced to three years in state prison, two of them suspended. He served three months."

I frown. "Why so little?"

"Overcrowding," he says. "It was a nonviolent crime, so they let him out when they needed his cell for someone worse. It's pretty common. But it wasn't long before he was back inside anyway. The following May he cracked a neighbor's head open with a baseball bat and was convicted of assault with a deadly weapon. He did eight years in Kern Valley, broke probation ten days after being released, and went back inside for nine more months. His penal records show that it was during this last stretch in prison that he started taking Bible study classes and announced that he had been reborn. I talked to his block captain from that time, and he said nobody bought it for a single second. It was, and I quote, 'Bullshit, pure and simple.'"

"Why would he pretend?" I ask.

"Judges have a tendency to look kindly on criminals who find God in prison and claim to have seen the error of their ways," says Agent Carlyle. "Not all of them, not by any means, but a decent number. And when you're a double felon who broke probation last time you were released, anything is worth a try."

"Desperate people do desperate things," says Doctor Hernandez. "I'd think you would understand that better than most."

No shit.

I nod.

"Whether it was a true-blue conversion or whether it was bullshit, we're not likely to ever know for certain," says Agent Carlyle. "But either way, Parson clearly decided to stick with it. In 2002, he joined a splinter group of the Seventh-Day Adventists called the Lambs of God and moved out to their compound in Nevada. He stayed for almost two years until he was forced to leave. Former members have told us that Parson denounced the group's leader as a servant of the Devil and tried to overthrow him."

"Sound familiar?" asks Doctor Hernandez.

I nod and give him a tight smile.

"Amos Andrews apparently left Nevada with him," says Agent Carlyle, turning the pages in his folder. "After that, there's no record of either of their movements until after they arrived at the Lord's Legion. I don't think we need to go over the rest of it again."

I shake my head. "I don't think so either."

Agent Carlyle smiles.

"So he was exactly what my mom said," I say. "A snake-oil salesman."

He nods. "She had him pegged. She saw right through him."

"Shame nobody else did," I say.

Neither man responds, but I can't blame them. There's nothing to say to that.

"Thank you for telling me," I say, when it becomes clear that I'm going to have to be the one to break the silence. "I appreciate it."

Agent Carlyle nods. "You're welcome."

"Do you want to continue with this session?" asks Doctor Hernandez. "You can go back to your room if you need time to think about what you've heard."

I shake my head. I've spent more than enough time in that room. "I'm good. Tell me what's going on outside."

Doctor Hernandez leans back in his chair as Agent Carlyle launches into a long story about how he got called into his daughter's school because she corrected one of her English teachers, and they got into an argument, and now the school is trying to suspend her. I listen and nod and smile in the right places, but my mind is elsewhere.

I'm thinking about Father John, about how so many people had their lives ruined and ended because they placed their Faith in a man as far from Holy as it's possible to be.

And although a little bit of me is proud that I saw through him in the end, most of me is thinking about what a waste it all was.

A terrible, pointless waste.

AFTER

I'm the last one now. I'm all that's left.

A couple from Houston came to collect Jeremiah this morning. I saw them waiting in the lobby as Nurse Harrow escorted me to Interview Room 1, standing nervously by the reception desk with a bag full of toys clutched in their hands and shiny hope on their faces. They've been to see Jeremiah half a dozen times over the last couple of weeks, but I hadn't seen them until today. They looked like nice people.

Doctor Hernandez let me out of our session for five minutes to say goodbye to Jeremiah. He gave me a hug in the corridor, and I hugged him back and told him to be good. He said he'd try, and I told him I guessed that would have to do, and he laughed and hugged me again. There was still a darkness behind his eyes that I didn't like, a remnant of the harm that was done to him, like a bruise nobody can see, but as he let one of the nurses take his hand and lead him into the lobby to meet his new family, I was able to convince myself that he might be all right, in time.

I *hope* he will be, him and all the others.

Including myself.

In twenty-three days, I will turn eighteen and officially be an adult. On that day I become legally responsible for myself, which doesn't sound quite as scary as it once did.

The investigation into the Lord's Legion—just as Agent Carlyle predicted—is not going to result in charges being brought against any of its juvenile members, including me. What I did inside the Big House has been recorded and filed away, and nothing is going to happen about it. I don't know whether they've decided not to believe what I told them or whether it's been marked down as self-defense or whether they've concluded they don't have enough evidence to prosecute me, but for whatever reason, it's done.

It's over.

Agent Carlyle wasn't able to tell me himself—the initial conclusions were issued on a day when he was in Dallas, and he didn't want me to have to wait until he got here to find out—so Doctor Hernandez gave me the news.

I cried for about half an hour. Not because I was sad, or even because I was happy, but because I was relieved. It felt like the end of something, as though I might finally be able to look toward whatever is ahead of me, rather than back over my shoulder. Because what comes next has started to occupy more and more of my thoughts.

About a week ago, Doctor Hernandez told me that I will be allowed to leave the George W. Bush Municipal Center—*if I want to, that is*—on my birthday. There are a whole lot of meetings I have to attend—about money and rent and identification documents and dozens of other things—before they let me go, and I'll have to check in with his office in Austin once a week, but once I'm out, I can go wherever I want.

I don't have the slightest clue where that might be, but I guess I'll work it out.

I guess I'll have to.

A
F
T
E
R

There are three days left until my birthday.

My morning sessions are every other day now, and there's no SSI anymore because there's nobody left for me to have supervised interaction with. I can tell Nurse Harrow that I need to see Doctor Hernandez, and he'll normally knock on my door within an hour or call if he's gone back to Austin, but I try not to bother him; he invested so much of himself in me and my Brothers and Sisters, devoted so much time to us all, that it seems only fair that he starts to get some of his life back.

Agent Carlyle is gone. He told me his boss had given him a three-month leave of absence, which seemed like the decent thing to do. His family must have missed him in those long, dark days after the fire, when he spent pretty much every waking minute either here or in the smoldering ruins of the Base. Especially his daughter, who is only four months younger than me; he told me several times that I would like her, and I'm sure I would. He gave me his card before he hugged me for the last time and said goodbye. He told me not to hesitate to call him if I ever need anything. I thanked him and told him I would, but I don't think I will. I think he's done enough.

They both have.

Most of the time my door isn't locked anymore. I can't leave the secure unit, and they still lock me in at night, but during the day I can pretty much come and go as I please. There's a library near the group therapy rooms that I sometimes go and sit in. Most days I go outside and walk around the yard. But I still spend most of my time in my room.

I've stopped drawing. The house and the cliffs and the water were something I could turn to when I needed them, something I could hold on to that was only mine. They served their purpose. Doctor Hernandez suggested I keep a diary, so I tried for about a week, but I didn't take to it.

I don't need to write down the things that happened to me, the things I've seen. They're burned into me, like scars that refuse to fade.

AFTER

Nurse Harrow says "happy birthday" to me as she opens my door just before ten o'clock. She didn't say it when she brought in my breakfast, but somebody must have told her in the meantime, and it's really nice of her, so I'm not going to say anything.

I smile and follow her into the corridor and automatically turn left toward Interview Room 1. But she turns right, toward the lobby and the canteen and the group therapy room. We never go that way anymore, not since Jeremiah left.

I ask her what's going on, but she doesn't answer, which is also weird. Nurse Harrow has been kind to me since the day I arrived, and I can't think of any reason why she would suddenly start ignoring me. I walk beside her in silence, and with each step, I put my feet down a little heavier than usual, so the sound of them thudding into the plastic floor tiles echoes down the corridor. I know she notices, but she still doesn't say anything.

We round the corner, and Doctor Hernandez is standing in front of the group therapy room door. He smiles at me as Nurse Harrow turns back, and I walk the rest of the way to meet him on my own.

"Good morning, Moonbeam," he says. He's standing very upright, and there's something oddly formal in his voice. "Happy birthday."

"Thank you," I say. "Everything okay?"

He nods. "Everything's fine," he says. "I'm sorry for the change in routine, but there's something I need you to see."

"All right," I say. "What is it?"

He gestures toward the door. "Wait in there," he says. "While you do, I want you to think about what today means, and I want you to make sure your mind is open. Remember that I'm right out here if you need me."

I frown. "What's going on?"

Doctor Hernandez shakes his head. "I'm right out here," he repeats, and opens the door. I walk through it, bracing myself for whatever is waiting for me, but the room I came to know really well over the last few months is almost empty. The tables and sofas are gone, as are the boxes of toys and piles of paper and tubs of crayons. Two plastic chairs facing each other in the center of the room are all that's left.

I turn back to ask Doctor Hernandez what this is all about, my frown deepening, but the door is closed.

I'm on my own.

I walk slowly toward the chairs, wondering if this is some last part of Doctor Hernandez's process that I don't understand, like a final test to decide whether they should actually let me out of here or not. I hear the door open again behind me, and I turn toward it, my increasing annoyance clear in my voice as I speak.

"I don't know what you want me to—"

435

My body turns as hard as concrete and as heavy as lead.

All the clocks stop ticking.

The world stops spinning through space, because my mom is standing in the doorway.

My mom.

She has a hand over her mouth, and there are tears in her eyes, and she's looking right at me. I can't move. I can't even think because it's *my mom*, it really is, I'm sure of it, and the first thought that manages to take shape in my mind, the only thought, is that I must be dreaming, because nothing else makes sense.

She looks much older than the last time I saw her, like she's aged more than she should have in the three years that have passed since she was Banished; her hair has streaks of gray in it, and her skin is pale, and there are lines around her neck and across her forehead, but the eyes—*her* eyes—are the same. We stare at each other, the distance between us as vast as the widest ocean. Memories and emotions crash against each other, pain and relief and anger and grief and joy flooding through me in a torrent that I can't process, can't swallow down. I can only try to breathe and hope I survive.

She takes a step toward me, and I'm sure I'm going to faint, going to collapse to the floor in a heap. The voice in the back of my head shouts that I'm stronger than this, that I didn't make it through everything I made it through to fall apart at the last minute, and I know it's right. I answer it with a silent scream that reverberates through my skull, and my head clears. Feeling returns to my legs, and I stand still as my mom comes toward me, as slowly and carefully as if she were approaching a wild animal.

When she's close enough that I could reach out and touch her, she stops. Tears stream down her face, and one of her hands is still over her mouth, and she looks at me like I'm not real, like she doesn't believe I'm standing in front of her.

"Little Moon," she whispers, and the sound of her voice cuts though me like the sharpest knife, splaying me open and exposing my insides to the entire world.

My face twists, and I start to cry, because I never thought I'd hear her voice again. I had come to terms with that awful reality, had done all my grieving and sobbing and cursing and weeping, and the relief that I was wrong is almost too much for me to bear.

"Don't cry," she says. "Please don't cry, Moonbeam. It's all right."

I shake my head because it's *not* all right. *Nothing* is all right. It's not all right that so many people died, that so many of my Brothers and Sisters were orphaned and left with wounds that will never fully heal, and it's not all right that my mom can come back to me while their parents are rotting in the ground.

It's not fair.

But I can't tell her that. I don't *want* to tell her that. Because all I want to do is hug her and hold on to her and never let go.

"Say something," she says, her voice shaking. "Please say something."

I open my mouth but nothing comes out, and she sweeps forward and pulls me against her and whispers two words in my ear, over and over again.

"I'm sorry. I'm sorry. I'm sorry."

AFTER

I don't know how long we stay like that, standing in the middle of the room with our arms wrapped around each other.

It feels like forever.

When we finally untangle, I go to the door and ask Doctor Hernandez to come into the room. My mom looks confused, almost nervous, as though she's worried I'm going to ask him to make her leave. But that's not why I want him. I want him to stand beside me while I ask her the only question that really matters anymore: *Where have you been?*

He gives me a tight smile as he walks through the door, an expression that's very clearly asking: *Are you okay?*

I nod, and then I stand next to him, and we look at my mom, and I ask my question.

She tells me that when I was sent out of the Big House after the decision was made to Banish her, Father John told her two things.

The first was that he had people in the Outside who were loyal to the Legion, people who would be watching her every day for the rest of her life, making sure she never went to the authorities.

The second was that if the police or any other Government ever arrived at the Base, he would assume it was because of her.

He would assume it was her doing, and he would have Jacob Reynolds take me out into the desert and gut me and leave me for the coyotes.

She never knew whether to believe his first claim, but she never doubted the second, not for a single second.

"He meant it," she whispers, her voice cracking. "Oh God, he *meant* it."

Doctor Hernandez takes a step closer to me as she talks, his face pale. I think he's getting ready to catch me if I faint. I don't think I'm going to, but I appreciate the gesture.

My mom tells me she was too ashamed to call her parents while I was still inside the Base, so she called a woman she had been friends with in Santa Cruz and asked her for help, a friend who had tried to persuade her not to go to Texas in the first place. She tells me she knows how stupid that was now, but that at the time she wasn't thinking straight. Not even close.

She tells me that her friend sent her enough money for her to rent an apartment in Odessa, from where she started planning how to get me out of the Legion. But the apartment was broken into three times in three months, and she felt like people were watching her, people she saw in her building or at the store. She started to believe her phone was bugged, and she started to leave her apartment less and less. And she started drinking. Started drinking *a lot*.

She stops and tells me she's not sure I want to hear this, not now. Doctor Hernandez says he thinks that's a decision I can make for myself, and I feel a surge of affection for him. I tell her I want to know everything, no matter how bad it is.

Be brave, whispers the voice in the back of my head.

She starts to cry as she tells me the rest of it. How she gave up the apartment in Odessa and fled to Dallas, how she saw Father John's people on every corner, in every diner and bar, in the strangers who smiled at her as they passed her on the street. She drank more and more, until she didn't really do anything else.

And for a long while after that, she was lost.

It took an ambulance ride to the emergency room, more than two years later, to wake her up. She had ended up living in Seattle, for reasons she tells me she can't remember, and she collapsed outside a drugstore on the south side of the city. Her heart stopped twice on the way to the hospital. My stomach churns as she tells me she was technically dead for six minutes, and when they released her, almost a month later, with the address of a shelter where she could stay, she finally started the journey back to the person she used to be.

She was halfway through a six-month residential addiction program in Oregon when the fire at the Base happened. Access to the news was carefully filtered, so as not to upset the patients' process—I glance at Doctor Hernandez as she uses the word—and nobody at the center knew she had any connection to the Lord's Legion. As a result, she didn't find out what had happened until two days ago, when the program ended and she was released.

She immediately started making calls, trying to find out what had happened to me, and within three hours, she was on a flight to Texas. She arrived in Odessa last night, and this morning—my birthday, of all days—Doctor Hernandez gave her the news she had stopped believing she would ever hear.

I was out. And I was safe.

She finishes talking and looks at me. My heart is aching for her, for the things she has been through, and I wonder if the damage that Father John caused will ever truly end, if his shadow will always be out there, creating pain and misery wherever it touches.

Doctor Hernandez asks me if I'm okay, and I tell him I want to go back to my room. My mom looks like she's going to start crying again, and she tells me she doesn't blame me if I hate her, that she failed me, that she let me down.

I shake my head, and I tell her I love her.

She does cry then, and she tells me she loves me too, that she never stopped loving me.

I'm going to try to believe her.

AFTER

I've been eighteen for just over a month.

I'm an adult now. I could go anywhere in the world I choose, but right now—for the time being, at least—where I want to be is here.

I'm sitting in the garden of my mom's little house on the outskirts of Portland, Oregon. She's gone into town to meet her sponsor, and then she's going to the store on her way home to get food for dinner. It always takes her about ten minutes to get into the car, to convince herself that I'm telling the truth when I say I'll be okay on my own for a couple of hours.

A mug of coffee is steaming on the table next to my chair. I'd never had coffee until I got here. I'm still not sure if I like it or not, but drinking it seems to be a thing that people in the real world do, and I don't want to be different. I want to be exactly the same as everyone else, at least for a while.

I take a sip and look around at the place my mom keeps telling me is my home. There's no cliff at the bottom of the garden, no water stretching to the horizon. The house doesn't have a chimney, and its wall aren't blue.

But it's okay. It's a start.

AUTHOR'S NOTE

After the Fire is a work of fiction.

The Holy Church of the Lord's Legion, the George W. Bush Municipal Center, the town of Layfield, and the characters that populate them are all products of my imagination. And as I hope will be clear from the text, the novel is not intended as an attack on anyone's religious beliefs. The belief structure of the Lord's Legion is far removed from the Christianity practiced by two and a half billion people around the world—deliberately so. This is a story about power and corruption and how charismatic figures can twist faith to serve their own ends. And ultimately, it's a story about survival; more specifically, one girl's way back after her world falls apart.

Like most writers I know, I don't go looking for ideas. The good ones, the ones that might be worth pursuing, that might even-tually turn into a story, usually appear out of nowhere. Sometimes (although rarely, for me at least) they're fully formed, with a beginning and a middle and an end already in place. Sometimes they're infuriatingly vague: a piece of action, a small moment, or the first outline of a character. And sometimes they are a direct response to something I read, or hear, or see.

This novel was inspired by a real event: one that I remember vividly, but that I suspect many reading this book will be unaware of. Things have a tendency to fade into history, even events that shocked the world when they happened.

On April 19, 1993, eighty-two members of the Branch Davidian religious sect and four U.S. government agents died after a standoff that had lasted almost two months and ended in a blazing inferno. It became known as the Waco siege (after the nearby town in Texas). At the time, I was too young to absorb the details of what had led to such a terrible loss of life and definitely too young to comprehend the existence of men like the group's Messianic leader David Koresh, the latest (at the time) in a long line of men (they're almost always men) who manipulated people's fears and beliefs to satisfy their own desire for power.

But I do remember my shock at watching footage from the fiery conclusion of the siege on the news. I remember watching the buildings burn, thinking how terrifying it must have been to be there, to find yourself in the middle of all that chaos. It seemed so entirely alien to me.

Years later, my girlfriend and I went to Washington, DC, on vacation. We visited the Lincoln Memorial, the Smithsonian, the Washington Monument, and on the day before we left, we visited a place called the Newseum. It's a museum of American journalism, from its beginnings to the present day, and it's fantastic. One of the exhibits was about the FBI and the press. It showed the coverage of Bonnie and Clyde, the agency's battle with the Italian mafia in New York, and the hunt for the 9/11 terrorists.

And in one corner, filling the entire wall, was the coverage of the Waco siege.

I hadn't thought about it for a long time. I'd remained fascinated by cults and organizations like Scientology that furiously reject the label, but Waco and the Branch Davidians and David Koresh hadn't crossed my mind in years.

I looked at the photos, and I watched the footage again—the armored vehicles, the black-clad agents with their automatic rifles, the burning buildings, the empty desert that surrounded it all—and I listened to recordings of Koresh negotiating with the authorities. His voice—so flat and ordinary as he discussed the end of the world—sent chills up my spine. I thought about Waco from the perspective of an adult, one who had twenty years more experience of seeing people do awful things to others, and I asked myself the most obvious questions: How did such a thing happen? How did David Koresh persuade people to lay down their lives at his command? How did he twist their faiths and beliefs until a violent end became inevitable? What led people to the point where they believed in such an obviously self-serving charlatan? How desperate must they have been, or vulnerable, or both? What was it like to live inside that compound, believing you were in mortal danger from the outside world? And what would such constant fear do to a person? Lastly, for the people who survived, what would it mean to discover that your whole life had been a lie?

On the way back to our hotel I bought a notebook, and in our room I scribbled the outline of a character. A teenage girl, who survives the end of her world but is still far from safe. A girl whose own faith has failed, but who is surrounded by the truest of true believers. A girl who has seen the truth, but not until it was far too late. A girl with secrets she has no intention of telling anyone.

And I already knew her name: Moonbeam.

But there was an immediate problem. I didn't want to tell a

straight fictionalized version of the Waco siege, for a pretty obvious reason—it would be disrespectful to the Branch Davidian survivors to retell the worst thing that ever happened to them as entertainment.

So I started researching in earnest, and as I read, Moonbeam's life became clearer and clearer. I read the Danforth Report, the U.S. government's investigation into the actions of the federal agencies during the Waco siege. I read Malcolm Gladwell's remarkable account of the negotiations between the authorities and Koresh ("Sacred and Profane," published in the *New Yorker*). And I discovered the work of Dr. Bruce Perry.

In the early days of the siege, Koresh released twenty-one of the Branch Davidian children, in an apparent show of good faith to the authorities negotiating with him. I don't want to give him more than a minimum of credit for doing so, given that about twenty more children, most of them fathered by Koresh with various female members of the group, were not allowed to leave, and most of them died with their father.

But twenty-one children survived. Broken, battered, abused, but alive. Although what chance did any of them have of really, truly surviving what they had been through?

Dr. Bruce Perry was the chief of psychiatry at the Texas Children's Hospital in 1993 and had formed a rapid response Trauma Assessment Team, intended to assist children who had been the victims of car crashes, shootings, and natural disasters. He offered his services after the Branch Davidian children (ranging from five months to twelve years old) were released and immediately traveled to Waco.

What he found were children whose hearts were beating at almost twice the normal speed—a symptom of the profound, intense stress they had lived under and were still experiencing. The children were now in the hands of the "Babylonians," the outsiders that Koresh had warned them about, and saw themselves as hostages rather than patients. He discovered the boys and girls were unwilling to sit together because it broke the rules. He found children who had been forced to fight each other as "training" for the apocalypse, who had been taught numerous ways to kill themselves if they were ever caught by "their enemies." Children who had lived in a state of almost constant terror.

Perry and his team worked with the children, trying to help them move on from what had passed for their childhoods, even as the siege ended in fire and shooting, in the awful end of the world they had been repeatedly warned about become real for their friends and parents and siblings.

I felt like I owed it to them and to all survivors of abuse to treat this story with honesty and sensitivity, to not diminish the horrors that Moonbeam had been through, but not to sensationalize them either. All I can say is that any mistakes in the novel, in terms of process and psychiatry, are the result of my own failures of understanding rather than a lack of diligence in research.

By the time I sat down to write the first draft of this novel in the summer of 2015, Moonbeam had grown into the strong, vulnerable, complicated, sarcastic, brilliant survivor that I hope I've done justice to in these pages. I hated having to describe some of the things that happened to her, but I never stopped wanting to tell her story.

I genuinely didn't know that I was going to give her a (reasonably) happy ending until I was almost finished writing. In the end, I was glad the story's final twists and turns went the way they did. I like to imagine her and her mother in their little garden, as they try to put themselves back together and move on.

As they keep surviving, no matter what.

Will Hill
London, January 2017

ACKNOWLEDGMENTS

All my love and gratitude, as always, to Sarah. My biggest and most loyal supporter, my first and most unflinching reader. My partner in everything, who tolerates me spending so much time with people who only exist inside my head.

My agent, Charlie Campbell, for everything you do and for never losing faith.

Rebecca Hill, Becky Walker, Amy Dobson, Stevie Hopwood, Alesha Bonser and all the amazing team at Usborne, who never cease to impress me with their creativity and passion.

Jessica Craig, who found this novel a home where it's set.

Annette Pollert-Morgan, Cassie Gutman, and everyone at Sourcebooks Fire. Thank you for taking this very American novel by a very non-American author to your hearts.

My three families. The one that raised me (Mum, Peter, Sue,

Ken, Mavis, Roger, Claire), the one I was welcomed into (Kay, Tony, Kevin, Jo, Tom, Pika, Ruby, Lola, Bill, Angela), and the one I chose for myself (James, Joe, Mick, Jared, Patrick, Kim, Tom, Lou).

Finally, to everyone who has read this novel. Thank you.

ABOUT THE AUTHOR

Will Hill grew up in the northeast of England and worked in bartending, bookselling, and publishing before quitting to write full-time. His first novel, *Department 19*—the first in a series of five—was a bestseller in the UK and translated around the world. *After the Fire* was published to widespread acclaim and has been shortlisted for numerous awards. Will lives in east London.

Learn more at willhillauthor.com.

FIREreads

 #getbooklit

Your hub for the hottest young adult books!

Visit us online and sign up for our
newsletter at FIREreads.com

 @sourcebooksfire

 sourcebooksfire

t firereads.tumblr.com